The Captain and the Lady Fair

Changing Times

By Quinne Darkover

Copyright blah blah blah

This is a work of fiction. Names, characters, places, and incidents are products of the author's imagination or are used fictitiously and are not to be considered as real, unless you are on very good drugs. Any resemblance to actual events, locales, organizations, spirits, or persons, living, dead, or undead, is entirely coincidental.

Published by Steaming Press
Printed by CreateSpace
Original print Aug, 2013. Rev June 2017

Dedication

I would like to thank the normal group of people to whom dedications go for the massive support. To the naysayers and those who gave no support, I give a big raspberry. A special thanks to my alpha reader Mame Wood. And thanks to Barbara Alsop, my beta reader for stepping up for my first revision. Last, but by no means least, because I'm still alive to have written this, and her support of my life, a grand thanks to Dr. Jennifer Cabreira-Steimle. She has talents and doesn't know it.

Thanks, Doc

Cover Art by

Homer Manansala

Thanks for the patience while I nitpicked changes
to the draft

1
Thursday
June 23, 1898
11:23 PM
The Dolphin

Alexandria gripped the armrests as hard as she could to keep from being tossed from her seat by the violent lurching and shaking of the passenger airship Dolphin. The fact the seats and tables were bolted to the deck kept the salon from being a total disaster. The lights had gone out a few minutes before. Lightning flashes from the night sky gave staccato views of pale, tense faces, swinging light fixtures, and glittering glassware rolling around the floor. Glassware that had shattered with the fall from the tables gave off diamond-like reflections. Alexandria's face was as pale as the other passengers' were, but she was not screaming. Her lips were set in a firm line and she had a look of determination on her face. The other passengers were clinging to their seats just as Alexandria was. Alexandria could hear the cries of panic over the racket of the wood creaking and the shrieking storm pounding the ship. Over the din, a baby's cries stood out.

A loud explosion and a hard shift to one side tossed Alexandria from her seat and up against the bulkhead. The flames at the side of the salon now illuminated the carnage and highlighted the red in Alexandria's pantsuit with its floor-length skirt. A smell of acrid sulphur filled the air briefly before the wind blasting through the now-gaping hole in the side of the salon whisked the smell and smoke away. Alexandria looked around at the chaos by the light of the fire starting to burn more brightly around the salon. Air from the hole fanned the flames making them burn faster and hotter. The smell of burning wood mixed with the odor of burning flesh became overwhelming. Wind carried blasts of rain through the wound in the ship, plastering Alexandria's black hair to her face and outfit. A blood-soaked woman lay on the floor just in front of her, with a baby clutched in her arms. The blood was in stark contrast to the woman's pale green dress. It was the woman she had seen boarding last. Alexandria crawled to her and lifted her head onto her lap.

"You're hurt. Don't move." A large splinter of wood protruded from the woman's side. Alexandria put her hand around the wood and over the wound to slow the flow of blood leaking around the shaft. The shard in the wound moved with every breath the woman took.

The woman looked up at Alexandria. Her eyes creased in pain; her pale skin and faint speech showed the wound to be mortal. "Take care of my baby girl," she pleaded. "Please." She stroked the baby's face, pushing the blonde hair from it, and cradled her closer. Her hand fumbled at the baby's diaper, tucking the small pink ruffled shirt into it. As she kissed the baby's cheek, she went limp. The splinter stopped moving.

"I promise I'll take care of her." Alexandria's sad voice held conviction.

Flames blew closer to Alexandria. She grabbed and clutched the baby to her chest. Alexandria pulled the unusual fabric of her skirt over them both, shielding them against the heat. Her heels pushed her along the deep carpet to get away from the flames. The ship's envelope, losing air, began to tilt nose-down and drop towards the sea below. Alexandria slid faster along the wall as the tilt increased; she half-curled around the baby to protect her from impacts with objects and people in the room. Keeping the skirt up she offered what protection she could. Another shift and tilt tossed Alexandria out the hole in the side of the ship. The fall of 30 feet to the water below knocked the wind out of her when she hit the water at an awkward angle.

The waves bobbed her up and down and made it hard to hold the baby above the water. It was even more difficult trying to shield the infant from the rain and waves. "Well, little one, we're in a fine kettle of fish." She had lost her grip on the skirt edge with the impact with the water, and the skirt kept tangling her legs as she kicked to keep high enough for both to breathe. "Okay precious, hang on a sec; I have to shift the skirt." Holding the baby with one hand, Alexandria reached down to her calves and curled her legs up. Grabbing the hem, she pulled the skirt up over the baby, shielding her from most of the water pouring down. "Now what, eh? I need to get you out of all this, but there is nowhere to go and I can't see a thing in the dark."

With sudden movement, she gave several kicks to get herself floating on her back. She flipped the skirt up and over, trapping air as a bubble, and pulled the drawstring at the hem tight under her arms, with the baby inside, against her belly. "That will keep you out of the worst, sweetheart. Sorry I can't get you dry." The trapped air helped keep her afloat. In a few moments, the baby stopped crying but still squirmed, seeking a comfortable position.

Floating on her back, she could see the airship Dolphin wrapped in flames. It dragged across the water as its bottom sank deeper into the sea. The airship's explosion lit up the dark, revealing an empty sea with a red dot bobbing in the water. Pieces of airship fell around them. Alexandria talked to the baby to comfort her, as well as herself. "Now the fireworks are over, I need to figure out what to call you. Something short and cute like you. Kira. That's it. Kira."

Every few minutes, timing the waves, Alexandria loosened the string to flap the skirt and catch fresh air for Kira. Alexandria kept running her hand over Kira through the skirt to feel the baby's movement and reassure herself. The baby was quiet but still moved about. "At least the water is not that cold. You're a brave girl, braver than I am. You're quiet and I'm ready to cry. We kind of have this backward; you know?"

Alexandria's head hit something hard floating behind her. Kicking around, she felt a large plank. "Thank you, Lord." Her words were whisked away by the wind. She grabbed at the plank. There was a flat sheet of wood at the end of the plank. She pulled herself partially up out of the water onto the sheet of wood, staying on her side, to not hurt the baby. The slamming waves kept trying to knock her back into the water.

Keeping up the chatter to Kira while she fought the brutal beating of the water to stay with the flotsam, Alexandria waited for dawn.

2
Thursday
June 23, 1898
11 AM
The Lady Fair

Joan shook her head and mumbled. "We're in for interesting times."

Joan and Victoria, at the rear of the bridge, watched the Captain, with his head down, pace back and forth across the obsessively neat and polished bridge. The coffee in his cup had gone cold and untouched, but he still carried it with him, on his trek to find an answer. Wood gleamed and brass shone. In front of the center of the panoramic window was a large domed compass on a pedestal. The Captain would pause on every other pass to stare down into the compass dome as if it were a crystal ball. The reflection of dials, gauges, levers and small wheels spread out on each side of the Captain's huge spoke wheel were ignored, as he stared past it all, deeper into the ball. Finding no answer, he paced again. A brown leather seat with arms, mounted on a swivel pedestal in the center of it all, beckoned him to sit but it was ignored, offering no comfort. A turn in his path would bring him to the large mahogany chart table with round holes in the base holding rolled charts, where he would stare down at the chart, seeking a course that wasn't marked. His footsteps were a regular rhythm across the light tan bamboo floor. His reflection in the polished floor followed his every step.

Joan and Victoria stood still, their eyes following his pacing. Joan was slightly shorter than average and her brown, shoulder-length, curly hair framed a pixie-like face. Although both women wore the same style of outfit, it did more for Victoria. Victoria towered over Joan and the tan overalls she wore over a ruffled white blouse highlighted her slender frame. Her bright red, curly hair, which trailed to her waist, contrasted with the tan of the outfit.

The Captain six foot tall, with jet-black hair that hung to his shoulders, and his trim frame, was always striking, no matter which suit he wore. Today was no different, in simple tan pants and a white, long-sleeved shirt, ready for any action or work, but, for now, it was only for pacing.

Joan could just hear Victoria's whisper over the background noise of an active airship. "Umm, Joan. I have to ask; why are we here and do you have any idea why he's pacing? I've been onboard a year and I've never seen him do that."

Joan turned to the slight motion that caught her eye in the hatchway. Avery and Chance had stuck their heads in to see the Captain still pacing. Joan gave a shrug and a slow nod to the two peeping toms, which made the brown hair brush her shoulders as it swung. The two men looked at each other and left.

Joan turned back to Victoria. "We're here because I like to know what's happening and I've only seen him do that pacing once, and that was just before you came aboard. Maybe over dinner, I'll tell you what happened. When he paces, it means something is about to happen. Speaking of dinner, I'd better get below and get started on chow or the crew will see if I can cloud dance." Before Joan could leave, there was a loud commotion on the deck below. All three went to the window for a better look.

The deck extended 200 feet beyond the bridge. It was flat, with only a crane and half a dozen hatches to break the surface. The crew on deck had been loading cargo, but the work had stopped and turned into a shouting match. In the center of the fracas was the Chief, towering over a slightly built man in a business suit with papers in hand. The man waved the papers in front of the chief, as if it were a magic talisman, to deflect his wrath.

The Captain yelled through the open window without the use of a loud-box. "What's the problem down there? Why have we stopped loading cargo?" The Captain's fingers were turning white with the grip on the spokes of the captain's wheel.

The Chief's voice spoke back with the same sharp tone. "Some foul-up by a ground-kissing, scrawny-necked, pencil pusher sent us stuff we didn't order. We get the monster loaded and now they're yelling for us to unload it and give it back. I've been telling them; if they want it, they can unload it."

"What is it, Chief? Anything we can use?"

"It looks like some kind of swing arm crane that can extend out and back in. We already have a crane that works just fine even if it's not that fancy to move in and out." The Chief put his hands on his hips. Grease splotched his gray overalls, but few would notice, as the eye was always caught by his size: six foot six and wide as a door, with all of it muscle. His bald head and gray beard would be noticed last of all.

The Captain's eyes stared blankly at the crane. He didn't move but stood still in thought. "Chief, I want that crane. How long will it take to replace ours?"

The Chief's mouth dropped open for a moment. His jaw moved up and down silently as if practicing the words to come. "Well, Captain, it's not as easy as that. First, we have to get these pencil pushers to quit fighting over it, and then it'll take two hours to get the old one out, and maybe four hours to get the new one in. They've already sent for the Harbor Master's supply officer and when he gets here, I'm sure he will have them unload it."

"Okay, Chief. At the best, how long will it take you to make ours work like that one, or make one?"

The Chief stroked his short beard a few times while walking along the length of the crane on the deck. The bystanders on the dock and the crew on the deck watched the Chief in his thinking mode, which featured him pulling his beard with an occasional grunt. With a slow turn of his head, he looked up to the Captain. "Captain, with my crew working full-time it'll still take an hour to get the old arm out, and using parts from it and scrounging up more parts, maybe another 24 hours. It looks like rain's coming and that will slow it down. Maybe we could start it tomorrow if the rain passes."

"What about the new stuff Tailor was painting on the skin of the envelope?"

"He finished everything except the rudder this morning. He woulda been done, but I pulled him for cargo load. This is the last load and all cargo we're shipping will be on. It came in a few days early. We'll be ready to lift on schedule Friday and still have three days to relax until then. No rush, Captain."

"Chief, use the entire crew if you need to, but we lift in twelve hours and I want that crane. Rain or no rain."

The Chief nodded and stroked his beard. Only Avery, who had just come to stand next to the Chief, heard him mutter, "Here we go."

Joan spoke to Victoria as she turned to the hatchway. "I'll go make sandwiches before I head out on deck. You might as well head on out; they'll be screaming for you any minute."

The Captain gave another order. "Joan, after lunch is set up, go into town and get Doc and the others back to the ship." He turned, strode to the chart table, and stared down at the laid-out map.

Victoria heard the Chief calling her name, telling her to get her opposable thumbs on deck. As Joan stepped through the hatchway, Victoria heard a faint, "Oh yeah, interesting times."

3
June 23, 1898
7 PM
The Galley

Victoria buttered a roll and her stomach took that moment to give a rumble for her to hurry up. She wolfed down large bites of the roll. The crew was always in wonder as to where she put all the food. She ate enough for two easily, and her thin frame never gained an ounce. As soon as she had swallowed, she spoke up, "The Captain still on the bridge?"

As Joan ladled a thick stew into her bowl, she gave a sigh. "Get that in you so I can hear myself over that stomach of yours, and yes, he's still up there, and I doubt he'll leave it anytime soon. I'll take him his dinner or he'll starve." She grabbed another bowl and filled it. "He probably won't eat it anyway."

"Take my advice and eat when you can and sleep when you can. When I saw the Captain like this before, we ran hard for two weeks then ended up in an airship fight with slave smugglers on the Osprey that about did us in. Sound familiar? We had parts wearing out, then lots of holes to patch fast before we dropped into the water. It was close, I tell you. After that, he collapsed in his chair and slept for 24 hours as we slowly made it to Arla Bay, the nearest port."

Victoria's head popped up from hovering over the bowl, her bright red, curly hair bobbing several times as only brushed-out curly hair will do. "A gun fight and Arla? That was when you got me off the slave ship!" She paused in her eating, her face became a shade paler, and her hand gripped the spoon tighter.

Avery and Chance came in, shaking water off their slickers, and, as always, Avery had something to say. "I'll never forget that run but it wasn't as bad as the Med run the year before that. Out of the blue, he orders up all manner of meds, and off we go through a heavy storm that shook our teeth out. The gasbags were getting soaked and they got heavier and heavier. Somehow we stayed up Then, in the middle of the storm, we hold over Tinker Town and unload supplies with that very hoist we tore apart today. I don't know how he knew two weeks ahead there would be a plague, but that's the Captain for ya. By the way, take what time you need to eat proper; then we have to get back on deck. You too, Joan. Not even Joan is immune on this one. We all know how things get when he's like this."

Chance had grabbed a bowl, filled it, swiped a roll through it, and then stuffed it into his mouth. "Them sandwiches were good at lunch, Joan, but they didn't last. Now this will stick and get me through. What do you think, Avery? Another four hours push?"

Avery mumbled his answer as a stew-soaked biscuit disappeared into his mouth. "Yep, I think so. If no one falls in this downpour and breaks a neck. That rain runs down the side of the bag and drops off right on my head while I'm at the crane."

Chance's lips were set in a straight line and his forehead showed lines of concern. "Victoria, when the Captain is like this, it's important to him. He never does anything without a reason. There'll be no stopping him anyway. You just rush to make sure you're ready to do your job. If he gives an order, never question it. Most times, he can't tell you what or why, but what he says always turns out important. If he trusts you, he'll never question you either. He paces; we race. I know you've heard stories, but this will be your first time to see it. You'll never forget it."

Victoria groaned. "I ache too much now. I just hope I can make four more hours. What does he need that crane for, anyway?"

Avery, Chance, and Joan looked at each other and smiled.

Joan refilled Victoria's bowl. "When we know, we'll tell you."

4

June 22, 1898

6 PM

Alexandria

Alexandria checked the laid-out clothes on the bed one more time and gave them a nod. Picking up the white dress with the full skirt and high, ruffled collar, she held it in front of herself and looked in the mirror. She declared to herself, "My dress for tomorrow." The perpetual smile on her face showed her eagerness for the coming trip. Her waist-length, jet-black hair was a stark contrast to the white of the dress. At five feet eleven, her long legs made the figure in the mirror look almost regal. As her hand reached for the first clothes to pack, a knock at her bedroom door stopped her. "Come in, Auntie."

Auntie entered wearing a smile that did not match her eyes. She was a short woman, with a slight figure and bobbed black hair. Her quick smile and eagerness to lend a hand endeared her to everyone she met. "Alex, I'm going to miss you so much; so will your Uncle."

"The conference only lasts a week. You know I would cut it short if I could, but I'm on panels all week. I'll be back before you know it. If Auntie Helen is good, I'll bring back a souvenir." Alexandria's chuckle was light and airy and her eyes had a twinkle.

"You're always such a smart mouth brat. Okay, Miss Perky, I handmade something for you." From behind her back, Helen pulled out a folded cloth. "I want you to wear this on the trip."

Alexandria took the bundle and let it fall open to reveal a one-piece, bright red, loose pantsuit with large pockets on the breast and legs. There was also a matching wrap skirt and a wide sash long enough to wrap twice and tie around Alexandria's waist. "Pants? You want me to wear pants? Ladies do not wear pants! Bright red? I'll look like a walking hot pepper."

"Please, dear, wear it for me. It's good, tough fabric but not too heavy. It's even waterproof. I put in a draw at the hem on the skirt, so you can draw it tighter around the calves, so it'll have the modern look I saw in Harrods. The fabric is made by that new company, Nomex. That's the company that makes the fire suits your uncle wears. It's special fabric."

"Auntie, I'll roast to death in this. I love you to pieces but why do you want me to wear it? And Pants?"

Helen's eyes took on a sad look and her lips frowned at the corners. Combined with her short, rail-thin stature, it was a pitiful sight. "I can't say, dear; just please promise you'll wear it and put all your important papers and money in the pockets. They seal and become watertight in case you're caught in the rain. Please."

Alexandria laid the pantsuit on the bed and crossed her arms over her chest. As she placed her feet slightly apart, she asked, almost in a whisper, "Why, Auntie?"

The deep, raspy voice of her Uncle John emanated from the doorway. "I told you so." As short as his wife, he still was a daunting figure, with large biceps and a barrel chest.

"Be quiet, John. All she needs to do is wear it for me. Is it too much to ask her to wear it after I worked so hard on it?"

"Tell her."

"Let it go, John."

"If you don't, I will."

Helen stood quietly, wringing her hands.

"It's her dreams, or I should say 'nightmares.' " John ran his hand through his thinning brown hair.

"John!" Helen took a deep breath. "Please don't think me nutty, but I've been waking every night for a month having nightmares and I don't remember what they're about. But then, I just had to make this and you just have to wear it. I just know it."

Alexandria stepped forward and wrapped her arms around her aunt. "Auntie, I said I love you to pieces and, if it'll stop your nightmares, I'll wear it."

The relief on Helen's face showed it was the right choice.

"When I get back from the conference, I'm going to tease you to death for being silly."

Auntie looked at Alexandria with glassy eyes. "Your mother would have been so proud. You're so beautiful and smart too."

"Dinner, then pack and to bed. Tomorrow will be a long day." John had a smile on his face.

"Uncle, you're right, and I love you to pieces, too." Alexandria gave him a peck on the cheek.

5
June 23, 1898
7 AM
The Airdrome

The airdrome was new and huge. The square building had a mooring at each corner, which allowed the docking of four massive airships at once. The top half of the walls and the entire ceiling were made of glass panels. Through the glass panels, two massive airships were visible. Shiny marble floors and massive granite columns made the airdrome feel cool and open. It was busy with passengers hurrying to and fro, getting boarding tickets, checking luggage, and generally being excited to be boarding the airship Dolphin. The Dolphin was the grandest airship in the PanAir fleet, luxury only the rich could afford, or someone with traveling expenses paid to attend a conference. A loud-box announced boarding to start on the Dolphin for New City in five minutes.

Helen stood and hugged Alexandria hard. "Take care of yourself."

"Auntie, why does everyone always say that? And yes, I will. Come on, Uncle, a hug from you too."

As her uncle hugged her as directed, Helen thanked her for wearing the suit. "I slept better last night. Thank you. I still feel pins and needles, but I feel better. I wish you wouldn't go at all, but I suppose I can't talk you out of this."

"No, Auntie, I have to go. It's important. You know I have to go and give my paper on aether and the generation of electricity to create an aether energy shield. It could protect cities from storms and save lives. You know that."

They walked to the boarding gate and Alexandria showed her boarding ticket and her passport. The attendant nodded and Helen spoke up. "Pocket, dear. It's raining now."

Changing Times

Alexandria shook her head and smiled as she put the papers in her breast pocket. "So it rains; I'm waterproof, remember?" Quickly walking up the ramp to the airship, she chuckled and said to herself "Make way for the giant red chili pepper!"

Alexandria passed through the hatchway and the Sky Attendant pointed her to the left. The passageway emptied out into a grand sitting room, with velvet-covered plush seats all around the room. Vast windows and hanging electric chandeliers provided plenty of light. She sat in a seat on the portside; she could see tables covered in white linen at the end of another passageway. Looking down at the colors of her pantsuit against the red velvet of the chair, she muttered, "Can it get worse?"

"May I get you something to drink, Miss? Coffee? Orange juice? Breakfast will be served just after we lift off if you wish to wait." The attendant in the powder-blue skirt and jacket placed a napkin on the short table in front of Alexandria's seat.

"No, thank you; I'll wait. Is the rain going to be a problem?"

"No, Ma'am, it's a light rain. It'll make us heavier and slow us down, but when you wake in the morning, we'll be in sunny New City." The Sky Attendant pointed to the passageway where Alexandria had entered. "Your sleeping cabin is down the passageway past the entry hatchway and your cabin number is on your boarding ticket. Enjoy the cruise."

Alexandria watched the people coming into the salon craning their necks looking at the opulent fixtures and décor. A young woman in a pale green, floor-length dress entered; she caught Alexandria's eye, as she was carrying a baby. She did not look around but went straight to the chair next to Alexandria, sat, and let out a sigh.

The baby's sleeping smile captivated Alexandria. She spoke to the woman. "A beautiful baby."

"She's the best in the world, of course."

Alexandria watched the baby sleep.

The last person to board was a short man in a rumpled tan coat carrying a large satchel. He took the first empty seat next to the outer wall and stared at the woman and her baby.

6
June 23, 1898
11:23 PM
The Bridge

Doc watched the Captain sitting in his chair with his head down and eyes closed. It was obvious he was not sleeping and his mind was somewhere else. His form rocked with the swing of the bridge, pushed by the wind and rain of the storm outside. "Captain, why don't I give you something to help you rest? You're all wound up. Nothing strong, just …."

Ignoring Doc, the Captain leaped up from the chair. "We're out of time!" Crossing the bridge in two strides, he flicked on the loud-box. "All hands to stations! All hands to stations! We lift NOW! Pilot Kathryn to the bridge! Chief, engines up and fill the bags! Move! Move! Move!" The Captain turned to Doc. "You're on standby and no thanks on the drugs."

From the loud-box, each member reported on station and ready immediately. The entire crew had been waiting at their stations.

Kathryn and Diana stepped onto the bridge from the passageway, where they had been leaning against the bulkhead, just out of sight. They both wore pilot uniforms of brown leather pants and a matching corset over a white ruffled blouse. Their leather flying jackets open to keep cool and their brown, bobbed hair was tucked under leather, flying caps.

"Course, Captain?" Diana looked out at the storm.

"We're going to run with the wind, Pilot."

Changing Times

Diana did not ask the destination but went to the controls and wheel instead. She read the dials and gauges quickly. "Captain, we'll be ready to lift in three minutes. Engines are ready, and gas is filling."

"Lift when ready." He once again spoke into the loud-box. "Victoria, Joan, Diana, Rigger, Tailor. Emergency lift! Grab axes and be ready to chop moorings at Pilot's command in three minutes. Everybody else stay below deck." He turned back to Pilot. "As soon as the engines and lift can handle it, give me full throttle to the stops, and turn us with the wind."

The bridge floor under the Captain's feet started vibrating as the engines came to life.

Pilot Diana grabbed the comm mic for the far talker. "Lady Fair calling Harbor Master; Lady Fair calling Harbor Master. Request permission for immediate lift."

There was a short burst of static, and then the reply came. "Negative, Lady Fair. The winds are way too high and you're not scheduled to lift for three more days."

Diana did not have to check with the Captain. "Harbor Master, repeating request nicely for immediate lift." Normally the Captain would have smiled at her emphasis on the word "nicely."

A one-word reply came back. "Negative."

"We tried to be nice. See you when we get back." Pilot Diana switched off the comm and spoke into the loud-box. "Release lines." Diana slowly moved the throttles on the six engines to full throttle. Ropes strained to hold the ship earthbound against the thrust of the engines and the increasing lift from the added gas. The axes fell on the lines. There was a pause, and then the ship lurched into the storm to begin a race with the wind. The engines kept the Lady Fair in position against the 80-miles-per-hour wind. She kept a firm hand on the wheel. Her lips tight in a straight line, her other hand controlled direction by adjusting the engine power and the rudder to turn the airship around and gain speed in relationship to the wind as she rose clear of the tower. As the Lady Fair turned broadside to the wind, she tilted to the side when the wind got a purchase on the lift bag. For a time, the Lady Fair moved at 80 miles per hour sideways, until Pilots Diana and Kathryn could get the airship completely turned around. The wind pushing from behind gave the Lady Fair an impressive speed over the sea.

The Captain's voice was firm but some of the stress had left it as the airship Lady Fair picked up speed and altitude with the storm winds pushing hard from behind. Using the loud-box, he set up the coming flight orders. "Chief, keep a good eye on the engines. Get one of the engineers to stand by to rest as soon as you can; he'll be your relief. All crew stay within the ship. I don't need anyone blown off the deck." He turned from the loud-box, "Diana go on standby; you'll be the relieving pilot in four hours." He turned to Pilot Kathryn. "Do I detect a tilt?"

"Yes, Captain. The rain has soaked the fabric on the tail, making us tail-heavy. Tailor didn't get to finish that stuff he was putting on. The rest is dry and so it's light. I'm sending in more air aft and will shift ballast as soon as speed picks up and I can let go for a minute."

The Captain paused and then, for the first time in days, a smile crossed his face. "You forget I was a pilot well before your time. Diana, I can do this, get yourself on standby." He strode with purpose to the ballast controls and started the pumps to transfer water from the aft to the bow. Slowly the nose lowered and leveled as the airship continued to pick up speed. He opened the portside door and stepped onto the walkway, in front of the bridge, and was instantly drenched by the rain. Both hands on the rail, staring off to an unseen point, he leaned forward as if to will more speed. Stroking the railing, he spoke to the Lady Fair "I need all you have." The ship shuddered and gained still more speed. His eyes became unfocused as he stared forward. His words were whisked away by the wind. "Hold on. I'm coming."

Changing Times

7
June 24, 1898
Dawn
Alexandria

Now in a habit of working with the waves, she opened the skirt but, instead of closing it again after a flap for air, her hand, with aching fingers, plunged to the sash at her waist. Her legs spread wide to keep from rolling off the makeshift raft, as losing the plank meant a quick death. Her words came out in gasps. "Come on, fingers, work." Reluctantly, the knot loosened and pulled free. The sash free, she closed up the skirt again, clung to the plank, and took a brief rest, such as it was. "Stay with me just a bit more."

For the first time in many hours, Kira began a soft cry. "I know you're wet and hungry. Sorry, I can't help that." Alexandria continued the chatter to Kira and the baby quieted again.

Throwing one end of the sash around a piece of wood jutting up from the flat bulkhead, she grabbed the free end as it swung around. Alexandria struggled against the tossing waves to tie it under her arms, securing herself to the only thing that could keep them alive. For the first time in hours, she did not have to combat the sea to keep from sliding off into the sea and certain death. Keeping the baby to her chest, she allowed the skirt to stay open a small amount to let in a constant flow of air. Exhaustion and the relief of not holding onto the plank caused her to pass out, yet her arms kept a tight hold on Kira, as a mother would instinctively. In her sleep, she began to mumble, repeating, "Don't worry, Kira; Thomas is coming."

8
June 24, 1898
11:00 AM
The Bridge

The Captain stood out on the widow's walk, his hands gripping the handrail and his eyes staring forward. Pilot Diana, the identical twin sister of Kathryn, was at the helm, keeping the airship running with the wind. Both pilots were in the habit of wearing the same outfit any time they were at the controls. Diana's bobbed hair showed signs of sweat at the ends, where it touched her neck. Doc stood out of the way at the back of the bridge, holding onto a grab rail next to Kathryn, sitting on the couch. She always wore a long-sleeved ruffle shirt and long, black skirt.

Doc's eyebrows arched together. "He's been out there all night and morning? That isn't good."

"I've been here all night short-shifting with Diana. Does sticking his head in to give orders to adjust course every half-hour or so count as coming inside?"

As if he had heard them, the Captain left the walk and re-entered the bridge. "Come to port ten degrees and hold steady." Over the loud-box, his voice carried throughout the ship. "Chief, I'm going to need you, your crew, and the deckhands on the crane. Use safe lines. Victoria, to the spotters' nest with far glasses; you've got the best eyes for spotting."

A short line of bodies could be seen running onto the deck to man the crane and stand by. The men's safety lines took on the look of a spider web as they hooked up to the safety railing. The Chief looked towards the bridge, waiting for orders.

The Captain took up a pair of far glasses and stepped back out onto the walk to scan the tossing sea. He yelled over his shoulder "Pilot Diana, reduce to half speed. Ease to port. Drop us to 30 feet."

Changing Times

Diana reduced the throttles and shifted the airship two more degrees to port. Kathryn joined her at the helm. The angle of the wind made her have to fight the wheel to keep steady and use engines to assist the control. The airship dropped lower as she released gas. She watched as Joan joined the crew on the deck. Time froze as all eyes searched forward, looking for anything to show where the Captain was guiding them. The salt-water spray from the wave tops lifted by the wind soaked them in just a few minutes. Even at half throttle, the Lady Fair still raced over the sea, pushed from behind.

The loud-box from the spotters' nest carried Victoria's voice yelling with excitement. "Something ahead just off port heading, about 500 yards!"

"Pilot, stay steady, full reverse. Slow us to the seas." Eyes fixed to the far glasses, the Captain searched the sea for what Victoria had seen.

"Captain, it looks like a red dot. Small. On a big square."

A wave crest brought the object up into the Captain's view. The Captain dashed inside and yelled into the loud-box. "Chief, attach a cargo net to the crane and be ready to launch to port."

Figures on deck burst into a flurry of activity, releasing the locks on the crane, while three other figures ran to a storage box, just within reach of the safe lines, to pull out a net. Scurrying back to the crane, the crew grabbed at the net and started attaching the corners.

"Chief, make one end low; we'll need it as a scoop." The Captain could now see a large rectangular piece of wood with a figure in red lying on top. "Pilot, can you see it?"

"Steadying onto it, Captain. Portside keeping."

Kathryn stepped to the side of her sister and moved in coordination to help with the maneuvers.

"Joan, to the bridge, and be eyes for Pilot." The Captain ran from the bridge down to the deck to join the crew and passed Joan running full tilt for the bridge. Leaning over the side, he could see the figure on the makeshift raft.

The Captain and the Lady Fair

"Okay, Chief, swing it out." As the crew shoved at the crane, the arm swung over the side and the net fell open like a mitt. The Chief joined the Captain at the rail to hand-signal the crew directions for the crane.

The engines could be heard changing pitch over the howl of the wind as Joan, on the portside walk, staring down at the sea, relayed to Pilot, directions to come up and slow on the figure in the water. Both pilots worked to keep the ship steady and under control as it no longer raced faster than the wind, but now turned into it and fought to stay in place. During the pirouette, the raft never moved from portside. The engines thrummed to hold Lady Fair in place now that they faced fully into the wind. The wind, now tearing past the rudder, improved control.

"Captain, that hunk of wood is going to be a problem. It'll poke into the net and we won't be able to get the whole thing in. He has to get off it and get to the net." The Chief leaned over the side rail and looked at the situation.

"He hasn't moved and he should have if he were conscious." The Captain stared down a moment. "My trust is in you, Chief." The Captain launched himself over the rail, splashing down into the waves below. Surfacing, he was blinded by the salt spray in his face. Fighting wind and waves, he swam hard to the makeshift raft. Finding the figure tied to the plank, he struggled with the knot. While working to untie it, he saw it was a young woman. A shiver ran through him. Knot freed, he left it wrapped under her arms and used it to pull her off the plank. He began to swim a one-armed backstroke to the net, towing her behind him with the sash. Sudden pain ripped through the Captain, as the plank, driven by the wind, slammed hard into his ribs. He gritted his teeth and held his grip on the sash.

As he drifted near and far from the action of the waves and wind, the crane arm shifted in and out to keep the net near him. The Chief hand-signaled instructions to the crew instead of trying to yell over the wind.

The net scooped the Captain and Alexandria up and, as it began to lift, he blacked out from the pain of every breath.

The Chief signaled for the net to be lowered onto the deck. Seeing the two figures unconscious, he yanked frantically at the net, as a man gone mad. "Get stretchers! Get Doc!"

9
June 24, 1898
The Sickbay

Electric lights lit the sickbay. The white metal cabinets with glass doors reflected light back into the room. The large room held four beds. Doc looked at the two unconscious patients stretched out on the beds. "Sorry, Captain, I think she needs me first. Chief, don't just hover; get his clothes off so I can check him." She turned to the young woman, saw the cord holding the skirt up under the arms, and untied it. A gasp escaped her lips when she saw the still form of the baby. "Oh, Dear God! No! No! No!" Touching the back of the baby, she felt the chill skin through the thin pink shirt. "Please, Lord. NO!"

She tried to pick the baby up, but the woman's arms were locked, with their hold protecting her from bumps and the cold. Trying to pry the arms away, she bent and talked in the woman's ear. "You can let go. You're safe now." She whispered it repeatedly as a mantra while the grip slowly relaxed enough to pull the baby away. She hugged the baby's head to her cheek. "I'm sorry, little one." Then she felt a small puff of air on her cheek. The baby was alive! Her back was chilled, but her front was still warm from being held against the woman. Doc yelled out to anyone who could hear. "I need another pair of hands in here!"

The baby woke with the shout and started crying.

Looking up at the commotion at the hatchway, it looked like the entire crew was trying to wedge in at one time. Seeing Joan and Victoria at the head of the mob of bodies, she gave directions. "Joan, get in here and strip off your top behind that curtain and dry yourself. Victoria, grab

21

a blanket and wrap it around her when she's got the baby. Everyone else out!"

To the crew, "out" meant just out of sight at the hatch, so they could hear what was going on.

As she held Kira out to give her a quick look over, the baby flailed. "Thank God. Cry your heart out, sweetheart; it'll warm you up." Doc laid Kira on the bed next to Alexandria and removed the cold, wet diaper. A necklace with a large, blue stone fell onto the bed. "Well, hello, young lady. You are as cute as a button, and you are learning fashion sense. Yes, you are. But that goes around the neck, not on your tummy." Doc kept up the chatter as she checked the baby for any obvious injuries, and then moved her arms and legs and found everything intact. She got a damp cloth and cleaned up the baby, getting the salt water off, and dried her.

"Okay, Joan, here we come, and if anyone can hear me, I need warm milk!" Doc took the baby around the curtain and put her in the arms of Joan. "Keep her to your chest to warm her." As she turned away, Victoria was already wrapping the blanket around the pair. Victoria moved close and wrapped her arms around both to add her body heat.

Doc returned to the side of the woman and worked at removing the odd pantsuit.

Chief moved to put his back to Doc, giving some privacy.

"This is strange stuff and the strangest outfit. Okay, young lady; let's see if you were as lucky as the baby." Doc quickly checked her over. There were only a few scratches on her face, and hands, mild signs of exhaustion, exposure, and dehydration. "Victoria, come wipe this lady down to get the salt off, then get her a blanket, too."

Doc turned to the Captain. The Chief had gotten his clothes off and covered him in a blanket. "Okay, Captain, let's take a look at you." Pulling the blanket back revealed a large area on the side of the Captain's rib cage taking on an ugly color. "Looks like you got the worst end of the deal." Touching the area brought a groan from the Captain and his eyes opened.

His voice was strained. "Easy with the poking fingers, Doc. The whole side hurts. Can't I just tell you it hurts without you poking at it?"

"Sorry, Captain, I'm checking the ribs and I have to touch to find out. Be the big, strong, brave Captain type and endure it a little longer." Doc continued to feel his ribs. "Looks like maybe two broken and the rest bruised. You're going to be hurting for days."

"Okay, a small plaster and I'm out of the sickbay. You know I don't like being down. Get me up and moving."

"Sit up and I'll wrap you." As soon as the Captain sat up with a little help from Chief, Doc began to wrap the ribs to keep them from moving. "I'd be wasting my breath to tell you to take it easy. I'll give you something for the pain."

The Captain ignored what Doc was doing and let her work. "Chief, what's our status?"

"I have no idea, Captain; I came straight here with you but she feels to be flying okay. Good call on that crane, Captain. Never would have managed to keep up with the old one."

Victoria spoke up. "When I left the bridge, Pilot was pulling us up and planning to do a quick search for survivors, then turn back for New City."

The Captain almost fell when his knees gave from trying to get up from the bed. Only the Chief's fast grab had stopped him from a full fall. The deep breath he tried to take was cut short and a groan slowly passed his lips. Standing straighter, he carefully slid with a shuffle towards the loud-box. "Pilot, set us on a course for home. It may be farther, but with the winds to fight returning to port it would take even longer."

The crew's voices were heard shouting from outside the hatch. "Home!"

10
June 24, 1898
Noon
The Sickbay

Alexandria stirred on the bed. Her eyes opened wide and her arms flayed about, searching. "Kira! Where's Kira? I lost Kira!"

Doc stepped quickly to the side of the bed. "Kira's alright. She's had a bottle and Joan will bring her another soon. Calm down now. You're both okay. I'll call the Captain and let him know you're awake and you can tell your story. You have a cute baby. I have hot tea for you while we wait for him. I'll also ask Joan to make you something."

"She's not mine. Her mother died on the Dolphin." Alexandria's voice was low and soft. Her eyes saddened with the memory.

"The Captain will want to know all about that, too."

Alexandria watched Doc move to the loud-box. Doc's naturally fluffy, brown hair, which hung to just past her shoulder blades, waved in the air as she moved. The long, black skirt with suspenders and white long-sleeve blouse looked professional on her five-feet-five, thin build.

Doc barely had time to pour and give her the tea when the Captain came in. "Welcome to the land of the living, Miss?" He paused, waiting for her to give her name.

Alexandria froze and stared at the Captain; she shivered and answered his implied question. "My name is Alexandria Castle." Her eyes stayed mostly on the baby but kept taking glances at the Captain. Over the span of 30 minutes, she told her story and had two more cups of tea. "I can't believe I drank all that tea and I'm hungry. How did you find me?"

"Good luck with that one, Captain." Doc turned to hide her grin.

The Captain stared at his feet. "We happened to be in the area and, as luck would have it, we saw you bobbing out there."

Doc's hard, short burst of laughter drowned out what he would have said next, had he not stopped talking during her outburst. Finally regaining control, she managed a contrite "Sorry, Captain, I just thought of something very funny and it just came out." The crew's snickers in the passageway seemed loud, now she was no longer laughing.

"You bunch of layabouts have nothing better to do than hang around outside hatches? I can find something for you." The full laughter from several voices faded as the crew made a fast exit.

"You and Kira were the only survivors. We're headed for our home Island, which is faster to get to than anywhere else."

"You sure do have a happy crew. I'm sorry; did I miss your name?"

"Thomas." Staring at his feet, he missed the startled look on her face as he continued. "Thomas Hewitt Edward Castellan at your service." His eyes finally met hers as he finished with an exaggerated flourish of a bow.

"Castellan? I haven't heard that name before. Where's it from?"

Head down, the Captain checked his shoes. "It's Old English." He had to speak louder over the new wails of laughter from Doc.

"Does it have a meaning?"

Doc grabbed a pillow and buried her face in it to muffle herself.

Captain sighed. "Yes, it means 'Captain of the castle.'"

Doc was bent over the empty bed in major fits, and her fists pounded the pillow.

"Doc, I could have Chief make a brig and toss you in if that will help with your condition."

Doc's muffled laughter did not abate.

Alexandria thought for a moment. "That makes it T.H.E. Castellan. Or …" Alexandria failed to suppress the chuckle bubbling up. "THE Captain."

Doc fell to the floor and no longer wasted the effort to try to hold back the laughter.

"Excuse me, ladies, I'm needed on the bridge." The Captain made a quick exit.

"I'm sorry, Captain; it's that it …." Alexandria's voice trailed off as she realized she was speaking to empty space.

Joan was bringing in food by the time Doc was getting control of herself. "What did I miss? What's so funny?" Joan placed the tray in front of Alexandria. "Doc said to make you something hot." The tray featured steaming French onion soup with a round piece of toast floating on top, covered in a grated cheese, and sliced green beans with small carrots and pearl onions with a melted, pale cheese. Thin slices of roast beef covered in a thick, brown gravy, and a thick slice of warm bread, with the butter in its final stages of melting, completed the meal. Tray settled, Joan turned to Doc and helped her off the floor. "Give."

"Patient first." Doc went to Alexandria and smiled down. "An excellent lunch, Joan."

"I'm sorry to put you out; you didn't need to make all this for me."

"My pleasure. Oops, I almost forgot lunch for Kira." She pulled a bottle from her apron pocket. Placing a napkin over her arm, she approached the bed and picked up Kira. "Your lunch is here, Mademoiselle."

Kira woke in the lifting arms and squirmed only for a moment. In seconds, she was sucking away at the bottle.

"I'm still waiting." Joan stared at Doc with a smile.

"Our young guest here has a very quick mind. He told her we just happened to be in the area, then she asked the Captain his name. He gave her his full name. She pegged it right away."

Joan started chuckling. "I like you already!"

"But I upset him. I was rude and laughed at his name. I have to apologize at once."

Doc spoke up. "Relax. He's used to it and he knows you weren't laughing at him. Just that, like everyone else, you found the combination amusing. He'll be over it before you finish eating. He also knows I was overdoing it just to poke him. It's odd he gave his full name so quick." Doc noticed the speed with which Alexandria was eating. "Hey! Slow down on the starving dog action you have there. You can have seconds."

"I didn't know I was this hungry." Alexandria looked at Kira. "Kira must have been starving. She had nothing to eat for so long. She was very good and hardly cried at all. You had a baby bottle onboard?"

Doc smiled. "I have 3 just in case. As long as she was held, she was happy and felt secure. Blind babies are often like that."

"What! Blind?" Alexandria's eyes snapped to Kira.

"You didn't know?"

11
June 24, 1898
Afternoon
The Sickbay

All afternoon, Alexandria held, rocked and talked to Kira. Members of the crew trickled in and out of the sickbay to say hello to Alexandria and to see Kira.

One by one, they would return and place a gift on Kira's bed. A hand-carved rattle from the Chief, teething rings made of rubber from the deckhands, even a small sleeping gown hurriedly hand-sewn by Victoria. No one would admit to the small lamb made from lambskin, its curly hair a pure white. Victoria also handed Alexandria some clothes: a white blouse with ruffles, a canvas corset, and a pair of dark brown canvas pants. Alexandria's cleaned undergarments completed the set. Victoria gave Alexandria a smile. "If you tell me your shoe size, we might find something for you."

"Thank you. I'll give these back when I can get a proper dress."

Victoria's face fell.

"I'm sorry. Please don't take it wrong. I've just never worn pants until this trip. It doesn't feel right on me. I wouldn't have worn it if it hadn't promised my aunt I would wear it. I guess I was lucky it kept us afloat and was as tough as it is. It probably saved us some pokes and scrapes and even some burns."

"You don't like it? I think it's wonderful!"

"I kept my promise and wore it and you've been so kind. It's yours."

"Really! I mean 'thanks,' but I could never. It's so nice and you might want to wear it again."

"Not in a hundred years. I insist. I'm going to get something for everyone anyway. They've been so nice to me."

"They like you, too. Don't be surprised to see them hanging around to talk with you. Saving a baby means a lot."

Doc came back in after doing a walk around the ship, checking on the crew. "Okay, time to get you up and out. There's a cabin for you. You can clean up with a shower and then I'll give you a tour of the Lady Fair. After that, it'll be dinner time and you can meet everyone at one time. I have a pullover shift for you to wear to your cabin."

"Shower?"

"Oh, I forgot. Cities only have tubs. Chief made pipes that pour water over you like rain. It's even heated by the engines. You stand under it and wash. It's marvelous. It pumps water from the ballast then drains into holding tanks so the weight and balance stays the same. Chief is a genius."

Victoria leaped up from the side of the bed where she had perched and headed for the hatchway. "Yikes! I forgot; I promised Joan I'd help."

12
June 24, 1898
Late Afternoon
The Bridge

The Captain sat quietly in his chair, watching Pilot Kathryn work the controls at the helm. They had flown out of the storm and the Lady Fair flew smoothly in the clear skies. After a long sigh, his body visibly relaxed. "Pilot, anything to report?"

"Calm air, on course, home by late morning and the message was sent out about the Dolphin and survivors."

"Go on standby. I'll take her. Tell Diana to report in eight hours. You both need the rest."

"You sure about that, Captain? I think Doc would get peeved if you don't rest those ribs."

"I'm sure and fine. Go." The Captain looked Kathryn in the eye. "You both handled that storm like the ace pilots you are. The best I've ever seen. You deserve better."

"Thanks, Captain, but being on the Lady Fair as your pilot is enough."

The Captain stepped up to the helm as Kathryn left the bridge and muttered: "Not nearly enough." Rubbing his hand back and forth across the wheel, he gazed out the window with a smile on his face. "Thanks, girl. You were fantastic. Home and some rest and we'll pass on the cargo to someone else to deliver. Chief and the boys can have a field day tending to you."

"You called?" Chief eased onto the bridge. "Good to hear we can relax for a while."

"Eavesdropping can get you into trouble, Chief."

"Keeps life interesting."

"Yes, I think a few days at home will do us good. I need to do some digging. Something's odd about the Dolphin."

"Oh?" The Chief's head tilted and his left eyebrow rose.

"She said the ship was in the storm and there was an explosion. If it were the gas in the bags, the whole thing would have gone, not opened a hole in the side. Then there was that sulphur smell."

"Okay, you have my attention. Sounds like a bomb."

"That's what I'm thinking. It may take a few days to get any answers."

"If it's going to take that long, my boys and I want to add some things to the Lady Fair. I had an idea to fix up Victoria's space."

"Permission granted, Chief; just check with her first."

"Already done. What do you think of our passenger?"

The Captain, freezing in place for a moment, didn't go unnoticed by the Chief.

"She's a brave young lady, she kept her wits and used what she had at hand. She was even calm when she woke to tell us, in good detail, what happened."

"Going to tell me you didn't notice she's a very good-looking woman?"

"What's this about, Chief? She'll be off the ship tomorrow and that'll be that. Why should she be any different than anyone else?"

Chief headed for the hatchway. "Things to do. I'll have Joan send up some coffee. I see you did notice she's a very good-looking woman." His quick stepping through the hatchway cut off any retort.

13
June 24, 1898
The Galley

The Chief entered the galley to see Joan busy at the large side table, working some dough with small clouds of flour puffing up. The galley was huge. Ice coolers lined one wall. A large ten-burner stove was at the center of another wall; dozens of utensils hung from a brass overhead rack. Pantries flanked each side of a large cast iron stove. Under the huge windows along the outside wall, a prep table ran its full length. The shadows and light beams swayed across the floor and room as the Lady Fair moved. A large pine table, surrounded by eighteen chairs, was in the center of the galley. A dozen overhead electric lights filled the space with light when needed. Victoria sat on a stool in the corner with a red pantsuit in her lap, working on it with needle and thread.

The Chief leaned over Victoria to see what she was doing. "Why are you here working on that?"

Changing Times

"I was supposed to help Joan, but she's on a mission and said I was in the way. I'm staying in case I can do anything."

"You could take coffee to the Captain on the bridge."

"Great, my fingers need a break. This stuff's really tough. I've broken two needles already. Take a look." Handing the suit to the Chief, she went to the brewing coffee and got out the largest mug to fill.

The Chief felt the fabric. Recognition crossed his face. "This is from that Nomax Company. It's the latest stuff for fire suits. I have one near each engine room. Yes, it's tough, but it's also waterproof and fireproof. No wonder she had no burns. By the way, the Captain said 'okay' to working on your space."

"It's going to be a wonder, Chief. Thanks. I'm off to beard the dragon." With that, she left.

The Chief crossed over to Joan. "Joan, what's got you so intense?"

"We seldom have guests and I want to make a special dinner for a special guest. A full, fancy dinner."

There was a chuckle in his voice. "She's special, saving the baby and all. The Captain noticed her. The question is 'Did she notice him?'"

"You saw a connection, too?"

"I would have had to be on the moon not to see it."

"We can watch them over dinner." A smile came to Joan's lips.

"Nope, he's staying on the bridge. Had the pilots stand down for eight hours."

"Rats."

Chief thought for a moment and then grinned. "I'll talk to the pilots. Maybe we can work something out to get him relieved for some grub. I'll even pass the word to dress for dinner. You pass the word to find something nice for our guest to wear."

The Tour

Alexandria was in awe as Doc gave her a tour of the Lady Fair.

The Captain and the Lady Fair

"The Lady Fair is 600 feet long and 120 feet wide at the widest. The gas envelope is 1,800 feet long, giving great lift." Opening a door, Doc showed her the lounge. It was 50 feet square. As with most of the outside rooms, large windows gave a beautiful view of the passing clouds and the sea below. The inside wall was lined with shelves filled with books on all subjects. A grand piano took center stage on the forward wall. Writing desks waited for people to sit and write home about their adventure. Several couches faced the windows. The rest of the room held scattered wingback leather chairs and a few tables for playing cards.

"This is just a sample of the ship. She's like this everywhere. The Lady Fair was a luxury airship before the Captain bought her. We seldom use the lounge; we all like the galley." Doc stared at the view out the window. "This is a great place to come and watch the clouds or stars. It's quiet, and you can think here."

"How did you come to be on the crew?"

"Not a very interesting story. I was working in a hospital. Being a woman, I was only allowed to care for minor injuries or lost causes. I was frustrated. One day, a patient died I had come to really like. I ran out, and when I hit the sidewalk, I ran into the Captain. Knocked him on his backside. There I was, tears streaming down my face, trying to apologize, and he just stared at me. He got up, brushed himself off, grabbed my arm and dragged me to a nearby park. He told me he would accept my apology if I told him what had upset me. I told him everything I had inside that had been choking in me for a long time. Then he said, 'Come be the Doctor on my ship.' He said, most of the time, there would be nothing much to do, but if anyone were to get hurt while flying, I would be the only help for days. From simple cuts to near death, it would all be my job. He said I could set up a sickbay, with anything and everything I wanted. I took the job then and there, and I've never regretted the decision a second. All the crew has about the same story but theirs are theirs to tell."

The tour of all four decks continued. The two bottom decks were for cargo. The upper two decks held luxurious staterooms, galley, lounge, sickbay, and a formal dining room. Doc explained that above the upper deck was the bridge with a meeting room attached to it on the aft end, and then the Captain's cabin behind that. As the tour ended, it was near the time for dinner.

"Let's get changed for dinner. I'm sure Joan made something nice."

"This ship is so beautiful. It must be wonderful to work and live here."

"The Lady Fair is our home away from home."

"How did the Captain afford all this?"

"Pick a rumor. He won it at cards; he blackmailed someone; he inherited a lot of money and he stole it. None of us knows. The Captain doesn't talk about himself."

"A rich hero who has a secret past; there must be a story there."

"I'm sure there is."

14
June 24, 1898
The Dining Room

The dining room was set up for a full spread with good linen. Fine china and crystal glasses sparkled. Silverware gleamed on a table large enough for 100. The dark wood paneling gave the room a warm feeling. The setting sun cast a reddish-orange light through the wall of floor-to-ceiling windows. Joan scurried about, making sure everything was perfect. One by one, the crew entered and took a seat. The men were clean-shaven. Victoria and Kathryn had their hair up. All the crew wore a formal white uniform with gold trim. No rank or insignia showed, only a patch depicting the Lady Fair on the shoulder.

The Captain entered, and all stood while he seated himself at the head of the table. "It seems my pilots think they give orders. I was ordered to dress and attend a formal dinner. Anyone care to explain what's going on?"

The crew glanced around at each other, but no one spoke up. They all looked to Joan as she entered with two large polished silver pots of coffee to place on the table. "What? Why are you all staring at me? What'd I do?"

"I asked what this is all about and they seem to be looking at you to answer."

"Captain, do you think I would let our guest think we have no class and no manners? Of course, we need a nice dinner for Alexandria. She survived a wreck and saved Kira. That deserves something."

"Why do I feel there's more to this?"

"Oh my! This is beautiful, Joan." Alexandria entered wearing a light blue dress cut low on the bodice. A darker blue corset showed off the curve of her waist. Her hair was flowing freely down her back.

The men stood, and the Captain pulled out the chair to his right. "The crew seems to have gone mad and overdone things a bit, but it's deserved."

"Thank you, Captain. Thank you, everyone." She gave a smile and a nod to each member. "I'm sorry, but I don't remember everyone's name I met today, but I'll catch up. This should be for all of you, not me. You saved Kira and me in a storm. I just floated around clinging to a piece of wood for dear life. I thank all of you."

"Joan, if you'll begin serving, I'll do the honors. Around the table, we have Chief, Henry to a select few. Kathryn, which means Pilot Diana is on the bridge. Melissa, also known as Doc. Victoria, then there's Avery and Chance, our Chief's engineers. Tailor and Rigger, our deckhands."

"I have so many questions. Why is it Pilot Diana or Pilot Kathryn sometimes and Diana or Kathryn at other times?"

"That's easy. Whichever one is acting Pilot is called Pilot. On this ship, it avoids confusion as to who has the pilot responsibilities at the time. It's also a show of respect. Some of the names are not names, but a kind of title gained through time and actions. Rigger here is the best I have seen at rigging lines. Tailor there, his name is Marcus. He became 'Tailor' after a small adventure he and the Chief had to patch holes in the lift bags. He bested the Chief in the speed of sewing the holes, which saved the ship."

"I'm surprised there are so many women onboard. I didn't even know there were women pilots."

"There aren't. But that's too long a story. That's a pretty necklace you have."

"Oh, it's not mine; it belongs to Kira. I borrowed it to wear. I don't know anything about it, but it's pretty. I couldn't make sense of the markings."

"Markings?"

"On the back. Look for yourself."

The Captain looked at the markings as she held out the necklace to the full length of the chain. His eyes widened. "Yes, odd, but, overall, a pretty piece." His cheeks flushed when he realized his line of sight put him in line to stare at her chest in the low-cut gown. He straightened back up quickly.

"I had a tour of the ship and it's beautiful. Why are there so many cabins, a large beautiful lounge, and this fancy dining room, if you only carry cargo?"

"It was a luxury ship. We kept these decks as they were and modified the decks below, which were the cheap cabins, and for cargo. From time to time we do carry a few important people under special circumstances, so it works out."

Joan served the mulligatawny soup made with celery, turnips, chicken, and curry powder boiled and passed through a colander. Pieces of roasted chicken floated in the golden yellow mixture. That started the evening on a good note. Each course was more elaborate than the last. The chatter stayed light. The crew kept sneaking looks at the Captain and Alexandria talking at the head of the table. Each time the Captain and Alexandria's eyes met, they would quickly find an interest in a water glass or another bite of food.

"Joan, the dinner was so wonderful. I've never had such food in my life. Something I'd expect in the grandest restaurant There had to be more than seven courses. I'll never forget this. Nor will I forget any of you after I leave tomorrow."

"I must return to the bridge. Alexandria, it's been most pleasant." The Captain spoke again as he passed through the bulkhead. "Very nice dinner … Chef."

Joan plopped into an empty chair, her eyes glistening. "I would have been happy with 'Cook' or 'Cookie.' "

"To Chef Joan!" Everyone raised their glasses in a toast.

15
June 24, 1898
9 PM
Alexandria's Cabin

Victoria followed Alexandria back to her cabin. The cabin was large, with a floor-to-ceiling window looking out at passing moonlit clouds. A table and four chairs, a king-size, four-poster bed, two dressers, and a loveseat furnished the room. The carpet was thick and lush. A full-length mirror was attached to the wall next to the door. A connecting door led to the lavatory and shower. Kira was still sleeping, but it would soon be time for a bottle. Alexandria picked her up and held her close.

"Thank you so much for the dress. I thought you were all about pants."

"On ship, yes, but dirt-side I like to be in a *proper* dress." The poke was said with a smile. "I see you two are getting attached."

"She's such a good baby; someone must miss her. Do you mind a few questions? I had a lot answered, but some raised a few more."

"Be my guest. I'll answer what I can."

Changing Times

"Why the big commotion about Joan?"

"You mean Chef Joan. As the Captain said at dinner, everyone gets a nickname or title, based on something they've done. Tonight, the Captain was saying her cooking was worthy of a Chef. We all agree. She's been with the Captain a long time and was hoping for some kind of recognition. She would have been happy with anything, but he declared her 'Chef'. The best. She deserves it, but to be called that now, as a title/nickname, well, she couldn't be prouder. Even when she cooks something simple, the taste is heaven on earth. You'll see."

"Tonight was unlike anything I've ever had before. I wanted to eat more of everything but wanted to try the next thing at the same time. She is a Chef."

Alexandria continued. "Maybe I'm not supposed to know, but what was that about the pilots aren't pilots?"

"Wow, that is a full story, but here goes a short version. They both wanted to be pilots since they saw their first airship drift over their heads. They studied hard with what little they teach in school to girls. Then they bothered boyfriends and anyone else to teach them math and more."

"I know how that goes. I had to pay tutors, and they were reluctant."

"Yep, same thing. They got into Pilots' school. I guess they got in because those in charge thought it would be funny to have two that would be the point of all the jokes. They were top in everything, but when it got time for Pilots' papers, they were told women aren't Pilots and thrown out. They ended up here because they heard there were openings. They wanted any job they could get so they could get in the air. Captain checked them out and found out about the school. The Captain is a ticketed Pilot, so we fly under his ticket, but they both do the flying. It works for them, but the Captain doesn't want them to feel bad about it, so he won't talk about it when they're around. I think he is rankled about it as a gross wrong to them."

"The Captain is something. He treats men and women the same." Alexandria paused in thought about that and the next question. "He was

37

sitting stiff at dinner. Is something wrong?" She sat on the bed and rocked Kira in her arms.

Victoria chuckled. "So you want to know if he's healthy? He's single, not seeing anyone, and sat stiff because he is taped up with a few broken ribs."

"Broken ribs? What happened?"

"Gossip flies around this ship, but something always gets left out. Doc patched him up while you were still out. They got broken while in the water to get you."

Alexandria shook her head. "I don't know what to say to that but I must thank him again. Another question. What do you do on ship?"

"You already thanked him. I suggest you don't make a fuss about it with him." Victoria paused. "Did you feel that?"

"What?"

"The engines picked up to full speed." Victoria dashed out the door, leaving Alexandria with a stunned look.

16
June 24, 1898
9 PM
The Bridge

Entering the bridge, Victoria saw the Captain, the Chief and both Pilots already there.

"Problem, Captain?"

"Not yet." The Captain continued his pacing. "Chief, that necklace had the symbols for Phoenix on the back. We need to get home to read it. Something is not right."

"We'll be ready for anything, Captain. I'll go do a walk-through."

"Victoria, I hate the feeling, but I think we're getting close to the time you earned your keep. Are you ready in case we do?"

"Yes, Captain, I will be."

"My trust is in you."

"I'll go get prepped to ready status, Captain. You call; I'll be there." Victoria left the bridge and walked quickly to her cabin.

Pilot Kathryn turned to the Captain. "Anything we can do, just let us know."

"We're okay for the moment. I'll be in my cabin. I need to change." The Captain stroked the bulkhead and continued out.

Diana took a deep breath and blew it out. She walked towards the brown, buttoned, overstuffed couch at the rear of the bridge. "I think we're in for more fun. I'm going to nap on the couch just in case. By the way, how did dinner go?"

"I forgot to tell you." Excitement tinged Kathryn's voice. "Joan is now Chef! The food was fantastic. Chef put on a show, and there was a lot between those two even though they tried to ignore it. You should have seen him go red when he stared at her chest."

"I can guess the two you're talking about and yes, it was great food. Chef brought me some of everything. Any guess on the troubles ahead?"

"The only thing I can guess is it's not with the weather."

17
June 25, 1898
8 AM
The Bridge

"Avery, Chance, to the spotters' nest. Crew, batten down." The captain turned off the loud-box and returned to pacing. "Status, Pilot."

Pilot Kathryn glanced over the instruments. "Full speed, on course, no problems."

The Captain and the Lady Fair

Chef Joan entered the bridge with a large pot of coffee. "Last pot until status relaxed, Captain."

The Captain poured himself a cup. "Thank you, Chef Joan."

The Captain was on his second cup when Alexandria entered to stand next to Chef Joan at the back of the bridge. At that moment, the spotters' nest reported. "Two craft appear to be heading across the horizon." Shortly thereafter, a new status report came. "Course change to head on, now three craft. Possible airsharks."

The Captain's voice over the loud-box gave new orders. "Gunner, you're up. Three unknown craft approaching bow-on. All hands, combat stations." He nodded to Pilot Kathryn. "Keep her steady so Gunner can get a good shot."

Alexandria whispered to Chef. "What's an airshark?"

"They're new flyers. They have no lift bags but wings sticking out. They're like sharks because they have to keep moving forward. If they go too slow or stop, they fall from the sky. They're very fast and can fly circles around us. They also always have guns."

Gunner walked with deliberate steps across the deck to the furthest point on the bow. A metal helmet gleamed and a long black duster coat reached to the deck but didn't blow in the wind. It hung stiff. Gunner carried a huge rifle, longer than the figure was tall. Resting the butt of the rifle on the deck, Gunner waited.

Alexandra turned to Chef Joan and whispered. "Who's that? I thought I met everyone."

"That's Gunner. Victoria."

Alexandria's eyes went wide and her mouth dropped open a moment.

As the airsharks came into Gunner's range, she lifted the rifle, clipped it to the wide leather belt crossing over her left shoulder and across her chest, settled it into place, and held an aim on the lead craft, waiting.

"What's she waiting for?" Alexandria's voice had a slight nervous tone.

"A reason to fire."

Changing Times

A stream of white smoke from guns firing trailed from the lead craft. Gunner fired. The report was easily heard in the bridge. Gunner was pushed back a step with the blast. Without waiting to see what had happened with the first shot, Gunner lowered the barrel to the deck and put in a new cartridge to raise the rifle again aim at the craft on the left. The first craft spewed black smoke as it spiraled down to the sea. Both remaining craft gave off white trails of smoke from the guns spewing bullets. Small craters peppered around Gunner. Slivers of wood flew in every direction. She fired again. The black smoke pouring from the second craft was immediate. More craters walked the deck until Gunner was knocked back a few paces.

"Oh my lord, she's hit!" Alexandria clutched Chef Joan's arm.

"Shhhhh." Chef Joan grabbed Alexandria on her arm and squeezed hard.

"But why are they shooting at her instead of the lift bag?"

"With the gunner out, they feel they have plenty of time to shoot up the bags. The idiots. God, I do hate this."

Gunner raised the rifle once more and, with no delay, fired as the craft was almost on them. The hit was more spectacular than the others were. The Craft exploded into small pieces. The whole action was over in less than a minute.

Gunner turned and slowly walked back from the bow.

Chef Joan relaxed her painful grip on Alexandria's arm.

"Gunner, to the bridge at your leisure. Spotters, keep station. Everyone else to standby." The Captain sat back in his chair.

Barely two minutes had passed when Victoria entered the bridge. "Yes, Captain?"

The Captain eyed the four bullet holes across Victoria's chest. "You've been hit! Pilot, call Doc."

"Wait! I'm okay. I'm not hurt at all, beyond some bruises."

"You did very well out there. When we're done here, I want you down to the sickbay and checked over by Doc. Are you truly all right? It was your first time as gunner and please explain the bullet holes that don't bleed."

"I'm okay, Captain. A bit shaken. The last one, I saw the man fly out. I feel bad about it, but I stand by my promise and I am glad I made it. When Chief added plating to protect the bridge, there was some left over. We sewed small plates of it into this coat. Neck down; front and back, I'm protected. For three airsharks I thought it best to use my gun instead of the ship's portable guns." She removed the coat and handed it to the Captain. His eyes widened at the weight. At the same time, Alexandria's eyes went wide at what was her old pantsuit, now a very tight, form-fitting outfit, leaving no doubt as to where every curve and crease was. Joan stood transfixed.

"I thought you said 'light'. This must be 60 pounds at least." He handed the coat back and saw her outfit. He couldn't stop himself from looking head to toe and back again.

"The weight is worth it and, if I need to, it comes off easy enough."

"Your weapon?"

"Chief and I worked it up months ago. It has a sling that goes over my shoulder and neck to support it, so all I have to do is aim."

"That's not a rifle, that's a cannon. I would say the ammo is not a standard issue."

"No, Captain, Chief and I made that, too. It has an explosive in the tip." Victoria pulled one of the shells from her pocket. It was the size of a good carrot.

18
June 25, 1898
10:30 AM
The Galley

Wearing the blue shift Doc had loaned her, Alexandria sat drinking tea in the galley with Doc, Chef Joan, and Victoria. Kira lay sleeping in her arms.

"It's been an exciting trip, but I'll be glad to get land under my feet. I'm going to miss Kira. I'm getting too attached; I tried not to, but she's so good and beautiful." She sighed softly. "I don't know how I'm going to get to the conference."

Victoria, now dressed in her usual canvas work clothes, gave her a smile. "Oh, I'm sure someone will see you safely."

Doc chuckled into her cup of tea. "Yes, someone will; I'm sure. It's going to be great to be home. Hubby will be so happy to see me."

"Hubby?"

"Yes, I'm married. Sometimes we're apart months at a time but it keeps us from arguing. It makes time together too precious to waste. We do go out for months sometimes but more often it is only a few days or a week or so."

"It never crossed my mind anyone aboard was married."

Doc smiled. "Oh, yes. The only ones not married are the Captain, Victoria, and Chef here. You have *got* to meet the Chief's wife."

"It must be hard on everyone being apart all the time. I think I'd want a more normal relationship."

With a glint in her eyes, Doc commented. "Depends on the man, now; doesn't it? You'll meet all the spouses at the party."

"Party? What party?"

A touch of happy excitement tinged Doc's voice. "Whenever we come home, the crew and spouses always have a big party on the beach.

Food, music, dancing till you can't move anymore. Of course, you have to be there. Some natives of the Island join us and play music."

"I wouldn't miss it. Victoria, you were amazing. I don't know how you could stand there with bullets flying and still hit them like that." Alexandria paused. "I'm not sure my aunt ever thought her pantsuit would ever be, umm …, so fitted."

"It's my lucky suit. It kept you safe; it'll do that for me. I do love it. Thanks again for giving it to me. As for hitting them, I was always a good shot growing up with my brothers. I would tag along when they went hunting and pestered them to let me shoot, too. I was good from the start. I asked Father every day until I got my own rifle for Christmas. I loved it and got so I seldom ever missed."

"How did you get on the crew?"

"I, uh, met the crew and felt good here; everyone is so nice to each other. It's like a home I've wanted since my mother died, so I asked the Captain to give me a job. When I finally said I could shoot as well as any man, he had me show him. He took me on as gunner. I try to help everyone until I'm needed as gunner. This was the first time I've been needed. I thought it would bother me more, but when I was out there, I got mad someone was trying to hurt my friends, the ship, and me. Then it was over." Victoria paused and looked down at her wringing hands as if they were trying to remove a spot. "I felt bad about the man I saw fall, but when he fired at us, any doubt left as to what I had to do. I had the Captain agree I wouldn't shoot anyone unless they shot first. I promised him I would protect the ship. He said that's best anyway. So here I am."

"Why didn't you tell me you were a gunner when I asked what you do?"

"Because I didn't want you to know. I thought you would think less of me if you knew I was a gunner. It's not a nice thing to have to kill people, but then you were happy with what I did and said I was amazing; that makes me feel good. I'm proud to now be an *active* protector of the ship." Victoria leaned over and gave Alexandria a hug. "Thanks."

Over the loud-box, a status from the spotters' nest came through. "Home sighted."

The Captain's voice responded without delay. "Good job. Stand down. All crew, stations for docking."

Victoria jumped up. "Want to see what docking looks like from the bridge? If we stay quiet in the back, it'll be okay."

Victoria and Alexandria left for the bridge.

Doc looked at Chef Joan, smiled a big smile, and had a twinkle in her eye. "I think she'll do. The Captain is trying too hard to stay away from her. What do you think?"

Chef Joan smiled the same smile. "Yep, I think the crew thinks so, too. We'll just have to see if a nudge now and then is needed. Sometimes I think fate is a real thing. After the fight with the smugglers/slavers, the first time he was needed, the old gunner walked off. Lazy bum thought it would be an easy ride. Then Victoria, rescued from that same ship, joins us. She fits in and won't quit. That's fate."

Doc smiled. "Victoria didn't really feel like she belonged until today. Now she looks happy and proud to belong. I just hope she has another year before she has to go to work again."

19
June 25, 1898
11 AM
The Island Of Paaku

The Lady Fair approached the bay for docking at an empty docking mast. Both pilots were together, bringing her in. The view of the Island was breathtaking, white sandy beaches backed by tall palm trees, a large mountain behind rolling hills covered in green, and white buildings dotted around with a larger building near the bay. The pale green water in the bay was still, with a glasslike surface reflecting the clouds above.

Alexandria's eyes scanned back and forth, trying to see everything. "It's so beautiful."

As Lady Fair drew near the docking mast, Pilot Diana used the loud-box. "Drop ground lines." Ropes dropped from each side for the ground handlers to help guide in the ship if needed.

Men scurried to the ropes, ten men to each line. Pilot Diana released small amounts of gas at a time to lower the nose of the ship to the level of the mooring ring. Pilot Kathryn played the throttles to slow the ship to a gentle bump into the mooring. The men below let out a loud cheer.

"I can't believe something this big could do that." Alexandria watched the men below.

Victoria leaned closer and whispered. "They're the best at docking. Look below and watch the lines near the bow."

The ground crew released all the lines except for the bowline once the mooring ring was locked. The men were tying something on. Slowly the bowline was pulled up. As it cleared the side of the ship, Alexandria could see a basket was tied on. Chance brought it to the bridge as soon as it was up.

"Pilots, your basket." Inside were fruits of all kinds.

"They give the arriving ships baskets of fruit. That's nice." Alexandria clapped and grinned at the pleasantry.

Victoria chuckled. "No, only the Lady Fair gets them for the pilots. They're the only ones that moor up so well, they have little to do unless there's a hard wind. They're also the only ones that come in that don't dump ballast on them. The ground crew loves them. It does get under the skin of other pilots that they're so good at it, but the ground crew says the other ships are getting better as they try to match them."

"Good for them."

"It really hit home when the pilots of one of the other ships were talking bad about them and the ground crew heard. Those pilots sported black eyes the next day. Then, to make it worse for them, the next time their ship came in, they had to wait a half-hour for the ground crew to show up and get them in. Those pilots couldn't even get close." Victoria laughed. "The commanders heard and put them on extra details and told them they had better learn to fly better than girls or they would be kicked out."

"I'm glad to hear more than this crew appreciates them."

"It gets boring from here on. They run out a gangway from the side of the ship to the loading platform. Once it's in place, they unlock the platform so it can rotate as the ship moves in the wind. We walk down a spiral staircase in the middle of the platform, then another gangplank to the dock area. Cargo and supplies come up by the deck crane." She paused and stared at the crane. "That's why he needed it."

"Who needed what?"

"Sorry, I was just thinking out loud. Nothing important. Everyone below is finishing up now."

Alexandria watched in amazement. "This is like a dance! Things and people moving in time with each other."

"I watch docking at home every time I can. Everyone will be making the ship set for 'at dock' status. The Captain will take you dirt-side as soon as everything is settled. You might want to change for the trip. Welcome to our home, the Island of Paaku."

20
June 25, 1898
4 PM
Admirals Office, Phoenix Building

The Admiral's office, on the top floor of the sand-white building, overlooked palm trees and the lagoon. The Navy ships harbored were impressive in size and armament. They were dwarfed by the two Dreadnaughts moored at the docking masts at the end of the lagoon. The Lady Fair looked small, docked next to them. The view out the large plate-glass window was tranquil, with the leaves of the palms barely moving. The room, paneled in bamboo, could easily hold thirty in a conference if the need arose. The Captain sat in a wingback chair in front of the large mahogany desk while the Admiral finished reading a new report.

The Admiral was middle-aged, with white hair and the beginning of a potbelly. He lowered the report. "This is very bad. The only woman with a baby to board the Dolphin was the wife of a Phoenix agent. She boarded at the last minute with no luggage. About the time she was boarding, her husband was killed. He was pushed in front of a local train and the killer escaped. The fact she has an encrypt necklace tells me she was acting as a courier. That she placed it on the baby says she knew the importance of it. Also, it's odd that a man boarded immediately after her, and had no luggage, only a satchel. Someone was willing to bomb an airship to stop her. Then, there's the airshark attack. Those airsharks had to have been air-launched. The only airship reported in the area was the Dorset. The Dorset is owned by the Garrote Company. So far, there's no link between the two attacks. Let's see what the encrypt has to say." The Admiral pressed a button on a box on his desk. A faint buzz came from the outer office.

Alexandria entered and offered the Admiral a slight smile. "Hello; how can I help? I don't know anything beyond what I've already told about the crash."

"Straight to business. I like that. I'm Admiral Archer, and I asked you here because you have information you don't know you have. First, I'll tell you we've sent word to your aunt and uncle that you're alive and well. Now I need to ask you if you know of anyone who may want to hurt you or stop you from your research."

"There are many that don't think women should be in science, but I don't know anyone that would go this far. My research into the aether energy shields could only help people, so I can't see why anyone would stop that."

"I can. Is your shield large or small?"

"It is a matter of applied energy. It can be made to any size."

Changing Times

"So a country could protect its cities and its ships, and attack anywhere, anytime with immunity from any defense offered, unless they had the shields. I'm military, so I think that way. There may be some other reason, but I can't think of any. If a country is working on the same thing, then they need to stop you so they would be the only ones to have it. If you announce to the world, all countries would have it and make war use pointless. Let's see what other information you have. May I see the necklace we asked you to bring?"

"Of course. I just have a hard time thinking anyone would want to kill me."

The Admiral took the offered necklace and worked to install it in a box on his desk. The box had two thin arms on top, which held the jewel of the necklace.

"I'm afraid there is more to this. The bombing of the airship is an action from a military mind. Total destruction. The airsharks are different and were probably a civilian action. Military would have gone straight for the lift bags. Now we'll see if we have any better clues." The Admiral closed the curtains over the large window and turned on the box; an arm rose from the side. A light appeared on the arm and projected through the jewel. "Based on frequency, messages can be read that have been encoded in the jewel." An image appeared on the wall with a short text, followed by a list of names. "My god, a list of moles within Phoenix."

"What's Phoenix?" Alexandria slowly sat down in the chair next to the Captain.

"Admiral?" The Captain raised an eyebrow.

"Her life's on the line; she might as well know everything."

The Captain cleared his throat and turned in his chair to face Alexandria. "Phoenix is a secret arm of the government. Works independently and has a wide range of powers. Actions deemed best to be out of the public eye are handled by Phoenix. Leaks of information could cause anything from embarrassment to massive casualties and disruption of a planned action. This Island is home base."

Admiral Archer nodded. "Captain Castellan was once an officer in Phoenix. He retired early with honors."

"I still do contract work for Phoenix from time to time and I'm kept on retainer. Our cargo hauls are legitimate and earn us extra cash."

"Captain, I'm going to put you under contract again. I want you to take Miss Castle to New City. We'll have a press meeting set up there to cover the energy shield she's working on. That might bring rats out of the walls, and our agents can do a protect action. With luck, we can catch one and get some information. We'll use only direct contact with the agents to avoid the moles. We need to leave them in place and track to whom they're reporting. Setting up the press means it'll be public and may mean you may be attacked at any time. Your skills may make the difference. I can't use military ships for this; it would tip our hand about the moles and show too much military interest. It would drive them all further underground."

"I'm not happy about putting Alexandria at any more risk, but she'll be at risk no matter where she is."

"We need to get you proper pilots for this mission. Find yourself two qualified ones."

"But there are …" Alexandria's comment was cut off by the touch of the Captain's hand on her knee.

"I already have two great pilots, Admiral. Tested and true."

"You do not have qualified, ticketed Pilots, Captain. My bosses are going to insist. This will be the first contract since your qualified ones left. How you fly as a civilian is your business but, under contract, it's mine."

Captain sat silently for a time and then spoke softly. "You know full well they're as qualified and are better than most. Just denied tickets because of gender, but you're the boss. As you know, the actual selection of any pilot on my ship is my decision." The Captain stood, placed a hand under Alexandria's arm to pull her to her feet, and continued speaking as they headed for the door. "I'll put out a posting, listing the openings. Maybe give it a two-week opening so I can choose from a larger number. Then do the interviews, which could take a week or two. I wouldn't want to rush into picking wrong pilots. Then I'll probably need to take them up to test the skills. As Captain, I can't take just anyone and I won't. Yep, can do Admiral." Reaching the door, he turned to the Admiral. "It's too bad it's only a matter of some silly papers. See you in five or six weeks when I have my pilots hired."

The door closed on a screaming Admiral.

"Won't you get into trouble for talking like that and delaying everything?"

There was a gleam in the Captain's eye and a lift in his step. "Nope. Let's go to a party."

21
June 25, 1898
6 PM
The Party

The staccato sound of drums, easily heard long before arriving, lifted their spirits. Following a path through palm trees and lush, flowering vegetation, Alexandria and the Captain were alone for the first time. They walked slowly; neither seemed to be in a hurry to join the party full of people.

"I'm overwhelmed by all that's been happening. Not just the Dolphin, but so many new things. There are completely new lives and ways of living I never knew. My tutors taught me math and science, but nothing of the world. Airsharks, women happy in pants, Victoria in my pantsuit, women flying airships, maybe people wanting to kill me. It's just so much."

"If anyone asked me, I would say you are doing fine and handling things well. I'm sure it's all new and strange, but it's up to you if you want to adapt or stay with your old life. No one will judge you, no matter which you choose."

"Captain, I'm sorry I laughed at your name. It was rude of me and I can understand if it made you angry with me."

"Angry at you? Why would I be angry when everyone does the same thing? If I weren't Captain of an airship, no one would laugh, but my life would be dull. I love being on the Lady Fair. I was never angry at you."

"Then why have you avoided me? The rest of the crew like talking to me, but you only talk business with me."

"I, uh …" He sucked in a deep breath, and then blew it out hard and stopped walking. Once again, he checked his shoes. "I have no idea what the crew has told you, but we weren't there to rescue you by accident. I had a feeling there was trouble and something pulled at me to get there in a hurry. I learned the hard way, long ago, to follow my feelings. Then, when I saw you, a shock went through me. I have no idea what it was, but I felt drawn to you and it …" He paused. "Well, it bothers me." He resumed his walk.

Alexandria followed, staying a step behind him. "I knew you were coming."

The captain stopped and spun in place to face her. "What?"

"I saw you in a dream. I thought it was just a dream when I woke in the sickbay. Then, I saw you and, I don't know, something in me knew it was you I dreamed was coming. Even your name sounded right."

The Captain stared at her for a moment. "I guess there are some things we'll never understand." He turned and walked at a slow pace until she caught up. They walked along the path a little closer together, hands brushing from time to time.

The path opened onto a small hill looking down on a beach lit by several fires. Dozens of people were walking about or dancing in a circle lit by a larger central fire. A dozen small huts dotted the beach. Most were open-sided and all had thatch roofs. One of the fires featured a whole pig roasting on a spit slowly turned by a laughing Victoria. Overseeing the spit and slopping on a sauce was Chef Joan. Three young women knelt near the fire, fanning the coals with their skirts to get the newly laid wood to catch. "Look at the colors! Everyone's clothes have so much color!"

"Come, let's join. I can smell the cooking pig from here."

A short brisk walk brought them to the center of the festivities. "Good to see you, Chief. I have good news; you have three days to tinker and feel free to hire as many men as you need to help."

The Chief grinned widely. "And here I thought the party couldn't be better! That's great news. Hello, Alexandria. Welcome to the party."

"Thank you, Chief. I kinda stand out in this plain dress."

"Easily fixed. NEENAA!" The bellow the Chief uttered might have been heard far at sea.

A petite, young woman ran up to his side, barely reaching his elbow. Her blonde hair, which hung past her waist, moved slightly with the ocean breeze. She looked about 16 years old. "And why does the great Chief yell my name?" The punch to his stomach hit with a loud smack, but the Chief didn't flinch. "Hello, Captain."

"Neenaa, let me introduce you to Alexandria, the baby saver. She thinks she stands out in that dress. Think you can help?"

"Of course." She grabbed Alexandria's wrist in a surprisingly strong grip and pulled her off through the party in the direction of a large hut on the far side. Passing a group of women, she yelled "Baby saver!" They all jumped to their feet and followed. "We've heard all about you and saving the baby. It's wonderful. Babies are so precious. All the wives have wanted to meet you. This is a great party." Neenaa chattered nonstop until all the women were in the hut. "She needs proper party clothes!" So many women talking at once made it impossible to understand anyone.

"Wait, wait; what are you doing? I thought you would just show me some clothes to pick." Hands undid Alexandria's clothes and pulled them off. The hands did not stop even at pulling off all the undergarments. "Stop, please."

Happy laughter and giggles continued as they grabbed different fabrics and discarded them until all seemed to agree on a pale green fabric with a bright red flower print. A rip and the fabric was in two pieces. The narrower piece wrapped around her chest and tied in the back. The wider piece wrapped around her waist and then tied at the hip. It was long enough to reach her ankles. Her party clothes looked no different from those of the rest of the women, other than the color and print. Neenaa reached up and pulled out the combs holding Alexandria's hair up, to let it fall loose. Again, Neenaa grabbed Alexandria's hand and pulled, this time back to the party.

"Wait; stop. I'm not covered. There's nothing over my middle and my leg shows."

"Right, now you're dressed like us. Relax. Besides, you want to get your man interested, don't you?"

"What? My man? No, no one is my man."

"Please do not call my husband a liar. If they say he's yours, then it is so."

"Who's your husband?"

"The Chief, of course."

Alexandria pinched her lips together to keep quiet and not say the wrong thing. They arrived back at the Chief and the Captain's side.

"Now you look like a native. Much better." The Chief bent down and gave Neenaa a hug. "Thank you, precious."

"Anything for you, O Great Chief." While still bent over, she grabbed his ears, pulled him down further, and kissed his nose.

The Captain's eyes did not leave Alexandria's as he smiled. "You look stunning."

Alexandria kept one hand on the side of the skirt to keep her leg covered and her other arm over her stomach as she blushed.

Silence fell in the immediate area. Alexandria looked around and saw a tall, thin, elderly man, wearing only a wrap around his waist and a wreath of leaves and flowers on his head.

Changing Times

The Captain gave a short bow. "Arku, you bless our party by your presence." The rest of the group also gave a short bow.

"I see the saver of life is among you. The Island's blessings are on you." His fingers poked down into a pouch at his waist and marked Alexandria's forehead with a circle and a wavy horizontal line with a black powder. "May your place in life find you soon." Saying no more, he turned and walked on through the party.

"That was the local head man and medicine man. He seldom leaves his home in the hills. I'm surprised by his appearance here."

"What was that about?" Alexandria looked bewildered.

"Neenaa, care to explain?" The Captain wore a small smile.

"He has put a blessing on you. The circle is of life or spirit; the wavy line is for the ever-changing lines of fate."

The Captain kept staring at Alexandria's forehead.

Doc walked up and handed Alexandria and the Captain each a drink in coconut shells. "This will help get you in a dancing mood. I would've brought Kira for you, but she's sleeping in the community hut, where all the babies and small children are watched over during parties."

Alexandria hesitated then used the hand over her stomach to take the drink. She took a sip then drank it down. "That's good. I was thirsty. Thank you."

There was mirth in Doc's voice. "You might go easy on that stuff. It'll sneak up on you. It'll make your legs wobble when you dance."

The Captain put his hand on Alexandria's back and guided her to the dancing area. "I can take a hint now and then. Especially when I'm hit over the head. Dancing it is." The music had slowed to allow couples a rest from the fast pace and more intimate dancing. As they danced, his hand started a slow, up-and-down caress of her back. "If I step on your toes, just tell me."

Alexandria quickly learned the new slow way to dance. At first, she squirmed a little at his touch, but the drink relaxed her enough to let go of the skirt hiding her leg.

22
June 26, 1898
9 AM
The Galley

Alexandria sat with Kira in her lap. A circle and a wavy line on Kira's forehead matched the ones on Alexandria's. One arm held Kira; the other, with an elbow on the table, held her forehead. Her face was close to the steaming cup of coffee as she whispered, "Why didn't someone warn me about the coconuts?"

"We did, but each time you said 'Okay, just this one.'" Doc sat down at the table with her own cup. All the women onboard were having coffee and relaxing as, in port, there isn't much to do.

Diana added to Alexandria's misery. "We all liked that nice, sultry dance you did before passing out. Holding on to the Captain like that. I'm sure he'll remember that forever."

"What? I did what?" Alexandria rocked her head and groaned.

The whole table broke out in laughter.

"Just teasing."

"I remember dancing. I remember eating and talking to everyone, then more dancing, then nothing."

"When you were staggering, Victoria and Chef Joan brought you back to the ship." Diana patted her shoulder.

Finishing her cup, Alexandria asked for more. "I've never felt like this. I'm going to die. When I woke, I was still wearing the clothes they put on me. I don't know what happened to your dress, Doc."

"It came back all safe and sound. Don't worry about it."

"Things are bumping in my head. Questions? I seem to be all questions these days."

"Like what?" Doc poured her another cup.

Changing Times

"I heard something about the Captain ignoring a feeling and something about retiring early."

"I guess it's not really a secret, just something not talked about much. A couple of years ago, the Captain was on active duty of some sort. He was a Captain then, too. There was a mission to guard against an invasion. He was at his assigned place. He got a feeling he was needed to the west, and it got stronger and stronger. He ignored it and stayed with his orders. A sister ship was ambushed and all 163 onboard killed. He blamed himself for not going. I guess they let him retire because he said he wasn't sure if he felt it again, that he'd obey orders. I think he's still haunted by it. He and the Chief retired, he bought this ship, and here we are. Those feelings took us to you. The need to get to you pulled at him hard. That's probably why he made that stupid leap over the rail. If he gets in a mood, we don't question; we just follow orders."

"Everything new I hear makes him more … special."

"Sorry to leave you, but we have to go start packing." Diana stood and stretched.

Kathryn gave Alexandria a hug. "Thanks for letting us know so we could be ready."

"Wait, ready for what and pack for where?"

Diana spoke in a saddened voice. "You don't remember telling us the Captain has to replace us? That's why we're here today instead of at home. Pack up and be ready."

"Oh my Lord in Heaven! I shouldn't have said anything. Please don't do anything until the Captain says something. He'll be angry at me for sure."

"No, he won't. He likes you too much. We should thank the Captain for letting us have our dream as long as it lasted. No one else would." The pilots left the galley, shoulders drooped.

Doc stared at Alexandria. "Replaced?"

"This coffee is not going to help how bad I feel."

23
June 26, 1898
9:15 AM
The Bridge

Both pilots entered the bridge to find the Captain sitting in his chair, watching the army of men working on the bow of the ship.

"Captain?" Kathryn's voice was soft.

"Pilots, good morning. I trust you had a good time at the party."

Kathryn stepped forward. "Yes, Captain, we did. We just wanted to say 'thank you' for everything."

"You're quite welcome, but for what?"

"Taking us on as pilots and treating us fair. That's more than anyone has ever done for us. We know you're of good heart and would find it difficult to give us the bad news. So we thought we would let you know, we already know and will be ready to go whenever you say."

The Captain looked back out the window; the angle blocked their view of his smile. "Care to explain what you're talking about?"

Diana stepped forward. "We know we aren't supposed to know yet, but you have to replace us and are hiring new pilots."

"Mind if I ask you a few questions?"

The pilots answered in chorus. "No, Captain."

"Have *I* told you, you're to be replaced?"

"No, Captain."

"Have *I* told you to be ready to leave?"

"No, Captain."

"Have *you* decided to start giving orders?"

"No, Captain."

"Have *you* decided I'm someone not to trust anymore?"

"No, Captain."

"Then if I'm still the Captain and I still give the orders, then your orders are to run as fast as you can to your homes and your husbands and do whatever you do. Have fun and relax. Try trusting me. Report back to this bridge in three days at eight AM sharp."

"Thank you, Captain, but …" Kathryn was cut off.

"Orders given. Now MOVE!"

Their running feet echoed in the passageway. "Do you think he's getting us a pilot job?" Diana's voice faded as they ran.

The Captain rubbed his sore ribs. "She can be a pain." A mischievous grin came to his face. "It's good to be King."

Chuckling to himself, he rose and left for the galley.

The Galley

The Captain entered the galley to find Alexandria, Chef Joan, and Victoria having coffee. "Well, it seems I need more coffee. Did you know the drinks last night made people crazy? Both pilots came to me to say they were leaving. Imagine that."

Alexandria's face took on a stricken look. "Captain, I'm so sorry. It's all my fault; I blabbed about them being replaced. Please forgive me. I'm truly sorry."

Victoria chimed in. "Please, Captain, don't be mad at her. It was the drink."

Chef Joan added her thoughts. "Captain, everyone makes mistakes. It was a big party and she isn't used to drinking."

"Stop. Stop." He put his hands behind his back and took a pose of serious thought. Turning his back to them hid the momentary loss of a stern expression on his face. "I must think on this. This is a serious breach of trust. In all honesty, this isn't the military and she isn't even an employee, but discipline and trust must be maintained on my ship. I guess I could have you leave the ship, but that wouldn't fix the discipline or the trust. There's also the fact you'll be gone soon anyway. Do you have any idea what I should do with you?"

Head looking down at the empty coffee cup, Alexandria's voice sounded small and hollow. "No, Captain."

"Perhaps if I see you can follow orders, that would help restore trust."

"Yes, Captain. I can follow orders."

"Very well. During the day, you'll tour the Island, in native dress. When you come on ship, you'll wear standard onboard dress: pants and blouse. I'll not order you to do any work, but if you wish to lend a hand, you may. Clear?"

"Yes, Captain. Clear." Alexandria chewed at her bottom lip.

"If you hurry, you might catch sight of the twins. If not, I'm sure you'll see a crew member that can point out interesting places on the Island."

"Kira is in my cabin, sleeping; can I take her along?"

"Of course. Kira's in your care from your promise, and I don't expect you to turn that duty over to anyone else. Why are you still sitting here?"

Alexandria left, running.

Chef Joan's face had a look of disbelief. "I had no idea you could be so mean!"

A short chuckle escaped. "Mean? That was not mean. First, it'll firmly put in her mind not to speak of things she shouldn't or doesn't have all the information about. Second, she'll remember not to try to do my job. Third and, I must say, the most important, she'll learn about a new way of living, a different culture firsthand and, with luck, it will help her relax about herself. This is the real world out here, not some big, stuffy city. Maybe you should get some clothes for her to wear."

Chef Joan nodded. "Since you put it that way. Victoria, will you help me get some clothes for her to wear on land and ship?"

Victoria grinned. "Maybe something fitting, like my lucky red suit."

Chef Joan chuckled. "I don't think even orders from heaven would get her into anything like that."

24
June 26, 1898
11 AM
The Village

Alexandria strolled down the market street, looking at all the colors of the clothes displayed. The light ocean breeze made the bright dresses and fabrics hanging out for display flutter and wave as if inviting people into the shops. She stopped on occasion to stare down the road toward the ocean. The path, where the road turned away, was lined with splashes of the brilliant colors of flowers against the dark green of shrubs. The pastel-painted shops on each side of the road added to the kaleidoscope of colors. Such a contrast to the drab browns and grays of her home city made it even more stunning. She had stopped holding the side of the skirt. Holding Kira and the skirt was too awkward. The more Alexandria saw, the slower she moved, taking longer to take things in. Even the huge mountain as the backdrop to the village kept catching her eye.

"I see you're going native." Neenaa greeted Alexandria with a lively tone.

"It wasn't my choice, but I'm getting used to it, as all the women are dressed the same."

"It's the heat. This is the coolest thing to wear. Big dresses and such get too hot and sticky."

"It does make sense, really, I suppose."

"If it wasn't your choice, why are you wearing it?"

"Captain's orders."

"Okay, let's go get a cold tea and an early lunch and you can tell me about the orders."

They found an outside table in front of a small lunch shop and having purchased drinks and sliced fruits, Alexandria explained while they ate.

The Captain and the Lady Fair

Neenaa started her questions. "So you accepted the orders. That makes little sense. Maybe it wasn't that you're following orders, but because you want to do as he asks to please him."

"Don't be silly."

"You two are something." Neenaa smiled as she shook her head.

Alexandria changed the subject. "I know nothing about the Island, so I don't know what there is to see."

"I'll walk you around. There isn't much to see on the Island, other than beautiful scenes and a small shrine. Beyond the local huts, there are fantastic homes dotted about. They're small and decorated on the outside to lessen messing up the views, but very nice."

Alexandria's eyes were once again drawn to the view of the mountain backdrop. "What about the Chief? Won't he miss you? You've only had an afternoon and night together."

Neenaa's eyes twinkled, and she took on a mischievous grin. "He's fine. He's out with his first love, the Lady Fair. I did make him promise he'd be home by five or it'll be cold supper and shoulder. He'll be home."

"How did you and the Chief meet?"

"I was working at the hospital. He came in with a bad cut and you would've thought he was dying the way he carried on. I was the nurse on his floor and got to know what a softie he is when he kept visiting the children's ward to play with them. He can be clumsy with women. I guess that and his size makes him scary to most. He didn't scare me. One thing led to another and we married. Around me, he's addlebrained. He treats me like I'm fragile glass." Longing showed on her face as Neenaa looked upon Kira. "If we're ever blessed …" A chuckle escaped her. "And I survive the birth of a monster of his; I expect he'll be a doting father."

"Excuse me for saying this, but you're so young. I mean he … you …."

Neenaa laughed. "We get that all the time. Yes, I'm near enough half his age. It's okay. Most are shocked by the size difference." She saw

Changing Times

Alexandria's face blush. "I thought so." Neenaa smiled and rose. "Let's get on with the day. Alexandria, any time you're ready, go ahead and ask me what you really want to know."

They left the shop, Neenaa leading the way. At the first shop with fabric, Neenaa turned in. Quickly looking over the fabrics, she bought two pieces. "Now to make you a real native," Neenaa said. She tied the two ends of the longer piece of fabric together and placed the loop over Alexandria's head. "Now, put your right arm through and we can pull it open and have a nice sling for Kira." Kira, in the sling, waved her hands around and gurgled. She seemed happy to be supported by the sling and resting low against Alexandria's chest. "Now, off with the heavy baby stuff and cover her with this lightweight piece to block the sun. Now you're a native and Kira is happy and cool."

"I can have both hands free if I need to. I like this. I could carry her all day and never get tired." Alexandria looked down on Kira's happy face, which swiveled back and forth, feeling the light breeze that carried the scents of forest and flowers.

"Now, we'll take a walk, then come back and do some shopping."

The dirt path led up into the hills behind the village. The colorful long-tailed birds sang them songs as they walked. The fresh smells of growing plants and sea air made the walk refreshing even though it was uphill. After a few minutes, a wide clearing with a shrine in the rear came into view. Stacked lava rock columns held up a thatched roof. At the center of the shrine was a pedestal surrounded by offerings of fruit and flowers. Arku stepped out of the bushes behind the shrine and greeted them. "Greetings, Alexandria, saver of Kira. You as well, Neenaa. Come sit with me and find peace and warmth of heart." Both Alexandria and Neenaa bowed to Arku then sat with him at the edge of the shrine. Both of their faces took on a peaceful, relaxed expression, with a hint of a smile, at the smells of life from the plants and flowers around the shrine. The soft melody of the sounds of the insects and bird songs made it difficult to speak and break the soothing atmosphere.

Arku held out his hands. "May I hold Kira?"

Alexandria freed Kira from the sling and placed her in his hands. "Of course you can. Thank you for the blessings at the party. This shrine, what God is it for?"

"It's not to a God. It is for the Island. This Island has been loved so much, for so long, the Island spirit grew in strength and now protects and blesses its people. I tend it, removing old offerings. Offerings here are more like a sign of respect and a show of thanks rather than gifts."

While they were talking, a new smell came, the smell of Jasmine and Gardenia wafted over them. Alexandria looked around. "Jasmine and Gardenias, but I don't see any of those flowers."

Arku smiled at her. "It is the spirit of the Island. The smell of those flowers means she is near."

Arku pulled Kira close, smiled down and traced a finger across her cheek. His finger stopped moving when Kira grabbed it. "Such a good heart grows in her." His eyes took on a distant look. After a moment, he spoke softly. "Soon, child. Soon."

Alexandria broke her silence. "What is soon?"

Arku looked up at Alexandria. "That is a secret between her and I. Everyone has secrets. Even you and Neenaa have them."

Alexandria and Neenaa spoke on top of each other. "I have no secrets!"

Arku extended his hand to Alexandria, asking her to place her hand in his. After a short time, he nodded, released her hand, and took Neenaa's. Again, a pause and then a big smile came to his face and his eyes widened. "Yes, you both have secrets. Perhaps you don't even know you have them."

Alexandria beat Neenaa by a fraction. "What secret?"

Arku offered Kira back to Alexandria. "If you wish it, I will tell you part of it."

"How can you know a secret I don't even know I have?" Alexandria put Kira back in the sling.

Changing Times

"How does not matter, but you have two loves that your heart and spirit have been given to, and though things may be difficult, you will never take them back. I will tell you one love is in your arms."

Alexandria laughed. "It's no secret that I'm attached."

"No, not attached. You love this child with all your heart and will fight for her. Take peace in knowing you do not fight alone."

"And who is going to help?"

"That is a different secret. Now, Neenaa, do you wish to know yours?"

"Arku, I trust you, and yes, please."

"You have been given your greatest wish."

Neenaa took on a puzzled look. "What?"

Arku sat and smiled. A kind of excitement made him sway. Not saying anything, he stared into her eyes. Alexandria watched both of them, her eyes going back and forth between the two.

After almost a minute passed, Neenaa jerked up straight, eyes wide and mouth open. "My greatest wish?"

Arku clapped his hands. "Now you know."

Alexandria couldn't contain herself. "What?"

Neenaa placed her hand on her stomach and fought to speak through a tight throat. A whisper came. "A baby."

The Village

Leaving the dirt path and entering the village, Alexandria couldn't keep quiet any longer. "A baby. That's great news, but how does he know?"

"The Island knows everything. I believe in the Island and Arku. You'll see he's right. Please don't say anything yet to anyone. I need to find the right time to tell the Chief and now is not the time. Many things are happening and, if he knew, he would be thinking of me and not his work."

"I promise I'll keep quiet no matter what. I'm afraid of what the next thing the Captain would come up with if he found out I blabbed a secret. I can understand babies are important but the people here are making such a big fuss. Why?"

"Babies are the future. There is a story that started not long ago, that a special baby would be saved from the sea, come to the Island, a baby who would have special sight, and be very important to the Island one day. Many think it is you and Kira. There is more to your rescue than you know but it isn't for me to talk about. The Captain will need to tell you in his own time."

"You're going to tell me that and stop there? That's mean."

Neenaa gave a full laugh. "Okay, shopping time."

"Hey, girls. Mind company?" Chef Joan's voice called from across the narrow road. She and Victoria waved, attracting their attention.

"Please join us! Alexandria was just going to ask me about the Captain."

"Why's everyone going on about me and the Captain? I've only known him a few days. I've talked to all of you more than him. There's nothing there, for goodness' sake."

"My, she is loud in protest. What do you think, Chef?" Neenaa examined a swaying dress.

"I think we should let her be. For now."

Neenaa's steps slowed, and the group halted to see what was wrong. "Maybe now is not the time, but it's important to all of us. You'll have decisions later of where you go. You can see that all the people around the Captain love him. He treats everyone like family. Maybe like a big protective brother. Don't get me wrong; he's not perfect, but what family is? Many women have vied for his attention, but all failed. They were not accepted by the crew as right for him."

Alexandria looked stunned. "Wait a minute. You're saying you're looking for a girlfriend for the Captain? That's wrong!"

"Slow down a minute and hear me out. No, we're not shopping and we don't introduce him to anyone. It's just approval or not of those he does meet. We just don't help women we don't agree is right for him, and he stays away from involvement anyway. It's not something we think about; it just happens that way. Call it protecting our Captain and big brother. I don't think, even with the right one, he'll act on it. Now the hard part."

There was tension in Alexandria's voice. "What hard part? If you're telling me I'm not for the Captain, then that's not hard and I don't mind at all."

"Remember when all the crew came to see you? The Chief told me all about it. Then they all spent time seeking you out to chat from time to time. Remember?"

"Yes, they were just being friendly."

"Friendly, yes, but also getting to know you. The hard part is …" Neenaa took a deep breath. "You're the one. All the crew thinks so."

"You're all nuts. Everyone on the Island is crazy."

"Yes, we are, I think. Nice, isn't it? Now, let's shop."

The goal seemed to be to visit every shop. Chef Joan and Victoria bought a few light dresses and a few of the native wraps and tops. Alexandria was surprised at how late it was when Neenaa announced she needed to leave. "Time for me to get home and start dinner. It's been wonderful and I hope we can do a proper tour soon."

"Thanks for a terrific day." Alexandria gave Neenaa a smile. "I have never spent a whole day like this."

Neenaa left them with a wave.

"I guess it's late enough to head back to the ship. I'll help in the galley."

"Happy to have you in my galley. There'll only be four of us onboard, so there won't be much to do. Dinner will be light, anyway."

Arm in arm in arm, they headed back to the ship.

25
June 26, 1898
5 PM
The Galley

Chef Joan and Victoria turned towards their cabins. "We'll dump these packages in the cabin and meet you in the galley if you'll start the coffee." Chef Joan skipped down the passageway, followed by Victoria.

Seeing the Captain sitting at the table, Alexandria hesitated at the hatchway.

"I don't bite. Come in and make yourself comfortable."

Alexandria walked in and started making coffee.

"Nice sling for Kira. Very practical." The Captain watched her make the coffee.

"Neenaa made it for us."

"I'm not the best with babies, but I would guess it's feeding time. Hand her over and you can make a bottle when you get done with that coffee."

"You sure?"

"I might as well get to know the little lady; we may be kicking around together for a while."

Alexandria passed Kira to the Captain. He moved with exaggerated care, taking her in his arms.

"First time holding a baby?"

"I've never had an occasion to before, so yes."

"Don't worry; people never drop babies." There was a pause. A smile came to her face. "Well, almost never."

The Captain, intent on Kira, did not notice it was a poke and tensed.

Changing Times

"I had a great time today. All the colorful shops. The people were all friendly. The weather so nice and the view of the beach and trees from the main street is breathtaking. That mountain is magnificent."

"I'm glad you had a chance to see the Island. You can see why the crew's always happy to return here. It isn't really a mountain. It's a dormant volcano. It's what made this Island."

Chef Joan entered just ahead of Victoria. "Hey, Captain. What do you want me to make for dinner? Anything special?"

"Nope, anything will do."

Alexandria, bottle in hand, started to reach for Kira.

"I can do that." He held out his hand for the bottle.

Chef Joan turned to stare at the Captain. "Captain, you're in a strange mood."

"The Captain isn't allowed to have a good day?"

Chef Joan crossed over to him from the prep table. Bending at the waist, she came close to his face, looking him in the eye.

"What're you doing?"

"Checking your eyes for drugs or drink."

Alexandria gave a short laugh.

"Okay, Chef." The Captained leaned back in the chair. "As you have so little to do that you find it amusing to look in my eyes, I have a job for you and Victoria."

"Thanks for dragging me into … something, Chef." Victoria nudged Joan.

"Tomorrow, go into the village and order up foodstuffs. I know we're still pretty stocked up from such a short run, but I want us topped up. Make sure to get fruits, especially the green melons I like."

"That's easy, Captain."

"There's more. I want you to make it separate batches for delivery. Even tote some back by hand to make it appear casual. I don't want it to look like we're stocking up. Maybe even box the orders to look like packages of some kind or another as long as it doesn't look like food stocks."

"You're up to something."

"Me?" There was a twinkle in his eye.

Alexandria spoke up. "Captain, I can help with that if I am allowed to board during the day."

"Consider it new orders then. Speaking of orders, are you dressed wrong?"

"On my way to change now, Captain." She dashed out the hatchway.

"Still being a little tough, aren't you?" Chef Joan pulled more food from the cooler to prep for dinner.

"Did you see she was more relaxed with herself?" He smiled.

"Yes, I did. She was pretty relaxed all day while we were shopping."

"You were together?" The Captain's head tilted and his eyebrows drew together in thought.

"Yes, we were shopping as ordered." Chef Joan wiped her hands on a towel and stared at the Captain.

"Ordered?"

"You did say to get her clothes."

A chuckle escaped him. "Okay, you got me there, although I didn't exactly say 'shop.'"

"Captain! You can't expect a lady to wear hand-me-downs forever!" Victoria stood next to Chef Joan and glared at the Captain.

"Okay, I yield." The Captain's speech slowed. "So, what did you ladies talk about?"

"Captain, you gave us all a fine example in discipline to keep our mouths shut. I think even Alexandria will keep quiet on that." Chef Joan gave him a mischievous smile.

Alexandria appeared in the hatchway. "What's with all the dresses, wraps, blouses, and pants on my bed?"

Victoria kept a straight face. "Tooth Fairy?"

"Change!"

Alexandria dashed at the bark from the Captain.

Chef Joan put the fresh cup of coffee down hard in front of the Captain. "Mean. Just plain mean."

Changing Times

The Captain played with Kira's toes as the baby giggled.

26
June 27, 1898
9 AM
The Deck of Lady Fair

The Captain walked up to the Chief, who was standing on the deck, watching a small army of men working. "Chief, I seem to be missing parts. Where's the bow?" Ten feet of the bow was gone. Men were welding braces while others dragged flexible steam lines across the deck to be installed.

"Morning, Captain. Just doing that fix-up you said I could do. It's down on the ground getting work done on it. You'll get it back. By this afternoon, we'll be putting it back on. We've already repaired the bullet holes in the decking, good as new."

"Nice to know. Anything else?"

"You do know we're being watched."

"I thought we would be, but haven't looked for them. The Admiral sent them. He wants to know if we're preparing to lift." He laughed softly. "I bet the missing bow has him in a fit. Take your time, Chief; just have it together by the morning of the 29th."

"Operation slow down. Aye, Captain."

"You have time if there is any other fix-up you need."

"Well, Captain, now you mention it, I was thinking. Maybe a cannon would be nice, seeing as we have people wanting to shoot us down. Extra firepower could be good."

"Where would you put it?"

"I was thinking topside, above the bridge. It would give full 360-degree coverage."

"It would be nice, but I don't want the watchers thinking we're gearing up."

"How long do you need to keep it secret?"

"Four days or so."

The Chief started rubbing his chin in thought. "That's easy, Captain. My friends in supply can get me one and, as a favor, be a week slow in reporting the requisition. Use that fancy crane and it can be lifted straight into place. All I have to do is prep a mount. I can hang a canvas down from the lift bag hiding the bridge and make it look like we're painting something. I bet I could hire a few ground handlers to set up near the crane and bang on scraps of metal to make it sound like any noise I make on the bridge is work on the crane. I'll also wager the watchers will only watch during normal day working hours. Could load it up tonight."

"Sounds good. Don't forget shells for it. If you will excuse me, I have to go do another jab in the Admiral's side and place a job opening."

As the Captain reached the dock, he heard the Chief's voice on the loud-box. "Avery, meet me on deck. I have a paint job for you. Chance, to the crane; you've got work to do on the base plate mount."

The Captain chuckled. "Miracle worker." He left the dock and went directly to the Phoenix building.

27
June 27, 1898
9:30 AM
The Phoenix Building

The Captain's shoes clicked on the polished floor as he walked down the hall, lined on each side with various specialty rooms. A wood wainscot, topped by clear glass, made each room open to view. The military idea was that being seen kept slacking to a minimum. He entered the employment requisition office.

Changing Times

"Good morning, Ensign; I need to place two job openings for the Lady Fair for a contract."

"Yes, sir; what specifics?" The ensign behind the counter grabbed a pencil and paper, ready to take down information.

"Two pilots, minimum one year experience, top five percent in Pilot school, some experience in combat, able to handle 80-knot winds, ready to ship in five weeks for extended periods, and can follow orders without question."

"That's pretty stiff, Captain."

"Oh yes, candidates selected for an interview will be notified in three weeks."

An edge of sarcasm came into the Ensign's voice. "Anything else?"

"Nope, that'll do it. Thanks." The Captain turned on his heel and left whistling. Stopping outside of the office, he pulled a paper from his pocket and appeared to be looking at it. Instead, his eyes watched, through the glass partition, the Ensign picking up the phone and making a call. Used to the glass walls, and being seen at any time, he failed to notice he was being watched.

The Captain next went to the message center and checked with the clerk, who was sitting stiffly erect in a white uniform one size too small for even her slight frame. The nametag proclaiming her to be Petty Officer Carter was thrust forward on her chest. It drew even more attention to the uniform. Her brown, short hairstyle cupped her face.

"Hello, Petty Officer Carter. Have anything for the Lady Fair?"

"Just a moment, Sir; I'll check." She turned and checked the slots behind her. "Yes, Sir. You need to sign, Sir."

"Petty Officer, isn't your uniform … um …."

"Yes, Sir. The men at the barracks thought it would be funny to switch all my uniforms to a size smaller. I have to get new ones at the quartermaster stores after work. Sorry, Sir."

"Don't apologize. It's not your fault, but you might tend to it at lunch hour if you can." The Captain's face showed his anger at the prank. He signed the slip attached to the envelope and handed it back to her. Opening the envelope, he scanned the letter. "Damn."

The Captain walked at a rapid pace to the village and went to the nearest fabric shop. The walk helped burn off some of his anger over the prank and the message. He visited three shops before he found what he wanted. He returned to the Phoenix building.

"Petty Officer."

The petty officer looked up to see the Captain holding out a small package. "Sir, do you need me to send that?"

"I found this while I was walking. I thought perhaps you might have a use for it."

Looking inside, she saw a red powder. "Sir?"

"I would be very cautious with that. I've heard just a thumb-size amount would turn a whole load of white laundry a shade of pink." He winked at her and left.

The open-mouthed Petty Officer watched him leave. "He should be the Commander."

28
June 27, 1898
11 AM
The Lady Fair

The Captain sat on the bridge, watching the workers and looking out at the boarding ramp. Alexandria, Chef Joan, and Victoria walked up the ramp, laden with wrapped boxes and chattered nonstop. A few minutes passed, then he rose to the loud-box. "Chief and Alexandria to the bridge, please." The Captain stood waiting for them.

Both the Chief and Alexandria entered at the same time.

"Captain, problems?" asked the Chief.

Changing Times

"Of a sort, Chief. I got a message from the Admiralty. The only thing they have so far on the bomber is that he was from Boschland. Probably military. There's a hint he was part of a special squad. They're still checking. The airsharks were a private hire by the Garrote Company. The hire was from high up. So far, it looks like someone had Alexandria as a target. There are hints three women scientists have been killed in the last year, but nothing solid, and no hint of the man at the top yet. So it looks like two different groups with the same target or targets."

"So we can be hit from two sides. That could ruin a picnic."

The Captain walked over to Alexandria and looked down at Kira. The back of his fingers brushed her cheek. Small wiggling hands grabbed at his fingers. "Now, the bad news."

Alexandria took a breath. "I'm not going to like this; am I?"

"A search on little Kira. We already knew both parents were killed. Her real name is Regina. The search shows she has no living relatives. She'll be placed in an orphanage."

Alexandria's eyes began to fill. "No, an orphanage is no good. Kira deserves better than that. I won't let them take her. Her name is Kira. I made a promise." She hugged Kira closer.

"It won't happen right away. Slow paperwork may take weeks. No one's in a rush to grab Kira. We have to trust fate will come up with something."

Alexandria walked slowly from the bridge, hunched over Kira and crying.

The Captain studied his shoes. "That hurt."

Softly, the Chief spoke. "She took it hard."

"Yeah, her too." The Captain took a deep breath and blew it out. "Any status updates, Chief?"

"The cannon will be delivered at two AM. Everything's on schedule."

"Thanks, Chief."

The Captain left the bridge, talking softly to himself "Sometimes it rots to be King."

29
June 28, 1898
2 AM
The Lady Fair

"How can I help, Chief?" The Captain stood next to the Chief, who was standing at the crane.

"Well, Captain, explain to Neenaa this is important so I don't get cold food over this. Failing that, watch for any nosey people dockside. We'll begin the lift shortly and all will be hidden in a few minutes." Chief signaled the crew at the crane and it lifted and swung out over the side. The arm extended until it was over the large truck parked below. A wave to the men at the truck sent them scurrying to pull back the tarp. Climbing up to the truck bed, the men hooked up the cables of the crane. At their wave, the Chief signaled his men, and the crane lifted the large cannon from the bed of the truck. As soon as it cleared the bed, the truck chuffed off.

"Big enough, Chief?"

"Big as I can fit. I'll have to add some kind of damper system to control the kick."

"I'd think so."

The Chief scurried up the ladder to the top of the bridge. With more hand signals, the cannon was lowered into place. The Chief signaled "all clear" after he disconnected the cables and the men returned the crane to its resting place on the deck. It took less than five minutes from start to finish.

The Captain joined the Chief at the cannon. "Not exactly invisible, Chief."

"Yet. Watch your feet." The Chief bent down and twisted a lever on the floor. Slowly, four sides rotated up from the sides of the bridge to form a box around the cannon just high enough to block any view of it from ground level. "Now it'll look like we have a slightly tall bridge. When the walls are down, it offers shielding around the bridge windows. There're slits for viewing out when they're down. I even found a very good artist. Rachael. She painted on details like portholes, even rivets so it looks like a part of the bridge. We'll get a shock system installed and bolted down before morning. If not, we'll finish it tomorrow morning in the o-dark hours."

"Chief, you never cease."

"It'll be preloaded with a stack of five rounds. After that, it will have to be loaded one at a time, unless you have a loader. We in for trouble?"

"I think so. Beginning to feel that way. Nothing firm yet. Things feel like they are still in motion. Fluid yet."

"You know, no matter what, we're here for you. We're better set than any other crew I know. At least for our numbers. The Lady Fair is tougher than her looks and name."

"Thanks, Chief."

30
June 28, 1898
9 AM
The Galley

"Good morning, Chef." The Captain entered the galley to find Chef Joan eating a late breakfast.

"Ready for breakfast, Captain? Bacon and eggs?"

The Captain poured a cup of coffee. "Coffee is good for now. Take your time and finish yours. I'll wait to see if anyone else comes in."

"Alexandria has already gone out for the day. Sleepyhead Victoria is still sleeping in, I guess."

"I have another job for you."

"Name it, Captain."

"Pick up some fruits or buns or breads. Wander to each crew member's home as if dropping off gifts. You may or may not be followed. Tell the crew to be aboard before sunup and stay below deck. That we may be lifting. Tell them not a word is to leak out."

"Simple enough, Captain. Sounds like the quiet life is over."

"Good morning, Captain. Morning, Chef. I smell bacon." Victoria pulled brown paper-wrapped bacon and four eggs from the cooler.

The Captain watched her place six strips of thick bacon and four eggs in two skillets. "How did you know I'm ready for breakfast?"

"Sorry, Captain." She added three more strips of bacon and two more eggs. "I'll make you some, too."

"Now I know why the food bill's always so high. Victoria, where do you put all that?"

"I exercise hard every day. You don't think I could lift my gun or wear that coat if I didn't, do you?"

"I've never seen you exercise."

"I stay in my room. I don't want to disturb anyone. I like to keep it secret how strong I am. Sometimes I even play the weak girl act."

"The cabins are big for the ship, but not that big."

"It's difficult, but I worked it out."

"Whatever you are doing, it works, I guess."

A grin came to Victoria's face. "Now I have to keep working out to stay in shape to fit my lucky red suit."

"I'm not going to try to understand how that suit helps. All I know is that it's … disturbing."

"Here I thought you were so enlightened." Victoria faked a pout.

With breakfast served, the Captain sat staring into space as he ate.

"Bad things coming, or thinking of Alexandria in my red suit?"

Chef Joan patted him hard on the back to help his choking, coughing fit.

Chef Joan and Victoria looked at each other while the coughing continued, saying at the same time "Red suit."

31
June 28, 1898
11 AM
The Deck

With coffee in hand, the Captain walked up beside the Chief, who was standing on the deck. "I see things are wrapping up nicely, Chief."

"A thing of beauty."

"Is the bow longer, or is it my imagination?"

"Just a few feet. There's a section that extends beyond the main body of the ship."

"Sometimes I'm glad I have no idea what you're doing."

"Maybe I have a touch of what you have, Captain. I get an urge to make something and can't help myself."

"That's just a sign of genius. I have an idea I want you to think about Chief. No rush. And I'd like it on the quiet."

"I love secrets. Especially when I know what they are. We lifting tomorrow?"

"If my plan and feelings are right, yes. Other than the crew knowing, it's one of those secrets. It boils down to if our next flight is sanctioned or not." The Captain's face went slack as he stared at nothing. "Sometimes I worry I am going to miss something. I'm getting confused, Chief. Before, I paid attention to the crew as a crew. Now I find myself wanting to get more involved in the very personal parts. Not nosey, just to help or do something right. I don't understand it."

"You've always cared for the crew as more than crew. Let me guess. This feeling started a few days ago? About the time of Alexandria?"

"I hate to say it, but yes."

"Sometimes even a small change in a heart can be confusing. You have shielded yours too long, my friend."

"Any idea what to do?"

"Trust in fate, your friends, and those you care about. Even those you haven't known long."

"I'm going to go try to rest. Maybe things will clear in my head."

"You should rest those ribs anyway."

"It is only a touch tender." The Captain grinned. "Doc is a lot better than she knows. I guess we all have our talents, Chief."

"We'll be ready to lift when you give the word. I almost forgot; I added a shielded box to the back of the cannon to protect the shells. If Gunner is doing her job, who will man the cannon?"

"Me."

32
June 29, 1898
7:30 AM
The Galley

The Captain entered the galley in his white dress uniform. "Thank you all for coming at this hour. I trust Chef has fed you all. I'm going to ask you all remain below deck for a little longer; there've been watchers on the docks trying to see if we're up to anything. It helped they only watched during the day. So far, we've done pretty well in looking like we plan to be sitting here for a good while; I want it to stay that way. Why I won't go into but, one way or another, we'll be lifting soon. The Chief will brief you on what we know of the attack on the Dolphin and on us. When we lift, we'll be headed for New City. The odds are high we'll come under attack. This time, you have a choice if you want to stay behind knowing the danger ahead. Any of you may leave the ship if you wish when it comes time to lift. You're civilians, not military, and I'll respect that."

Several voices rose about staying with the ship and the Captain.

"Thank you all in advance. Chief, if you please, watch the boarding ramp and if we have any guests, escort them to the bridge. Pilots, please meet me on the bridge in dress uniform." He picked up a cup, poured some coffee, and grabbed a handful of croissants from the table. "Now for some fun."

The pilots followed the Captain through the hatchway and turned to their cabins to dress.

Soon the pilots joined the Captain on the bridge. "Please have a seat and be comfortable. We shouldn't have to wait long."

"What're we waiting for, Captain?"

"Diana, you and your sister will just have to wait. I can't guarantee things will go as I hope." The Captain leaned back in his chair and glanced out the window now and then.

They left the Captain in peace. The coffee pot had just gone empty when the Captain straightened in his chair. "I see we have company," he said as he stood. "Pilots, you might want to stand for this." Reaching over, he turned on the loud-box and put his finger to his lips.

The Lieutenant entered ahead of the Chief. "Greetings, Captain. I have a package for you from the Admiral." He held out a large square envelope.

"Lieutenant, what's your name?"

"Fausworth, Sir."

"I take it you know the contents and heard a few less than polite words from the Admiral."

"Yes, sir, on both counts."

"Then I suggest you open that envelope and present them properly." He pointed to the pilots.

"Sir?"

"Did I stutter?"

"No, sir." He gritted his teeth as he opened the envelope and turned to the pilots. "Kathryn and Diana Anderson, I hereby present to you by Presidential order …." He paused.

"Continue, Lieutenant."

"By Presidential order, Pilot tickets effective immediately." He handed the documents to the pilots, not concerned if he handed the right document to the right new Pilot.

Both pilots stared, dumbfounded.

The Chief looked wide-eyed at the Captain as cheers could be heard all the way from the galley.

The Captain reached into his pocket and approached the pilots. "I thought they would send a low-level, incompetent idiot, so allow me the honor. Congratulations." His hand opened to reveal two Airship Pilot pins; he proceeded to pin one on each pilot.

"How the heck?" The Chief's stunned look matched both pilots.

"Secrets, Chief. Secrets."

"Sir, may I tell the Admiral you'll take the contract?"

"Lieutenant, you may tell him anything you wish as long as it includes telling the Admiral the lift was delayed by your slow-moving butt. Chief, if he's not off the ship when we lift, let him cloud-dance home. And Lieutenant, I suggest you always show proper respect to any member of my crew and, if you have any friends, you might pass that on. Am I clear or did I stutter again?"

"Loud and clear, Sir. My apologies, Pilots."

The Captain leaned over the loud-box. "Lift the ship." Feet pounded in the passageway, including those of the Lieutenant.

33
June 29, 1898
9 AM
The Bridge

Activity had settled into a routine. The airship was at cruising altitude and on course for New City. The flight was smooth through the light blue sky, which held scattered clouds.

As soon as the Chief stepped in through the hatchway, Alexandria dashed past him up to the Captain, kissed him on the cheek and then ran out.

"Well, I guess that represents the feeling of the crew." The Chief looked towards the Pilots, who still had to keep wiping their eyes to see the instruments. "I'm honored to be flown by the only Presidential pilots in the world. Captain, you know my curiosity is killing me."

"I was not allowed to do the contract without qualified, ticketed Pilots. They really needed the contract without delay. I guess the Admiral decided it would take too long for me to get them. The school would not feel pressure to give in as they're not under any military authority. It would take a day to fly airsharks in relay to the President, who happens to be over the Aviation Ministry. A day explaining the need and get them made up and signed, a day to fly back and then make delivery the next morning, a total of three days, I would think."

"That's why you didn't want his watchers to see we were ready for a lift. He thought you were really going to take a long process of hiring pilots."

"I imagine his face was very red when he got the call about my job request with the qualifications my pilots already have. Tough to match."

"You can be an evil man."

"I wonder if he hurt himself when he saw us lift and realized he'd been had."

Kathryn turned to the Captain, trying to get words to come out past a tight throat. She failed.

"You're both welcome. Don't you ever forget; you truly earned those. Chief, be so kind as to get frames for the tickets next time we are in some port."

"Gold-plated, Captain." The Chief grinned broadly, as any proud father would.

"I think we're good for today and tomorrow morning. After lunch tomorrow, I'm going to need two spotters at all times and we'll be running dark at night. We'll also increase altitude, so things will get thin and cold. Pilots, I'm going below. Call if you need me."

"Aye, Captain."

"My trust is in you."

Still sniffling, both Pilots stood straighter.

34
June 30, 1898
2 PM
The Bridge

The Captain sat in his chair, staring out the window, with occasional glances at Pilot Kathryn at the helm. "Altitude?"

Pilot calmly answered as if she were not aware he knew full well the answer already. "Holding at 15,000 feet, Captain."

"Thank you." His leaning forward in the Captain's chair, eyes fixed out the window, staring ahead, along with his stiff posture, telegraphed tension.

Pilot turned on the loud-box. "Sis, bring some coffee to the bridge please."

"Since when do you call her 'Sis' like that and ask her instead of Chef?"

Changing Times

"What's wrong with it? We *are* sisters."

Below deck, Diana passed the word things must be close. All the crew went to stations. Victoria, already in her lucky suit and coat, went to the hatch that led to the deck and waited. It was not to be a long wait.

The spotters reported in. "Captain, ship on the horizon, just off port by 20 degrees."

The Captain grabbed his far glasses and stepped out on the walkway. Before he could get the glasses to his eyes, he saw Gunner, in her black duster, walk out on the forward deck, open a hatch at the bow, and climb down.

"Captain, we've been spotted; they're turning."

Before the Captain could get all the way back to the bridge, reports of "on station" were coming in. He turned on the loud-box. "Just for formality. All hands to stations."

He looked to Pilot, who looked back, smiled, and shrugged.

"I thought we had an agreement that I give the orders."

"Me, Captain? When did I ever give orders?" She turned back to the wheel, took a deep breath, and let it out to settle herself for any coming actions.

Diana walked in and stood at her sister's side, ready to be a second set of hands.

The spotter reported an update. "Captain, it's a Dreadnaught. At speed, they'll be on us in ten minutes."

The Captain spoke to himself. "They wasted no time." Activating the loud-box, he made an announcement of orders. "Crew, stand by for ballast drop and gas. At this altitude, we can climb and turn faster than they can. When you feel the shift, get your air masks on. It'll get very thin up there. Be ready for hard maneuvers. They'll be on our starboard side."

The Captain put on his fur-lined jacket and went to the cannon. Once he freed the cannon lockdowns, he cocked the cannon and waited. "Chief, bless your oversized heart; you have your own Talents."

The Dreadnaught had gained altitude and was slightly higher than the Lady Fair. Shooting out or down was the only option as shooting upward endangered the lift bags. The Lady Fair needed to be in a position to shoot down.

"Maintain course and speed. No sense in running; they would chase anyway." The Captain waited until the huge Dreadnaught, four times the size of Lady Fair, was almost broadside. He yelled over the wind into the loud-box. "Emergency lift!" Ballast poured out the keel, and the lift increased with the Pilots adding gas. Knees giving with the increased weight, he held onto the cannon's grip to keep from falling. A puff of smoke shot out from the side of the Dreadnaught. The shell passed under the Lady Fair making a whistling sound. "Free to open fire when you have a target." The Captain put on his air mask.

He twisted the handle in the floor and the sides dropped free, protecting the bridge and exposing the cannon. Aiming down on the Dreadnaught, he pulled the trigger. The buck back of the cannon was a surprise and his shell raced at the Dreadnaught to make impact on the side from where the smoke had come. Small-arms fire erupted from the cargo deck portholes of the Lady Fair as the crew used their own weapons.

Victoria

Inside the bow, Victoria swung the nose to starboard and rotated down to keep an aim on the Dreadnaught. "Too tight in here." She flipped her coat open and over the back of her seat. When the smoke belched from the Dreadnaught, she pulled the triggers and both barrels threw out streams of bullets at a rapid pace. Steam that powered the guns poured out of the exit ports at the bottom of the bow. Empty brass shells spun in the air to land at her feet. Her yell competed with the noise of the guns. "You will NOT get me! You will NOT get my friends! You will NOT get my ship!" Her first stream tore at the bridge, blowing out the windows and making unwanted peepholes for them. Seeing men on the deck of the Dreadnaught running for a gun station, she aimed at them. "Oh no, I'm not going to let you get there that easy." They ducked out of view. Aiming the stream higher, she sent a storm of bullets at the bags. The men on deck made a dash to the guns and now bullets peppered her shielding, adding to the noise with a pinging sound. She kept her aim on the bags to kill the Dreadnaught. Fans in the bow barely kept up with the smoke from the guns. The pile of empty shells at her feet was getting deeper. Pain ripped through her as one shell made it through the view slit, glanced off the wall beside her, and sent a shard of metal into her left arm. Victoria kept up the fire one-handed for a short time and then passed out.

The Captain

The Captain saw the carnage of the Lady Fair's guns and kept up his own attack on the big guns on the side of the Dreadnaught, silencing them one at a time. He looked at the bow of the Lady Fair to see the bow bent 90 degrees to starboard and rotated down. The barrel of the gun was swung to point directly at the Dreadnaught. He loaded another shell and fired again, aiming for the closest engine.

The dreadnaught was trying to rise to get above the Lady Fair. The Captain fired shell after shell, creating massive damage on the Dreadnaught, but as it was so large it could take a pounding. Shells from the Dreadnaught just missed the keel of the Lady Fair as she climbed, keeping above the Dreadnaught. Figures were running across the deck to the rapid-fire guns on the deck. A stream of bullets made them dive for cover. The bullet trail raised and raked the lift bags. Dozens of holes appeared and the Dreadnaught's ascent with the Lady Fair slowed. The men on the deck reached the gun and bullets streamed in return, aiming for the bow of the Lady Fair to silence her gun. The bullets of the Lady Fair continued to stitch the sides of the Dreadnaught's lift bags. The numerous holes in the Dreadnaught's lift bags began to rip open in large tears. It dropped away fast.

Bullets from the Lady Fair's bow stopped as the men on the Dreadnaught finally got the range and peppered the bow from where

Gunner was firing. The last bullet stream raked holes in the Lady Fair's lift bags. The bullet stream from the Dreadnaught stopped as it plunged nose down towards the sea far below.

The Captain yelled down the loud-box. "Tailor, we have holes! Pilots, keep the gas. We need to keep all we can." He swung the cannon to its rest position and turned the lever, bringing the sides back up. Once secured, he returned to the bridge.

"Everything okay?"

"No, Captain." Both pilots pointed to the bow, which was still bent to the side and rotated down; it looked very wrong.

The Captain hit the loud-box. "Chief to the gunner's station on the run."

As the Captain reached the deck to run to the bow, the Chief came through the hatchway. Seeing the angle of the bow, the Chief ran harder, and then let out a rare cuss word. "Damn."

Reaching the bow, the Chief skidded to a stop and pulled open an access panel just short of the bent bow section. Pulling at small levers inside caused the sounds of steam motors to start making the nose raise and rotate back into place. Now that the bow was level with the deck, the Chief went forward the last few feet to the gunner's hatch. The Chief pulled it open and looked inside. "Hey, lady, you okay in there?" He got no reply in return.

"Vicki!" Chef Joan was running full-tilt across the deck to reach the hatch.

The Captain moved Chief away from the hatch and looked down into the gunner's station. Victoria lay slumped to the side. The blood splatters across her left arm and chest gave the Captain pause. Shell casings buried her feet up to her ankles. Her coat lay draped over the back of the seat. The noisy fan's whir kept the smoke out, but the thick sulphurous smell of spent powder clung to the air.

"Vicki!" Chef Joan was pushing at the Captain to get at the hatch. "Vicki!"

The Chief held Chef Joan back.

"Chief, I can't get in there to get her out. You sure aren't going to fit with her in there."

Doc arrived, breathing hard, med bag in hand. "I do believe someone forgot to call me. Now let me in there." Doc lowered herself down the hatch and squeezed in beside Victoria. "She's alive!" Opening her bag, she pulled out bandages to wrap Victoria's arm tightly. "Just her arm is hit, but it's bad. She's lost a lot of blood. I can push her up if you can reach down and pull her out, Chief."

Chief looked at Chef Joan. "If I let go, will you stay put, so I can help Victoria?"

"Help Vicki. Yes, Chief, you help Vicki."

The Chief bent over the hatch and extended his arms down. Once Doc had lifted Victoria to an almost vertical position, the Chief grabbed and pulled her out like a doll, and laid her on the deck.

Avery and Chance arrived at that moment with a stretcher. The Chief scooped up Victoria and, as soon as he laid her on the stretcher, Avery and Chance lifted it and headed at a quick pace to the sickbay.

Chef Joan was half-trotting to keep up while holding Victoria's hand. "It'll be fine, Vicki. You'll see. Doc will fix you up good as new." She continued talking. Her tears kept falling during the entire trip to the sickbay.

35
June 30, 1898
3:30 PM
The Bridge

"What went wrong, Chief?"
  "It's all my fault. I didn't design it safe enough."
"Chief, am I going to have to go out there and look for myself?"

"One bullet got in through the view slit. The shielding stopped everything else. I guess one was all it took to get her."

"One bullet. Chief, there are risks to the job and only one bullet tells me it was as safe as it could be. She would have been fine if she had kept her coat on. I can't wait like this." He hit the loud-box. "Doc, any status?"

Shortly the Doc's voice came back. "You might as well come down."

"Coming, Chief?" the Captain asked.

"Want to try to stop me?"

Both left the bridge.

"Chief, when did you add to the passageway? I don't remember it being this far."

Chef Joan sat on the deck in the passageway, her knees pulled up and her head down, with her face buried in a sopping wet handkerchief. An occasional hiccup of sound escaped her.

"I am sure you can go in soon, Chef." The Captain knocked on the closed hatch.

"Come in, Captain."

The Captain entered with the Chief staying behind him as if the Captain could block the view of his large form. Chef Joan was right behind the Chief and his form did block her.

"Good and bad. She'll live, but the arm's a mess. Looks like a thin piece of something sliced through her bicep. I have the bleeding stopped, but the muscles are sliced. She won't have the use of the arm and, if infection sets in, she'll lose it."

"NO! Doc, you have to do something. Everyone knows you're the best. You can fix it!" Chef Joan's teary-eyed face was twisted in anguish. She pushed past them all to take Victoria's good hand in hers. Chef Joan talked to the unconscious form. "She'll fix ya. Doc is good. Please, Vicki, be okay. I'll make your favorites."

"Can you do anything at all?" The Captain asked Doc as he watched Chef Joan.

Changing Times

"I have cat gut and very fine needles, but it's a matter of seeing what I'm doing and a lot of delicate sutures. Suturing muscle wouldn't be easy. It would expose her to a greater risk of infection. Plus, she's lost a lot of blood. She wouldn't survive a major surgery."

The Captain blew out his held breath. "So you can do something. That's great. So do it."

"Hear that, Vicki? She's gonna fix your arm up good as new. Told ya she was good."

"Does no one listen to what I really say? I said I can't see and the word 'infection' was in there; so was 'loss of blood.' "

The Chief looked down at Doc. "If it is a matter of seeing, I can fix that." He turned and left.

"Doc, can it wait for a while before a final decision?" The Captain's face showed his effort to think through an area beyond his knowledge.

"She needs to be stable anyway before I can do much of anything."

"Nothing you can do about the blood?"

"Well, I do have an idea, but the risk is very high."

"Good; then, when she's conscious, we can talk to her about it."

"Hear that, Vicki? You can say 'yes' and be all fixed."

Doc crossed to a cabinet and removed a pill from a bottle. She got a glass of water and went to Chef Joan. "Here, take this."

Chef Joan swallowed the pill. "What's it for?"

"My nerves."

36
July 1, 1898
9 AM
The Sickbay

The voices woke Chef Joan. "You knocked me out! I can't believe you. I've slept all afternoon, evening, and night!"

"Yes, I did keep knocking you out. You start up again and I'll do it again, and next time you wake up, you'll be locked out of here even if I have to post a guard. Get control of yourself. You aren't doing anyone any good acting like you belong in a padded room."

"It's just that Vicki is so hurt and I …."

"Shut it."

"Joan, have you been bad?" Victoria looked at Chef with a small tired smile.

"You're awake!" Joan's face lit up.

"Sharp as ever, I see."

"Chef, keep quiet for awhile so Victoria and I can finish talking. Thank you. Well, Victoria, that's how it is, as best as I can explain it. The Chief says he has an answer for one problem and is on his way. If he has, then the choice is yours."

"Not a hard choice to make. I wouldn't be much use as a gunner or anything else with only one good arm."

"Well, we shall see what we shall see soon enough. I talked to the pilots and Diana volunteered to assist me."

"I'll assist!"

"Chef, I know you want to, but do you really think that would be a good idea?"

"No, I guess not."

When the Chief arrived, he was carrying odd spectacles with many loops attached. "This should work for you, Doc. The frames hold the different magnifiers. By turning them in front of your eyes, what you're looking at gets bigger and bigger. Try them."

Doc put them on and rotated one set of lens, one for each eye. "Everything is blurry, Chief."

"Think 'microscope.' Look at your hand up close."

She brought her hand up to her face and rotated another set of lenses down and looked again. Still another set brought her hand into an even closer view. The ridges of her palm were now mountains. "Good work, Chief. That does solve the problem of what I'm seeing. But there's still the problem of blood."

"What do you need?"

"Someone to give blood."

The Captain was quick to answer. "That's easy; I can give you mine."

"Sorry, Captain. I don't think you'll work. I think Chance is the only one on the ship."

"Why Chance and not me?"

"I can't explain it. I just know Chance is the one."

The Captain crossed to the loud-box. "Chance to sickbay. As quick as you can."

A few minutes later Chance entered, out of breath. "Yes, Captain?"

Doc patted a bed beside Victoria. "Have a seat, Chance. I need to explain some things and ask for your help."

"No need to say anything, Doc. Just tell me what to do."

"No, Chance, I need to explain. Victoria was hurt bad. She lost a lot of blood and, if I try to repair her arm, she wouldn't survive the surgery. I need your blood. That's something no one has the right to order. You have to volunteer."

Chance looked over at Victoria and thought for a while. "She's a good one, Doc. She stands her ground and protects the ship. She's needed. When do you want to start?"

"To get everything ready? About an hour."

The Captain walked to the hatch. "Well, I'm not needed here. My trust is in you, Doc."

Chance stood up from the bed. "Okay if I get something to eat?"
"That would be a great idea, Chance. Come back in about an hour."
Chance walked out slowly. "She's worth it, Doc."

37
July 1, 1898
10 AM
The Sickbay

The Chief came back to the sickbay just short of an hour later. "Anything else you need, Doc? I figured I'd check one last time before you start."

"When I need it, can you put the needles on the hose?"

"Sure, Doc."

"You'll need to scrub your hands and use lots of hot water and soap. Then I'll pour some alcohol over your hands to make sure everything is as clean as we can make it."

Chance entered, looking around. "Where do you need me, Doc?"

"Over there on the bed next to Victoria. We'll start soon." Doc turned to Victoria. "Okay, young lady, time for you to sleep and when you wake, we'll see how things went."

"Doc, thanks. No matter how things go, I know you'll do your best."

"Say 'goodnight.' " Doc gave her a pill from the same bottle as she had given Chef Joan. It didn't take long before Victoria was sleeping.

"Chief, time to clean up and fix the needles. Chance, one needle will go in your arm and the other in hers. The needles and tube are small, so it'll be slow but steady. I'll stop the flow if things look good and restart it when she needs more. The boxes on the bed and pad over there are to get you higher so the blood will flow easier."

"Just do what you need to do when you need to do it, Doc. I've made ready."

Diana entered, her face pale. "I'm here, Doc."

"Put on that clean apron I put out for you and clean up like the Chief is doing. I'll start the blood, let some flow in a while, and then we can start."

The Chief attached the needles and left.

Soon enough, Doc was at work on the arm. Stitch by stitch, the muscles were connected. It was slow and tedious work. Diana stayed pale but handed over everything Doc asked for. Chance stared up at nothing.

38
July 1, 1898
11 AM
The Bridge

"We should be at New City in three hours, Captain." Pilot Kathryn was relaxed at the helm.

"When we get within sight of land, start doing slow circles. I don't want to try to moor up while Doc is doing surgery."

"Why didn't she wait till landfall and do it at a hospital?"

"I asked that. She said they're disease pits. That her sickbay was better than anything they have and there was nothing there she needed."

"I hope it works out. Victoria's a good kid. Think Chef Joan will make lunch? I hear she's out of it with worry. I can understand concern; we're all concerned about Victoria, but Chef's nuts."

"I was just going to see about her and lunch. Joan and Victoria are close. They've been best friends since Victoria joined and neither has anyone else in life. No family, so in a sense they're family to each other. I'm going to hunt down Chef." He left the bridge at a slow pace, headed for the sickbay.

The Captain saw Chef Joan sitting on the deck as she had been before. "I thought you'd be here."

The Captain and the Lady Fair

Chef Joan got up off the deck. "No news yet, Captain."

"And there won't be for a long time yet. Doc told you it would take several hours. Now let's see about lunch. You do still have a job to do."

"Captain, I left out stuff for sandwiches for the crew. They can help themselves. I'd rather stay here."

"Chef, your job's in the galley, waiting. Throwing out loaves of bread on a table is not why you're here. I'm being polite here, as I know you're stressed, but it's not really a request. Being here won't speed anything up or change anything. Victoria did her job; now do yours, or should I tell her you slacked off? Come on. I might even lend a hand."

"Captain, you know you can't cook."

"Maybe not, but I can sample real good."

Chef Joan cracked a smile. "Okay, Captain."

Entering the galley, they found all of the crew that was on standby sitting around the large table. Some sat drinking coffee and some played cards, but no one was talking. They all looked up expectantly.

The Captain looked at each member. "No news yet. I think that means good news."

They returned to what they were doing.

"Chef, something light to poke at. I don't think anyone is a mood for anything heavy."

"I'll make salad and fruit trays then." Chef Joan went to work. She visibly calmed with the concentration of prep work.

Soon the crew had trays in front of them. There were only halfhearted attempts at eating.

The Chief entered and fixed a plate of salad. "Bow's fixed and cleaned up in case it's needed."

"That took longer than I'd have thought."

"I worked on it by myself. I just couldn't let anyone else do it."

"Chief, you heard her. She took the coat off because she felt it was getting in the way. She did a good job. She took them out."

Tailor joined in. "They went all the way down. I saw it hit."

Changing Times

"We were lucky is all. If they could have gotten a full broadside on us, it would have been over. Good job on those patches, Tailor." The Chief patted Tailor's shoulder.

"Chief, the only luck involved was they underestimated us. They thought a broadside was all they needed. They even had their limiters set too low to avoid hitting their own bags. They didn't have gunners in place at the start and only one crew made it to a gun. We gave them too many surprises with the cannon, the nose gun that could aim back and down at them, and the rate of our lift to keep above them. It was us being ready, Chief, nothing to do with luck. They thought a luxury ship would be an easy target."

Tailor looked up at the Chief. "It was 100 percent my fault, Chief."

"What? How?"

"I should have taken her place."

"That makes no sense. You're not a gunner. It wasn't your fault at all."

"Well, I am thinking it wasn't your fault, either, Chief, but if you're wanting to take the blame for it, why can't I?"

The Chief stared at Tailor. After a moment, he blew out a breath. "You're right, I guess."

With nothing to do, Chef Joan began to pace and mumble.

The Captain grabbed her shoulders and stared into her eyes. "Chef, she's in the best hands. You know Doc's the best. You can't make a seven-course dinner in five minutes, so relax. Give Doc the time she needs."

"Easier said than done, Captain."

"It's going to be a long afternoon. I'm off to the bridge." Taking a tray for Pilot, the Captain left the too-quiet galley.

39
July 1, 1898
The Sickbay

The work was slow and tedious but, even though her back ached and burned as if on fire from being bent over, she kept at it without pause. Finally, after six hours, the work was done.

Doc pulled the needles out of Chance's arm and patted him on the shoulder. "Thanks, Chance."

"I'm alive!"

"Of course you are. What are you talking about?"

"I thought she needed my blood. All of it, I mean."

"Oh my God! I didn't explain well enough. She just needed some to replace what she lost. You thought we would take your life for hers?"

"Umm, of course not. That would be stupid to think that. Okay if I go to the galley?"

"Yes, of course. For the next few days, rest a lot and drink lots of water and juice."

In his haste to leave, he didn't notice the paper drop from his pocket.

Doc crossed over to the loud-box and called the bridge to announce she was done. She saw the piece of paper on the floor, picked it up, and read the neat script on the outside. 'For my loving wife, my final words.'

Doc's eyes became glassy. "What an idiot. A giving, wonderful, loving man. But an idiot."

40
July 1, 1898
The Bridge

The Captain was slumped in his chair on the bridge. "Pilot, if you want a break, I'll relieve you for. You've been at it too long without a break."

"I'm good, Captain. I don't know what I'd do. At least for now I have something to help occupy my mind. It doesn't help a lot, but it does some."

The loud-box clicked on. Doc's voice came through. "It's all done. It went well. Better than I expected. She's good for now. Yes, Joan, you can come down and sit. Just keep it to a dull roar."

"Six hours. That was a long six hours. I'll be in the sickbay. You good for taking us in?"

"Sure, I feel better now"

"I'll be back before hitting dock." The Captain headed to the sickbay, stopping at the galley along the way. Checking the cooler, he found a full tray of fruit. Taking that and some bread and butter, he made his way to the sickbay.

Doc was resting in the chair at her small desk.

"Good work, Doc." He put the food down on it in front of her. He looked over at Chef Joan, who was once again holding Victoria's hand. "I see the cook forgot to bring you something to eat."

Chef Joan looked up, ashen-faced. "I'm sorry, Doc. I'll get you something right away."

"Relax; the assistant to the Chef took care of it." He pointed to the food on the tray and smiled. "I hear he's a pretty good sampler, too."

"Did you make this, or did Chef Joan?"

"I bring you food and you question me? Chef Joan made it and had it in the cooler. I could have done it. Just chopping up fruit isn't hard."

"Captain, you could peel a banana and ruin it."

"Thanks, Captain. I really am sorry, Doc. I should have thought."

"It's okay, Chef. She will be out for maybe a half-hour or more."

"Thanks for fixing her up, Doc." Chef Joan started whispering in Victoria's ear, ignoring Doc and the Captain.

"What's the whole story, Doc?"

Doc raised her voice enough to make sure Chef Joan would hear. "It went well. I lost count of the sutures in there. I made them as small as I could. They'll dissolve in just over a week and I'm hoping the muscles will attach themselves in the meantime. I strapped her arm down to prevent movement during the healing. Full rest on that arm for two to three weeks. I prefer bed rest for most of that time. Then we'll see." She lowered her voice. "Infection is my worry now."

"Doc, I've said it before and I'll say it again. You have talents you don't know."

"Just hard work."

"That and Talent."

The Chief poked his head into the hatch.

The Captain looked at the Chief, and then at Chef Joan. With a quick tilt of his head, he indicated the Chief should get Chef Joan out.

"Hey, Chef, you can see she's okay. Why don't you come make me something good to eat? Make everyone something good to eat and we'll celebrate."

Before Chef Joan could say anything, the Captain added his support of the idea. "Good idea, Chief. I'm sure everyone will be hungry. Joan, she won't wake for a while yet, and the Doc can call you when she does. Let's get out of her hair and let her do Doc stuff." Then he added, "It'll make the time pass quicker."

"Yes, Captain." She bent over as if whispering again, but the Captain could see the kiss on the forehead. She left with the Chief.

"Okay, Doc, I am sure you know your business but I suggest you get some rest."

"I can't just yet."

"Sure you can. She's not going to run off anywhere." He pulled a chair over beside the bed. "You sit here and rest your head and, if she moves, it'll rouse you. That simple."

"I don't know about that."

He helped her up and guided her to the chair. "Here, you sit. You can rest your head." Once she was seated, he picked up her hand and gently laid it over the bandage on Victoria's arm. "If she moves it'll rouse you and you can do Doc things. Just dream good things, like how those muscles will heal up and connect just fine."

"Alright, alright. Go away then."

"Okay, Doc. I'm going back to the bridge for docking."

Forty minutes later the bulkhead door slowly opened. Chef Joan's head came in just far enough to see around the door. Doc was sleeping with her head resting on Victoria's bed. Opening the door, just enough to squeeze through, she walked, as a cat stalking a bird, across the room to Victoria's bed. Once on the side away from Doc, she took Victoria's good hand in hers. She whispered to Victoria so as to not wake Doc. "I am sorry for being such a mess, Vicki. I was just so afraid of losing you. I know it's wrong and all, but I can't help it. I love you." At that, Victoria opened her eyes wide, looking at Chef Joan.

"Oh, Lord!" Chef Joan covered her mouth as she ran out.

Doc jerked upright. "What happened?"

"Just a dream, Doc. Just a dream. Nothing to worry about."

41
July 1, 1898
6 PM
The Galley

The Captain, the Chief, and Alexandria, with Kira, sat in the galley, forming plans for the days ahead.

"Chief, any more changes you want to make?"

"No, Captain. Nothing comes to mind."

"Good. I told you before I had an idea I wanted. Now's the time. You can work here, or we can move to the overhaul yards if you need. Here's a plan for Cabins 22 and 23." He slid a folded paper across the table. "There's also a list of items to add to the space."

The Chief looked over the paper. "I don't see how this will help the ship, Captain, but if you want it, you'll have it."

"Chief, this is one of those secrets. Alexandria, you're scheduled for your media event on the day after tomorrow. I'm sorry you missed the whole conference. The good news is you'll be center stage now."

"I'm ready for it, but nervous. Do you think anything will happen?"

"If something does, I'll be there. So will a lot of Phoenix personnel."

"Okay to do shopping?"

"Sure, just make sure you have two crew with you at all times. Do you think, with the Chief's help, you could actually build a shield big enough for the Lady Fair?"

"I think so if we can get the parts."

"Chief, make the shield top project and only the three of us to know. You can farm out any other work you need to. I'm hungry. Where's Chef?"

"I haven't seen her since she snuck away from me and went to sickbay."

"I had a talk to her before about her job. This isn't like her."

Alexandria started to get up. "I can go get her."

"No, never mind. I'll cook us up something."

"Captain, if you don't mind, I'll cook. I don't want to die just yet." The Chief turned to the ice cooler.

"My cooking's not that bad."

"Says you."

Alexandria giggled. "Gentlemen, if you don't mind, I'll fix something. One of you take care of Kira while I do?"

The Captain took Kira carefully, so as not to awaken her. "She sleeps all the time. Is that normal?"

"Eating and sleeping are her two biggest pastimes but, when she's awake, she can be a handful. She likes to wiggle and grab at things she brushes against. I see there're some fruit and slices of pork in the cooler. Salad, fruit, warmed pork, warmed potatoes, and Brussels sprouts okay?"

"Anything is fine by me, as long as the Captain doesn't have a hand in it."

"Doc said everyone onboard is married except the Captain, Chef, and Victoria, but when the pilots got their certificates they have the same last name. Aren't the married?"

The Captain laughed. "They married twin brothers."

"Oh. I bet that is a sight to see all four together."

As Alexandria started gathering things, Doc entered. "Perfect timing, I see. I was just coming to see what Chef Joan had made for dinner. Victoria's hungry, which is a good sign, and she is not in pain. Where's Chef?"

"We thought she was with you. The last Chief saw of her was when she slipped away to go to sickbay a couple of hours ago."

"I woke up, and she was running out and never came back."

"I guess I'll have to look into that. Did Victoria say anything?" The Captain's voice was tinged with concern.

"I asked her and she said it was just Joan being silly and that's all she'd say."

"After we eat, I'll go look for her. Chief, make a list with Alexandria on what parts you'll need tomorrow." The Captain sighed. "Chief, remember the quiet days?"

"Yep, they were dull; weren't they?"

42
July 2, 1898
9 AM
The Garrote Company Office

"You have another chance to eliminate that upstart of a woman. I expect better results." Maxmillian Dartin stood with his fists on the massive executive desk. His voice tight with anger, he continued to badger the man standing stiffly in front of him. "I expected you to handle things yourself, not hire some idiots to use airsharks. You'll handle this yourself. She'll be at a news meeting tomorrow to make her announcements. You should have no problem to get at her at the New City Town Center. You'll see to it she never says a word. Ever again. Am I clear on what I want?"

"Yes, sir."

Maxmillian sat down and leaned back. "Don't let anyone get in your way."

"My bullet will hit its mark."

43
July 2, 1898
9 AM
New City

Standing at the end of the boarding ramp, Alexandria, the Chief, and Avery looked back at the airship.

"I don't know anything about airships, but I think she's the best."

With the sound of pride in his voice, the Chief agreed with Alexandria. "There's no doubt in my mind she's the best."

"Where do we start, Chief?"

"We go to some special supply houses I know. After that, I need to go into the city proper to get something."

"Good, I need to get something, too, and I'll need your advice."

On reaching the street outside the port, the Chief flagged down a passing steam carriage for hire. The chuffing of the engine was a familiar sound, but it was in stark contrast to the Island, where the only noise was laughter and bird songs. The racket of the hard wheels on the cobblestones added to the distraction.

"I miss the Island already. Why did I ever think it was so good living in a city?"

"I miss the Island and my Neenaa already."

"Maybe she spoils you."

"I do my best to spoil her, so she'll never want to leave me for someone better."

"Trust me, Chief; there's no one better for her."

"Better safe than sorry, I say."

It took three supply houses to find all the parts they needed and have them sent to the ship.

"That's taken care of that. Now, I need to find some gold frames for the Pilots' certificates."

"How the Captain worked that out is amazing."

"The Captain's wanted that to happen for a long time. Sad that even though they have them, they'll never be Pilots anywhere else. Even with the tickets, no one will hire them. It does mean a lot to them, though, and they can stand up to any Pilot now."

The Chief waved down another steam carriage, and they chuffed to the art shop.

"It would've been nice if the Captain could have joined us, but he left early to go talk to some high ranks." The Chief swayed with the jostling carriage.

"It seems like he's always up to something."

"Yep, that's him alright; keeps his nose in everything."

The carriage wound through the cobblestone streets past plain gray shops. Soot coated every building. Shades of gray and black hid any color that may have been painted on when the buildings were new. The streaks in the soot made the buildings look as if they were crying. The carriage stopped in front of a shop that looked the same as all the others they had passed.

They were greeted as they entered. "Welcome to my shop. How may I be of service this fine day?" The short, rotund shopkeeper behind the glass display case gave them a huge toothy smile.

"I need frames for these. Gold-plated ones." The Chief unrolled the certificates onto the display case.

"Gold-plated, you say? They must be special indeed. Let's see what you have and I'll measure them up. I doubt I have anything ready-made in stock to fit, but by afternoon I could have something made up." The shopkeeper measured up the certificates for size but didn't notice what they were. He spoke louder towards the rear of the shop. "Marie, bring out the gold frame samples." A young girl in her mid-teens with tightly curled red hair, and wearing a tan, muslin, long-sleeve shirt, and a tan, muslin skirt, placed six pieces of frame on the display case.

"Here you are, Father." Looking up at the three standing before the case, she remarked, "It must be for something very special." Looking down at the certificates a moment, her eyes grew wide. "Father, look! That's a President's seal! It's for Pilots! And look, those are women's names!"

"Yes, Marie, that's nice. Now go on back, and I'll call you if I need you."

"But, Father, that means I could be a Pilot too!"

Alexandria grinned. "Yes, you can, if you study hard and learn lots of math and you find the right Captain. By the time you are old enough things may have changed."

"Poppycock. Women are not Pilots."

The Chief leaned over the counter to look directly at the shopkeeper. "I think, good sir, the documents before you belie that. I think my Pilot friends would be offended to hear you say they are not Pilots."

Sweat shone on the shopkeeper's forehead. "I meant no offense. I've just never heard such a thing."

"Now you have heard and seen such a thing. Young lady, you can be anything you want to be, no matter what anyone says." He put emphasis on the word 'anyone' as he stared hard at the shopkeeper. "You, sir, will be the talk of the town when you tell others you have seen such a thing with your own eyes." Straightening up, the Chief gave him his best smile. "Now, let's see what we have here to chose from." The Chief's choice was the most ornate one, with engraved curves and scrollwork.

"Yes, Chief, I like that one too."

Avery spoke up. "Count me in on that one."

They agreed on a time to return to pick up the frames and left to make the next shopping trip.

"The Captain has really rubbed off on you." Alexandria smiled up at the Chief.

"Maybe. Okay, Alexandria, what do you need to buy?"

"A gun."

"Excuse me? You want a gun?"

"Not for me! For Victoria. A get-well gift. I thought a gun would be better than anything else I can think of. I'm sure she has a gun already, or lots. I just thought something special would be nice and cheer her up."

"She only has two, the rifle we made together, and an old handgun that belonged to her father. She inherited it when both her brothers were killed."

"That's terrible. What happened?"

"A skirmish at a border war a few years back. I'm sure you asked around about why the Captain retired or heard the story. That airship he didn't go help, Victoria's brothers were on it. The Captain doesn't know that. When she found out she became more determined to be a good member of the crew and help him be where ever he thinks he needs to be." The Chief paused and changed the subject. "I think you're right. A nice gun would be just the thing."

"Do you think she's still doing okay?"

"With Doc watching over her and Kira to keep her distracted, I'm very sure."

At the gun shop, Avery chose to remain outside. The bell over the door gave a high-pitched tinkle as Alexandria and the Chief entered. Guns of every shape and size filled the cases; the walls were covered in rifles and shotguns and the dimly lit shop smelled of gun oil.

"Good afternoon. May I help you find something?" The thin, balding gunsmith in a tattered vest beamed his best smile.

"Yes, we are looking for the newest and the best handgun. Usable, not something for display that gathers dust."

"Just over here, sir. The Pony Company's newest. Fifty-caliber, six-shot revolver. It's nickel-plated to wear well. Stop an elephant. Here you are, sir. Feel how well it fits your hand."

Hefting the weapon, the Chief smiled down on it. "Yes, very nice. But it's not for me. It's for our lady friend."

"I do apologize, sir. I assumed wrongly." He snatched the weapon from the Chief's hand and replaced it with a derringer. "For a lady, sir. Fine scrollwork and pearl handles. Just the thing for a lady."

Changing Times

The Chief roared a short laugh and handed it back, holding it with two fingers. Even Alexandria was chuckling. "If I gave her this toy when she got done beating me to your size, she would come here and ram this down your throat. I think, for our wellbeing, we should stick to the larger one." The Chief leaned over the counter and gave the gunsmith a cold stare.

"Chief, it's huge and I'm sure she'd love the idea of knocking down things as big as elephants. It's perfect! I don't think I've anywhere near enough for it."

"Not a problem. I think the Admiralty can pick up the tab on this one."

"Then I could get her a nice holster for it!"

"A holster and 200 rounds if you please."

"Sir, I am sorry; I only have 150 in stock."

"Can you wrap it all as a gift?"

Alexandria was still laughing as they left the shop with the package wrapped in plain, brown paper.

44
July 2, 1898
3 PM
The Sickbay

Alexandria slipped into the sickbay. "I see you're awake. Did you take good care of Kira for me?"

"You're funny. You know I can't move. She and I had long talks though."

"I bet Doc will have you up soon."

"She did good. I'm down to a dull ache and I can move my fingers."

"I brought you a present to help you get better."

"I do like presents."

"Sorry, but it's heavy, so I think I better unwrap it for you. If that's okay."

"Heavy? Sounds like something good."

Alexandria unwrapped the package and placed the gun in Victoria's right hand. "A big gun for a big girl."

"It's beautiful! I love it. You shouldn't have, but I'm not giving it back!" Victoria repeatedly raised the gun with her arm extended, cocked the hammer back, and then eased it back down as she lowered her arm. The double click back and single click down had a sharp, crisp sound to it.

Doc came to the side of the bed. "Nice. I'll give you ten minutes to play with it. Then I get it until I leave the sickbay, and then you can play more. That clicking will drive me nuts."

"Doc, it's great for me to exercise my good arm. I should exercise, shouldn't I?" There was a teasing tone in Victoria's voice.

"Yes, exercise is good. You can exercise all you want with it. When I am out of the room."

Alexandria chuckled. "I'm glad you like it, but I think I'll put the bullets and holster in your room."

"Holster? A holster, too? Let me see; let me see." A child at Christmas would have looked sad next to Victoria's expression and tone of voice.

Alexandria pulled the holster from the box and laid it next to her.

"That'll look so good on my hip! Could you do me a favor and get my sewing kit and the leftover fabric from the suit?"

"Sure, I'd be happy to, but what'll you sew and how are you going to sew with one hand?"

"Trim on the holster, and I can hold it with my knees if I have to. It sure beats laying here staring at the ceiling."

"Okay, not a problem then. I'll get your stuff and pick up Kira when I come back."

Doc gave a slight wince with each click that had not stopped or even slowed. "You're doing fine. The wound looks several days old already and I'm not worried about infection anymore. You're still not to move that arm. If you mess up my work, I might be mad enough to leave it messed up."

"Yes, Ma'am."

Alexandria's voice lowered. "You can tell me it's none of my business if you want but I have to ask. The whole time I have been on the Lady Fair, you and Chef have been together all the time. What happened?"

Victoria was quiet a moment. "I was sleeping, woke, and she ran from the room. I guess you'll have to ask her."

45
July 2, 1898
3:30 PM
The Galley

Alexandria was met by the rich smells of baking when she entered the galley. "Hello, Chef. I see you're all alone. Anything I can do to help?"

"Hi, Alexandria. Not much to do. The crew is going dirt-side for dinner tonight. Chief told me you're going, too. I'm just making some cakes for late night raids on my kitchen."

"I wish I knew about a dinner in town."

"I am sure he'll say something when he sees you. How did shopping go?"

"We got gold picture frames for the Pilots' certificates and we got a huge pistol for Victoria and she liked it."

Chef Joan whisked the batter in the bowl faster. "Maybe you and Chief can have some of my cake when you get back and think of more stuff to buy."

"Yes. We can do that." Alexandria poured herself some coffee and sat at the table taking tiny sips and watching Chef Joan.

"I can feel your eyes boring in my back. What is it?"

"Well, since you asked, I'm worried about Victoria. She didn't look well. She was covered in sweat and could barely lift her arm to touch the gun."

"What?" Chef Joan slammed the bowl down and started pulling off her apron as she moved to the hatch.

"Stop right there, Chef! She's fine and playing with her new toy. Even going to do some sewing."

Chef Joan froze at the hatch and turned to stare at Alexandria.

"Mind fixing Kira a bottle?" Alexandria was gently bouncing Kira and playing a grabbing game with Kira's hands.

"What was that all about? Why did you say that?"

"I thought the 'I don't care' attitude was fake. You just proved it. So why don't you fix a bottle, sit down, and we can talk about it."

"Nothing to talk about."

"It is not my business, but I asked around among the crew. You two have been side by side since the day she came onboard. Best friends. Now you hide away."

"I'm not hiding. I've been busy." Chef Joan grabbed the bowl and started whisking again. This time, the motion was fast and hard.

"Okay, so you don't want to talk about it with me. I can understand that. You don't really know me. I'll tell you the Captain is bothered by it all."

"He told you that?"

"No, but he was looking for you last night."

"He could have found me at breakfast."

"No, Chief said he left early. I guess before breakfast."

"He'll get the same answer."

"Tell me. Have you ever seen him not get his way?"

Joan's shoulders slumped. "No." Her whisking slowed.

Alexandria changed the subject. "I've been asking the crew how they came to be on the Lady Fair. Mind telling me how you came to be onboard?"

Changing Times

"I was street vending. I worked for a nasty man and sold oysters, like most the other vendors. Mine were special because I cooked mine. Cooked oysters are safer than raw ones unless you know they're really fresh. I did a good business and sold everything every day. The Captain bought some and started to walk away. I was watching him because he was so nice looking in his clean white uniform and everyone else was in second-hand clothes. He ate some, stopped, turned around, and watched me cook while he ate. Do you think the Captain is handsome?"

Alexandria blushed. "I haven't really noticed."

"After he ate, he left, but when I was done for the day, I looked up, and he was standing there. It was night by then, but he didn't scare me. He just smiled and said 'I want you to be the cook on my ship.' He told me where his ship was and said I would have the galley to myself, and it would always have fresh food, and I could cook anything I wanted. He told me I would have my own cabin. Of course taking off in the night with a stranger would be stupid, so I said I would think about it. I went to the docks, where he said his ship was, and there was the Lady Fair. Such a beautiful ship, and fancy for rich people. I thought I didn't belong on something as high class as that. I turned to leave and bumped into Doc. She looked like a proper lady, but she was dressed like someone that worked on the ship. I must have had a silly look on my face because she laughed. Then she said I must be the cook that was coming, and said she would show me the ship. I told her I was just looking, and not there to take the job. She took me by the hand, showed me all around the ship, showed me a cabin, and said it would be mine. Then she showed me the galley. How could I say no? She just stared at me while I thought about it all, and then she went to the loud-box and announced to the Captain the cook was onboard, and he could have bacon in the morning. He does love bacon. I can't think of being anywhere else now. There are lots of books here that have all kinds of recipes and every day I read about a new one."

"Ahh, the missing Chef." The sound of the Captain's voice stopped Chef Joan's whisking and story.

Both Alexandria and Chef Joan greeted the Captain as he entered and got himself a cup of coffee.

"Alexandria, we're going into town for dinner. We'll go to Bernard's. It's where we all tend to go when we're here. We'll probably run into some of the crew."

Alexandria muttered "Better late than never."

"What?"

"Never mind. It's not important. Chef is making cakes to have later."

The Captain gave Chef Joan a stern look. "Chef, we need to have a talk. We can have it when I get back from dinner. On the bridge. It'll be empty."

"Yes, Captain."

"Good. You two go on with your conversation. I need to go see Doc."

46
July 2, 1898
4:00 PM
The Sickbay

"Doc, how's our patient?"

"Hello to you too, Captain. She's doing better than I hoped. Really well."

"When will she be able to go back to her cabin instead of laying about here?"

Victoria stopped her sewing, but still held the holster wrapped in a piece of red fabric with her knees. "Laying about? You make it sound like I'm being lazy."

"Sorry, Victoria. I'm just distracted and not thinking as well as I should. Doc, when will our patient be well enough to be up, instead of stuck in bed?"

"Like I said, she's healing well. She could be up tomorrow, but only for short trips. I just don't want her on her own yet. She needs to be watched in case something comes up, and I still don't want her going around getting her own food and such."

"So all she needs is someone to watch over her."

"Yes, and help her with any needs."

"Good news, Victoria. You get your freedom tomorrow." The Captain left before they could ask any questions.

Shortly after he left, his voice came over the loud-box. "Chief to the bridge, please."

"He can't be thinking of having the Chief help me, can he?"

47
July 2, 1898
7:00 PM
Bernard's

Bernard's, with white-clothed tables and waiters in the new style of tuxedos, showed its desire to be an establishment of class. The food and prices showed a desire to have more business than the rich alone would bring. Young men would save up to bring a date to impress, but it wasn't so expensive as to make them broke. The fabric-covered walls and thick carpet absorbed excess noise, which made for a quiet and comforting mood. The secret to its finances, which were better than most would expect, was the bar in a separate walled-off area that even had its own door to the street. It was not as quiet nor as calming as the dining room. The walls held numerous drawings and painting of famous airships, and even of a few current captains of distinction. The bar was popular with sailors and flyers alike. Once the bartender learned a face, even a tab was allowed. Heavily salted garlic breadsticks were a free staple that kept the men thirsty. A wall and a doorway separated the two worlds.

Women around the room of the restaurant turned one by one, to stare at Alexandria as they entered the restaurant. "My head on backward?"

A big grin came to the Captain's face. "No. I think it's more that you look stunning and …."

"And what?"

"You seem to have forgotten you've gone a little native. I doubt anyone here has seen a baby carried that way before."

"Oh my gosh! I forgot all about it. It just seems so right to have her close and my hands free when needed."

Through a chuckle, he said, "I'm sure it'll be a fashion with mothers soon."

"Good evening, Captain. We're so glad you've come to visit us again." The host, standing stiffly in his tuxedo, gave a short bow. "I am truly sorry, Captain, but your table isn't ready just yet. Perhaps twenty or thirty minutes. If you would care to wait in the bar area, I can fetch you when it's ready."

"Thanks." The Captain, Alexandria, and the Chief made their way to the bar.

"Look. There's the crew. Let's join them." The Captain stopped short behind a man in a white dress uniform who was standing at the crew's table.

"Just because your pretend Captain got you certificates doesn't mean you're Pilots. Women Pilots! What a joke you are. You'll go crying to Momma as soon as anything happens. Women should be at home cleaning and taking care of babies."

"Well, Lieutenant Fausworth, I see you didn't learn anything from our last meeting."

The Lieutenant spun in place, his face ashen. "I was just teasing them, Sir."

Changing Times

Standing beside the Captain, the Chief's hands formed into fists, his biceps bulged enough to stress the jacket, and the veins on his neck throbbed.

The Captain stared at the Lieutenant and watched his Adam's apple bob up and down. "That was not a good idea, Lieutenant. What brings you here from the Island?"

The Lieutenant reached inside his jacket and brought out a sealed envelope. "From the Admiral, Sir." He handed over the envelope.

"Isn't that nice? Mail from home." The Captain slid the envelope inside his jacket.

"Aren't you going to read it? I mean, you might want to, in case you want to reply."

"It can wait unless you want to tell me the contents."

"The admiral didn't tell me, Sir, but it might be important."

"I'm sure it is. Your job is done. I think you're done. I suggest you leave the area in case the pilots and my crew wish to answer your teasing with some *punch* lines."

"Yes, sir." He left by the bar door leading to the street.

They joined the crew at the table. "Pilots, you just ignore that weasel."

A quiet voice came from behind the Captain. "Excuse me, Sir."

The Captain turned to see a young man in a casual shirt and pants standing straight as if at attention. "Yes?"

"I overheard the comments by that lieutenant. I just wanted to say something, if you don't mind, sir."

"I take it you're Navy."

"Yes, sir. Sorry, sir. I'm Lieutenant Meyers, sir. Pilot for the Dreadnaught Peregrine."

"Relax and drop the 'sirs' to one a day. Go ahead; what's on your mind?"

As the two were talking, three more men came up behind the Lieutenant.

"I heard about the events you and your crew have been through. Taking off and flying through a storm. Fights with airsharks and a

Dreadnaught. My brother was in Pilot school with your Pilots. He said they were best in everything. Natural flyers. I just wanted to say …" He turned to the Pilots. "My brother didn't say enough. You must have two of the greatest Pilots for all that."

The Captain smiled at the men. "You probably haven't heard; they are ticketed Pilots now."

"The school gave them tickets?"

"Nope, they're by Presidential Order, seal and all."

Lt. Meyers saluted the pilots. The three men standing behind him joined in the salute.

Both Pilots' eyes were glassing over. "Diana and I thank you," said Kathryn.

"We request permission to buy a round of drinks for you, your crew, and fellow ticketed Pilots, sir."

"Granted, but only if you all join us."

The Lieutenant headed for the bar and the others pulled up chairs near the pilots and started asking questions about their adventures.

The table was a full roar of stories and laughter when the host came to get them for dinner. Shown to a table, they soon had drinks in front of them and were waiting for the meal. Before the food could arrive, women began to come up to the table, asking about the baby sling and chatting with Alexandria about how clever it was to have the baby so close. Alexandria smiled happily, explaining how to make one, and said she was thinking of sewing in two pockets, one for a bottle and one to carry some spending money.

The Captain and the Chief leaned back in their chairs, keeping out of the way. "Maybe it wasn't such a good idea to get her to go native." The Captain tilted his head towards Alexandria

"It was a good idea, Captain. The question is 'Is the rest of the world ready?' Do you think it's safe enough to be here like this?"

"Whoever's behind it all has to have time to get people in place. Each attack has been in a place we were predicted to be. The only two places they can plan on are the ship and the media event. The media event will be the next target. The two crew rule is just in case."

"Makes sense."

The waiter arrived at the table with the food and the visiting ladies scattered back to their own tables.

"I'm not sure I like being the center of attention, but that was fun. Did you see Diana and Kathryn's faces? They were so happy. What's with that slimy Lieutenant anyway?"

"That's a fair question. I wish I knew. Chief, what's your opinion of the Lieutenant?"

"After he's around, I feel like I need a shower."

"That's my feeling, too. I need those magnifiers you made when we get back."

"Sure, but why?"

"He was in a rush for me to break the seal. Plus why would he be here with it instead of bringing it straight to me? I want to get a close look at it before I open it. And yes, Alexandria, the pilots were very happy, and they deserve it. You still nervous about tomorrow?"

"With everything that's happened I shouldn't be, but yes. How many people do you think will be there?"

"It's for the media, maybe twenty people."

"I am hoping some of the scientists show. The information needs to get to them, and a news report won't have all the information they'll need."

"If they're interested, they'll show, too. No one will be kept out. Chief, did you get the projects done I asked you about earlier?"

"All done and quiet. I had to have help to get it done quickly, but it's done and still quiet."

"Thanks, Chief. I had a quiet talk with Doc before I left. I told her of my plan. As it happens, she told me something very interesting. Because of that, I need you to make another trip into town. Later, I'll draw up something to show you what I'm wanting."

"If it is something to be made, I'll make it if I can. If I can't, I'll get it made for you. Not a problem, Captain."

"Thanks again."

Alexandria jumped into the conversation at the pause. "What plan?"

The Captain took a sip of his drink. "Sorry. That's on a need-to-know basis for now."

"Captain, I have so much to thank you for, Kira's and my life, more than once. Letting me see the beautiful Island I'll never forget. What'll really happen to Kira when I go home after the conference?"

"There's no hold on you. You can go home if you want, but I suggest you stay with us. We don't think the conference will stop the attacks on you. You'd be safer with us. The talks I had this morning were about you and your safety. There are leads being followed, but we need more time. As far as Kira goes, like I said before, no one is rushing anything."

"That would mean more time with Kira and maybe time on the Island. I'm very happy with that if I won't be in the way."

"You won't be."

48
July 2, 1898
9:30 PM
The Lady Fair

The Captain studied the envelope with the Chief's magnifiers as the Chief stood by. "It's been opened. There is a hint of re-melted wax on the bottom edge of the seal, and there is a faint water stain along the edge of the flap from being steamed open." The Captain straightened and read the message. "Intelligence says there'll be an assassin in the area for the press meeting. No specifics, but a postscript says to watch my back."

"Does that mean the assassin is after you?"

"No. To just read it like that, you would think so. The Admiral would have said that straight out. From him, like this, it means someone close is not to be trusted, and because it gives no name, it tells me he feels the same as we do about the Lieutenant. We'll have to deal with him. I'll have to figure out some nice bait. In any case, tomorrow, after breakfast, I'm going to talk to some locals and make some plans for the press meet."

"Sounds good. Let me know if you need anything."

"Thanks and goodnight, Chief."

As the Chief left, the Captain used the loud-box. "Chef Joan to the bridge, please." The Captain paced the bridge, waiting.

"Yes, Captain?" Chef Joan stood just inside the hatchway, slump-shouldered, and with a saddened face.

"Come on in. Sit if you want."

Chef Joan flopped onto the couch at the rear of the cabin under two gold frames holding the Pilots' certificates. "I know I've disappointed you with my work, Captain."

"Chef, do you think so little of me, that you think I wouldn't understand you were upset over your best friend being almost killed or maimed for life? I can understand that, but you're acting way out of sorts. There is more to it than that. Care to tell me?"

"Nothing to tell, Captain. That's all there is."

"I was hoping I was someone you could trust and talk to. I'm saddened you feel I'm not. Your actions at the bow were extreme, but that isn't the issue. What you've been doing since is. Dodging your work, dodging me, and even avoiding your friend to the point of having others take food to sickbay is. There's something going on between you two. Some kind of tension happened and you don't seem to be doing anything to work it out. Do you wish to leave the Lady Fair?"

"No, Captain! This is home to me. Please don't kick me off the Lady Fair."

"Alright, I won't, but I'm confining you to your cabin. Food will be brought to you. You'll be confined there until I am satisfied attitudes have changed."

"Yes, Captain." She rose to leave. "I'll go now, Captain."

"That's fine, but there is one more thing. Your cabin is now Cabin 24."

"Captain?"

"Later, you'll have help and an escort to your old cabin to get your things."

"Why the change, Captain?"

"Call it cruel and unusual punishment. I'll go with you to make sure you get there."

It was a slow walk to the new cabin. "I feel like I'm headed for the brig."

"At first you might prefer a brig. I'm ex-military and some answers come to me that way. As a civilian Captain, sometimes I can do more and sometimes less than the military. In this case, I think this is best for now."

Chef Joan froze when she opened the door and saw the inside of the cabin. It was one of the nicest cabins for guests. The furnishings were more for the rich than for a crew member. Light-colored wallpaper with intricate patterns, polished tables and chairs, brass lanterns, and two double beds still left room to move easily. The white curtains were closed over the floor-to-ceiling windows. Her eyes weren't fixed on the room, but on Victoria, who lay on one of the beds with Doc sitting at her side.

Doc stood. "Good, the nurse is here. Victoria, I'm not going to spend my time watching over you. Let me introduce you to your new nursemaid. Victoria, this is Chef Joan, your nursemaid. Chef Joan, this is Victoria, your patient. Bye now." Doc slipped from the room.

"Go on in, Chef. You now share a cabin with Victoria and will watch over her. When I decide you both have ironed things out, then the confinement will be over." The Captain left, closing the door behind him. He stopped and leaned his back against the door for a moment. "I hope it's the right thing."

49
July 2, 1898
10 PM
Cabin 24

"I can't get up and walk out, so it's going to be a very long night if we don't talk to each other." Victoria tried to push herself up into a sitting position. "You need to help."

Chef Joan got up from her chair, helped Victoria to sit up, and fluffed up her pillows. Not saying a word, she sat back down.

"If you think I'm going to make this easy on you, then you'd better rethink it," said Victoria. "You left me lying in sickbay with just Doc. If the crew hadn't stopped by all the time, I would've gone crazy. My best friend wouldn't even bring me something to eat."

"I'm sorry." Tears flowed down Joan's cheeks.

"That's it? 'I'm sorry' is all you have to say?"

"You were awake. You heard me. I'm so sorry. I was keeping it secret. I didn't want you to feel awkward or uneasy around me. I couldn't lose you like that."

"Does it sound like I feel awkward? Well, maybe I do a little, but avoiding me is even worse. I think you forgot some things."

"Like what?"

"Slave ship."

"What about it? We got you off safe and sound."

"No, you didn't."

"What?" Chef Joan looked up and, for the first time, looked her in the eye.

The Captain and the Lady Fair

"I was rescued from the ship and given a safe place, but I wasn't sound. Doc knows because she treated me. Joan, that was a slave ship, not a luxury cruise. What do you think they did to the women whenever they felt like and however they felt like? Sometimes they did things just to humiliate us for fun. If we refused at all, we were beaten."

Victoria paused. "There was a buyer or leader there all the time; he was the worst of them all. I don't know which he was, but he gave the orders and he kept me for himself. He escaped. I still have nightmares of him now and then. I can talk about it now because of Doc. She would just sit and hold my hand. Let me talk or not. I saw how the crew here liked each other, helped each other, cared for each other. It felt okay. I felt I was in the middle of a family and I needed that. When the Captain took me on, it wasn't out of sympathy; it was because I had a skill. I would be a useful part. Not a freeloader."

Victoria sat up straighter. "Joan, the first time I met you was right after I was off the ship. I was a mess. I still had the stink of him on me and in me everywhere. I mean everywhere. It even hurt to sit. While the crew got others off the ship, you took me to the galley and wrapped me in a blanket when you saw me shiver. I wasn't cold, but the blanket helped. Then you put a hot, full loaf of bread in front of me, tore it apart in small pieces, and fed me a little at a time. You cared about me. You cared for me and asked for nothing. Not even for me to talk. After that, I stayed close to you because I felt safe."

Joan had tears in her eyes. "I was just trying to help. I didn't understand about what happened."

"Even better, it wasn't sympathy then. After all that, how do you think I'd feel if a man were to touch me? You know, with desire."

"I guess I'd feel bad."

"You were always touching me. My arm, my hands and my back."

"Yes, I'm sorry. I shouldn't have." Joan looked down, avoiding Victoria's eyes.

"God, you *are* dense. Didn't you notice I didn't pull away and even did some touching back?"

"What?"

"I guess I have to be bossy and more outspoken. I was never interested in men that way. Didn't you like my red suit?"

"I loved it."

"How did it make you feel?"

"What? I can't say things like that."

"Joan, tell me. Tell me now or get out."

Joan hung her head. "I wanted you."

"That's why I made it. That and my own desire to show the world I was strong and not broken. We can take all the time in the world. We can talk, hold hands like we used to, or whatever. It's new to me, too, but the difference is I don't care what others think." Victoria held out her hand.

Chef Joan took it.

50
July 3, 1898
8 AM
Cabin 24

Doc opened the cabin door. "Oh good, no bloodshed. Come on in, Captain."

The Captain entered, carrying a large tray. "Here we are; breakfast is served. I wanted to do the eggs yolk-up, but they broke, so they're scrambled. I'd taste them before adding salt. They might be salty already. The toast is good. I scraped off the burnt parts. The bacon is nice and crispy. Extra-crispy. Maybe over-crispy. The coffee's great."

Chef Joan stared open-mouthed from her chair next to Victoria, who was just waking. "You cooked?"

"Of course. We're short a Chef in the galley, and I couldn't ask anyone else to do your job. Did you sleep in that chair?"

"Yes, we're talking just fine. Everything is fine. We talked all night. I'll go cook a decent breakfast."

Doc went to Victoria, checked her over, and was satisfied to see she was still mending. "No worse for wear. I guess there was no fighting."

"Good, Chef is a good nursemaid and can keep it up. Chef, you're still confined. As for my cooking, you can eat it or not. Maybe it'll speed things along."

"Confinement is one thing. Torture is another. Let me go cook."

"Nope."

Victoria struggled to sit up. "Why can't I have good food? I need good food to heal. Doc can tell you that; just ask her."

"It might not be tasty, but you can live on it. Sorry, Victoria, I can't tell the Captain otherwise."

"I'll go plan lunch. It might be late, maybe one o'clock, even later if I have to do it over again. Have a nice morning. Let's go, Doc."

Doc and the Captain both left, leaving Joan and Victoria staring at the tray.

"I'll never heal. His cooking may even kill me."

51
July 3, 1898
8 AM
The Engineering Room

The Chief entered the engineering room, mumbling to himself, and found Alexandria already there, at his worktable, working on drawings. Kira was wrapped in a light blanket, sleeping in a wooden box on the floor next to her. The worktable sat against the back wall of the large room, which featured one wall lined with shelves of wooden boxes holding parts and supplies. Along the opposite wall were: a metal lathe, a drill press, a tube bender, a small hammer machine, and a large sheet-metal cutter. Being an inside room, the light was provided by electric lights. "Good morning to you. Those the plans for the machine? When did you start them?" asked the Chief.

"Yes. I started about two this morning. I couldn't sleep. All I did was think about the press meeting tonight. I think I'm almost done. They're just sketches, not engineer drawings, but good enough, I think." Alexandria arched her back and rose. "My back is telling me I worked on them long enough, and my stomach tells me I need to eat. I'll go to the galley and see what Chef has."

"You won't find Chef Joan there. She's confined to quarters. You just missed the Captain making her breakfast. That was something to see. It's make it yourself day. Lucky for me, Neenaa taught me some cooking."

"He must be pretty angry at her."

"Angry? Nope, but he is concerned and is taking measures to resolve things."

"I thought the Captain doesn't cook. I could have made something up if he had asked."

Chief gave a short laugh. "I think his cooking is part of the plan to speed a resolution. He was making something, but if I hadn't watched from the start, I wouldn't be sure what it was supposed to be. If he ever cooks something, never, and I do mean never, eat it. Tell me where to get started and then go get something to eat."

Alexandria spent the next half-hour going over the sketches and what needed to be done. "The only hard part I see is locating the six coils to generate the shield. On the Lady Fair, it could be difficult, or at least the top one will be."

"I'm sure by the time it's ready to go up there, I'll have thought of something. The rest can be mounted inside the hull. The wood won't affect the energy fields."

"Chief? What makes the Captain the way he is? I know everyone on the crew is supportive of each other and I guess the Captain rubbed off on everyone, but what I mean is, why is he so strong about supporting women?"

The Captain and the Lady Fair

The Chief plopped down on a stool next to the worktable. "We were all pretty open-minded when we came aboard and being with the Captain made us even more so, and pretty strong-headed about it. As for the Captain, that's a mystery I'm not sure about. It's hard to get anything out of him about his past. I only know about him from when we met up in the military and the years we've been together. He was that way when I met him. I do know it had something to do with a girl he knew when he was very young. She died, but how and why, I don't know."

"Maybe it's none of my business, anyway."

Chief smiled at her. "Someday he might tell you about it if it's important for you to know. You already know what you need to know about the Captain and even the rest of the crew. You know what the crew risked to get you and to bring you this far. Have faith in them as they have in each other and the Captain. I will say he can take risks when it comes to women. Like when he hired on the twins. Straight out of school, no experience, no tickets but he hired them anyway. I can't see that anyone else would have given them a chance. Of course, now we know, they are the best. I guess he gets a feeling about things and he just jumps in, no matter what grief it may bring him. The only two onboard that had any experience are me and Doc. I have no idea how he talked her into signing on, but that is another case of getting the best. He somehow gets a feeling about people. Sometimes he feels someone is special and hires or helps them. Go get something to eat and we'll see how far we can get with this wonder machine."

"Okay, and if Chef isn't back to work by lunchtime, I'll make us something." Alexandria left quietly, so as not to disturb her own thoughts.

52
July 3, 1898
12 PM
The Sickbay

The Captain strolled into the sickbay with a big grin on his face. "Afternoon, Doc. Time to go check on your patient."

Doc was reading from a medical journal. She glanced at the clock on the white wall. "It's noon. I thought you said one o'clock. Are we stopping by the galley to pick up the lunch?"

"I didn't make lunch. I'm hoping I won't have to. If things went well, Chef can start back to work and make lunch herself."

"I still don't understand what's going on. I've gone along so far because it's good for Victoria to have a more comfortable place, but if I'm to help anymore, I need to know what you're up to." Doc leaned back in her chair and crossed her arms over her chest.

"I guess I can explain it to you, Doc. If I do, you can't say anything to either one, or anyone, if it doesn't work out. Pact?"

"Yes, I'll agree, but only if it doesn't put them at risk."

The Captain paced, rubbing the back of his neck. He started to speak, stopped, and tried again. "I'm pretty sure I know what the problem was between those two. Knowing them both as I do, Chef Joan would avoid Victoria, and Victoria wouldn't try to get closer. They would stay apart. We both know Victoria had a bad experience. The crew treats her like a sister to watch out for. Chef Joan has a nurturing spirit. I think being around Chef has helped heal her. Because they got close, when Victoria got hurt, it brought out feelings in Chef she couldn't control. Chef Joan isn't doing her job and I worry the strain between the two, might affect Victoria in hers. It would kill either one of them to have to leave. They both love the Lady Fair. The problem is, they love each other too, but I think they were keeping it secret from each other."

The Captain and the Lady Fair

Doc came halfway out of her chair. "What are you talking about? Sure, they love each other. They're best friends and close."

"Doc, in case you haven't noticed, I'm not the best in relationships. It's best I don't get involved. On the day Victoria was shot, why was Chef the only one acting like that? We were all concerned, but no one else acted that crazy. All day she was a basket case. Ask yourself. If you weren't a doctor, and it was your husband in the turret, do you think you might have acted almost like Chef did?"

Doc popped the rest of the way out of her chair. "Yes, I probably would be frantic, but that's my husband. He is my partner in …" Doc grew silent, thinking. Her eyes swiveled back and forth as if reliving scenes from the past. "You're saying you think that Chef … that she … that they …?"

"I'm pretty sure, yes. It's the only thing that makes sense from the things I've seen. I'm positive Victoria knew that day Chef Joan ran out of sickbay. When Victoria didn't protest my putting them in the same room, I figured she was okay with it. That cabin is a make-or-break, and I felt it was going to be a make situation." The Captain picked up a hand towel from the stack on the med trolley and wiped his brow. Twisting it in his hands, he looked over at Doc. "Let's go find out."

Doc rose and followed the Captain through the hatch. "Why early?"

"I'm hoping a surprise is best. You'll need to go in without knocking and make sure the ladies are decent."

At Cabin 24, Doc took a deep breath, opened the door and walked in. A few seconds passed before Doc called the Captain in.

Chef Joan yelped. "No, wait!"

The Captain stepped in and saw them both in Victoria's bed. Chef Joan was holding the covers up to cover herself. Her clothes were draped over the chair.

"Captain, it's not what you think. I was just…."

The Captain held up his hand, cutting her off. "What I think doesn't matter. What *is* important is that you're both important to this ship and crew. Chef, your confinement is over and I'm hungry." The Captain turned to leave. "I almost forgot. Victoria, Cabins 22 and 23 are both yours to use. Doc, go through that connecting door and check it out and let Victoria know what she can and can't use in there. If you both want, this cabin is yours now, or you can go back to your old ones." He continued out the door and closed it behind him.

Victoria tried to speak. "Doc, I … we … this …."

"The Captain figured it out, not me. I guess he's okay with it all or he wouldn't have gone to the trouble. Best I can figure out, for him it's like if he had a son or daughter that gets into trouble. A good parent doesn't judge but supports. Now, I'm going to peek in the other cabin and see what he was talking about."

While Doc passed through the door to the connecting cabin, Chef Joan got up to dress, and then to help Victoria to get up and dress.

After looking through the connecting door, Doc took a half step backward, back into the room. "My stars. You have to see this."

Chef Joan, hopping on one foot while putting on the canvas pants, looked through the door. "What *is* all this?"

"I wanna see. I wanna see." Victoria was struggling to get up.

Chef Joan hurried back and helped Victoria to the door to look. The wall between Cabins 22 and 23, as well as all the furniture, had been removed. The two large cabins were now one grand one. The room was full of equipment, a medicine ball, a rowing machine, free weights, pulley weights on the wall next to a large mirror, a padded horse, Indian clubs, and more.

Chef Joan stepped in. "Who would use all this stuff?"

Victoria stood with tears flowing down her cheeks. "Me." She wiped at her tears with the back of her hand. "Damn that Captain. How can he act so mean one minute and then do all this?"

53
July 4, 1898
3 PM
The Press Meeting

The Captain, the Chief, and Alexandria rode in a steam carriage to the Town Center. It rattled and bounced on the paving stones. The chuffing of the steam engine added to the noise, making conversation difficult.

The Captain raised his voice over the din. "Alexandria, we'll be on either side of you at all times. If either of us drag you off, don't resist at all; just go. The press meet might be important but it's not worth your life."

"Thanks. I was feeling fine until now. Please, anything else you want to add to make me nervous, go ahead and tell me now."

Alexandria felt the Chief touch her knee. She looked at him and saw his lips move, forming one word. "Trust." Only the one word. After a moment of looking in the Chief's eyes, she nodded and relaxed back into her seat with a half-smile.

The Captain gave the Chief a puzzled look.

"Secrets, Captain. Secrets." The Chief crossed his arms over his chest and settled back as if he had no cares in the world.

Arriving at Town Center, they were happy to leave the noise of the carriage. An official from the police met them at the top of the steps leading up to the center. "Hello, Captain. And you must be Miss Castle; I'm Officer Martin. We've had to use the main hall, as the turnout is larger than we expected. Not just the media came, but most of the scientists in town." Officer Martin guided them inside and down a long set of hallways to the rear stage area of the main hall. "This hall is also used for opera, so the sound carries well. Even so, there's a loud-box on the podium set up for you." The officer pulled back the curtain so they could peek through. The hall was over half-full, with more than 200 people. The hall had a high domed ceiling, and the seats were arrayed in a fan pattern as they went back from the stage. "A larger group than expected. Captain, as you asked, around the hall and in the balconies … they're all the officers we have that were off duty and many from on duty. They're all in civilian attire and all armed. Good luck, Miss." Officer Martin left to go stand at the side of the stage and watch through the curtain.

The Captain touched her elbow. "Any time you're ready, you can go out and start. Chief and I will be right beside you. It seems they came early to get good seats."

"Captain, thanks for everything you've done getting me here." Alexandria parted the side curtain and walked across the stage to the podium, flanked on either side by the Captain and Chief, who were dressed in black business suits. Bursts of light flashed as the photographers' bulbs went off. Alexandria paused at the side and just forward of the podium for a moment to allow the press to take pictures. Her hair was up in a bun and her neck was circled by white lace extending up from the bodice of her black, floor-length dress. The dress fit her figure well. Matching white lace adorned the cuffs of the long sleeves. A long row of silver buttons from the neck to the hem at the floor sparkled in the flashes of the photographers. It was an image of a professional and a lady in one. The Captain and Chief took up positions on either side of her, each about two feet away, as they had promised. There was not a sound from the audience other than a murmur or two. Alexandria began her speech. "Thank you all for coming to this special presentation. First, I will say the technical information needed will be available for a penny at newsstands tomorrow. Those pennies all go to pay the contracted printer. Making it available this way ensures it gets the widest possible dissemination." As she spoke, the audience settled in with more attention. Each revelation on the abilities and possible uses for saving lives and homes garnered more attention.

The Captain and the Chief stood as if they were statues, with only their eyes moving, constantly looking over the audience and balconies.

The Captain and the Lady Fair

The Chief would glance at the Captain after each scan to see if he had any hint of trouble. The hint came when the Captain's eyes stopped scanning and became unfocused. Now watching the Captain, he saw his fingers moving. They were counting down from five. One at a time, his fingers curled up into a fist. When the count reached one, the Chief let his vision go back to the hall to watch for any movement or sign. From the corner of his eye, he saw the Captain spin and dive at Alexandria, wrap his arms around her, put one hand behind her head, and knock her to the floor. Just as the Captain wrapped his arms around her, a shot echoed in the hall. The Chief saw a muzzle flash in a balcony to the left. He leapt over to the podium and bellowed for all the police officers to hear. "Balcony! Third from the left!" Reaching under the podium, he pulled out a handgun that had been placed there for just such a situation. He placed himself in front of Alexandria and the Captain. The hall was in chaos with shouts and people trying to get out through the back.

Alexandria felt the Captain collide with her and hit the floor hard, but the hand behind her head kept her from being knocked out. The captain lay on top of her, not moving. In a dazed state, she was surprised at how good he felt on top of her. As her mind cleared, she realized he was not moving. She couldn't get the leverage to push him off. "Chief! Help!"

The Chief spun at her shout and rushed over. He pulled the Captain off Alexandria. The Captain was unconscious and bleeding from his left shoulder. A knot was already forming on his forehead where his head had hit the floor. As plain-clothes officers ran to their side to surround them, the Chief was already shouting orders. "I need a carriage to get him to the ship!" The officers wanted him to be taken to the closer hospital, but the Chief ignored them as he scooped up the Captain in his arms and carried him offstage, with Alexandria close at his side.

Changing Times

54
July 4, 1898
5 PM
The Galley

The crew sat in silence in the galley, waiting for word from Doc. Only Alexandria and Victoria still on bed rest were missing. Each was absorbed in their own thoughts. The silence was broken when the loud-box announced there was an Officer dockside, waiting to come aboard. The Chief answered the hail and then left the galley to go greet the visitor. He returned with Officer Martin in tow and invited him to sit. Once he was settled at the table with a cup of coffee, he spoke up.

"How's the Captain?"

The Chief shrugged. "No idea yet. Doc is still working on him. Did you get the shooter?"

"Yes, that's what I came to let you know. He's with people now asking him questions. You did us a favor. Knowing where an assassin is going to make it a lot easier. Chief, your shout took us right to him. It seems he's the assassin we've been looking for that's been responsible for over ten other murders."

"He'll stay quiet and not say anything; I'm sure."

"He'll be talking for all he's worth by morning. Special people are asking him questions in special ways. No one will be coming to help him because we told the press he was killed resisting arrest. He had his payment in his pocket, money in an envelope from the Garrote Company. Officers will start a quiet dig for information in the morning."

The loud-box clicked on, with Doc's voice coming through. "Chief to sickbay, please."

The Chief left at a run. In the passageway on the floor, outside the sickbay hatch, was Alexandria, with her knees up and head down sound asleep. He quietly opened the hatch and slipped in.

The Captain was awake but groggy. "That you, Chief?"

"Rest there a while, Captain. What's the news, Doc?"

"He'll be fine. The bullet is out and it did no major damage. His thick head seems fine. He'll stay here a few days so I can watch him."

The Captain's voice was stronger this time. "No, Doc. I need to be up tomorrow."

The Chief put a hand on his good shoulder. "No, Captain. The police caught the man and found a link to the Garrote Company. They start an investigation in the morning. There's nothing to do but relax and heal up."

"I need to be up while it's all still fresh. There's still a military group out there and there's the matter of Mr. Slimy. Chief, trust me and back me up for Doc's help."

Doc shook her head. "Nothing more can be done. You're patched up. Rest and time will take care of the rest."

The Captain took a deep breath. "How is Alexandria?"

"Passed out from exhaustion. She didn't sleep last night and it caught up to her. She's in the hall, but I'll take care of her." The Chief moved over to an empty bed next to the Captain, lifted it, and put it up against the Captain's bed. Going to the passageway, he lifted Alexandria, brought her in, and placed her on the bed. "Doc, you might want to loosen those buttons later, so she can sleep better. I'll leave Kira in the care of Victoria and Chef Joan. Captain, you're crazy, but I'll back you if need be."

Doc smiled. "You can back him all you want, but it won't change anything."

The Captain sighed. "Doc, for the next hour I want you to trust me and do as I ask. No argument and I promise I won't even try to leave the sickbay unless you say I can."

"If it'll keep you quiet, it's a deal."

The Captain smiled and winked at the Chief. "Doc, I want you to pull up a chair next to me and get comfortable. Then I want you to rest your hand on my shoulder and wait one hour, just like that."

"The bump to the head must have been worse than I thought."

"A deal was a deal. I am up and out of here."

"Wait! Calm down. I'll do it."

When Doc had settled in, he continued. "How is Victoria healing up?"

"She's doing fine. Why?"

"She's not fine. She's great. I bet her wound looks weeks old, not days."

"That's true. She's lucky and heals fast."

"We'll see." The Captain relaxed back and remained silent, waiting out the hour.

The Chief went to Alexandria's side and placed her hand on top of the Captain's. "Trust me."

55
July 4, 1898
6:30 PM
The Sickbay

The Captain moved his arm around slowly, testing how it felt. "Much better."

Doc grabbed his arm to hold it still. "You'll open your stitches!"

"Doc, remove the bandage and check it."

"It needs to stay like it is, and your hour is over, and I say 'stay.' Any questions?"

The Chief came to Doc's side. "Doc, do me a favor and check his wound."

"Chief, did you hit your head, too?"

"You're saying you don't trust me? Please do it as a favor. It really is a favor for you, too."

Doc gave a heavy sigh. As soon as she saw the wound unwrapped, she collapsed back onto her chair. "This can't be."

"Doc, you know some people have a Talent, just as I do. Now, you know yours."

"Victoria."

"That's why I had you rest with your hand on her that day. You're a Talented healer, Doc. If it'll make you feel better, I'll stay the rest of the night here. I'll go to the galley, grab a bite, and come back here for the night. That okay with you? While I'm gone, make Alexandria more comfortable."

In a daze, Doc agreed.

When the Captain entered the galley, followed by the Chief, everyone broke into cheers. Officer Martin was still there and staring at the Captain.

"What is it, Officer?"

"I thought you were shot."

"Only a graze. The big deal was the bump on the head. I'm fine now. The Chief tells me you caught the assassin. If you don't mind, I'll come by in the morning and see what information you've gotten."

Still staring, Officer Martin rose. "I just stayed to hear how you were doing. I'm glad you're doing fine. I'll see you in the morning."

After getting something to eat and telling the crew Doc ordered him to sleep overnight in the sickbay, he left.

The Captain saw Alexandria was still sleeping but was now under sheets and a blanket. Her black dress was folded and laying on a table. "I see you made her comfortable. Thanks, Doc." He climbed into his bed next to Alexandria's. "If you want to talk about all this, I'll be happy to."

"You can start by telling me how you knew and why you didn't tell me before this."

"It's better if you learn it slowly on your own. That way a person with talent is more willing to accept it. You have tended to the Chief and me many times. We always healed too quickly to be normal. It seems the longer you're in contact with a person, the faster the healing. I don't know if thinking about what you want helps too or not, but I suggested it for Victoria just in case."

As the Captain and Doc talked into the night, the Captain slowly slid his hand over and took Alexandria's.

56
July 5, 1898
8 AM
The Galley

Breakfast was more like a feast and a party combined than anything else. Everyone was there, including Victoria. Laughter and good spirits were on the agenda. Bacon, eggs, pancakes, sausages, hash, skillet-fried potatoes, biscuits, gravy, cut ham, small steaks, fresh bread, slices of several fruits and oatmeal were on the table.

The Captain stood and banged his empty coffee cup on the table. "Crew of the Lady Fair, I have orders to give this morning, but there are a few things first. I want to take this time to first ask if anyone needs anything or has anything they wish to say."

The table fell silent. The crew looked around at each other, waiting to see if anyone would speak up. Doc stood. "Captain, I would like Victoria to spend the day in my sickbay, so I can make sure she is progressing as well as can be."

"Good idea, Doc. I'll feel safer when she's ready to go back to work."

Victoria remained seated. "I'm ready now, Captain. I still have a good right arm I can shoot with." The crew laughed with her.

"Anyone else?" When he was greeted with blank stares, he continued. "I have an announcement, then some orders. Chance, come up here with me." As a confused Chance made his way to stand next to the Captain, everyone watched and wondered what was happening. "Not long ago, our Chance was asked to volunteer for a secret mission. At the time, he thought he might not survive. He accepted without hesitation and, as a result, a life was saved. I can't give any more details than that and I expect you all to respect that he is not allowed to talk about it. Chance, I'm sorry; official channels can't recognize your actions, bravery, and self-sacrifice, but I can." From his pocket, the Captain pulled out a shiny brass medal that was two inches across. It was a sunburst with an enameled red heart in the middle. Below it, on a short pair of chains, hung three plaques. Each was engraved with one word. Bravery. Self-sacrifice. Honor.

The crew clapped and cheered while Chance stood, beet red with confusion. "Thank you, Captain." As he passed Doc, she touched his elbow to stop him a moment. He heard the whisper in his ear. "Bravery and willingness to sacrifice are the same in any form. Only the Captain and I know." She slipped the piece of folded paper he had dropped, into in his hand.

Chance looked at her face, saw her smile, and give him a slight nod. He quietly returned to his seat and quickly busied himself with the food.

"No rush, but after breakfast, all hands, except Doc, Chef Joan, and Victoria, will give Chief a hand. They're making something that may defend our ship and will need your help. I don't know the details, but Chief will handle that anyway. I do understand a lot of cable needs to be installed. I am sure the Chief agrees with me it should be hidden away and not laying around on the floors. I'll be dirt-side, finding out all I can about the attack last night. Alexandria, you take care of Kira as usual. I know Chef Joan and Victoria were happy to have a guest last night, but they have other things to do."

"Captain, I'll be busy helping the Chief. Doc, could you watch Kira for me?"

"Of course; she and I will have a great day."

Chatter resumed around the table. Alexandria filled the Captain's cup. "Thanks for saving me again. Is this going to be a habit?"

"I hope, soon enough, you won't be in danger anymore."

It was a great breakfast.

The Sickbay

Doc held the sleeping Kira close. "Let's see what we can do for you."

Doc sat with Kira for two hours. While Kira slept, Doc kept her hand resting lightly on Kira's face.

The Captain entered the sickbay to find Doc sitting next to Kira on the bed. Her head was down.

"Doc?"

When she turned, he saw the red eyes and the tear-streaked face. "I was going to ask you, but I see you had the same idea."

"What good is a talent when it can't help Kira?"

57
July 5, 1898
10 AM
Police Headquarters

"Good morning, Officer Martin. Here I am, like I said I'd be." The Captain shook the officer's hand. He looked around the office, which was a simple box shape, with a small desk and two chairs in front of it. On the walls were plaques and awards. The office on the third floor looked out on a courtyard.

"You're looking good, Captain. I was right about him talking. He was a direct hire by the boss of the Garrote company, Maxmillian Dartin. He was paid for the attack by airsharks on your ship. We've also got information out of him on other women scientists he was hired to murder. According to him, Maxmillian hates women with any strength or power. He also says there is a rumor Maxmillian ran a smuggling/slave ship."

The Captain sat stunned. "The Osprey."

"What was that?"

"The Osprey was a slave ship we fought last year. At the time, no links were found of any ownership."

"We'll look into that, too, in case there's a link. The hard part is that even with the word of the assassin, we can't do much. We have to dig and find hard evidence but, at least now we know where to look. If he thinks he's safe, thinking the assassin is dead, he won't go anywhere."

"If there's anything we can do to help, speak up anytime."

"I'll remember that. There's news that might interest you. An airship came in yesterday right after the press meeting. It caught attention because we seldom get a gunship dock here, and it was in a big hurry. Came in much too fast and nearly caused a crash of a passenger ship leaving. We had a few street people watch it. Some crew went straight for the hall but turned around when they got there and it was all over. Then, this morning, the same crew went to newsstands and bought dozens of copies of Miss Castle's paper. They boarded the ship then pulled out."

"Do you know what country's flag she flew?"

"Boschland."

58
July 5, 1898
1 PM
The Galley

The Captain heard the galley, which was full of chatter while the crew lingered over lunch before he passed through the hatch. "Afternoon, everyone." A chorus of responses greeted him. "I trust the work is going well and I am glad everyone is here." The Captain continued to talk as he made a plate at the prep table. "I have some news and I think you should know what we're up against. There's a powerful man out there that wants Alexandria dead. He's tried twice now, the airsharks and the assassin. There's a military group that's after us and or Alexandria. I'm saying, soon this ship may be a target again. I'm working on some plans, but nothing is set yet. Again, I offer that anyone that wants off ship before that happens is free to go."

"I can't leave, Captain. You can't cook and you would starve." Chef Joan patted his stomach.

"I can't leave you by yourself. You can't hit a thing unless you use a cannon." Victoria mimed a fast draw.

"No, Captain. I can't leave. You can't sew holes fast enough and you'd go down fast."

"Captain, thanks for the offer but I doubt you can patch a hole in yourself. I've already had to do that for you."

Chief spoke for the rest of the crew. "Captain, you need all of us. We've been through plenty together. We're not leaving because it may get exciting."

"Alright then. I am tired of being a sitting target waiting to be hit. It's time to make things go more in our favor. Victoria, how's the arm? Can you handle that new sidearm?"

Doc interrupted. "If it's important, she'll be ready by this afternoon."

Victoria sat up straight, smiled and nodded. "Whenever you need me, I'll be ready. That's my left arm; my right arm is fine, so it's not a problem and I've been practicing quick draws for fun. Chief gave me a few minutes to modify the holster and make it faster. I just haven't practiced firing it yet."

"Chief, Alexandria, how long before that thing of yours is ready?"

"Working like we are, tomorrow afternoon or evening. We can't push like we did the crane, or things may go very bad with any mistake." The Chief looked at Alexandria, who nodded in agreement.

The Captain gave the orders for the day. "Victoria, I'll need you ready to go with your sidearm at 2:30 AM. I can't believe I am saying this, but … wear your lucky suit. Chief, take your time and make it work. While you're working, see if you can think up more defenses. The bow gun, cannon, the one portable gun, and handguns out the portals may not be enough. Chef Joan, check what you need and restock. We may be lifting in three days. Doc, restock as well. We've used a lot of your supplies lately. Go crazy and overstock whatever you think we could possibly need if things go bad. It all goes against the Admiral's account."

Alexandria stood. "Captain, thank you for taking care of me, but I think all of you and the ship would be safer without me onboard. I should leave."

The Captain laughed. "Why would you be so mean to your friends here? How do you think they would feel if something happened to you when they weren't there to protect you? No, leaving would be a very bad idea."

The Captain summed up. "People have declared war on us. Now it's our turn."

59
July 5, 1898
3 PM
Police Headquarters

The Captain knocked on Officer Martin's doorjamb, as the door stood open. "Have a minute to spare?"

"Come in, Captain. How can I help you now?"

"I need a favor in the early hours this morning."

"Sure, but why me?"

"Because you're more than you try to appear. Ordinary officers don't have an office. They aren't kept informed with all the latest information about captured assassins. They aren't free to move about as you are. Most of all, I trust you."

The conversation only took 30 minutes and plans were in motion. The Captain left the office with a smile.

The steam carriage to the office for the Navy made the trip in five minutes. At the desk in the lobby, the Captain asked where he could find

Lt. Fausworth and was directed to an office on the second floor. The Captain didn't knock, but simply opened the door and walked in. "Lt. Fausworth, I have a job for you."

"Excuse me, Captain, but I don't think I take orders from you."

"You do work for the Admiral, and he has shown his trust in you by giving you a message to bring to me. As he has your trust, I thought you should be the one to take a message to the Admiral. If I'm wrong, I'll find someone else, as it's urgent."

"No, if it's for the Admiral, then, of course, it's my job."

"This is a rush delivery and must get to him right away. Can you get it there quickly?"

"Of course, sir; leave it to me."

The Captain handed over a wax-sealed envelope and left the office.

"Next stop, Army Ordnance." The Captain hailed another steam carriage and took the half-hour trip to Army Ordnance outside of town.

The Depot sat in a large field and was made up of six huge buildings of metal and a brick office building. Surrounding the field was a high metal mesh fence, which hummed. At the gate entrance, he had to wait for clearance and an escort to see the Commander. An open steam carriage slowly chuffed up to the gate. A sergeant in a gray uniform stepped down. "Captain Castellan, I'm here to escort you, sir."

"Thank you, Sergeant. I have no idea about this particular depot. Do you just store ordnance or do they do research here as well?"

"There is a research section full of people so smart they have no room left over for common sense. We have to watch them close, or they'll blow themselves up." The sergeant kept chuckling for the rest of the ride.

The Commander was a cordial, middle-aged man of average height. His eyes were striking. They seemed to miss nothing and conveyed a great intelligence. "Welcome, Captain. It's unusual for a civilian, even one under Navy contract, to visit us here. What can I do for you?"

The Captain settled into a chair in front of the Commander's desk. "There's no reason for you to know me or my ship. I'm a simple captain, and my ship is a converted luxury ship. During this contract for the service, we've been attacked by airsharks and a Dreadnaught. I'm in need of an idea for defense if I'm to keep my crew alive. I know all the Navy ordnance, but nothing about what the Army has. I don't want the ordnance. Just a tour in case there's an idea I can use."

"A tour is no problem. We often give them to various officials and your credentials of contract can qualify you for that. The sergeant that brought you to my office will take you around. When you're finished, please come back to my office."

The Sergeant gave the tour of the storage area and explained the weapons the Captain didn't recognize. Of the most interest was the research section, a large space just inside a large sliding door filled with raw explosives and chemicals. Four scientists huddled around a table. In the center was a small tube two inches in diameter and eight inches long. A vise held the tube upright. Two wires came from the top of the tube. The wires ran to a small control panel. Next to it was a one-square-foot metal block. "Sergeant, do you know what that is? Assuming you can talk about it."

"No secrets there, Captain. You're looking at fireworks."

"Excuse me?"

"That metal block is magnesium. It's a very lightweight metal, so it works in fireworks. Magnesium makes those bright sparkles. They take metal shavings from it and stuff it in the tube. Light it and you have a torch that can burn metal. Once it's on fire, there is no putting it out."

At that moment, one of the scientists tried to reach across the bench and bumped the control panel. There was a soft click and smoke rose out of the top of the tube. The smoke turned to flame, and then a jet of flame with sparks flying in every direction. Sparks fell on the block and it started to spark and burn. The scientists ran out the door, yelling for everyone to run.

The Captain looked around for anything to push the metal cube outside of the building. He saw a piece of lumber four feet long in a small pile of wood, which once had been a crate, near the door.

Grabbing it up, he ran back to the table and swung the wood as hard as he could at the block. The block of sparking metal flew out the door, rolling and bumping across the ground, and stopping 30 feet from the door.

The Commander's office seemed very quiet after all the noise at the research building. The Captain was back in the seat he had used before.

"You're no simple Captain. You saved my research building from idiots. If that burning magnesium had stayed in there, the whole building would have gone up. Large explosions may have even caused fatalities. I owe you."

The Captain's face lit up with his smile. "In that case, may I borrow some magnesium?"

60
July 6, 1898
2:30 AM
The Dockyard

"I need this man alive. Other than that, I don't care. Don't shoot unless you know for sure it's the one we want. There will be an Officer around here somewhere that will take away the one we're after." The Captain spoke in whispers to Victoria. Both were in the shadows, waiting for someone to show up. "This dock is deserted at this hour, so there's no danger of a bullet hitting anyone behind him. Just wait. I need to see if I can get anything out of him first."

"Captain, I told you; I've had no practice with live rounds. I can't guarantee I can hit what I aim at unless I'm close."

"I trust you at any range, but you'll be close enough. I'm hoping seeing you will distract him enough for you to get a clean shot."

The Captain and the Lady Fair

Victoria was in her lucky red suit, which now had a matching holster on a wide belt sitting low on her hip.

"Hello, Captain." A whispered voice in the dark behind them startled Victoria. She spun and drew her gun in one move so fast it was a blur.

Officer Martin, with his hands raised, stepped close enough to be seen in the weak light. "Lady, you scare me and I don't scare easy." Looking at the barrel of the gun, he backed up a step. "Mind introducing us before I'm blown in half by that thing?" His mind registered the suit Victoria wore, but his eyes couldn't leave the barrel.

"It's all right, Victoria. This is Officer Martin."

Victoria slid the gun back into the holster. Giving it a pat, she smiled at Officer Martin. "Nice to meet you."

"I've done some research, Captain. This must be your gunner. I've never had much occasion to see weapons drawn other than practice, but, Christ, that was fast. I would tip my hat if I wore one. If my guess is right, that's a 50 cal. Most men can't handle that, but I promise, Miss, I'll not question you."

Victoria chuckled softly, not much louder than a whisper. "I didn't draw it." Victoria slowly placed her hand on the butt of the gun, and then pushed back and down. The holster split in the middle at the front and the barrel swung up and free. One motion and it was ready to fire. She placed it back in the holster and cocked the hammer back so the next time a slight pressure on the trigger would set it off. "I practiced and found out; it was too slow and awkward to draw, so I fixed it." A smile came to her face and she turned to watch the dock area.

They leaned against the wall, waiting for the three AM meeting. They didn't wait long before they heard footsteps. "He's early, of course." The Captain stepped from the shadows into the light of the warehouse dock and waited.

"Lt. Fausworth, you're early."

"Just hand over the encrypt, Captain." Lt. Fausworth held a small-caliber pistol aimed at the Captain's stomach.

"I'm guessing you're going to shoot me anyway to keep me quiet. I also think you would ignore me if I asked who you work for… if he pays enough."

"I'll tell you, so you know you've been a fool. I'm paid very well, thank you. As to whom I work for, he's a nobody general, with delusions of grandeur, who thinks with enough information, he can take over a country and have allies in his debt. He's an idiot, anyway. Crashing into the dock and too late to make the speech was stupid." Lt. Fausworth took another step forward. "Your message said you had an encrypt that was going to be disguised by a music box maker. That you were going to meet him here. That was a trap, wasn't it?"

"Smart, aren't you? Are you smart enough to know you should give up now?"

"I'll just silence you and be on my way if that's okay with you."

"I don't think Victoria likes that idea. Do you, Victoria?"

Victoria slowly walked out from the shadows, just far enough into the moonlight to be seen. Only ten feet separated them. She stood in a relaxed stance. Her hand was on her waist, above the butt of the gun. "No, I don't think I'll allow you to shoot my Captain."

"What is with you and women? Women playing at being Pilots. Now a woman who wants to be a gun shooter or something. I'm not sure what. It's too bad you won't live long enough to find out that big gun is more than you can handle. You have to die with the Captain." His eyes kept roaming up and down her red suit, ignoring the Captain and the gun on Alexandria's hip.

The Captain smiled. "I've heard enough."

A loud explosion immediately followed the words out of the Captain's mouth. Holding level at Victoria's hip, the gun barrel let curling smoke drift up and away.

Officer Martin spoke with a stunned voice as he stepped from the shadows. "My God."

Lt. Fausworth's gun was gone. So was his hand.

61
July 6, 1898
12:30 PM
The Galley

The crew sat around the table having lunch. All the work had been going well.

The Captain leaned back in his chair and sipped at his coffee. "Chief, you haven't said anything. Does that mean you haven't come up with a new defense?"

The Chief sighed and lowered his head. "Sorry, Captain. I've been concentrating on the job at hand. We should be done about the middle of the afternoon. After that, I'll work on it."

"Chief, I know you've been very busy. This'll scare you, but I have an idea. After the device is installed, we can take the Lady Fair out for a short run and do a test away from prying eyes. When we get back, you and Victoria can get with me and see what you think of my idea." The loud-box, announcing a visitor dockside, interrupted the Captain. When the Captain found out it was Officer Martin, he told the dock guard to send him up, as he knew the way.

"Thank you for seeing me, Captain."

"Sit; have coffee; join us for lunch."

Chef Joan was already up and making a plate for Officer Martin.

"I'm here on business. It's about that lieutenant from last night."

Victoria rose from her seat. "I'll go with you, no problems."

Officer Martin looked at her with a blank face. "What? Why would you go with me, and to where?"

"To jail. I shot a man."

"Victoria, isn't it? You shot in self-defense of your Captain and yourself. Just because he hadn't pulled the trigger yet means nothing. You did right. I was aiming at him, but I would have gone for a bigger target, his chest. Most likely he would have died. You saved at least your Captain and perhaps yourself. Please relax. Let me ask a favor. Please never get mad at me." He gave a broad smile.

"Captain, I brought you notes on the information we got from Fausworth. The Navy has him now, and he'll never see the light of day again. Treason and attempted murder are just the start of his crimes. They'll find more, I'm sure."

Chef Joan placed a plate in front of Officer Martin. "Really, I shouldn't."

Victoria stood. "My friend made you a plate. It would be rude to refuse." Even though she was in her canvas trouser work clothes, she placed her hand above her hip. "Shall I growl?"

Both the Captain and Officer Martin broke out laughing. "I yield!"

The Captain heard the new information and sat back to think on it. Officer Martin had finished his plate.

"Miss Victoria, thank you. Without your … encouragement I would have missed this food. Captain, do you all eat like this, all the time?"

The Captain grinned. "Chef Joan is the best."

"Captain, I'm thinking your entire crew is the best."

The Captain poured himself another cup of coffee. "Now that Mr. Slimy has been taken care of, that leaves Boschland and the Garrote Company. You might be able to help with the Garrote Company."

"The investigation has just started. It'll be some time before anything can be done." Officer Martin's tone conveyed his disappointment at not being able to act sooner.

"What if information was leaked to him you had a source that had proof of his slave dealings? That we would be transporting the informant, the proof, and Alexandria to a safe holding. Now, if he thought that, he would also know you could arrest him anytime. He would want to run, he would also want to get rid of a source and the proof, with a bonus of getting Alexandria in the bargain. He's already tried twice."

"I would say it was too risky. Your ship wouldn't stand a chance."

The Captain looked around at his crew. "Anyone agree it's too risky? That we don't stand a chance?" He was met with silence.

"So, it's a matter of timing. I'll let you know when it can all start. Would you like to join us?"

"If that were to happen, and that is a big 'if', I would love to come, but with a few of my men as well."

"That's settled then. Everyone, shall we get back to work? It looks like a war is being scheduled."

62
July 6, 1898
4 PM
The Engineering Room

The Captain entered the engineering room. The Chief was at his drawing desk, going over the plans to make sure they weren't missing anything that needed to be done.

"Brought you a coffee, Chief. Everything ready?" He sat down on a crate next to the desk.

"As ready as we can make it. Just some work at making it all neat. We could have been done earlier, but I wanted to hide the cables and wiring. It didn't seem right to mess up the Lady Fair with junk strung everywhere." The Chief took the offered coffee and relaxed back into his chair. "What do you need, Captain?"

"Why should I have to need something to bring a coffee?"

The Chief smiled at the Captain. "We've known each other a long time, Captain. We've been through good times and bad ones. I know you well enough to know when something's on your mind."

"I've decided to delay lift for an extra day. I want you to build something to test while we are out testing this generator thing. I've drawn a sketch showing what it should do and how."

Changing Times

"Captain, when you explain how something should work, I get worried."

The Captain put a few sheets of paper on the desk in front of the Chief. They featured simple drawings of a tube with a long tail and a fuse at the end.

"Fireworks, Captain?"

"Exactly, but with a difference; it would have a bigger batch of magnesium in the head to burn. Launch it at a gas bag and start a fire."

The Chief stroked his chin, looking at the drawing. "It's very risky, Captain. If anything goes wrong, you could burn your own toes."

"It would be a strong weapon though. With the nose gun, cannon, and this, we'd have a better chance of surviving a fight."

"Okay, I can work something up for a test. Now tell me what's really on your mind."

"That's all there is, Chief."

"When are you going to admit to yourself that those two drive you crazy?"

"Joan and Victoria can be distracting at times, but they don't drive me crazy."

"Captain, I don't know of a single other man that would do what you did for them. They took me by surprise, but I should have seen it. I'm not talking about them though. I'm talking about Alexandria and Kira.

"Captain, around Kira you turn into a softie. I know that lambs wool came from the lining inside of your jacket. Around Alexandria, you stiffen and close up most of the time, but now and then you start to relax, and then stop yourself."

"Chief, I have an airship to run and people that rely on me for a job and to keep them safe. I don't need distractions." The Captain stood up to leave. "She's a good woman. She's smart, brave, and is good to other people. Okay, I'll even admit she's beautiful as well. She doesn't need me and I don't need complications. Let me know when the firework is ready." He left with a quick step.

The Chief sighed. "Captain, you're as hooked as a fish. You just need to be pulled in."

63
July 8, 1898
1 PM
The Bridge

"Prepare for lift." The Captain stepped away from the bridge loud-box. "Alexandria, you look nervous."

Alexandria kept twisting a handkerchief in her hands. "Yes, I am. This will be the first-ever try. Theory doesn't always work in the practical."

The Captain placed his hand on her shoulder. "Then cross your fingers."

The Chief spoke to the pilots. "What we added shouldn't affect flight. We added coils, port, starboard, fore, and aft. One is in the bilge and the other is atop the bag. It makes the bag heavier, but it should be no more than a person standing up there."

The pilots gave the Chief a nod.

The lift was smooth and normal. An hour later, they were well out to sea and away from prying eyes.

"Pilots, take us up to 10,000 feet. I want room in case we need it. Bring us to a full stop." While the pilots followed orders, the Captain went to the loud-box to address the crew. "We're just about to start the shield generator. If it goes well on start-up, we'll try a few things and see how it handles. We waited an extra day, so Chief could work up a new defense weapon. We'll test it and if it works, it'll get refined and all of you will be trained in its use. The weapon test will be off the bow. I'll announce it so you can watch and know what to expect."

The Captain leaned up against the chart table. "Alexandria, the show is yours."

Changing Times

She crossed to the new panel installed to the left of the pilot station. She threw switches and turned a dial. Indicator needles moved back and forth and then settled down. Everyone felt their skin tingle.

The Captain suppressed a laugh when he saw the hair on both pilots stand out like porcupine quills. "I think it's working."

"That should do it, Captain."

The Captain used the loud-box. "Time to test it, Chief."

Pilot Diana was staring hard out the window. "I don't see anything."

The Chief walked out onto the deck, to the port side. He turned sideways and leaned back. Snapping up and swinging his arm, a ball flew out of his hand. Forty feet later, the ball bounced back, as if it had hit a wall. The Chief watched it fall away. It took on an arc under the ship and disappeared from sight under the hull. He did the same at all four compass points of the ship, with the same results each time. He walked back from the deck and climbed the ladder to the bridge.

A big grin on his face showed what he thought. "Works!" He went to the loud-box. "Tailor, do your test and come to the bridge."

They waited for Tailor to climb to the top of the lift bag.

"It bounces back at about thirty to forty feet. It's hard to tell with no reference. I couldn't see it at all."

The Captain took a deep breath. "We're standing still but safe. Let's try lifting. Release some ballast."

Seconds passed. Nothing happened.

"Fill the bags." This time they rose but not as fast as normal.

The Captain looked out the windows at a few clouds. He watched for a while. "We're drifting with the air current. Pilots, give me half speed."

At half throttle, the ship began to move, but at a walking speed.

Efforts to turn to port or starboard using the rudder did not work at all. Using the engine thrust worked well.

"Anything else anyone wants to try?" The Captain waited for a response. "If not, then, Alexandria, lower the shield."

As soon as Alexandria shut it down, the ship lurched upward. "Pilots, if you please. I don't like this."

The Captain and the Lady Fair

Releasing some gas stopped the rising, and the ship was stable once more.

The Captain let out a breath. "That was unexpected. Caught me by surprise." After thinking a few moments, he turned to Alexandria. "What would happen if we were ten feet above the water and started the shield?"

After a pause, she spoke slowly, as if still thinking it through. "It should just enclose the water within the bottom of the shield."

"How are we on gas Chief?"

"Full tanks; we filled them like we always do in dock."

"Pilots, take use down to ten feet."

The Pilots followed the order and stole glances at each other. Once the Lady Fair hovered over the sea, the Captain gave the order to start the shield. The Captain avoided looking at both of the Pilots' hair. Alexandria indicated the shield was on and stable. He glanced at Alexandria, she was trying to pull the loose ends that had escaped the tight bun, back behind her ears.

"Pilots, ignore the fact we have an overweight load. Fill the bags for 10,000 feet in one feed, then stop."

Pilot Kathryn looked at the Captain, stunned. "Captain, you know that's not how to do it. The gas would be a guess. You slow-feed and adjust."

"Try it my way. I trust you both."

Pilot Kathryn fed the gas in a flood and shut it off. The Lady Fair creaked and groaned louder than the Captain had ever heard before as the Lady Fair tried to lift. The noises stopped when the stresses evened out.

The Captain addressed the crew on the loud-box. "All hands. We're about to try a new maneuver, and it may be violent. Sit down on the deck and hold on to something that's bolted down. One minute to maneuver."

The Captain waited. "All hands, maneuver is now."

Changing Times

He nodded to Alexandria to turn off the shield. His knees buckled as the Lady Fair surged upward. The sea below rapidly receded. At 10,000 feet, the altitude gauge showed the Lady Fair was still climbing at a high rate of speed. Pilot Kathryn reached for the gas release lever.

"No! Let her rise." At 11,000 feet, the Lady Fair's climb slowed. At less than 12,000 feet, the Lady Fair stopped climbing and started to drop. The Lady Fair settled at 10,500 feet. "Great guess on the gas, Pilot."

The Captain informed the crew that the maneuver was over, and the Chief's test would begin.

The Chief's firework test was problem-free. It raced away with a trail of white smoke and in the distance exploded, bright sparks bloomed out then arced to fall towards the sea. Everyone breathed a sigh of relief when they didn't shoot their own lift bags.

"Pilots, back to port, please."

The Captain led the group to the galley. Alexandria made a detour to get Kira.

"Chief, when you teach the crew to use the weapon, make sure you tell them to aim well away from our own bags."

"Victoria named it 'the Sunburst.' " The Chief grinned at the name.

Alexandria came into the galley a short time later. "My shield was interesting, wasn't it?"

"Very, and now I know what the ship can and can't do, but I don't know why."

Alexandria held out Kira to the Captain. He took her without hesitation. Kira, who was just beginning to stir, grabbed at the Captain's finger that brushed her hand.

Alexandria talked while she made a bottle for Kira. "We're moving the 'bubble', not the ship."

The Captain waited for more explanation, but there was none. "That cleared it up for me. How about you, Chief?"

"As clear as glass."

Alexandria turned to see the men looking at her with blank faces. "Think of it as if you had your engines and propellers inside the ship."

The Chief smiled. "Now, that I can understand."

"Good." Alexandria nodded. "Now think of your ballast as being more than the ship can lift, on a rope, thirty feet below the ship."

"I can see that. You cut the rope, you lose the ballast in an instant, and we would pop up faster than letting ballast out slowly through the valves."

"Right. Now a bit harder. A donkey with a carrot on a stick."

The Chief laughed. "I knew science didn't have to be hard. The engines are slow because it is circulating the air and not pushing it away clearly."

"Top marks for the Chief."

"So, we'll have to drop the shields to shoot and move. Raise them to hide." The Captain reached out for Kira's bottle. "That will make it interesting to figure out tactics. Can you raise and lower the shields faster?"

"Now that I know the settings, yes. Perhaps two seconds for the shield to build, almost an instant to drop it."

"That'll have to be fast enough." The Captain held Kira's fingers as he fed her. He addressed Alexandria. "I want you and Kira off the ship when it comes time to start all this."

Alexandria shook her head. "Kira, yes. Me, no. You need me for the generator in case anything happens. I want to help keep everyone safe. Fighting me on this will waste your breath." Her hands on her hips and her expression left no doubt there would be no getting her off the ship without an army.

He gave up the idea of getting her off the ship. "You just want me to save you again." He sat silent for a few minutes, watching Kira work on the bottle.

"Chief, I have an idea for the Sunburst. How long will it take to make enough for the crew?"

"Two days, maybe three. The rockets are not a problem. The problem is setting range, near or far."

"Good enough, Chief. Alexandria, stop glaring at me and sit down. You can stay."

64
July 8, 1898
The Lounge

As the Lady Fair cruised back to port, the Captain sat on a couch in front of a large window in the lounge, his feet propped up on a low table. The clouds were few and the sea below was calm. The late-afternoon sun made the crests of the waves sparkle. The only quick change to the view was when a sea bird would pass by the window to find a resting place on the Lady Fair.

Alexandria, with Kira in her sling, walked into the lounge and sat next to him. "May I join you?"

The Captain was startled from his thoughts and looked around to see if they were alone in the lounge. "I don't mind. A view like this should be shared now and then."

"Captain, I wanted to thank you again for saving me. You've done a lot for Kira and me. You even paid for the parts for my generator. I've tried to stay out of your way, but I have questions I want to ask you."

"Ask all you wish; I'll answer what I can. You should be proud. The shield works just like you said it would." The Captain returned his eyes to the view out the window.

"I know you were shot. That was no graze of a bullet. How can you be fine? How was Victoria healed so fast?"

"I guess you've seen too much to pass it all off as minor scratches.

He got up and went to the bar at the end of the lounge. "We call it Talent. Some people have a natural talent for things, a natural talent for music, art, or any number of things. Doc has a natural talent for healing. Since she has been onboard and started living on the Island, her Talent has increased."

He walked back with drink in hand. "She didn't know she had a Talent until she healed me this last time. The Chief and I had to open her eyes to it. She's like you, all science and proof. Please don't say anything to anyone about it. If people learned about Talents, there would be no peace for anyone."

"Your Talent was to find me?"

"Sometimes I feel I have to be someplace; sometimes I know when danger is coming. I wish it worked all the time, but sometimes I wish I didn't have it at all."

Alexandria was quiet for minutes, looking at Kira. "Captain, do you think Doc would mind if I asked her if she could help Kira?"

"She would never mind being asked to help someone." The Captain looked down at the sleeping Kira. "She already tried when she was watching her while you were working with the Chief. Nothing happened. I'm sorry."

"Don't be. It was wishful thinking, anyway. When I think of her future, I worry. How will she live; how will she support herself when she grows up? What kind of life will she have? Who will take care of her properly if she's taken away? I want the best for her but I don't know what that is." Alexandria took a deep breath and let it out slowly as she stroked Kira's hair.

"I would think she needs what all babies need and don't always get. Love and support. As long as you're in her life, she'll have plenty of both."

Alexandria thought for a moment. "Captain, what happened to make you the way you are? I mean helping."

The Captain stood up. "The same thing that happens to everyone: life. That and I grew up. I'm just like most of the crew. Lost too much too soon. Most of the crew are orphans from an early age and had to make it through on their own. Excuse me; I should go check on the bridge." He finished his drink and left as quietly as Alexandria had entered.

Tears welled up in her eyes as she spoke to Kira. "I'm sorry; I wish I could help you. I can't even help myself. The Captain has to keep saving me, and he doesn't even like me."

65
July 8, 1898
4 PM
Cabins 22-23

Victoria, in her lucky red suit, was practicing fast draws, twenty times standing, then twenty times on one knee. Each time, she aimed the revolver at a spot on the wall. Twenty times, her arm stretched out aiming, and then she aimed twenty times from the hip. Victoria kept on repeating the practice sequence without pause.

Chef Joan, wearing only underwear, was sweating and breathing hard while she worked on the rowing machine. Her words came in short bursts as she gulped air. "Why am I doing this?"

"Because I like to see you sweat, and you sound so cute when you grunt. Keep at it."

"This isn't fair. I don't need this to cook."

Victoria stopped her practice and walked over to Joan. She stopped Joan's rowing efforts. "I'll spell it out for you. I want you healthy as can be so you'll live a long life. A life as long as possible with me. Besides, if you're in shape and toned, we can play longer and harder when we want." Victoria paused. "I'm sorry; do you *want* to be lazy and tire out on me quickly?"

Joan's answer was to attack the rowing machine with a vengeance.

The Captain and the Lady Fair

At the knock on the door, Victoria walked into the cabin, closing the exercise room door behind her. "Coming!" Opening the door, she saw the Captain on the other side. "Need me, Captain?"

The Captain looked at his shoes for a moment and then took a deep breath. "I came to see you both."

"Wait a moment." Victoria went back to the exercise room and returned shortly with Joan, now in a floor-length robe. "What about, Captain? A special job for us?"

"No, I came because there's something I need to say." He continued speaking haltingly as they made their way to the room's chairs and sat down. "I came to apologize to both of you."

"What for?" Victoria had a puzzled look.

"For the way I treated both of you by forcing you together like I did. I abused your trust in me as your Captain."

Victoria and Joan looked at each other, startled a moment by the apology. Joan spoke first. "Captain, I admit I was a mess and acted like a fool. I didn't do my job and didn't do Vicki any good either. If you hadn't acted, things would have gotten worse, and I might have even been kicked off the ship. I don't know if there was any other way to get this result. You didn't abuse my trust. You used it to help me. I haven't thanked you yet. Thank you."

Victoria reached over and took Joan's hand. "Captain, you didn't abuse my trust either. Joan is my family now, for life, I hope. Without you, that might not have happened. You made me realize something else. You're my family, too. The whole crew is family, they've accepted us as who we are without a word. But you're special, Captain. From the very first day, you have treated me with more respect than I ever had before. You've been just like a big brother of the best kind."

Joan nodded in agreement. "I never had a brother. But I do now. You never think of yourself, always of the crew. I think that means you think of all of us as family one way or another."

Victoria took a deep breath. "How did you know?"

He sighed as if he had been the one to take the deep breath. "I'm not good with relationships, but my first clue was the kiss by Joan in sickbay."

Victoria's head snapped to the side to look at Joan and see her blush.

"I have no idea what caused Joan to run away and hide from you but it made me start thinking wondering what happened. The overreaction only fit when I thought of someone that more than cared for someone as a friend. It was the only thing that fit."

The Captain visibly relaxed in his chair and nodded at them. "I'm truly glad it worked out. Now, if you'll excuse me, I have Captain things I have to go do."

After the door shut behind the Captain, Victoria turned to Joan. "Now it's time to make you sweat and grunt."

"What? Now? I'm all sweaty."

Victoria laughed and strode into the exercise room. "The rowing machine won't mind."

66
July 9, 1898
6:30 AM
The Bridge

The Captain sat in his pedestal command chair, staring out the window at the early morning sky. If any of the crew came on the bridge and saw him like this, they would turn and leave. They all knew this was his thinking position. More often than not when he finished he would have a plan or two in mind to put into motion.

Chef Joan entered the bridge with a pot of coffee. She always brought in a pot early and would set it on a steam plate that would keep it hot. The Captain and the Pilots would have coffee on hand anytime that they wanted. She saw the Captain in his chair staring, set the pot down quietly, and turned to leave.

The Captain rose from his chair and stretched. He turned and saw Chef Joan about to leave. "Good morning, Chef. Would you like to go with me to Feast Town later this morning?"

"Yes! I've always wanted to go there. I'll go change."

"Hold on. I said 'later this morning.' I have an errand to run first. I'll come back and then we can go. First, let's have some breakfast."

They both went to the galley, with Chef Joan chattering nonstop about all the things she hoped to find in Feast Town. Entering the galley, they saw the Chief and Victoria already there at the table, having coffee. Chef Joan chatted on about going to Feast Town while she prepped to make breakfast for the crew.

"Chef Joan, could you please make me just bacon and eggs now? I want to leave about the time the crew gets here for breakfast."

"More plots and plans, Captain?" Alexandria entered the galley, with Kira in her sling. "Lucky Kira woke me, or I would have missed hearing a new plot."

"Sorry, no new plots. Just some simple shopping for today. Would you like to join us?"

"Us?" Alexandria started making a bottle for Kira.

"Chef Joan and Victoria. Chef will be looking at everything, and Victoria will be bodyguard."

"I'm invited?" Victoria was wearing her normal shipboard canvas outfit and white blouse.

"Going to Feast Town, and I want you to be bodyguard." After another sip of coffee, he turned to the Chief. "Chief, keep working on the starbursts. I think I'll have an answer for quantity this afternoon." The smile on his face showed he did have a scheme in mind.

Changing Times

8 AM
Officer Martin's Office

The Captain knocked on Officer Martin's door and was beckoned in. "Ah, hello, Captain. What is it today?"

"I think it's time to see if we can get Maxmillian to show his color."

"I have a few men watching his office, and a few watching the hangar where his airship is stored. Nothing's happened yet. I have a couple of street people that can let the information leak in the right places. As a slaver/smuggler, he'll have his own people in low places. I'll have it released tonight. What's the lift date?"

"Three days sound good?"

"Sure, I have five men I would like onboard when you lift."

"You've met my crew. What do you think of them?"

"That's out of the blue." Officer Martin leaned back in his chair. "Sharp, loyal. I've only seen Miss Victoria and the Chief in action, but if they any indication of the rest of the crew, I would say all are highly skilled. That woman is scary. How did you get such a crew together?"

"Some by invite and some came to me. Do you have any vacation time?"

"More out of the blue. Plenty; I seldom take any."

"When this Maxmillian thing is put to rest, I'd like you to take a trip with me to a nice Island."

After finishing up with Officer Martin, the Captain made his way to Navy headquarters.

The Captain didn't have to wait long in the Commander's outer office before he was shown in. The Commander was young for the position, and looked very fit in his white, starched, and pressed uniform. The stress of the job did not show in his blond hair, blue eyes, and smooth face. "I was wondering when you would stop in for a visit. You should visit me more often, or I might think you don't like me anymore."

The Captain laughed while he shook the Commander's hand. "I have to avoid you. If any of my women saw you, they would leave my ship for you."

"That crew will never leave. You're here for the information from the lieutenant?"

"I can guess some of it, but I'd rather have confirmation."

"General Tarki is the problem. He was here the day of Miss Castle's speech. He left the same night. Word is he has two or three other gunships with him. His moles are in every country and feed him information. He's building a power base with the other countries so he can take over his own country. He didn't want anyone else to get the information for the shield. Now that the information is out, he has no reason to keep after Miss Castle. It makes no sense that he tried to kill her on the Dolphin before he got the shield information."

"He didn't."

"You know something?"

"Yes, my Admiral already has that information, and I can't go into it. In any case, he may not be after Miss Castle, but he might be after me at some point. He might be angry I took out his Dreadnaught and protected Alexandria. Keep an ear open for me, will you? Let me know if anything comes up."

"For almost a year, everything was quiet. Now, all this. What happened?"

"I guess fate decided my vacation was over. To put it another way, a woman happened."

67
July 9, 1898
10 AM
Feast Town

The steam carriage took them to the outskirts of Feast Town. It was a short stroll to enter the congested streets.

Alexandria pulled on the Captain's sleeve. "What's Feast Town, a place with lots of things to eat?"

Chef Joan jumped in before the Captain could answer. "It's a great place, full of shops selling everything. Beautiful clothes in bright colors, all kinds of strange foods, odd toys, medicines, furniture, gifts, all kinds of stuff is on display and sold. It's called Feast Town because everything is from the Far East."

The carriage stopped and they got out. There was a marked difference between New City and the entrance to Feast Town. New City, drab and gray, Feast Town with a bright red large wood arch over the road. Chef Joan's eyes were drawn to flashes of color as they entered the town.

The Captain stopped and spoke to them all. "When we go in, I have to ask you to stay behind me. Chat with each other, but always talk in a quiet voice and don't talk to me, unless I talk to you first. I know it sounds strange coming from me to say, but it's important."

They stared at him but said nothing. Falling in behind, they entered Feast Town.

The streets were filled with people, not carriages. Women wore long, slim dresses of silk with intricate patterns of cherry trees, dragons, moons, strange symbols, and lettering covering the bright red, green, and blue dresses. The shop fronts were at the edge of the street, and there was no sidewalk. Colorful flags high above the doors waved and proclaimed, in a foreign language, what was inside. Round, red lanterns hung on lines crisscrossing the street from the rooftops. At the first three shops, he went inside alone and asked for directions. At the third shop, he had the directions he wanted.

The Captain led them slowly down the street, allowing the ladies plenty of time to look and wander in and out of the shops. Victoria and Chef Joan bought silk pajamas and robes. Alexandria bought some items, but the Captain didn't see what she bought. At one clothing shop, the Captain again asked them to wait outside the shop. After a few minutes, a short woman, with long, jet-black hair, wearing a deep red dress of silk, came out and stared at the women. She nodded and re-entered the shop. Five minutes later, the Captain came out empty-handed.

They all looked at the Captain for some indication as to what that was all about, but he said nothing and led them further down the street. Turning down an alley, the Captain entered a shop. Well-lit by electric lights, the shop was filled with odd-looking paper tubes of various sizes on long, thin, sticks.

The shopkeeper came out through a curtain behind the counter. He was a short, rail-thin man in what looked like a long robe with huge sleeves. The Captain bowed slightly to the man and spoke in a strange singsong language. The shopkeeper gave a big smile, returned the bow, and spoke in an excited voice to the Captain. They talked back and forth for several minutes before the Captain handed the man money. The shopkeeper looked at the women behind the Captain and spoke again. The Captain laughed and spoke back. They bowed to each other, and the Captain left the shop with the women in tow.

On the street, the Captain could hear Alexandria making a soft long keening sound in her throat. The Captain turned, seeing she was trying hard not to speak first, but frustrated by not being allowed to ask questions. He put a finger to his lips and smiled. "You'll know when we get back to the ship. I'm done with my shopping, so if there's anything you want to look for, just ask me."

Chef Joan was fast to reply. "Food."

"I thought that might be a request. I did ask where that area is, and it's just a few blocks down and over. Let's go."

Changing Times

Stalls of food lined the street. Alexandria and Victoria didn't recognize any of it. Chef Joan clapped her hands, and looked at and touched everything she saw. Smells of cooking food drew them to a side street lined with stalls cooking food in shallow bowls. Chef Joan watched, with intense interest, how the food was prepared and cooked. One cook let her taste-test the sauces. The Captain bought them each something different to eat. Giving up the idea of eating with two wooden sticks, the women used their fingers. They eagerly sampled each other's lunch and made happy eating sounds. The keepers in the stalls hid their smiles behind their hands. It was obvious to the Captain that the keepers were happy that their food was enjoyed and were amused the women couldn't use the sticks. The Captain smiled as well, as he wolfed his lunch down, using the sticks properly.

They returned to the food market street, and Chef Joan bought strange foods. bottles of spices and sauces until they couldn't carry another thing. Joan's prize purchase sitting on top of the stack she carried was a large wide bowl shaped skillet. The Captain led them back outside Feast Town to catch a steam carriage back to the ship.

68
July 9, 1898
4 PM
The Engineering Room

The Captain sat with the Chief at the worktable with pieces of paper with crude drawings scattered around it.

"The plans for the Sunburst look fine to me. I even understand them. Thanks for showing me. Chief, what would you say if I could give you 200 small Sunbursts tomorrow night?" The Captain leaned back in his chair and waited for the Chief's answer.

"Two hundred would be great, but where are you going to get them?"

"I ordered them in Feast Town. They're being made now and will be delivered tomorrow night. A sergeant at the Army Depot said something that stuck with me. Fireworks. In town, I found a shop that makes them and just described a Sunburst, and they're happy to make them with extra magnesium. I did ask if they have very fast and short fuses. They won't be as large as yours, but in numbers, they should do the job. If they're made to fire five to ten at a time, set up one group on each side of the bow, each side of the roof of the bridge and one on the stern; it will make a big surprise when fired. With those, plus a few large ones, the crew will have good flexibility."

"Fireworks; only you would turn a toy into a weapon. I like it." The Chief picked up a scrap piece of tubing and laid it on a short piece of board. Picking up his pencil, he laid it at the end of the tube and stared at it. He found another flat piece of wood and held it above the first piece and the tube. "Yes, it can work. Five across on a piece of wood; hold it in place with some wax on the stick, near the fuse. I could use an electric spark to light some flash powder in a small paper sealed with wax. That would light the fuse; the firework would melt the wax on the stick in a flash, and off it would go. With spacers, I could make it five high. That would be twenty-five set off five at a time. Sorry to say there's a problem. Those are made to fly up a good distance before exploding. If they miss, they'll explode too far away. If they hit, they'll bounce off the bag and fall away before exploding."

"Ever go fishing, Chief?"

"On the Island, yes, and you know that. We've fished together many times, but what does that have to do anything?"

"You have a hook around here?"

The Chief dug into a drawer next to the desk and then looked in another. "Here's one." He handed it to the Captain.

The Captain put the hook in a vise and used pliers to straighten it. He handed it to the Chief. "If that is on the nose, it'll pierce the bag cloth and hold on. That also takes care of the range problem; it holds on until it explodes."

Changing Times

"Captain, you'll be an engineer yet. Did I mention you can be evil?"

"I'll agree he can be evil." Alexandria entered, followed closely by Victoria and Chef Joan. "I'm waiting for an explanation of what happened in town. Why the 'shut up and follow?' Why did that woman come out of the shop and stare at us, and what was that man saying in the shop?"

"Chief, protect me. There are three women in here declaring war on me," the Captain said, smiling. "We showed we were making an effort to respect their culture. It makes dealing with the people easier and more pleasant. I was asking the woman for more directions. I mentioned I was with three beautiful women, so she wanted a look. The gentleman commented that you three were very beautiful and properly obedient. I told him one was a bodyguard, and all three were more dangerous than pit vipers."

The Chief laughed while the three decided to be mad or not. Alexandria calmed. "Captain, I don't think you lied, but I don't think you told the whole truth."

"While you decide what's missing, let's go have dinner with the stuff Chef Joan bought."

The Captain headed out the hatch and heard Alexandria shout after him. "What was that language, how do you know it, and what are those stupid sticks?" He kept walking.

Once in the galley, Chef Joan started cutting up vegetables into very small pieces and setting each aside. She left the young peas in the pods but trimmed the ends. When the vegetables were prepped, she started working on a large chicken, removing the skin, and then the meat. She cut both into bite-size pieces.

Alexandria sat glaring at the Captain, waiting for his answer.

Holding up his hands, he finally answered. "Okay, okay, I yield. Let me ask a few questions first. How do you know all that stuff about making a shield?"

"I studied; now, answer the question."

"Wait. Victoria, how did you learn to shoot so well?"

"Practice, Captain."

"Chef Joan, how did you learn to cook so well?"

"Books, practice, and lots of time."

"There's your answers. Practice and time. The language is a common language in the Far East. Pilots that travel far often run into it."

"That's an answer but, at the same time, it doesn't answer anything. I suppose it's all I'm going to get," Alexandria added under her breath. "For now."

The crew filtered in, looking around for what was to eat. The only thing they could smell was rice cooking. Chance spoke up. "You haven't started cooking yet? Will it be late?"

Chef Joan leaned back on the stove. "It'll be ready when everyone's here. It'll be something new, so I can't promise it'll be any good."

Once the full crew was in, Chef Joan pulled out the new skillet and started cooking on a burner turned up so high that the flames curled around the edge. Rapidly different things were grabbed and tossed in. Sauces and spice were added and, at the last minute, rice was added as well. Stirring it all around for a minute, she turned off the flame and started scooping large portions onto the plates.

The crew looked down at the plates and hesitated. Victoria scooped up a large mouthful and started in. With her mouth full, she sat back and clapped. The rest of the crew dug in and cleaned their plates.

The Captain looked at the Chief. "She does have a Talent."

69
July 10, 1898
3 PM
The Bridge

The Captain relaxed by polishing brass on the bridge, a mindless chore he often performed when he wanted to let his thoughts drift. The highs and lows, since the rescue of Alexandria, had kept him from taking time to relax. Every time his mind drifted to Alexandria, the corners of his mouth would curl up into a small smile. The image of her lying next to him when he lay recovering from the gunshot wound stirred him in many ways. He had lain staring at her face until he realized she was naked under the sheet and blanket. He had turned away and tried to sleep.

"Captain." Alexandria's voice pulled him from his daydream.

"I didn't look!"

"What?"

"Nothing, nothing, never mind. What brings you to the bridge? Do you want something?"

Alexandria sat down on the couch with Kira. "No, just nothing to do other than feed Kira."

The Captain put down his polishing rag and crossed over to sit next to her.

"Captain, what happens now? I mean, what's next?"

"If all goes well, soon we'll lift, have it out with Maxmillian, and then go back to the Island and try to figure out if the General is a threat anymore."

"No, I mean, what's next for Kira and for me?" Alexandria watched Kira work at the bottle.

"That I'm not sure about." The Captain reached over and teased Kira's toes. "Kira has no home; so far, no one seems to be paying attention to her. If she's lucky, she'll be lost in paperwork and you two will stay together. What you do is what you want to do, and where you want to go is up to you." The Captain hesitated. "You could stay on the Island."

Alexandria sighed. "The Island is beautiful, but what's there for me?"

"You could learn about the Island and the people." Another hesitation. "You could learn more about me. I mean, we could get to know each other better."

"Captain, for a Captain of an airship and having fought battles, you're worse than a schoolboy." Alexandria smiled while she said it.

"Yes, well, I have something to do in town. It won't take long. We'll have dinner together."

Alexandria chuckled. "We always have dinner together."

"Yeah, we do." The Captain flashed a smile and left.

The Town Of New City

Diana pushed Kathryn flat up against the wall. The town streets were busy with people shopping and steam carriages rumbling and chuffing by. "Isn't that the Captain coming out of the jewelry shop?"

Kathryn looked at the back of the departing figure. "Only the Captain walks like that. Yes, it's him. Why did you pull me? We could have said 'hello' and kept on shopping."

"Aren't you curious as to why he was in there? What he was buying? Come on, let's go find out." Kathryn in tow, they entered the shop. The overhead lights made the stones in the jewelry sparkle. Cases were full of rings, pocket timekeepers, broaches, and necklaces and, still, there was more to see.

"Good afternoon, ladies. How may I be of help? Looking for something special?"

"Our Captain was just here and we want to buy a gift too. We wouldn't want to pick the wrong thing. Could you tell us what he bought?"

"Of course you would want a perfect gift for a wedding. He bought two silver wedding bands to be engraved. I would think anything in silver would be a fine gift."

70
July 10, 1898
4 PM
The Galley

As Chef Joan approached the docking ramp, she saw Officer Martin talking to the guard in his hut. "Officer Martin, what brings you our way?" She spoke to the guard. "It's okay; I'll take him up."

"Thank you. I was just going to have a word with the Captain, nothing important."

Chef Joan had a light chat with Officer Martin as they made their way to the galley. Alexandria and the Chief were there, having coffee while they waited for dinner. "I'll call the Captain on the loud-box. I'm sure he'll be here in a minute." Chef Joan headed for the loud-box.

"He's not here; he went into town. He should be back soon though, he said he'd be here for dinner." Alexandria teased Kira with the wooly lamb toy. Kira would grab at it when it touched her nose and giggled each time.

Chef Joan put a cup of coffee in front of Officer Martin. "There you are. Dinner will be quick. I'm making a dish like the one they have in Feast Town. I made a chicken version last night; tonight is beef."

"I couldn't, I have much to do, and I wouldn't want you to have you go to any trouble."

As Victoria walked in, Alexandria called to her. "Perfect time to drop in. Officer Martin just refused Chef Joan's food again."

Victoria crossed over to Officer Martin at a fast pace. Bending down, she got very close to his face. "Big mistake."

"Yes, you're right. What was I thinking? I would love some Feast-style cooking, especially since Chef Joan is making it." He put on a smile.

The Chief laughed. "What in the world did you do to the poor man? That's twice you've bullied him."

"I didn't bully him, Chief; we just have an understanding."

"Yes, Chief, we have an understanding. I understand she's lightning-fast with her cannon and she understands she scares me to death."

"Vicki, you shouldn't bully him."

"It's all right. He likes me."

"Respect, very much. Like? Well, the whole crazy crew is growing on me," he added quickly, while holding up his hands, palms out, to Victoria. "I mean 'crazy'; in a good way."

"Vicki, I mean it. Stop picking on our guest or you'll get no supper."

Alexandria threw her head back and let out a scream. "Something's wrong!"

Kira started crying at full volume. Victoria stepped to her side and took the baby. Alexandria grabbed her head and continued to scream that something was wrong. Victoria thrust Kira into the Chief's arms and ran from the room.

Chef Joan ran to the loud-box. "Doc to the galley! Emergency!"

Alexandria fell out of the chair and onto the floor. It was hard to hear anything over Alexandria and Kira both screaming. Doc ran in and knelt down by Alexandria's side. "Alexandria, calm down. What's wrong? Talk to me."

"It's wrong. It feels wrong. Where's Thomas? What's happening?"

"Shhh, the Captain will be here soon. I'm sure he was on the way when he heard the loud-box."

"No! He's not here! He's gone." Alexandria rocked back and forth on the floor.

The Captain was pleased with himself as he made his way back to the ship, whistling a tune. As he entered the dock area and passed between buildings, he started to turn at a noise behind him. He felt a sharp pain in his head, saw an image of Alexandria in his mind, and the world went black.

71
July 10, 1898
4:30 PM
The Galley

Victoria ran back into the galley wearing her holster belt with the revolver, a red bag hung on her left hip. Alexandria was on the floor, whimpering instead of screaming. Kira had calmed to a quieter cry. Victoria went up to Officer Martin. "Where would the Captain be?"

"What? How would I know? I'm sure he'll be here soon."

"I don't have time to explain but, if she's acting like this and even little Kira crying, something happened to the Captain, something bad. You're the cop; now think. Who would hurt the Captain?" She lowered her voice. "And if he's alive, where would he be taken?"

The Pilots entered the galley, laughing, and stopped when they saw the scene. Kathryn spoke in a worried voice. "What's going on?"

Victoria answered. "Something's happened to the Captain."

"He's not here? He should have been back before us. We saw him in town and left after he did."

Victoria stared at Officer Martin. "Start thinking out loud."

"Assuming something happened and assuming he was taken somewhere, there are only two people that would be after him, the General and Maxmillian. The General isn't anywhere near. That leaves Maxmillian. Other than his office building, he has a hangar with an airship."

"Where's the hangar?"

"Close, five hangers west of here."

"Let's go."

The Captain and the Lady Fair

Martin held up a hand. "Wait a second. If he's there, Maxmillian might be planning to leave in his airship. Pilots, I'm not your Captain but, if I were, I'd say 'Get ready for a lift in case we have to chase Maxmillian's airship.'"

The Pilots ran out; the Chief handed Kira to Chef Joan. "Want me to get her to sickbay, Doc?"

"Thanks, Chief. After that, go do what you need to get the ship ready."

Victoria took a moment to talk to Alexandria. "Don't you worry; we'll bring him back."

Victoria trotted out, with Officer Martin close behind. Their voices carried as they went down the passageway. "You're civilian, so follow my orders."

"Uh-huh, whatever you say."

As they reached the bottom of the docking ramp, Avery, Chance, Tailor, and Rigger were just approaching. Victoria broke into a full run and called over her shoulder. "Prep emergency lift!"

Officer Martin fell behind as Victoria outran him. He caught up to her at the fourth hangar, where she crouched, looking around at the fifth. Breathing hard with his mouth open to keep from making noise, Office Martin panted, "How can you run that fast?" He looked around. "There should be four of my men in the area. We've been watching Maxmillian. We can contact them and, if anything is going on, they can help." He cupped his hands to his mouth and made a bird sound. There was no response. He tried it again. "Something's happened to them."

Victoria ran to a side door on the hangar. Slowly, she opened the door a crack and looked in. After a moment, she opened it wider and entered. Next to the door, unconscious, bound, and gagged was one of Officer Martin's men. She quickly checked him. She whispered, "He's alive."

"That's a relief. I'll say this again; you're civilian. Follow my lead and do as I say."

"Uh-huh."

Changing Times

A large airship, in the middle of the hangar, was almost touching the floor with the hull. Victoria moved along the wall. Officer Martin stopped her with a hand to her shoulder and took the lead. After a few slow steps, a shot rang out and Officer Martin dropped to the floor, holding his stomach. Victoria heard steps on the stairs in front of her leading to the second-floor walkway. A man six feet tall and dressed all in black, with a black hood covering his face, stepped down from the stairs and stopped ten feet in front of her.

"I see I have something nice to play with. I'm going to enjoy you."

"You shot a friend of mine."

"He was a threat. Looks like police to me."

"Why didn't you shoot me?"

The man laughed. "A woman? You're no threat, and the boss would not like it if I wasted cargo."

From the floor, Officer Martin groaned. "Big mistake."

Victoria's revolver roared, and the man dropped, with a hole in his chest. She turned and checked on Officer Martin. The stomach wound was off to one side, but it was bad.

"Friend, eh? Thanks."

"I have to get the Captain, and then I'll get you some help."

"I guess saying 'get out of here' would waste my breath."

"Look at you, finally learning." She patted him on the head and headed for the airship.

A figure jumped out from behind a barrel and she fired before the figure had a chance to aim. "How many are you? Can't be many or I'd be swamped by now." Stopping, she stayed crouched and listened for any noise as she used to listen when hunting with her brothers. Seconds passed. A noise came from behind her. She rolled to her right and shot behind her to distract whoever it was. As she turned into a kneeling position, she saw a figure in black slowly fall forward onto his knees, and then fall face down.

As she neared the airship, a shot rang out, and a bullet pinged off the floor. Spinning in a crouch, she saw a man on the second-floor walkway and fired one shot. Without a pause, she boarded the airship. The interior was familiar. It was the same as the slave ship she had been on before. "I know where you'll be, Captain." Her palms began to sweat. After a moment of hesitation, she wiped her palms on her canvas pants, and moved on, with her lips in a tight, straight line. She heard gunfire outside the ship. "I hope that's help that's arrived." She stopped moving forward and reached into the pouch at her waist. Pulling out four bullets, she replaced the spent ones in the revolver.

In the passageway leading down to the hold, two figures leaned out from doorways on each side. Victoria's revolver roared twice, and both dropped straight down, with just their heads and shoulders in the passageway.

When she reached the hold, she saw cages, just like the one she had been locked in when she was a prisoner on the Osprey. Inside each cage was a naked woman huddled in a corner. Their ages ranged from teens to late twenties. Across the hold, she saw the Captain on the floor, unconscious.

"Look, Captain. Someone has come to your rescue. Your Captain thought he was so smart. I know he was behind the false information about any proof. The ploy of lifting would have been a good one to make me chase the proof. Since there wasn't any, the lift was a bad plan on his part to get me to come after him. It just shows how stupid he is." Maxmillian Dartin stepped into the light from a shadow, to the right of the Captain.

Victoria froze. It was the man who had claimed her as his own a year ago on the slave ship.

"Nothing to say? Good, I like my women quiet." He reached down, grabbed the Captain's collar, and started dragging him forward. The light caught a reflection in Maxmillian's right hand. A gun. "Let's have a closer look at you. I heard your Captain is weak, and he surrounds himself with useless women. Are you his pet too? I think I am going to enjoy you. That stupid woman he's been protecting will be mine too. I'm going to enjoy teaching her what her place is."

Changing Times

With each word he spoke Victoria's right hand opened wide then closed into a fist. She suddenly let out a breath and smiled.

"He must like stupid ones." Now, fifteen feet away, he stopped but continued his taunting and insults. "You're here alone. You're a woman and that makes you just a plaything. Your weapon isn't drawn, and you can't count. You're out of bullets. I heard that thing of yours blast away six times, the last one just upstairs, and you came down too fast to have had time to reload."

Victoria broke her silence. "You don't remember me. I remember you. You love to talk, so I'll talk, too. I'll tell you my Captain didn't make a mistake but you made four. His plan worked, you did go after him. Your first mistake was you hurt my Captain. Second, your thug upstairs hurt a friend of mine and, as he works for you, and that makes it your fault. Third, you hurt me. Fourth, as a friend just said to one of your thugs, 'a big mistake'. I reloaded early." With her last word, her gun snapped up from the holster and roared.

Maxmillian dropped his gun and fell forward to a kneeling position, wide-eyed, holding his crotch, as blood poured to the floor.

72
July 10, 1898
5 PM
The Lady Fair

Chance, Tailor, Avery, and Rigger met at the exit hatch; each armed with their own handgun. The Chief approached them.

"Don't try to stop us, Chief."

"I wasn't going to try. We're prepped and ready. Might as well go see what's going on out there. I'll stay here and keep an eye out. Head for the fifth hangar to the west. I wanted to say I'm proud of you all, and the

Captain would be, too, once he got done chewing you out for being dumb."

They took off running. When they reached the hangar, they saw light coming through an open door, they entered and stopped just inside. An officer was unconscious on the floor. A moan came from the right. Rigger and Tailor dragged the first officer out the door. Going to the right, Chance and Avery found Officer Martin. They picked him up and carried him back to the door and out. The unconscious officer had a lump on his head.

Rigger looked over at Officer Martin's stomach wound. "This one is okay, just a lump on the head. Officer Martin looks bad."

Chance paused. "Get Officer Martin to Doc. We'll go in and see if we can help. Victoria's in there alone." Chance and Avery went back in as Rigger picked up Officer Martin. Slowly circling the hangar near the walls, they had made it halfway around when a shot barely missed Chance's head. They both dove flat on the floor, trying to see where the shot had come from. Finally, they spotted a head peering up in the bridge of the airship. Lights on the bridge silhouetted him. Slowly, the figure rose and raised a gun to point out the window. Both Chance and Avery aimed and fired two shots each. The figure dropped out of sight. They waited, but the figure didn't appear again. They heard Victoria's revolver fire twice. Chance broke into a run for the airship. Avery followed.

Chance stopped just inside the airship. "Which way?"

"Cabins, galley, and lounge would be stupid; it must be the cargo hold." They knew they were going the right way when they found bodies. Avery shook his head. "Victoria's pretty angry, I think."

As they neared the hatchway to the hold, they could hear Victoria talking, then Victoria's gun spoke. Standing at the side of the hatch, Chance yelled down. "Victoria, you okay?"

After a few seconds, Victoria answered: "Come on down."

When they reached the deck of the floor, they saw Victoria untying the Captain. Once they got closer, they saw Maxmillian, lying curled up on his side, and holding his crotch. There was a pool of blood under him. Both men winced at the sight.

Victoria had finished checking the Captain for injuries when he groaned. She looked up at Chance and Avery. "He'll be okay. Get those women out of the cages."

Finding tools to pry open the doors, Chance and Avery set to work. As the women got out of the cages, they went to Maxmillian and kicked and stomped on him. Victoria let them vent. "Chance, Avery, if they're all out, go up to the cabins and grab sheets for the women to wear." Chance and Avery ran up the stairs. Victoria finished untying the Captain. "Big brother, don't make me have to rescue you again." She sat on the deck, with the Captain's head in her lap. The moans and noises from Maxmillian stopped and the women still stomped and kicked. Victoria yelled to the women "Vent it out and take back yourselves!" She waited for Chance and Avery to return.

Looking up at the sound of footsteps running down the stairs, Victoria saw several police officers. Leading them were Rigger and Tailor. When they reached the bottom of the stairs, the only thing they could do was bend at the waist and pant big gasps of air. The officers removed their jackets and covered the women as far as the jackets would allow. They saw a dead man on the floor, every inch of him covered in blood.

Tailor tried to talk between gasps. "All that running, and we missed everything."

The Captain was coming around. Dazed and confused, he asked the timeless questions. "Where am I? What happened?"

73
July 10, 1898
5:30 PM
The Sickbay

Doc was still talking to Alexandria. Alexandria had calmed down, and only occasionally whimpered. Chef Joan held Kira close, rocking and making noises at her to keep her calm.

"What's wrong with her, Doc?"

"Remember how the Captain felt her, and we did that crazy rescue?"

"Yes."

"She felt him."

Rigger and Tailor burst through the hatch, carrying Officer Martin. "Gunshot to the guts, Doc." They laid him out on the nearest table and dashed back out.

Doc ripped open the officer's shirt. "What a mess."

Officer Martin's voice was weak. "Sorry, Doc. It's a gut shot. I know I probably won't make it, so don't blame yourself if I don't."

"Shut up, and don't tell me my job."

"Do me a favor, Doc. Tell Victoria she can lead the way next time."

Doc went to a cabinet and got the same bottle of pills she had used on Chef Joan and Victoria. "Take this and keep quiet." She pressed the pill past his lips. As soon as he was unconscious, she set to work and talked at the same time. "Joan, loud-box Chief to come take Alexandria to her cabin, please. She's calm enough now. Joan, you go as well. Settle Kira down and get Alexandria in bed."

The Chief came in, picked up Alexandria, and left for her cabin. Chef Joan followed closely with Kira. Reaching the cabin, Chef Joan pushed past the Chief, put Kira in the top drawer of a dresser, went to the bed, and pulled the bed covers back. The Chief laid Alexandria on the bed and left, closing the door.

Changing Times

She talked to the unconscious Alexandria as she undressed her. "I bet the Captain would rather do this." She chuckled at the thought of the Captain blushing. "So, you felt he needed you. I guess you're bonded." When she had Alexandria tucked in, Chef Joan placed a chair next to the bed, lifted Kira out of the drawer, sat down, and talked baby talk to her. Alexandria stopped whimpering, relaxed into the bed, and fell asleep. "I knew the Captain would be okay. That means my Vicki is okay too." Kira giggled and relaxed into a sleep, tired out from the crying. "Are you bonded, too? Nothing to worry about, young lady. He tries to hide it but I can tell he likes you."

By the time Doc was finished, the Captain and all the rescuers were back sitting in the galley. They had been swapping stories of their adventures. Doc entered the galley and grabbed a cup of coffee. "Martin will make it fine. Let me look at you, Captain." She crossed over to him.

"Only a bump on the head and a headache, Doc. No big deal."

"Why does everyone want to tell me my job?" She checked the lump on the back of his head and held his head in her hands for a few minutes while she heard the stories about what had happened, but Victoria sat quietly.

"Captain, I think you need to see me tomorrow. I'll take a better look at that head. Go see Alexandria, so she knows for sure you're safe."

The Captain left the galley.

Doc smiled at Victoria. "Anyone else notice Alexandria went kind of nuts like Joan did?"

The Captain knocked and entered Alexandria's cabin. Chef Joan got up and offered her chair. "She's still sleeping; keep her company and hold her hand, Captain. That way she'll know you're okay." She placed the sleeping Kira in his arms. As she left, she added a comment. "By the way, she's naked under there." She saw the Captain's face turn beet red before she shut the door.

74
July 10, 1898
9 PM
Cabin 24

Chef Joan entered the cabin to find Victoria on her bed, staring at the ceiling. "Is something wrong?"

"No, just relaxing."

"Really?" Joan stripped down to her underwear, carefully folding her clothes and laying them on her own bed. When she went into the exercise room, she left the door open. Working on the rowing machine, her grunting was extra-loud with each pull. After five minutes, she stopped and returned to her cabin to see Victoria in the same position, and still staring at the ceiling.

"Vicki, I know we haven't made any promises to each other about anything. We're just letting things happen. But I expected better."

"What are you talking about?"

"I strip naked in front of you; I go exercise, which I don't do unless you push me to get started, and I even make the extra loud grunts you like. Here you are, still staring at the ceiling, even when I'm talking to you. All of that together means you lied to me. You're not *just* relaxing. It hurts that you would lie and pull away."

Victoria's eyes turned to look at Joan. "I'm sorry. I just … I just …."

"I heard the stories and can guess. Two things are bothering you. One is killing those men; the other is the memories brought up by those women in cages."

"There's another. It was Maxmillian. He was the one. The one from before."

Joan thought a moment. "I know you won't listen to me, but I'll try anyway."

"Joan, I'll be okay."

"Yes, you will." Joan stood legs apart, with her hands on her hips. "I'm not going to tell you I understand all you feel. I've only had two bad things happen in my life. My parents died in a fire when I was eight and when I thought you had died. I understand it in my head, though, and given time, things heal and we move on. It's up to us to decide how long that is. It's okay you feel bad about taking lives. Better than okay; it's a good thing. It means you respect life. Those men had to be stopped. They were shooting at you or were about to. Officer Martin, a good man, is alive because of you. That slaver deserved what he got. He didn't care about life and enjoyed ruining others. Those women are safe now because of you. Sure, it has bad memories, but you rose out of it. You even got some revenge. He can never hurt you in any way again. He's not even a ghost out there in the dark, waiting to take you again." Joan took off her underclothes and slid under the covers of Victoria's bed. "Get undressed for bed and get under the covers. I'll give you all the time you need to move on with this. As long as it's by morning." Joan held Victoria's head to her shoulder until the sun rose.

75
July 11, 1898
9 AM
The Sickbay

The Captain, Doc, and the Chief stood quietly while Officer Martin listened to his commander.

"It's a good thing one of the crew of this airship let my men know you had been carried off here. Looks like the Doc did a good job on you."

"Commander, what of the women?" Officer Martin's voice was strong.

"They'll be fine. They had been collected up to be sold, but other than being stripped, nothing had happened to them."

"Thank God." As Officer Martin spoke, the three watching quietly let out a sigh of relief.

"Maxmillian Dartin is dead. No loss there. No issues about how he died either. With the testimony of the kidnapped women and the evidence we found in his private cabin, it'll be a closed case. The evidence also tells us who the buyers were and have been. Those in this country will be arrested this afternoon and, with luck, we will find the women they bought. The ones from other countries will be handled by the countries concerned. You're on sick time for a month. I'll not be blamed for allowing you back to work so soon that you didn't heal properly. The man who caught an assassin we've been after, and a slaver, deserves some rest time."

"Sir, I don't need a month. Maybe two weeks and I can be walking."

"No, I talked to your doctor, and she says a month. As long as she's willing to be your doctor, I see no reason to have you moved to a hospital. Good work, Martin." The Commander thanked the Captain and Doc for taking care of Martin and left with a wave.

"Doc, a month?"

"Maybe a little sooner." She looked at the Captain, who nodded.

"If you gentlemen will leave us, I think I'll have a long talk with Officer Martin." She laid a hand on his stomach.

The Captain smiled. "I think you have the time to visit an Island now. As you'll be with us awhile, why don't we just call you Martin?"

"Martin is fine with me. Thanks for all the help."

"Captain, ask Chef Joan if she would make us that Feast dish for lunch we didn't get last night." Doc smiled down at Martin. "You'll love it."

"Doc, don't tease me. I know I'll be eating soup for days."

Doc laughed. "If you insist … Doctor Martin."

Changing Times

For three hours, Doc sat with Martin, getting him to talk about himself, and she talked of the beauties of the Island. Her hand rested on his stomach the entire time.

"Doc, about Victoria. She scares me. She's so fast. I saw her shoot a man dead center that was behind her and she hadn't even looked. She outran me by a mile and wasn't even panting."

"If you were a pilot, you would be in awe of our pilots. If you were an engineer, you would be in awe of the Chief. If you were a Captain, you would be in awe of the Captain. Because you're a cop, Victoria is the closest thing, and you're in awe. They take things very serious and practice, learn, exercise, or do whatever it takes to be better."

"Why do I get the feeling that if I were a doctor, I would be in awe?"

"Me? I'm just a simple doctor, good with bandages."

"Doc, what was that pill that knocked me out so fast?"

"Just something I made for emergencies. The drug is normal, but I made it so it would dissolve as soon as it hits the tongue. Much faster than waiting for it to get to the stomach and dissolve. 'Stomach' makes me think. Let's go for lunch, shall we?" Doc stood and put the chair back at her desk.

"Stop teasing me. Go get yourself some. I'll be okay on my own."

"The Captain once said 'Did I stutter?' " She moved to the side of his bed and offered her hand. "I said 'get up.' We don't deliver food to people that can get it themselves. It's lunchtime."

Martin hesitated but took her hand when he realized that she was serious. He slowly sat up, waiting for pain to strike; when none came, he stood up carefully. "You must have some great drugs, Doc."

They entered the galley to find the crew around the table waiting for Chef Joan to finish making lunch.

Victoria was the first to see them enter and greeted them. "Doc, Martin, glad you could join us. Martin, thanks for going after the Captain."

"They only thing I did was get in your way and get in the way of a bullet."

The Captain and the Lady Fair

Victoria laughed. "Next time, you'll follow orders, right?"

"I thought you should know; I heard this morning, nothing happened to those women other than being stripped. They were saved in time."

Victoria smiled. "Thanks for telling me."

Alexandria nudged Doc and whispered. "I think Kira can see a little."

"What?"

Alexandria continued in a whisper. "When I feed her she reaches for the bottle before it touches her. Watch." Alexandria slowly lowered the bottle towards Kira's mouth when she reached both hands up to grab at it. "See."

Doc watched closely as she repeated the motion and the same thing happened. "That's very odd."

"Odd? It's great."

Doc picked up her napkin, folded it lengthwise and gently laid it over Kira's eyes. "Do it again."

As Alexandria lowered the bottle again, Kira did the same thing, a giggle and a reach for the bottle.

Doc leaned back in her chair and kept her voice low. "Somehow she sees the bottle, just not with her eyes. When you showed me, I noticed her eyes didn't follow the bottle, she just reached. I have no idea how she's doing that, but it's not with her eyes. At least it means she can somehow 'see' around her. Let's not make a big fuss yet and just see how things progress."

"I'm sorry, Doc, I just thought she could see."

"Alexandria, this is great. I think in some way she can see better than we can. Give it time. Let's just keep it quiet for now."

Chef Joan served up the Feast-style dinner they had not gotten the night before. The crew started eating with no hesitation. The Captain reached over and took the fork from Alexandria's hand, replacing it with two thin, wooden sticks. "You said you wanted to learn."

"No, I said 'What are the wooden sticks?'"

"Now, you'll find out." The Captain smiled and showed her how to hold them.

Changing Times

Doc looked at Martin with a frown. "You're not eating?"

"It looks and smells delicious, but I'm waiting for the soup. I know it's too soon to eat solid food with a stomach wound. Telling me to eat this is teasing me."

Joan turned from the stove. "Victoria, it sounds like Martin is refusing my food again and even ignoring Doc. Please fix that."

Across the table, Victoria put down her fork and stared at him.

"I'll eat. I'll eat." He ate slowly, waiting for pain at any moment. As soon as he felt satisfied, he stopped, not wanting to eat too much. He felt no pain and looked at Doc. "Even though I'm not a doctor, I'm in awe. I guess I can go back to work."

Doc chuckled. "Victoria, could I ask for your help? It seems you're the only one Martin listens to. Explain to him he's on sick leave and can't leave the ship until I say so. If he argues and tries to leave the ship, shoot him in the leg." She got up and patted him on the head. "Be good, or I'll make it confined to sickbay with Victoria as a door guard."

Martin shook his head. "I was right. You're all nuts."

The Captain stood and addressed the crew. "Now the excitement has died down, we'll take today and tomorrow to make sure everything is good onboard, and everything topped up. Do some shopping if you want. We'll head home the day after tomorrow at sunrise. Anyone have anything?"

The Chief nodded. "Your order came last night in the confusion. I'll be working on the Sunbursts."

"If this is going to keep up, I want more rounds." Victoria patted her hip where her revolver would be. "If you go anywhere, let me know; I'll go with you as bodyguard."

"Sorry, Victoria; I have to go someplace where I don't want you going. The Chief will go with me."

Victoria leaned over and whispered to Joan. "Brothel?"

76
July 11, 1898
8 AM
New City

Chef Joan entered the gun shop. The high-pitched tinkle over the door announced her. The gunsmith was behind his counter, cleaning and polishing a rifle. "Good morning, Miss. How may I be of service?"

"I have a friend that could use a belt for a holster. It needs to have a way to carry bullets. For now, she's carrying them in a bag and a regular belt." Chef Joan smiled, hoping he could help her get the perfect thing.

"Of course. I am sure it would be awkward for a lady. Here is a nice one and we can add loops of leather to fit any size ammunition." He pulled a narrow belt from the case that was imprinted with flowers and had fake jewels scattered around it. Handing it to Chef Joan, he smiled.

"Oh, this won't do at all. It needs to be heavier." Looking in the display case, she saw the same model revolver Victoria had. "It needs to hold a heavy gun. She has that one." She pointed to the 50-caliber revolver in the display case.

The gunsmith blanched, grabbed the belt from her hands, and tossed it over his shoulder to bounce off the shelves behind him. "I'm sorry, my mistake." He opened a drawer and pulled out a wide leather belt. "If you tell me about what the waist size is, I can cut this to length, add the loops, and have it ready this afternoon." He presented a nervous smile.

"I do have a few requests. Can you dye it red to match as close as you can this color?" She pulled a small scrap of cloth from her pocket.

"Yes, I'll be very happy to."

"My Captain also said to see if you have any more ammunition for her gun since he was here. He wants 200 rounds."

The gunsmith looked nervous. "That's a lot of rounds."

Changing Times

"Well, lately it seems she's needed to go through some and, if it keeps up very long, she would need more."

"That's no a problem. I'm sure with practice she'll learn to handle it someday. Anything else?"

"Yes, there is. Could I ask you to deliver them to the Lady Fair at the airship docks this evening? I have so much to do; I won't have time to get back here."

"I can do that as well. I'll just total this up for you."

"Would you mind making a second holster? One for the left side and a belt for it. I'll be paying for that. The Captain's account will pay for the ammunition, and that as well." She pointed to the matching 50-caliber revolver.

"Excuse me, but are you sure? The one she already has is very capable."

"If she gets mad again, it might be handy." She smiled a knowing smile.

He stammered. "Please don't send the big man around. I'm here to please." He scrambled to gather everything together.

As Chef Joan left the shop in a happy mood, she gave him a word of advice. "It's not the big man you should be worried about." Closing the door she turned to go back to the ship and heard her name being called.

"Chef Joan, good morning! Where's Victoria?" Pilots Kathryn and Diana waved.

"She's on the ship. I wanted to get her a gift, to make her feel better, and understand that the shootings were okay. You two out shopping too?"

"Well, we lift tomorrow, so we thought we'd look around in case there's anything we need, but forgot."

"Enjoy the day; I'll head back. I want to make some cakes."

They parted ways and the pilots went on their way to a bookshop. When they entered, they were struck by the musty smell of paper and the distinctive smell of leather from the bindings. The bookbinder at a worktable nodded to them and kept working, allowing them to browse.

The Captain and the Lady Fair

He was a man well into his years, with gray hair thinning on his head, and a permanent hunch from long hours of working at the table. A leather apron protected him from the glues.

"Excuse us; perhaps you can help. We're looking for a wedding gift or gifts."

"Is there anything you have in mind?" His voice was soft but loud enough in the quiet shop.

"Yes, two large diaries, leather-bound, one black and one brown."

The bookbinder rose and went to the back. He returned with a thick, leather-bound book with a leather binding cord to keep it shut. "I have this one. I have the stock to make a matching brown one." He ran his hand over the leather, showing his pride in his work.

"Could you have it ready today?"

"I'm sorry; I can't do it that fast. Sometime tomorrow, if I rush."

"That will be too late. We leave on a ship in the morning."

"A wedding gift, you say?"

"So they can record things that happen, adventures together and just being together."

The bookbinder smiled. "I wish we had kept diaries; I would have things to read to help my memories of my Charlene. Young people today too busy rushing about to take time to write down memories." The bookbinder laughed. "Don't look so surprised. I was young once. You'll have it at sunrise. Just tell me where to bring it."

Leaving the shop, they saw the Captain across the street, headed deeper into town. They crossed the street and caught up to him. Kathryn pulled on his sleeve. "Good morning, Captain."

"Good morning."

"Aren't you supposed to have a bodyguard?" Kathryn teased.

"I think I'm safe enough for now. I slipped out." He wore a mischievous grin as he said it. "Last minute shopping?"

"We're just looking around in case we need anything. Any news, Captain?" Diana smiled with a look of anticipation.

"Nope, a quiet day to relax."

Changing Times

"Okay, Captain, we'll just let you walk and shop, then."

Both pilots giggled and laughed as they walked away.

Shaking his head, he continued on his way to the jewelry store, where he picked up the rings. He stopped a steam carriage to take him to the frame shop the Chief had told him about, the one where the shopkeeper didn't believe in women pilots.

"Welcome to my shop. How may I be of service this fine day?" The rotund shopkeeper wiped his palms on his pants.

"I hear you do good work, and you are quick to the customers' needs." The Captain flashed him a smile.

"I try my best to please. Anything special you need, sir?"

"Yes, though it's not a frame exactly, you may have what I want. I am looking for a nice presentation tube with a stand to hold an important document."

"Actually, sir, I do carry a few. I can also engrave it if you want." He yelled to the back. "Marie, bring out the certificate holders."

Marie came out carrying five tubes with stands. She laid the wood, copper, pewter, brass, and silver tubes on the counter. She looked up at his clothing. "You work on an airship!" Her face took on a glow.

"Yes, I do. I'll take the silver one and please engrave it." He slid a piece of paper across the counter.

"I can have it ready by early this afternoon, sir."

"I'll be on business most of the day. Could you deliver it after you close up for the day?"

"Of course, sir."

The Captain turned to address the shopkeeper. "Please bring Marie. I'm sure she would like to see an airship up close."

Marie had a beautiful face, brimming with happiness. She bounced on her toes.

"Very nice of you to offer, but she has no need of that."

Marie's face fell and her head dropped.

"I like people seeing the ship I work on. I'll be very disappointed if I can't let her see it. Perhaps I should find a friendlier shop, then." The Captain reached to take the paper back.

"Oh, no sir, I just didn't want to burden you. Of course, she'll be there."

The Captain made his way back to the ship. "Yes, a very special look at the ship I work on."

77
July 11, 1898
6:30 PM
Dockside

The crew relaxed, sitting on wooden crates on the dock near the guard hut. Alexandria played touch-and-tickle games with a giggling Kira in her lap. The shadows were long, and the sky was turning orange with the low sun. The keel of the Lady Fair hovered a few feet above the ground.

Looking around, the Captain noticed a crew member was missing. "Where's Victoria?"

"I asked her to change into her lucky outfit and wear her gun for me." Chef Joan had a grin that let on that there was more than a simple outfit change.

"You asked, and she did it with no questions. Why should she wear her gun?"

"She asked lots of questions, and I had to bribe her. I think someone might learn something tonight. No matter what happens, it'll be fun." Chef Joan's grin got bigger.

Victoria returned, sat down next to Chef Joan, and asked questions that were ignored. A man approached the guard hut carrying a package. The guard poked his head out and yelled over to the crew. "A package for Chef Joan!"

Changing Times

As Chef Joan got up, she pulled Victoria along.

"Captain, that's the gunsmith I told you about." The Chief got up and headed over to see what was going on. The Captain followed. They said nothing, but stood to one side and listened.

The gunsmith extended his hands with the package. "Here you are, Miss." His voice trailed off when he looked at Alexandria. "So this is the lady that likes big guns. I thought she would be bigger, much bigger. As thin as she is, I doubt she can lift that thing out of her holster. She even put clothes on it to pretty it up. That outfit is obscene."

The Captain balled his fists, and the Chief was turning red.

Chef Joan's tone was light and amused. "Victoria, would you let the man get a look at that holster? Please, sir, take a closer look. You might learn something."

The gunsmith bent at the waist to look. "I doubt it." As his eyes drew level with the holster and looked from a foot away in one blink, the revolver was pressed against his nose. He froze in place a moment, and then dropped to his knees, covering his head with his arms. "Don't shoot!"

Victoria spoke with contempt. "It's magic fabric. I wager you didn't even see it move from the holster. Still want to make snide comments?"

"No. No. I'm sorry."

Chef Joan enjoyed the view. "The Chief, the one you call 'big man,' told you that you didn't need to worry about him, I told you, too. You should have paid attention when you were warned. Some nasty men, just the other night, didn't take her seriously and paid the price. One even lost his manhood and died less than a man."

"That was her? I heard a crew of police had a shootout. That was her?"

"Yes, and she was by herself. Women are stronger than you think. Don't be rude to women and don't make the mistake of thinking women weak again. Please."

The man slowly raised his head to look and saw Victoria tilt the revolver to one side, letting the cylinder fall open. She calmly reached into the bag at her waist and pulled bullets out to load the empty revolver. "Oh, please, do get up. While you were looking, I just thought you'd like to see that I can handle it. You can sell women bigger guns than you thought they could handle. Bigger guns can mean bigger profit."

He was calling over his shoulder as he left in a hurry. "Yes, thank you. Come to my shop anytime."

Victoria and Chef Joan were in a full laughing fit as they went back to their crates. The Captain just shook his head and sighed.

The Chief's hand over his mouth hid his grin. "Starting to take after you."

Before returning to sit back down and enjoy the evening, movement caught the Captain's eye. "I see we have another visitor." A young woman approached, carrying a very large package. The Captain greeted her in her native language, which he had used in Feast Town. She handed him the package, turned to leave, and nearly bumped into the frame-maker, with his daughter wide-eyed behind him.

"Feasters ought to stay in Feast Town and stay out of the way." The frame-maker glared at the woman.

The Captain spoke again in the singsong language, and she laughed and went on her way.

"What was that about? Was she laughing at me?" The frame maker's voice was tinged with anger.

"Of course not. I was only giving her my prediction for the future. Marie, what do you think of the ship I work on?"

Marie was wearing the same outfit he had seen her in before. Her hands clasped over her chest, she whispered. "It's beautiful."

The Captain turned to the seated crew, looked at the pilots, and yelled out. "Can I get two volunteers to give this young lady a tour of the bridge? Marie wants to become a pilot someday." Both Pilots jumped up and hurried over.

"Hi, I'm Kathryn and this is Diana. Let's go." They grabbed Marie's hand and pulled her to the boarding ramp. Alexandria got up and followed.

"Really, it's not necessary. No need to waste anyone's time, and I'm sure the Captain of the ship would disapprove of having girls roam his ship. Here you are sir, your purchase delivered as promised."

The Chief bit his lip.

"The Captain approves, I assure you. Let's go have a drink and let the girls have some fun." The Captain nodded at Martin to come along. The Captain led the way slowly up the boarding ramp and guided the frame-maker to the galley. "I do apologize. I don't know your name."

"Marcus. What would be your name?"

"Thomas."

Martin poured himself a coffee and sat down, not saying a word.

"This is a grand ship. I'm sure the rich people enjoy taking trips in this."

"Yes, she's a fine ship."

The Captain offered Marcus a glass of wine from Chef Joan's cooking supplies and kept him distracted with small talk.

The Bridge

"It's so beautiful. It's so big and everything gleams." Marie was so happy to see the bridge she was close to tears.

"Look around at everything, and then we'll tell you about the controls and what everything does."

Alexandria sat down on the couch at the back and whispered to herself. "Good for you, Captain."

Marie looked out the window at the view of the foredeck, then turned to look back at the bridge, to take it all in. She saw something on the wall that looked familiar, crossed the room and looked closely at the frames and certificates. She spun in place, open-mouthed. "You're them!"

The Captain and the Lady Fair

Kathryn laughed. "Yes, we're them." Marie was speechless, staring wide-eyed at the pair.

Diana spoke up. "Come on over here and we will explain about how it flies." Over the next thirty minutes, Kathryn and Diana explained the controls.

As Marie heard about the controls and relaxed, eager to see and hear everything, she began to get ahead of the explanations by reading the nameplates over the dials, gauges, and levers and guessing at what they did.

"Have you read much about airships and flying?"

"No, Father won't let me read stuff like that. I'd like to leave a note for the Captain of the ship thanking him for allowing this. It's been a dream to be here. Father would never let me be a pilot. He needs me to work in the shop since Mom died. He doesn't care about me. Only the work I do. The shop used to belong to my real Dad, but he died." Her expression took on a sad look for a moment.

"If my guess is right, you can thank him yourself soon enough." Kathryn nodded to Diana, who nodded back.

Marie was looking at the map on the chart table. As she traced her fingers along the lines and looked at how small some Islands on the chart appeared to be, she heard her father's voice.

"Well, Marie, that's enough of this nonsense. I hope you can stop going on about airships."

The Captain and Martin followed Marcus through the hatch.

Before Marie could say anything, the Captain spoke. "Tell me, Marie. Still want to be a pilot?"

"More than ever."

"Have you reached your majority?"

"Yes, six months ago."

"What does her having reached majority have to do with anything? She's still a silly girl with her head in the clouds." His voice was tinged with anger again.

"Pilots, what do you think?"

Changing Times

"Pilots? They're pilots? Women are not pilots."

Kathryn ignored Marcus and nodded as she spoke. "She's smart and quick. Might even be a natural. I can also say there are no anchors."

Marie's eyes flicked between looking at the Captain and the Pilots.

"Marie, how would you like to start learning to be a Pilot in the morning?"

"What? I can't. Father would never approve."

"You're right about that. How dare you fill her with such ideas?"

"She said she reached majority; you agreed she has. Seems to me as an adult, by law, she can make any decision she wants without your permission."

"No, she can't. I'll report you for interfering with my daughter."

"Marie, be a pilot or not. Just tell me."

"I want to be a pilot, not a shopkeeper."

"Fine then. Kathryn, will you please find her a place to bunk?"

"You can't do this. I'll report you as kidnappers."

"I'm sorry, did I forget to introduce you to Officer Martin? He's an officer with the police, not the military. He was witness to her majority that you confirmed and her desire to stay."

"I want to speak to the Captain. He'll put a stop to this."

"That woman at the dock. I told her the future; it just wasn't hers. It was yours. I told her your helper would leave, and you'd never be able to hire another and you'll be out of business within six months."

The Captain stepped to the loud-box. "Could I please have a volunteer come to the bridge and throw this man off my ship?"

The loud-box produced a quick answer from the Chief. "On the way, Captain." Victoria's voice followed immediately after. "My guns are loaded and I'm on my way, Captain."

Both Marie and Marcus stood open mouthed. Marcus was very pale.

"The owner will hear about this!"

"I already know, thank you."

The Captain turned to Marie. "Welcome aboard, Marie. Just call me Captain."

78
July 11, 1898
7:30 PM
The Galley

Chef Joan was plating dinner when Victoria entered, still in her lucky suit, with two belts that matched the color of the suit. Shiny brass cartridges filled the loops on both, and the large 50-caliber revolvers filled the holsters on both hips. "Thank, you Joan. I love it." She spun a pirouette that would have done a debutante at a ball proud.

Officer Martin looked at Victoria. "Thanks for getting her that stuff, Joan. I'm not scared of her anymore. Now I'm terrified."

Kathryn and Diana escorted Marie through the hatch as Victoria finished her spin. She wore a pale green, short-sleeved dress. Marie's eyes opened wide, and she stared at Victoria but said nothing. Kathryn sat Marie at the table between herself and Diana.

The Captain stood and banged the table with his coffee cup. "Everyone, I introduce you to Pilot Trainee Marie. She begins her training tomorrow. Pilots, you have permission to do training maneuvers as we head for Paaku. Did you get Marie a place to bunk?"

"Captain, it's not a bunk. It's huge, has a fancy soft bed, huge windows, even a private privy and a thing that makes rain to have a wash. It looks like it's for royalty. It's fine for tonight, but tomorrow I'll be ready for a proper place to bunk."

"I can see you are going to be a delight. You appreciate things. Do you think my Pilots made a mistake and put you in a wrong room? That is your room now. Marie, trust the Pilots; for that matter, trust the crew around you. We may poke each other now and then, but we never pull pranks or make fun of each other. Any questions you ever have, feel free to speak up. The hardest thing you will learn is not to hold yourself back." The Captain introduced everyone around the table as Chef Joan finished setting out plates.

The Chief smacked his lips. "My favorite. Thick, slow-cooked beef stew, mashed potatoes, green beans, hot-out-of-the-oven rolls, and cooled melon. That fancy stuff is great, Joan, but I like food that sticks. Marie, you're not that big, so if you can't eat all that, just slide it down to me." The crew laughed.

Chef Joan nudged the Chief. "Save some room; there's chocolate cake and angel food cake for dessert."

Victoria couldn't hold her curiosity in anymore. "Captain, what did you get in those packages?"

"Just something I thought might come in handy."

Victoria knew not to push for a better answer.

The crew worked on eating, and the Captain, with a full cup of coffee in hand, spoke up. "Alexandria, Victoria, Joan, I'm going to delay lift. Please take Marie to town and get her proper onboard attire for a pilot. As she came to us empty-handed, she'll need everything. A few dresses as well. When we get to the Island, we'll figure out a trip to get things for her to wear there. While you're getting the work outfits, order up a formal uniform as well. Can you be done by noon?"

"It'll be rushing things, but we can do it." Alexandria's tone conveyed that she took it as a challenge.

Marie's face had a stricken look.

"What's wrong, Marie?" The Captain's voice had a worried tone as if he had said something wrong.

"Captain, I have no money. I can't buy anything. Diana even loaned me this dress. I don't even know how I'm going to pay for training."

A relieved Captain smiled. "All uniforms, from work clothes to formal attire, are taken care of by the Lady Fair. The other stuff is on me as I gave you no warning or chance to fetch anything. You'll work on the ship. It will be hard and may stress you at times, but do it right and it'll be fine."

"What will my work be?"

"The hardest you will ever have. Learn. Become a great Pilot that will make the Lady Fair proud. Besides being a Pilot, you can learn anything you want, time allowing."

79
July 12, 1898
7:30 PM
Dockside

A hunched-over old man waited, pacing near the guard hut. Both Pilots came down the boarding ramp to meet him.

"Thank you so much for bringing the diaries."

"It's my pleasure. I hope they're used well." He handed over the package. "If you ever need more, let me know. When I asked for you, the guard told me you were the pilots of this ship." He reached out and touched Kathryn's hand. "I wish I had children. I would want them to be just like you two." He turned and left to go to his shop. Kathryn and Diana re-boarded. In their cabin, they opened the package to re-wrap them in colorful cloth. They found, on top of the diaries, two ornate wooden pens, and two cut-glass bottles of India ink. There was a note under the bottles. Diana read it aloud. "Something extra as my wedding gift. May they have even more happy years than we had." They agreed they would have to visit him again. They left the cabin and went for breakfast.

Most of the crew had already eaten and left. Alexandria and Victoria sat next to Marie as she was just finishing her breakfast.

"Chef Joan, this was so good. You make even breakfast taste wonderful. I've never had food this good, or so much."

Chef Joan laughed. "Just you wait till I get fancy. Finish up, now; we have to get going."

Changing Times

Kathryn touched Marie's shoulder. "When you get back, come to the bridge dressed properly. Be ready to see your first lift in the Lady Fair."

Marie finished up quickly and hurried behind Alexandria, Victoria, and Chef Joan to begin the shopping trip. They had a plan in place as to which stores to visit, and what to purchase at each one. Marie was in a daze by the time the shopping was done. The four had their arms full with packages as they made their way back to the ship.

Victoria winked at Marie. "We bought those horrid bloomers, but next time we'll go to Feast Town and get some nice silk underwear. Of course, you don't have to wear any. I don't most of the time."

"What?" Marie was wide-eyed and open-mouthed.

"Welcome to the world." Alexandria chuckled. "Less than a month ago, I was the same as you. You're going to love the new life you've chosen. There are so many more shocks yet to come. I still get surprised all the time. Try to relax with it and trust us." They arrived back at the Lady Fair by 11:30. They put things away in Marie's cabin while she changed into her new pilot attire: tan canvas pants, a white blouse, brown calf-high leather boots, and a brown leather cap. "I'm not sure about wearing pants."

Alexandria giggled. "Neither was I. When we get to the Island, there'll be more surprises. Remember, I went through all this, and I survived. You will, too."

Marie headed for the bridge.

The Bridge

Marie stood behind Kathryn and Diana, watching them prep for lift. Each move they made they explained not only what each control did, but also how each one worked and why they did it. By the time they were done, and waiting for word from the Captain, Marie's head felt full, but the delight of being there had not worn off. They chatted while they waited.

"Why is the Captain doing this for me?"

The Captain and the Lady Fair

Kathryn smiled. "That's the way the Captain is. Why he's that way, no one knows. I guess you'll have to ask him. I can tell you; he won't answer that one. He seldom talks about himself. He's good to all the crew. He says 'please' and 'thank you' all the time. If he says 'jump over the side,' just do it. Never stop to question an order. I'm sure, soon enough, the crew will tell you all the stories of the things that have happened onboard. That'll help you understand."

The Captain entered the bridge. "Understand what?"

"Just how the ship works, Captain."

He crossed to the loud-box. "Chief, warm up the engines, please. Crew to stations to release lines." He stopped short of asking Marie if she was ready for her first lift when he saw her bouncing on her toes. "You look good, Marie."

She offered a shy smile. Her eyes kept looking around at everything, so she wouldn't miss anything.

"Pilots, give the order to cast off and lift when ready."

Kathryn nodded to Marie. "Okay, time to work. We showed you the comm; ask the Harbor Master for permission to lift. Then use the loud-box and tell the crew to release lines."

The Captain stepped out of the way as Marie approached the comm. She hesitated, took a deep breath, and let it out. "Lady Fair, requesting permission to lift, please." The reply was swift. "Anytime, Lady Fair. Good weather to you."

"Thank you." Marie gave a deep sigh and used the loud-box. "Cast off lines, please."

The crew members at the bow waved and cast off the lines.

The Captain patted her on the shoulder. "Well done." He left the bridge.

After the Lady Fair had cleared and started her flight to the Island, Diana lay down on the couch. "I'll rest here. Wake me for your relief."

Pilot Kathryn stood back and gave Marie instructions for change of speed and heading. Once Marie was comfortable doing that, Kathryn gave her commands to increase altitude, and then to return to the original altitude.

"You've done great, and it's six, time for dinner. Go eat and relax. Be back in the morning."

"I'm not tired; I could come back after I grab a bite."

"First, you never grab a bite with Chef Joan's cooking. It would hurt her feelings unless it's an emergency. Second, I remember what training was like. Right now, you feel fine, but you've had a long day of exciting shopping and then your first lessons. That's a lot of stress. You'll feel it after you wind down. I'll come down soon enough after Diana takes over."

The crew enjoyed Chef Joan's cooking, then sat and talked after eating. The Captain watched Marie slowly lower her head to her arms, fall sound asleep. "Chief, after you have your second helping of dessert, would you be kind enough to take our trainee to her quarters? Alexandria, will you make sure she's comfortable?" He smiled at the sleeping trainee and left for the bridge.

80
July 13, 1898
7 AM
The Galley

"I'm embarrassed. I know it was stupid and rude to fall asleep like that." Marie sat at the table, wringing her hands in her lap and staring down at her untouched plate.

The Captain looked at Marie. "Marie, while in training status, you will seldom get direction from me. Kathryn and Diana are your trainers and only they will give you orders, instruct you, or lecture you. But, on this one occasion, I'll speak up. Tell me ... if you knew the Chief worked all night on something the ship needed, would you think he should be embarrassed if he fell asleep at the table?"

"No, of course not, but I didn't work all night. Not even a full day."

"Do you think any crew member should be embarrassed if they fell asleep after giving their all at something?"

"No, but like I said, it wasn't a whole day and I didn't do anything."

"Pilots, please take over."

"Yes, Captain." Kathryn, sitting next to Marie, laid her hand on Marie's shoulder. "What the Captain is trying to tell you, not very well, is that you did a great job on your first day."

Marie started to speak, but Kathryn held up her hand. "The morning was exciting and took energy. All afternoon you worked with me, learned, and actually flew the Lady Fair. You took everything very serious, paid attention, and concentrated very hard. All that drained you and I even warned you. Remember?"

"Yes. You did and I didn't listen to that part."

Kathryn patted her on the back. "Welcome to the real world of life on an airship."

Chef Joan walked over to stand behind Marie's chair with her hands on her hips. "If you don't stop being so whiny about falling asleep after wearing yourself out and eat that breakfast I made, I will not be happy." Chef Joan lightly slapped Marie on the back of the head. "Stop it, eat, get to work, and cheer up."

Martin laughed. "That wasn't embarrassing. Let me tell you about the time I was shot because I didn't listen to Victoria and she did the job for me."

The crew laughed over breakfast as each one told an embarrassing story.

The Bridge

"Today, we'll do the same things as yesterday. There's no need to stress yourself. You did the same thing yesterday just fine. Today you'll take a two-hour lunch. After doing everything, we're going to practice controlling engine speed some more. The Lady Fair has mass, so things take time to happen. You have to think ahead. We've plenty of time. We won't arrive at Paaku until tomorrow night. Tomorrow you'll do a split shift. Work until noon, and then I'll call you when we're close. It'll be dark by then, so you can see what it's like on the bridge at night." Kathryn began the lessons.

They spent the day practicing maneuvers. Marie had a gentle hand on the controls and learned a deft control of the engines quickly. Everything from full throttle to dead slow and reverse. She practiced docking with small clouds.

Diana walked onto the bridge. "It seems you took her through the paces today. I could feel the changes. They all felt smooth and not jerky at all. Dinner will be in about an hour. Why don't you send Marie out on the deck, to feel the wind and the ship under her feet without the distractions of trying to fly? Then she can get cleaned up for dinner."

"I didn't know what to expect, but this ship is beautiful and the crew is so nice. Thank you both for teaching me."

Diana giggled. "Let's see if you're so eager to thank us when you're dead tired and still have to work."

Marie walked out onto the deck near the bow and stood with her hand on the railing, feeling the breeze and the vibrations under her feet. She closed her eyes and stood silently, taking in the sensations. Soon, she noticed the clean air. It smelled slightly of salt and felt cool on her face. "A beautiful day and a wonderful and beautiful ship." She felt a small surge of speed in the ship.

81
July 14, 1898
11 PM
The Bridge

The knock on the door woke Marie from a light sleep. She heard the Captain's voice. "Marie, you're wanted on the bridge."

Marie scrambled into her work clothes and ran to the bridge. On the bridge, she saw Pilot Diana at the helm and Kathryn sleeping on the couch. "Did I miss anything?"

"No, we're still an hour out. We'll go in for a close look so you can see it at night. Then we'll go back out to sea and do circles until dawn when the ground crew comes into work."

"So we can't dock at night?"

"We could if we wanted to have them wake the ground crew, but there's no reason to wake them and dock so late. The Captain treats the ground crew as friends and tries not to put them out too much."

Marie's eyes grew accustomed to the dimmed lights on the bridge, with everything in a red glow. "Why are the lights red?"

"It helps the eyes adjust and see at night."

The moon was bright enough to see the Island. The moon's reflection in the water raced ahead of them. Marie could see the bay and the white, sandy beach. Even the mountain was visible.

"See that green light?" Diana pointed to the light on the docking mast. "That one would be our docking mast if we were going in. Okay, let's do a gentle turn and head back out to sea, 180 degrees from the heading we're on now." She stepped back a pace from the helm and waved her hand for Marie to take control.

As Marie started the turn, the comm gave a burst static, and then a voice. "Airship approaching Paaku harbor, are you docking?"

Changing Times

Diana used the comm. "No, Harbor Master. This is Lady Fair; just showed a new pilot the look at night. We'll go out and circle until dawn. No need to wake anyone."

Before the Harbor Master could respond, another voice erupted. "Harbor Master, this is Dreadnaught Falcon; get them up and let them earn their pay."

There were a few moments of silence. "Harbor Master to Lady Fair. As they're going to be up, they can bring you in, too. You'll be first. Welcome home."

"You'll dock us first." The voice was arrogant and impatient.

"Are you declaring an emergency?"

"No, but we're priority."

Marie looked at Diana during the exchange and continued the turn.

"One of the nasty pilots you'll run into. Thinks he's so important. Wake Kathryn for me, please."

The Harbor Master's voice came over the comm again. "Falcon, if you don't have an emergency, then I need the mission priority code for you to cut in."

"You don't need any such thing. Just do it."

The Harbor Master's voice showed he was not concerned or ruffled. "Young man, I'm the Harbor Master and I decide who and when people dock. You can push it to dock at night and wake the crew, but I decide where, and in what order. Stay at sea until I clear you. Harbor Master out."

Kathryn, half-awake, shook her head. "It's never a good idea to make the Harbor Master upset."

Marie steered in slow wide circles while they waited. Kathryn and Diana walked around the deck, dropping the control lines over the side. Forty minutes later, the comm came to life. "Lady Fair, come into dock. Your mast is lit. The ground crew has been advised of the situation."

"Okay, Marie, put us back on the original heading for the Island. Take it slow."

As Marie finished the final turn, Diana let out a burst of gas, bringing the ship lower. "Being ahead a little bit means we don't have to adjust as much when we get close." Kathryn stepped up next to Diana. Diana took Marie off the wheel and placed her in front of the throttles. "Okay, Marie, your first test of what you've learned. You're in charge of the throttles. It's just like you practiced."

"What? Me? I can't."

Diana gave Marie a hard look. "Going to disobey an order by your instructor already?"

Marie turned and stared with concentration at the now-visible light. She waited for instruction from Diana. She felt the speed was too fast and pulled back on the throttles to quarter speed.

"Good, you had me scared. I thought after all the practice of docking with clouds, I was going to have to tell you what to do." Diana smiled at Marie.

Marie relaxed, knowing Diana would take over if she messed up. She pulled back on the throttles more.

Diana and Kathryn lined up the altitude and direction, keeping the nose in line with the docking ring just above the light.

Maria pulled the throttles back to idle and watched the light. Thirty feet away, she put the engines in reverse and gave a nudge to the throttles. By five feet from the ring, the Lady Fair was moving as fast as an old man with a walker. Just before they touched the docking ring, she gave a burst of power in reverse, and then put them in neutral, allowing the propellers to stop spinning. There was a soft bump and the Lady Fair was docked.

Diana shut down the engines. "Let's go say 'hello' to the ground crew." As they reached the starboard side of the ship, the crew was putting a ramp in place. Diana and Kathryn waved and the ground crew applauded. When they reached the ground, a member of the ground crew stepped forward with a basket of fruit.

"The Harbor Master told us you wanted to wait until morning. Thanks for that. You two did a beautiful dock as always."

Changing Times

"No, not tonight. Tonight there were three of us. Meet Pilot Trainee Marie. She handled the engines all on her own."

Marie smiled at the man and blushed as he handed her the basket. He glanced at Diana and Kathryn and saw them give a smile and a slight nod.

"Join us in a late snack. We have juices, sliced fruit, fresh bread, and butter." The man led them to an area the ground crew used for meals and waiting for work between ships. There they saw a long table surrounded by dozens of chairs, with one end covered in cloth with baskets and jugs atop it. The crew sat and nibbled at the impromptu feast.

Marie was speechless at the hospitality but was worried they would get into trouble. "Don't you have another airship to dock?"

The crew laughed, and the foreman got up and went to a nearby post with a box mounted on it. He opened the box, reached inside, and flipped a switch. He was already seated before anything happened. From the box could be heard the irate pilot of the other ship. "Isn't that lazy crew ready yet?"

"Sorry, no. They have a priority unload to do. May take a few hours."

"Get another crew then, and hurry up."

The ground crew all chuckled and laughed as the conversation continued.

"Sorry again. The contract we have only allows for one crew at night. I'm sure they're working as fast as they can. If you want, you can try to hit the ring without the ground crew's help. The Lady Fair just did. As usual."

The last comment was greeted with silence, and the ground crew roared with laughter. "I think that unload job we're on just might take till dawn. I'd even say by mid-morning there will be some very unhappy people."

He leaned back in his chair and smiled at Marie. "Tell us all about Pilot Trainee Marie."

82
July 15, 1898
7 AM
The Bridge

The Captain was sitting in his command chair, drinking his coffee and relaxing, when conversation drifted over the comm.

"Harbor Master, this is the Falcon. Is that crew ready yet?"

"Falcon, no, not yet. Is it a problem?"

"Just get that crew ready for me. I want to dock now. You ought to have a second crew by now."

"Sorry, Falcon. No second crew yet."

There was silence for a few minutes.

"Harbor Master, this is the Captain of the Falcon. Please accept my apologies for an over-eager pilot in training. It was his first night solo on the bridge. Please also extend my apologies to the ground crew for waking them for no reason."

"Falcon, you're clear to dock."

The Captain laughed into his cup. "Pompous pup, you don't know it, but you're in the fire now."

The Captain left the bridge and headed for breakfast. He was greeted by laughter around the table. "What did I miss?" He looked to Kathryn, Diana, Marie, and Joan for the answer.

Kathryn stopped laughing long enough to answer. "Telling Joan about the fun last night." She proceeded to tell him what had happened.

"Marie ran the engines, then. Good job." The Captain relayed what he'd heard on the comm, and they all broke into laughter again.

Diana stepped close to the Captain and whispered. "You should know, she is months ahead in learning. She has a natural feel and touch for it. A Talent for it I think."

Changing Times

The Captain's stood straighter and his chest puffed up. "A good decision then."

When the rest of the crew arrived for breakfast, they told the story again.

The Captain had finished eating and asked what Alexandria had planned for the day.

"Well, I am sick of cards for a while. Playing card games all day with you can do that when I lose every hand. Chef Joan, Victoria, and I will take Marie into town for some local clothes and show her around. Everyone else is going home to husbands and wives."

"At least we didn't play for money. Enjoy the shopping. Have you told Marie about the local … colors the women wear here?"

Alexandria laughed. "No, but she'll know soon enough when we all change for shopping."

Marie perked up. "What about the clothes and colors?"

The Captain left for the Phoenix building while Alexandria tried to avoid giving a straight answer.

The Phoenix Building

The Captain stopped at the message center and saw a young petty officer at the desk. It wasn't Carter. The Captain felt age creeping up on him when he noticed how young the man looked. "Petty Officer, do you have any messages for the Lady Fair?"

The petty officer checked and found one message.

The Captain read the message from the Admiral asking him to see him as soon as he was able. "Where's Petty Officer Carter?"

"In the brig, sir; she's waiting for a court martial."

"What? Do you know the charge?"

"I think it was insubordination, conduct unbecoming, and destruction of property, sir."

The Captain and the Lady Fair

The Captain walked down the hall at a brisk pace. Finding the office he was looking for, he knocked and entered without waiting for an answer.

"May I help you?" A lieutenant sat behind a clean desk with only a few papers on it.

"I understand you have a court martial coming up. I'd like to speak to the defense attorney assigned."

"Who are you, and what business is it of yours?"

"You don't need to know either one."

"I'm sorry, sir, then I can't help you."

"Interesting." The Captain left, slamming the door behind him.

He rapidly reached the message center. "Petty Officer, I need your phone."

After a short conversation on the phone, he hung up and strode back down the hallway. Reaching the legal office, he went in without knocking. He stared down at the lieutenant behind the desk, who was saying a lot of 'sirs' on the phone.

The Captain watched the lieutenant hang up the phone. "Are you ready to take me to the defense lawyer now?"

"Yes, sir; sorry, sir."

"Lieutenant, if I ever hear you obstruct like that again, I'll see you brought up on charges. Am I clear?"

"Understood, sir."

The Captain entered the office the Lieutenant had pointed out.

"Good morning, Sir. Something you need?" A young lieutenant greeted him.

"Yes, a chair to sit in for a moment. It seems I keep running into idiots, and I need to calm down to be civil."

The Captain sat in the chair and took a few deep breaths. He looked around and noted there was a stack of papers on the desk. "Thanks for waiting. I understand you're the defense for Petty Officer Carter. What is the case about?"

"I'm Lt. Mason; I can't discuss the case, but I can tell you the charges."

"I heard the charges, but what are the charges based on?"

"I can say that. Everything is based on an incident with damaging a few ensigns' uniforms; they pressed for charges."

The Captain laughed. "They didn't like pink, eh? Did she tell you why she did it and where she got the idea and the dye?"

"You seem to know a lot about this case. Care to explain?"

"I gave her the idea and the dye. Now, did she tell you why she did it?"

"Yes, but it won't help. There's no proof."

"What? She never reported any of the harassment?"

"She says she did, but there is no documentation, and when I requested a subpoena for the Assistant to the Admiral, Lt. Commander Whelps, it was denied. He's responsible for harassment complaints. They said, as there's no documentation, then there's no need for him."

"As you have no sworn testimony and no proof, let's keep my involvement quiet. Do her a favor. Tell her I came by. Tell her I asked she give you permission to tell me everything about this case. Tell her to be strong; she's not alone."

"I'll do that, but who are you?"

The Captain stood up straight. "Thomas Hewitt Edward Castellan, Captain of the Lady Fair." He left and headed for the Admiral's office.

The Admiral's Office

The Admiral's secretary greeted him as he entered the door. "Good morning, Captain. I hear you've had more adventures."

"Nothing big. The Admiral in?"

"Yes, sir, but he's busy with the Captain of the Falcon."

"I think I can help with that." He walked past the secretary's desk and entered the Admiral's office.

"Good morning, Admiral."

"Captain, I'm busy at the moment; please wait outside."

The Captain and the Lady Fair

"Admiral, I think I can help clear up the mess here. Hello, Captain Grieves."

Captain Grieves was in his late forties but still kept in shape. He stood stiffly in his white dress uniform in front of the Admiral's desk. Standing off to the side was a young lieutenant. He appeared to be unconcerned with what was happening.

"How would that be, Captain?" The Admiral's voice let on he was not happy with recent events.

"I can tell you what happened and guess why. I know Captain Grieves is a good officer and sticks up for his men, even when they mess up. He prefers to handle discipline himself."

"Captain Castellan, I thank you for your concern, but I can handle this."

"Captain Grieves, like I said, you're a good officer. Sometimes you shouldn't protect someone that isn't worth it. Save your strength and credibility for those that deserve it. Admiral, this young man was rude and demanding of the Harbor Master. I take it this young man is the pilot from last night."

"He is."

"He also demanded to be allowed to dock ahead of the Lady Fair. He made very demeaning remarks about the ground crew. Early this morning, he again started a tirade. He was, again, refused permission to land. I'll guess he didn't mention to you or the Captain his ship was offered to be allowed to land if he could dock unassisted as the Lady Fair had just done. The Harbor Master gave permission immediately on hearing from the Captain a polite request to land and apologies to the Harbor Master and the ground crew. I'll also wager the Captain had told him to circle until morning, but he wanted to dock to try to impress the Captain."

"Did I leave anything out, Lieutenant?"

The Lieutenant, embarrassed, was now upset. "The Harbor Master has no right to refuse permission to land. That ground crew wasn't doing anything. They were just ignoring me. They should all be fired and replaced with men willing to work."

"Captain Grieves, how long has this Lieutenant been in training to be a pilot?"

"Just under sixty days."

"Lieutenant, why didn't you take the ship in and dock unassisted?"

"Because that's stupid."

"May I point out my Pilots do it with every docking? I'll also point out I have a new Pilot trainee that throttled the Lady Fair to a perfect dock ring lock. The ground crew did not have to assist in any way."

"I'll be able to do that soon enough."

"My trainee has two days of training; it was her first docking of any kind, let alone at night."

"Her?"

"Captain Grieves, I'm sorry, if you feel I stepped out of place. If you do, I apologize. This man is not worth it and I think the service would be best if his commission is not confirmed."

"Captain, you were right about there was some information I was not told and that he disobeyed orders. I was going to address that later, but it seems there are many issues here. You are right in saying that the commission should be denied."

The Admiral had relaxed back in his chair and had watched things play out. "That takes care of everything, I think. Petty Officer, you'll be given a new assignment later today. Go fix your uniform to your new rank."

"You can't do this; do you know who my father is?"

"Yes I do, an idiot for letting you live. Get out of my office, or you can have brig time added to it."

Captain Grieves shook hands with the Captain and left.

"You saved his backside. He was willing to take a career hit for that moron." He sighed. "I guess I'll also have to do something about the Harbor Master."

"Admiral, I suggest you simply tell him the pilot is now a Petty Officer. The Harbor Master may have dragged his feet on purpose, but he did nothing outside his authority. Perhaps you might put on some civilian clothes and go talk to him and the ground crews about the ships and pilots. They can give you good information about the good and the bad. You might find there are ways you can improve things. I got your message. Let's talk about what you have for me, and then I have a request."

Martin

Martin strolled along a natural path, listening to the birds and taking deep breaths, breathing in the scent of the flowers. The sun, through the trees, made streaks of light filled with the flicker of reflections off the dust and pollen. Insects danced in the beams. A rustling noise near a bush to his right made him stop. He slowly approached the bush and looked behind it. A bird with a broken wing was hopping on the ground, guarding a nest under the bush.

"Hello, little bird. I see you have some babies there." Martin stayed very still in a squat. "I don't think you'll let me fix your wing, but maybe I can help."

Martin walked up the path, looking for fallen trees or large rocks. Finding a fallen tree that had been rotting, he pushed it aside and found grubs squirming underneath. He picked up a large leaf and placed all the grubs he could find on it. When he returned to the bush, the bird was still there. Very slowly, he slid the leaf with grubs towards the bird near the nest. He stepped back and watched. The bird stopped hopping and watched him. After a time, the bird pecked up a grub, hopped over to the nest, and fed it to a waiting mouth.

"I'll come back tomorrow with more. It's the best I can do."

Carefully he backed away and then continued down the path.

The bird stopped feeding and looked at a bush nearby. The bush parted. Two slim, tanned hands came towards the bird with palms up.

The bird had watched the slow progress of the hands and did not move. Inches away, the hands stopped, with the back of the hands resting on the ground. The bird took a few hops forward and settled in the hands. The hands carefully folded over the bird and stayed that way for many minutes. The bird didn't struggle in the hands but settled down as if sitting in a nest. The hands opened and tilted, letting the bird go. It hopped a few times, then flapped and took to the air. The hands withdrew and were gone.

83
July 15, 1898
11 AM
The Chief's Home

The Captain strolled along the path to the cottage set back in the clearing. The visible part of its walls was white; lava rock covered the rest of the walls, to blend in with the background. The tan, thatched roof stopped the sun from heating the wooden roof underneath. He knocked on the arched door made of polished wood. The Chief answered the knock.

"Welcome, Captain. Come in and join us." The Chief held the door open for the Captain and they joined Neenaa at the table, a large, polished slab of wood on a tree stump pedestal. The white-painted walls featured a few painted scenes of the Island and wooden shelves.

"What brings you out here, Captain?"

"I need to ask Neenaa for some favors."

Neenaa teased him. "O Great One, I get to work for your boss. Will I get paid more because I eat less?"

The Captain smiled. "Thanks, I needed some humor."

"What's wrong, and how can I help, Captain?"

The Captain and the Lady Fair

"First, I need you to get all the wives, because this needs to be quick. Go to the Phoenix building and ask questions of all the women there. I need a list of names of all the women that have been harassed. Make note of any that made a harassment complaint. We only have this afternoon and tomorrow."

"What's it about, Captain?"

The Chief laughed. "His usual, of course; saving someone's day."

"You got me, Chief." The Captain smiled a boyish smile.

"Captain, there aren't many women at the Phoenix building. I can do it myself. Women do talk to each other; each one will probably have a name or two of others. It shouldn't take much time at all."

"That's great news. You can tell them they won't have to testify if they don't want to."

"Okay, what else do you need?"

"This doesn't go beyond this room … I need you to set up a wedding. All the fancy stuff, I've no idea about. You know, make-the-bride-happy stuff."

"It's about time, Captain!" The Chief rose and slapped the Captain on the back.

"Control yourself, Chief; the question hasn't been asked yet. I also need two tents for dressing, one on each side of the clearing. Plan on just before sunset in three days at the shrine."

Neenaa nearly yelled. "You haven't asked yet? Are you crazy? You don't plan a wedding before you ask the question!"

"Neenaa, Chief, I'm asking you to trust me on this. Just keep it quiet. I've already talked to Arku. I know better than you the risk I'm taking, but I just feel it's the right thing to do. I have to figure out how to get everyone there without announcing it's a wedding."

Now the Chief spoke up. "Wait; everyone is going to show up at a wedding they don't know is a wedding and that even the bride doesn't know about? Captain, you've done some crazy things that I haven't questioned, but this is insane."

"I know. One more thing, Chief: I want you to give away the bride."

Changing Times

Neenaa

In her nurse's uniform, Neenaa didn't draw any attention as she walked through the halls, stopping to chat with the women whom she passed. She made her way to the women's lavatory. There was enough room for four women at a time. White tiles on the floor and light blue tile on the walls reflected the light that came through the frosted glass windows near the ceiling. She didn't have to wait long before a young blonde ensign entered.

The ensign looked up in surprise. "I know you. You took care of me when I had appendicitis. You've come a long way to use a lavatory."

"I'm glad you know me. It makes this easier. I don't have a lot of time and I need to ask as many women as I can if they've been harassed and then ask if it was reported. No one has to testify if they don't want to."

"This is about Petty Officer Carter, isn't it?"

"Yes, I'm trying to help."

"I reported mine and nothing happened. It still happens. I know several others, too. You stay here and I'll send them here. It's the best place to talk as long as you don't talk too loud. I don't mind testifying if something will happen this time."

By late afternoon, Neenaa had the names of fourteen women, eight of whom had filed complaints. It was too late in the day to shop. Arriving home, she found the Chief sitting on a bench in front of the cottage. He was staring at the bay through a gap in the trees. She sat down on his lap and put her arms around his neck. With her head resting on his shoulder, she spoke quietly to him. "It's bad. There are a lot of women being bothered. There's everything from nasty comments to being grabbed and fondled. I have the names the Captain wanted. I hope he can do something."

The Chief held her closely. "If anyone can make something happen, it's him; you know that. I'm more worried about his wedding plan."

"Alexandria's right for him. She's like us. She doesn't have to be with him every minute."

"Kira is her problem, I think. She wants to keep Kira, but she's afraid to file papers. She fears it'll cause attention, which, if left alone, might not be a problem."

Neenaa sighed. "I guess the most we can do is make the wedding as beautiful as we can. I'll get fruits and flowers, maybe some cloth to put on the altar, and wrap the posts. I'm afraid this could be a big disaster."

The Party

The Captain sat under a tree at the edge of the beach. He watched the preparations for the party for the crew and their families. His head was down and he slowly moved sand around with his foot. He turned at a sound next to him. "Arku, it's still early for the party."

"I came to tell you everything will be ready for the wedding. I have a few women that will help with the dressing. I can see that is not where your mind is."

The Captain continued to move sand around with his foot. "This is such a beautiful Island. Everything is peaceful and happy. I found some ugly things, and it bothers me."

"Yes, bad things can be brought to the Island from the outside. Like weeds, they are removed one at a time. It can take hands of more than one man. Remember, it always starts with one pair of hands. I have a pair of hands I will lend." Arku left as quietly as he had arrived.

The sun lowered, and the sky turned pink with streaks of red.

"This is where you're hiding. Starting the party early?" Alexandria sat down next to the Captain. She didn't try to hide her leg as the fabric slid. "The Chief said to give this list to you."

"No, just thinking. I've fought many battles, but now I face one I'm not sure I can win." He took the list and glanced over it.

"Captain, I've seen you plan and seen you fight. You make a plan and then take the actions you need to. I've never seen you worry. It's not like you to worry. Does worrying help?" She rested her hand on his leg.

"You're right. It doesn't help."

"Just do your best."

"I will. Alexandria, there something I want to ask you."

"Captain! Captain! The Admiral is looking for you." Marie arrived, out of breath.

"Now?"

"He's by the roasting spit. He doesn't look happy."

"What now?"

As the Captain got closer, he could see the Admiral was in shorts and a flowered shirt. He was talking with Chef Joan and both Pilots. "Looking for me, Admiral?"

"Captain, you've always been a man I could count on and you've also been a big pain in my backside. I even let that trick of yours with the taking weeks to get Pilots slide because they deserved tickets. Now you've stirred up a nest."

"I haven't done anything, Admiral."

"You told me I should go talk to the ground crews. I just came from there. I seem to have a number of crews who are out of hand and, when out of my sight, show a total lack of professionalism and respect. Now I have to fix this. It seems the Harbor Master has complained before to my assistant, but I never heard a word. I can't get rid of all of them, or this place would be empty."

"Admiral, it's worse than that. The court martial I talked to you about … I had some checking done. I have a list of names of women that have been bothered and even turned in complaints. The complaints were ignored, handled by your same assistant. I think we need to make some plans. I'll come to your office in the morning. Stay and have some roast pig. I think you should get to know the crew better."

"Thanks, Captain. Pilots, things have happened quickly and I haven't had a chance to tell you. Congratulations. The ground crews don't want to stop talking about you two. They had some good words for the Pilot trainee you have. I wish my crews were as skilled."

The party started and, as the Captain walked off to find Alexandria to dance with, he gave a warning. "Don't let Marie touch the coconuts."

84
July 16, 1898
8 AM
The Galley

The smell of cooking bacon filled the galley. Chef Joan hummed as she cooked. The Captain had a cup of coffee in his hand as he watched her. "Don't forget; I'm a good sampler."

Alexandria got up to refill her cup. "Why not just have bacon for breakfast?"

Chef Joan laughed. "You'll get some bacon soon, Captain." She noticed Marie and Victoria coming through the hatch. They both wore the wrap of the Island. "Good morning."

"Marie, how was your day yesterday?"

"I never would have dreamed a place could be as beautiful as this. There are so many colors and all the growing things. The air is clean and smells nice. I wasn't sure about the walking around naked though."

The Captain coughed into his cup. "What? You went naked?"

"I might as well have been. My naked leg was hanging out, and my naked belly was showing too. If a good breeze had come up, the world would have seen me naked under there, too."

"Please stop; I don't need that in my head." His eyes did a quick up and down look at Alexandria.

"It's okay, Captain. Everyone else was dressed the same way. No one stared and it's very cool to wear in the heat. I like it."

"Chef, is my bacon ready?" He rested his head in his hands, with his elbows on the table. "I need to get you a guard to keep you out of trouble, boys are going to be chasing you."

Alexandria stepped to the side of the Captain. The split in her skirt pressed against his arm. "Captain, are you starting to notice girls?"

Changing Times

Admiral's Office
11 AM

The Admiral stood looking out the window to the bay while the Captain talked. "Admiral, it comes down to the training and supervision, or should I say the lack of it. The senior staff have gotten complacent. Too many of the junior officers are from money, were raised poorly, and think they're privileged. The seniors need a kick in the pants and the juniors, too. The worst ones should go. Promote within the ranks and fill in the bottom with new blood."

The Admiral turned. "I'm one of the complacent senior officers. I should kick myself out of the service."

"You're not complacent anymore. The service needs you to turn things down the right path. From what I've seen, those same troubles aren't just here."

There was a knock on the door and Arku entered. Both the Admiral and the Captain bowed to him.

"Is something wrong, Arku? You've never visited my office before."

"Soon you may need my strength to help."

"Help with what?"

"To clean the Island. If you have people that will not listen to you, and what you need to do, tell them I said that if the Island is not cleaned, all must leave." Arku bowed indicating there was to be no further discussion and left.

"What was that about?"

"Admiral, it's about pulling weeds and extra hands. The first weed pulling starts tomorrow. We need to get a good start on this before I go out hunting the general that wants Alexandria or me dead."

"I admit I had my doubts about the court-martial tomorrow, but it's all a symptom of a disease."

The Captain and the Lady Fair

The Brig
12:30 PM

The room was bare, except for four chairs and a table. "Petty Officer Carter, is it okay if I just call you 'Carter?' "

"Sir, that's no problem. You're a civilian."

"Most of the time, yes. Call me Captain. Are you all right? Need anything?"

"Just a job. I know tomorrow will be my last day."

"Giving up?"

"No, sir, but I've been outgunned. I'll get it on record as to what happened, but it's obvious where this will go."

"I stopped by to let you know you're not alone in this. Let's talk about what you do and what you want to do. What you would like to really do in the service." They talked until the guard told them their time was up.

The Chief's Home
1:30 PM

Neenaa washed dishes while the Captain and the Chief talked. "Chief, I need you to do something for me. It won't take long. You're the only one I can ask. I need you to talk to someone and get some information for me."

"Not a problem, Captain."

"There's something else. I need a guard for Marie."

The Chief tensed up and Neenaa stopped washing. "Someone gunning for Marie?"

"No, Chief. She needs to be protected from herself."

"I'll help, but I don't know what to do."

"She's of age, but she's still very young and has never been on her own. Neenaa, will you help the Great Chief look out for Marie?"

"Me?"

"I'm not doing this right, and you can say 'no' and it won't be a problem. Can you take her in?"

"If that is what she wants. She's a young woman and will be fine. Don't get so overprotective you smother her. Besides, I think you'll find it impossible to get her off the Lady Fair if what Chief tells me is true."

85
July 17, 1898
9 AM
Court Martial

The courtroom was a plain room, with large windows opened to allow the air to breeze through. A large, raised bench at the front could hold three judges, but only one was in place for the court martial. Next to it, at a small table, sat a court reporter. At the two desks in front of the judge's bench were six chairs each. Lt. Mason, Petty Officer Carter, and the Captain, in his white dress uniform from the Lady Fair, sat at one. At the prosecutor's table were the attorney, Lt. Manson, and the four accusers, Ensigns Carver, Hackett, Booth, and Leach. They sat smiling as if they had no cares in the world. Behind the tables for the court was an array of two dozen empty chairs. A guard stood at the back of the room, next to the door.

The Captain sat with a blank face as he ignored the reading of the formal charges and the opening argument by the prosecutor. He started paying attention when Lt. Mason rose.

"Your Honor, the defense pleads 'not guilty' on the grounds of self-defense." He sat back down as Judge Lt. Commander Wells exploded in a verbal tirade.

"That's the most ridiculous thing I've ever heard. I already reviewed your plan of defense and told you it was unacceptable to this court, as there's not a single shred of proof that the actions your client claims against the accusers ever happened. I'll accept the plea of 'guilty' now so we can get on with our day."

Lt. Mason rose back to his feet, unruffled by the judge's rant. "Your Honor, I do have witnesses to call who can verify Lt. Carter's claims."

"There are no witnesses; the only subpoena you requested was denied. Who are these supposed witnesses? The prosecutor must be made aware of any witnesses so he can interview them. As there has been no filing, I can't allow it. While we're on the subject of what's allowed, what is Captain Castellan doing here?"

"He is here as a friend to the court, your honor. As to the witnesses, I couldn't and can't supply the names, as I don't know them."

Judge Lt. Commander Wells turned red in the face. "You mock this court. I'll have you up on charges."

"I would like to call my first witness, that I did request a subpoena for, Lt. Commander Whelps."

"That subpoena was denied."

"Your Honor is correct; it was denied, but he is here to testify. The subpoena only forces a person to court. He's here without a subpoena. Of course, you can deny it and then I'll file for a mistrial and a new trial can be set up."

The judge clenched his fists and gritted his teeth. "Very well; I'm sure the only thing he'll tell us is there is no documentation and that the claims were never submitted. When he's done, I expect an immediate change of plea to 'guilty'. Guard, see if the witness is in the hall."

The Captain and Carter sat calmly. The Captain wrote a note on the pad in front of him and slid it over so she could read it. "*Trust me. Help is here.*"

The guard opened the door and looked into the hall. He snapped to attention and held the door open. Lt. Commander Whelps came through the door, followed by the Admiral. The entire courtroom stood and came to attention. Expectations were that the Admiral would tell them to take their seats and resume, but that didn't happen. The Admiral indicated that the Lt. Commander take a seat on the stand.

"I heard that a subpoena was requested, but it never showed up. I thought I would save this court some effort and brought along the Lt. Commander." He turned and sat at the defense table. Seeing the note the Captain had written, he picked up a pencil and underlined its words. Petty Officer Carter sat, wide-eyed and nervous.

"Please, continue."

They all resumed their seats. The Judge cleared his throat several times. "It seems you have a witness. Ask your questions."

Lt. Mason rose and addressed the witness, who was squirming in his chair. "Lt. Commander, do you recognize the accused?"

"Yes, I have seen her at the Message Center."

"Let's not tire the court with games. You know what and why I asked? I'll make it easy on you. Did the accused come to your office and make a complaint of harassment?"

"Yes."

"In writing?"

"Yes."

"When asked if you had any documentation, you said there was none. Is that correct?"

"Yes."

"Still going to play games, I see."

The judge banged his gavel. "Show some respect to a superior officer."

"Why is there no documentation if she made a written complaint?"

"I decided there was no merit to it and threw it away. There is no documentation."

"Was the complaint against the accusers in this courtroom?"

"Yes."

"Lt. Commander, I'm sure you're an intelligent man and can see ahead as to what is going to happen out of all this."

The Lt. Commander's head drooped. "Yes."

The judge banged his gavel again. "This court does not believe in crystal balls and predictions. Please keep your questions germane to the case at hand."

The Captain wrote another note: "I think I can see his future."

The courtroom was quiet, except for birds chirping outside, the breeze through the windows felt cool.

"Lt. Commander, how many others made complaints against the accusers?"

The judge banged the gavel one more time. "That is not relevant. Only the complaints relevant to this case apply. Any other accusation would be a separate matter, and separate cases, should they come to trial."

The Admiral spoke up. "I want to know the answer to that and stop banging that gavel! Well, Lt. Commander?"

"There were over twenty in all, over a period of the last six months."

"And you decided they were not founded, even after twenty complaints?"

"It was a matter of priority."

"Priority? Please explain that."

The Lt. Commander sighed and slumped into the chair. "The complaints were by female petty officers against ensigns. If the petty officers wish to leave the service, they can. The ensigns are just starting careers, and I saw no reason to destroy careers over something so trivial."

Lt. Mason was quiet for a moment as he took that in. "Lt. Commander, you were given the function of hearing harassment complaints. Doesn't that imply you were to represent the harassed, not the accused?"

"My job was to make the complaints go away. The service doesn't need this kind of trouble."

Lt. Whelps looked back at the Admiral.

"Do what you need to do, Lieutenant." The Admiral gave a slight nod.

"Lt. Commander, did the Admiral tell you to make the problems go away?"

"No, I just knew it was best for the service."

"Does the prosecution have any questions for my witness?"

"Just one, Lt. Commander … you weren't subpoenaed, so why are you here?"

"The Admiral asked me to come to the court."

"Why did he ask you to come?"

"You would have to ask him that."

The prosecutor sat back down. All the smiles at the table were gone.

The judge paused. "Since there're no other questions for this witness, he may be excused. Is that all, Lt. Mason?"

The lieutenant looked down at a note that the Captain had written before. "Your Honor, I have a few more witnesses I wish to bring in at this time."

"I thought you said you don't know who they are."

"I still don't, your honor. They're in the hall, waiting."

"I can't allow no-name witnesses to …."

"I'll go bring them in." The Admiral cut the judge off in mid-sentence and rose to go to the door. He opened it and waved to unseen figures in the hall. Fourteen female petty officers filed in and took seats behind the defense table.

The accusers' faces went pale.

"Your honor, these women have been harassed, slandered, and groped by the accusers. It is clear that the accusers have been doing this for some time and feel they can get away with it. We can spend all day talking to these women, but I think the accusers know what they will have to say. The look on their faces tells me they know full well what will happen if they start speaking in this courtroom. This all points to what Petty Officer Carter has stated. She has been harassed and, when she complained through proper channels, nothing happened. In her defense, she attacked to get them to stop. That, your honor, is self-defense."

The Admiral rose. "Lt. Commander, I think we're done here. Now bang your gavel and find the defendant 'not guilty.'"

The judge, with gritted teeth, did just that.

The Admiral walked over to the prosecutor's table and looked down on the four ensigns. "Your fun is over. I hope you enjoyed it because it has cost you. I suggest you have your resignations, accepting a reduced rank or request for discharge, on my desk in the morning. You will not be confirmed to 'ensign.' If I have to go through the court-martial proceedings, I will, but then that allows for brig time. Your choice."

All four accusers sat slumped in their chairs.

"Captain, I see now why you win your battles. You hit hard and don't play by the rules." The Admiral patted his shoulder.

The petty officers behind the defense table all rose and saluted the Admiral.

The Admiral smiled at Petty Officer Carter. "You have a good friend sitting next to you. Relax today, but please come to my office this afternoon. Call my secretary for a time. I'll be busy this morning, pulling weeds with the Captain."

86
July 17, 1898
10:00 AM
The Admiral's Office

When they entered the office, the Captain took a seat, and the Admiral went to stand in front of the window. "Captain, I envy you. You have a great deal of freedom, still get to fly, and have a great ship and a greater crew. Today wasn't flying an airship into a battle, but today felt as good as one. I can see I have many battles yet to come."

Changing Times

The Captain nodded as he spoke. "Yes, and the coming ones will be just as important, if not more so than any fought in the air. It'll be much easier if you can get the full backing of the President."

The Admiral turned away from the window, sat behind his desk, and wrote a note. "First, I need to clear my afternoon and set up appointments for the judge who is not going to like the meeting at all and Petty Officer Carter who will. She did everything right, and I failed her with my choice of Harassment Officer."

"Might I make a suggestion, sir?"

"Since when did you get so formal with me? Tell me any thoughts you have as I need all the help I can get."

The Captain chuckled. "Maybe I felt you deserved just a bit of special respect from me for your help this morning. You could have avoided a lot of headaches by just letting it happen."

"But it wouldn't have been right."

"A wise man told me recently, a job is easier with many hands. You need people that will tell you the truth even if it isn't comfortable. You need to be able to trust them. Perhaps even give suggestions."

"Yes, I do; just where do I start? This is new for me."

"Look at it like anything else, even a war plan, and it's easier. You assign people and just oversee it enough to keep it going the right way. You know I hated committees and all that but, in this case, I think you need a committee to get together, make suggestions, and perhaps review all the fitness reports."

"Fitness reports? Before I forget, how did you get those witnesses so fast, or were they even witnesses?" The Admiral rose with note in hand, crossed to the door, and signaled his secretary to take it.

"They were real witnesses, sir; all had been harassed and several filed complaints. That's why all parties involved gave up so easily. As for the information on who, I asked my Chief's wife to roam around the building and see if she could find any women that had been harassed."

The Captain and the Lady Fair

"Chief Henry Marshal. A good man there. What a pair he and Neenaa are. I hated to lose him when he left. So, you let Lt. Neenaa Marshal do the work."

"Admiral, you may get a lot of grief from many directions, but I think you already have the makings of the committee at hand. Those witnesses this morning, I think they would be happy to dig hard on fitness reports to see if the women are treated fairly or are being passed over for 'men with careers,' and to do the work needed for the reviews. They might be heavy on their opinions, but I think less so than any others you could pick. After a time, if things are corrected a little at a time, they'll be fair."

"Do you have the list of names of the witnesses?"

"Of course." The Captain patted his chest where the inside pocket was.

"Please give my secretary the list and tell her I want to see all of them at three this afternoon. I want to see Lt. Marshal at two and to make the appointment of Petty Officer Carter at one. I'm going to make Lt. Marshal my Harassment Officer."

"I strongly suggest you ask, not order it."

"Good point."

The Captain rose and headed for the door. "One more thing. You might have them check to see if any of the women want to train in a different career. I'll have the Chief come see you at 12:30."

The Chief's Home

"Neenaa, you did a great job. The Petty Officer has been cleared, and the accusers will be demoted or kicked out." The Captain took a sip of his coffee.

"That's great. I'm glad I helped."

"I'm going to tell you something I shouldn't, so when you hear it, please act dumb. I think you should have time to think on it."

"What would that be, Captain?"

"The Admiral is going to ask you to be the new Harassment Officer. You'll get notified shortly that he wants to see you this afternoon."

"Me?"

"I said it would take some thought."

"No thought needed. I'll do it. I'm just surprised he wants me."

"Chief, the waters seems right for you to see the Admiral at 12:30."

"Captain, you and the Admiral are making a lot of changes. They might not be well received, but I'm still with you. It needs to be done."

"If things go right, this Island base will become a dream posting, with only the cream of the crop."

"Captain, Neenaa and I want to know. Have you asked yet?"

"No."

The Admiral's Office
1:00 PM

The Captain strode into the secretary's office. "Is Petty Officer Carter here yet?"

"No, sir, but I'm sure she will be any minute now." She looked behind the Captain and smiled. "You could just turn around and say 'hello.' "

"Captain, I didn't get a chance to thank you properly. I can't believe what happened, but I know I didn't have a chance without your help. Thanks."

"I'd say the Admiral had a big hand in it."

The secretary interrupted the conversation. "You can go in now."

Petty Officer Carter snapped to attention in front of the Admiral's desk and saluted. The Admiral smiled and returned the salute.

"You already know the Chief. We've had an interesting conversation about you. It seems you're wasted in the message department."

The Chief, seated in a chair, gave the petty officer a smile.

"Thank you, sir. Thank you for your help this morning. Thank you, Chief, for the visit yesterday. It helped take my mind off things."

"The Captain visited you and he asked the Chief to talk to you. There was a motive in it. I have a new assignment for you, effective immediately. You're to set up a plan for training women in non-traditional roles in the service."

"Sir?"

"There are many women in roles in the civilian sector the service doesn't allow. I want to change that and have women in all roles. You are to undergo training in a field more suited for your desire and abilities. While doing that, make note of things that work and don't work, and how best to train women to get them started. Once the roles are accepted, they'll be trained the same as the men. First, you'll learn your new job. Once you're trained to your trainer's satisfaction, you'll oversee other women in training, perhaps train them yourself."

"Sir, I understand you want me to train in a new job, but what job? And who is my trainer?"

The Admiral grinned. "You mentioned to the Captain you had joined hoping to be assigned as an engineer, but were assigned to administration instead. He asked the Chief to talk with you to assess your aptitude. You'll need to go to supply, where you'll be issued new uniforms. Although not effective yet, I have a lot of paperwork to do; you'll need uniforms to reflect your proper rank, which will be needed to do the job of planning and training for the new program. Ensign Carter, you'll be an airship engineer. You've already met your trainer, Chief Marshal."

87
July 18, 1898
8 AM
The Galley

The Captain, Alexandria, Victoria, Martin, and Marie sat at the table while Chef Joan made breakfast. It was to be eggs, bacon, and pancakes topped with a whipped cream and slices of chilled, fresh fruit.

The Captain had just poured a cup of coffee when the loud-box from the dock announced there was a visitor at the dock asking for the Chief. The Captain stood. "I'll take care of it. I'll be right back. Chef Joan, extra bacon, please."

Everyone chuckled as Chef Joan commented, "Thanks for telling me. I would never have guessed."

The Captain returned with Petty Officer Carter in tow. "Everyone, this is Petty Officer Carter, soon to be Ensign Carter. She's the Chief's trainee. Onboard, she'll be called Carter. The rank makes it too much of a mouthful. Sit and have some breakfast. We can do introductions and chat."

"I'm too nervous to eat, but thank you." Carter held up her hands to refuse.

"The Chief's at home, so there's no training today. That can start tomorrow. Today is a 'relax day', get to know some of the crew, and get to know the Lady Fair. After breakfast, we'll get you a bunk."

Chef Joan began serving up breakfast. "If the Chief's her trainer, does that mean he's back in the service?"

"No, I have a contract to train her. Marie, as part of the contract, you'll get ground school on the station. When ground school is done, and the pilots say you're ready, then we can see about getting you a ticket."

"Really! Thanks, Captain, I'll do my best to make you proud."

The Captain and the Lady Fair

Chef Joan placed a full plate in front of Carter. Before she could protest, Chef Joan warned her. "I get very upset when people don't eat my cooking. Victoria over there," she said, pointing to Victoria, "can get real scary when I get upset about people not eating."

The Captain spoke through the laughter. "Chef Joan, go easy; she hasn't been here fifteen minutes."

With the first bite of the pancakes, Carter's eyes widened. She had no problem cleaning her plate.

"Alexandria, would you please go to all the crew's homes this morning and tell them I need them and their families at the shrine just before sunset? Tell them to come dressed in formal uniform. Carter, you'll come too, as you're part of my crew now. Martin, you'd be most welcome as well."

"I'll do that. What shall I tell them the occasion is for?" Alexandria asked.

"Tell them … tell them the crew of the Lady Fair is being blessed and we should give a proper acknowledgement by dressing up."

As the day went on, the Captain got more nervous.

The Shrine
Sunset

The shrine had a white cloth on the altar. White cloth draped from each corner of the shelter. Two local women stood at each tent erected several feet to the side and in front of the shrine. A table had been set up off to the side, covered in white cloth and holding breads, fruit, and juices. As the crew and families arrived, Arku stepped out from behind the shrine. Following him was a slim woman, with jet-black hair falling past her waist and carrying a large basket of breads. Her dress was white, with a print pattern of small pink flowers. She walked to the food table, set the basket down, and stood quietly behind the table, watching Arku.

Changing Times

Arku placed a metal cylinder on the altar, turned, and stood waiting in front of it. He was dressed in a long, white robe. On his head was a thin band of gold.

Martin, frozen in place, stood staring at the woman behind the table.

When all the crew arrived, the Captain went over to Victoria and whispered in her ear. She nodded and went to the tent on the left. He spoke quietly to Chef Joan, who then went to the tent on the right. He made his way to the tent that held Victoria.

"Victoria, I have something to ask you, and I only want a 'yes or no' answer, and no questions. Do you wish to spend your life with Joan?"

Victoria's mouth dropped open. She stood stunned for a moment. "What is that question about?"

"Yes or no?"

"Of course; yes."

He opened the tent flap and spoke to the two women as he held open the flap. He pointed at a package at the rear of the tent. "Please help her dress." He left, headed for the other tent.

"Sorry to keep you waiting," he said when he arrived at Joan's tent.

"What's this about, Captain?"

"I have a question for you and I want only a 'yes or no' answer. Do you want to spend the rest of your life with Victoria?"

Chef Joan's face had the same open-mouthed look Victoria's had had. "What?"

"'What' was not an answer option. Yes or no."

"Yes, you already know that."

He opened the tent flap. "Ladies, please help her dress." He pointed to a package at the back of Joan's tent.

He walked over to the Chief. "Chief, good news."

"What's that?"

"Come with me." He started walking to Joan's tent. "So far, I'm still alive. I sort of just asked, and she said 'yes.'"

The Chief looked over his shoulder at Alexandria standing near the altar, with Kira cradled in the sling. "Just now?"

"Yes, the bride is inside this tent changing. When I signal, take her right arm and escort her to the altar. Before I forget, here." He reached into his right pocket, pulled out a ring, and handed it to the Chief.

He looked up again and Alexandria was still at the altar. "Who's in the tent?"

"Joan."

The Captain returned to Victoria's tent. "All dressed?"

"Yes, Captain."

He entered to see Victoria in a ground-length dress with a short train. It was form-fitted and plain white. The right shoulder was bare; the left arm wore a long sleeve to the wrist.

"What's all this about, Captain?"

"Let's go find out, shall we?" He took her left arm in his and walked out of the tent. He waved at the Chief. When the Chief emerged, both pairs slowly walked to the Altar. As they walked and were noticed, a hush fell over the crew and they cleared a path for both to the Altar. Both wore the same style of dress, except for the fact that Joan's featured a bare arm on the left and was long-sleeved on the right and Victoria's was the opposite. Joan and Victoria stood bare shoulder to bare shoulder.

Arku raised his arms and his voice as the crew moved closer. "Friends of Joan and Victoria …" he paused a moment as he took a deep breath of the scent of Jasmine and Gardenia in the air. "As the sun sets on the day, there starts a new beginning." He took Victoria's right hand and Joan's left and joined them.

Kathryn and Diana looked at each other in shock. Carter and Marie stood with open mouths.

Both Joan and Victoria were too stunned to say anything.

Carter looked around to see if she could spot anyone to explain what was happening.

Arku spoke to Joan first. "Joan, have you given your heart and spirit to Victoria?"

"Oh, yes I have."

"Victoria, do you accept what is given to you?"

Changing Times

Victoria was quick to answer. "I do and have."

"Victoria, have you given your heart and spirit to Joan?"

"I do, and I have."

"Joan, do you accept what is given to you?"

"Yes, yes I do."

"You are witnesses to the merging of two spirits to become one in life." He drew a circle on Joan's forehead. "The circle of life." He drew another, so the circles were linked. "Two lives joined." He did the same to Victoria. "Your friends bless your join, I bless your join, and the spirit of Paaku blesses you. Your spirits joined, shall be stronger than alone."

He paused and looked at the Captain, who nodded.

"Our ways are simple; the spirits are now one, but your world is different and we honor that here. Who gives this woman, Victoria, to be joined this day?"

"I, her friend, do." The Captain let go of Victoria's arm and took a half step back.

"Who gives this woman, Joan, to be joined this day?"

Taking the hint, the Chief followed the Captain's example. "I, her friend, do." He took a half step back.

"You both have been given. Do you, Victoria, accept what is given to you?"

Tears streamed down Victoria's face. She managed to get out a whisper. "I do if she'll have me."

"Joan, do you accept what is given to you?"

Joan's crying was coming close to open sobbing. "I do; yes, I do."

"Spirit has been given and received. Now a symbol of the joining."

The Captain pulled a ring from his left pocket and handed it to Victoria. Victoria looked at the silver band and saw the inscription inside, which read "Two spirits as one." She slid it onto Joan's finger.

The Chief handed Joan a ring. She slid it onto Victoria's finger.

Arku turned and picked up the silver cylinder. He presented it to Victoria and Joan. "Your document from the Island, showing you are joined here today."

"Crew of the Lady Fair, welcome the joined spirits of Victoria and Joan."

They all applauded and cheered congratulations. Conversations were lively as they talked over the food.

Martin stepped forward, drawn to the woman whom he had been staring at throughout the ceremony. "Hello, my name is Martin and I have no idea what else to say."

She returned his smile. "I'm Tala; welcome to Paaku."

"Thank you. It's a beautiful Island. I wish I didn't have to leave."

"Why do you have to leave?"

"I have a job I have to go back to."

"Anything else to go back to?"

"No, just work."

"Perhaps you need a new job."

They continued talking well into the night.

The Captain felt a pull on his arm. He turned to see Victoria and Joan staring at him. Victoria hugged him, then whispered in his ear, "When we get back to the ship, I'm going to shoot you."

Joan hugged him and whispered, "When you eat next, I'm going to poison you." They both left, laughing.

The Chief and Neenaa walked up and stared at him. Finally, the Chief spoke. "You're either very brave or crazy. Why didn't you tell us? We asked you if you had asked."

"I didn't lie; I hadn't asked them if they wanted this."

"You knew we thought you meant Alexandria."

"I didn't lie. I didn't ask her, either."

"If those two don't kill you, we will."

"Stand in line; stand in line."

88
July 19, 1898
8 AM
The Galley

The chatter at the table stopped when the Captain came through the hatchway. Alexandria, feeding Kira, paused, then paid more attention to Kira. Marie and Carter looked around at everyone at the table with a puzzled look. Victoria and Joan stared at him.

The Captain looked confused. "Did something happen?"

Victoria rose. "Excuse me; I forgot my revolver."

Joan got up and went to the stove. "Captain, I have a special batch of bacon for you."

"Wait! Wait! I can explain everything." The Captain was backing up, with his hands raised.

"That's fine, Captain. Sit and eat your bacon while we listen." She brought the plate to where he stood. She picked a piece of bacon off the plate, held it to his mouth, and gave him a smile. "Your favorite, Captain. I made this special batch just for you."

The Captain kept his lips tight and shook his head.

Joan pouted. "Victoria, do you see that? He's refusing to eat my cooking."

Victoria stepped to his side and put her arm around his shoulder. "Captain, what's wrong? Please eat Joan's cooking."

The Captain stood still and then ate the bacon.

Victoria ran to the loud-box. "Doc to the galley! Hurry!"

The Captain began spitting out the bacon.

Joan and Victoria went back to the table and both started to eat the bacon from his plate. The crew broke out in laughter.

Joan finally calmed enough to talk. "That was payback, Captain. Doc is at home."

"I'm just going to keep quiet." He sat at his customary place.

Joan put a plate of breakfast in front of him. "Eat up, Captain."

Martin walked in and sat down, yawning.

The Captain grinned. "Late night, Martin?"

"We got to talking, and next thing I knew, it was early morning."

"That can happen. Was she pretty?" The Captain watched Martin to see if he would take the bait.

"She's beautiful and easy to talk to." Martin sat with a smile on his face. "I'm meeting her again today. She's going to give me a tour and tell me about the Island."

"I think the Island's charm has a hold on you."

"It does. What's the plan, Captain? When will we be leaving again?"

"There's a lot happening still. We'll lift in four days. Marie will be in ground school and, until then, the Chief is stopping by to work with Carter and I'll be working with the Admiral on a few projects."

"I think I may stay awhile longer. Now that I'm here, I'll ask. Why did you want me on a vacation here so badly? It's not like we're best friends or you owe me anything."

"I wish I could tell you. You just needed to be here. We'll leave it at that. Joan, do you and Victoria have any plans for the downtime?"

"We thought we would do what we always do: relax, walk around, and chat with people. Nothing special. I'll start checking stocks and resupply before we lift."

The Captain thought for a moment. "Alexandria, why not join me with the Admiral this morning? I think your opinions may help."

"As long as we have a picnic on the beach, Kira and I will be happy to help."

"That takes care of today's planning." The Captain ate slowly, hesitating with each bite.

Kathryn's Home

Kathryn answered a knock at the door. "Joan, Victoria, what brings you here? Is something wrong?"

Changing Times

"No, but we need your help with something. Diana would be of help, too." Joan, followed by Victoria, entered and sat at the kitchen table.

"She'll be dropping by soon. We always get together while the men tend the gardens. Want to wait to tell me what it's about until she gets here?"

They sat chatting about the men and the garden they worked to supply food for themselves; they sold the extra produce at the market in town. Kathryn's kitchen walls were a cool white; shelves around the walls held books, some spices in labeled jars, and small items she had collected at the different ports she had visited. There was a knock at the door and then it opened, with Diana letting herself in. She saw Joan and Victoria seated at the table. "Trouble?"

Victoria laughed. "Yes, but not for us. We think the Captain needs a lesson in meddling without asking first. We need your help with a plan we came up with."

"How can we help? Diana and I will do what we can if it's not going to put us in bad graces with the Captain."

"You'll be fine. We just need you to ask the Admiral for some help. The Captain will be mad at us." Joan perked up. "We have a new trainee working with the Chief, we lift in four days, and Martin has a crush."

"Trainee and a crush? Wait a minute; we have something for you." Kathryn dashed from the kitchen and returned with two wrapped gifts. "These are your wedding gifts. I'll be honest; we thought the Captain was going to get married, so we ordered them. They'll be perfect for you."

Joan and Victoria opened one to see the diaries, pens, and ink. "These are nice."

Diana told them what they had been told about writing down the good things of each day for the future.

Victoria's curiosity was too much. "What do you mean, you thought they were going to get married?"

"We saw him at a jewelry store and asked the shopkeeper after he left. He said he ordered wedding rings. We naturally thought it was for marrying Alexandria."

Joan shared the story about the Captain and a shopkeeper's odd behavior in Feast town at a dressmaker's. Once the stories of the Captain's doings were done, Joan talked about what she knew of the coming lift, the trainee, and Martin's crush on an unknown woman. She explained what she needed from the Admiral, but not the why. Joan and Victoria had put the first steps of revenge in motion.

The Village

Martin and Tala strolled through the village, paying more attention to each other than to the surroundings. Martin was so fascinated with Tala that he failed to notice that the villagers would bow slightly as they passed. They bought some fruit to eat when they went to sit on the beach. The lower the sun got, the closer they sat to each other. When the sun met the horizon, his lips met hers.

89
July 20, 1898
8 AM
The Galley

The Captain interrupted the small talk at the breakfast table. "I see the whole crew is here for breakfast. Anything I should know?"

The Chief spoke up. "We heard we're going to lift soon, so everyone's here to make sure everything's ready, and to meet the newest trainee."

"Yes, we're lifting in three days. I'm sure word will get to General Tarki. Since you're all here, again, I offer any crew that wants to stay behind can do so with no problems. I'm going to cruise around and let the General find us. It'll be dangerous."

Once again, the entire crew refused to be left behind.

"Captain, I'm a trainee pilot, but I'm going. I might not pilot but, if needed, I can be an extra hand at patching holes." Marie smiled and gave a nod of conviction.

Carter added her vote. "I'll do whatever the Chief wants; I can even patch holes too."

"You're all as crazy as I am. Marie, you'd better finish breakfast and get going to class. Martin, you're not part of the crew and don't have a job onboard. I suggest you stay on the Island."

"Captain, as much as I would like to be useful, I think I'd be in the way. I'll stay behind; I just need to find a place to stay while you're gone."

"I'll arrange quarters for you on the station. If you would like, I'll talk to the Admiral and see if he has a use for your observation skills while we're gone. I'm hoping it will be only a few days. I guess that's all for now."

Engine Room 1

Carter, on her back, was deep in the engine mounts of the engine, checking the filter and a pressure line; her legs, from the knees down, were the only things visible. "Chief, the new filter is installed and the pressure line is tight. I think we need to check the part that controls the set speed. The test run didn't feel smooth to me. It felt like it was surging."

"You done under there?"

"Yes, Chief." She started to squirm back out.

The Chief grabbed her ankles and pulled. She slid out with a surprised look on her face. "Thanks, Chief." Her short, tousled hair framed her face. A smudge of grease adorned the end of her nose.

"So you felt a surging. Let's take a look, then." The Chief handed her a rag to wipe her nose.

They took apart the governor and found a little speck of dirt that made it stick on occasion. "Good job, Carter. Let's go on to Engine

Two. We should be able to go over all the engines by tomorrow afternoon."

"Chief, it might be none of my business, but I have a few questions about the Captain. Is he fancy?"

"What?" The Chief was startled by the question.

"I've heard he has never dated a woman; he arranged Joan and Victoria's wedding and set them up together in a cabin. He supports them, so I wondered if he was so understanding because he fancies men."

The Chief laughed hard during the walk to Engine Two.

Phoenix Building
Navigation Class

Marie sat in her assigned seat at the back of the classroom. She was wearing her Lady Fair Pilot uniform. Her red hair was in bright contrast to the tan blouse.

"Gentlemen, I'm your instructor, Chief Ecker. We'll be covering navigation in its two main forms, dead reckoning and celestial. You most often will be using dead reckoning as getting a celestial fix means going to the top of the lift bag to get a clear view. We'll start with dead reckoning. Young lady, you can knit or whatever you normally do. Please don't disrupt the class with silly questions."

Marie's face turned a shade of red in anger but, before she could say anything, the door opened. The Admiral stuck his head in and indicated for the instructor to step outside the classroom.

Chief Ecker smiled at the Admiral. "Sir, how can I help you?"

The Admiral's face turned close to a shade of purple. "First, you can snap to attention when addressing a superior officer."

The instructor dropped the smile and came to stiff attention.

"Why is there a woman in your class?"

"You ordered it, sir. I still have your written order."

"What exactly were those orders?"

Changing Times

"To accept that woman in my class."

"That woman has a name. It's Marie Holmes. She was sent here to learn navigation. It appears, from what I overheard, you have no intention of carrying out my written order. Reread it and you will see it says 'accept and train.' "

"Sir, I just thought this was some joke or something. You can't be serious about training her."

The Admiral stared hard at Instructor Ecker. "So now you've decided which orders to take seriously and which to ignore. You've decided you know better about what I want than I do. In case you're too slow to figure it out, you now have my attention. Your career and future lie with Miss Holmes. Once her classes are done, the best pilots I know will test her to see if she makes the grade. If she fails, we'll be having another talk. I promise you that you will not like it. I suggest you spread the word to all instructors and anyone else that, the next time I find someone not following my orders or deciding what they think I really meant, I'll throw them in the brig first and talk about it later, at my convenience. Have I made myself clear this time, or do you have questions?"

"Clear, sir. I'll ride her to be good, sir."

"You must want the brig. I said teach her, not ride her. I will be checking. Get back in there, apologize to her, and show her respect at all times."

"Yes, sir!" Before the two short words were out of his mouth, the Admiral turned and stormed off. Chief Ecker muttered to himself. "Women pilots; what is this world coming to?"

The class sat in stunned silence as Instructor Chief Ecker stammered his apology.

90
July 20, 1898
7 PM
The Galley

The smells of fresh bread and roast beef filled the galley. Chef Joan had finished serving up dinner and sat down at her usual seat. "How was school today? Was it fun?"

"You make it sound like I'm in my first year of school. It had a bad start, but after the Admiral stopped by, it was very good. The instructor knows what he's talking about and goes over everything very well. I wish I could learn it faster, so I could be of more use here."

"Relax; it'll come soon enough." Joan patted Marie's arm. "Carter, how did your day with the Chief go?"

Victoria laughed. "She sure does sound like a mother."

Chef Joan slapped Victoria's hand. "Don't you start or I'll make special food just for you."

Victoria stuck her tongue out at Joan and laughed. "Not afraid of you. So, Carter, how did your day go with the Chief?"

Marie paused between bites. "Now there are two mothers."

The Captain cleared his throat. "Enough teasing; just tell them how your day went."

Carter giggled. "Yes, Father. It went really well. We fixed a few things that would've been problems later. Chief says I didn't do well on tests for my application when I entered the service because I don't know the names of things. He said I'm worth training, so that's good enough for me."

Alexandria nudged the Captain's arm. "How does it feel to be a father?"

"Can't a man eat in peace?" He sighed heavily and looked down. No one could see his grin.

Victoria changed the subject. "Captain, where's Martin?"

Changing Times

"I imagine he's busy with a certain young lady that caught his interest."

7 PM
The Beach

The sun had set, and the moon was up reflecting off the water. Birds had gone quiet for the night, but the insects still buzzed. Gentle waves made a hiss on the sand as they washed up the beach. Soft breezes from offshore brought the salty smell of the sea.

"Tala, I umm … have strong feelings for you. I know it's fast, but I do. I have a job I have to go back to, but I want to stay here with you. I don't know what to do, other than be honest with you."

"I have feelings for you, too. Things always happen for a reason and I'm sure it'll all work out. I've told Grandfather about you and he's happy with it. He said there might be a job on the Island for you, but he didn't tell me what. Let things happen as they will. When the time comes for you to decide, you'll make the right one."

Martin sat for a while with his arm around Tala's shoulders. "Tell me about the Spirit of the Island."

"I'm sure you have already heard the stories. When you have seen for yourself the power of the Spirit, then I can tell you more. Telling you now would just be a story; after you have seen things, it will have meaning."

"I'll stop asking then. The Captain and crew love this Island. I can see why. It's so beautiful and alive. No gray soot, no loud noises, or people talking too loud."

"The married crew members have homes here; they've all married Islanders."

"So, to have a home, a member has to marry someone from the Island?"

Tala snuggled on Martin's shoulder. "No, someone could live here without marriage, but it hasn't happened. It might someday if it's the right thing."

"More of the Island Spirit story?"

"Part of it, yes." She paused and stared out at the moonlight sea. In a quiet voice, she spoke again. "Martin, there's a storm coming. Stay away from the station."

"What's that about?"

"Just a feeling. If you care for me as much as you say, just do as I ask and don't ask questions."

"Big storm?"

"One that brings death."

91
July 25, 1898
9 AM
The Bridge

The Lady Fair traveled in slow circles for two days, waiting for General Tarki to make his attack. Joan sat on the couch with Alexandria, watching the Captain pace back and forth across the bridge. "It's starting."

Alexandria looked around, confused. "What's starting?"

"He paced like that just before we went to rescue you. Something will happen soon, and it won't be good."

Before Alexandria could ask her another question, the Captain gave orders. "Pilot Kathryn, bring us about on a course for home, engines full." He stopped in front of the loud-box. "All hands to stations. Sunburst crews to stations. Don't raise them in place yet; let's keep it a surprise."

Changing Times

Pilot Trainee Marie, at the chart table, gave the pilot a heading. "Take a heading 100 degrees, at full speed; we'll make the Island in thirty minutes."

Figures ran across the deck to stations. Victoria, carrying her rifle and wearing her long coat and lucky red suit, strode to the forward Sunburst station to man both launchers.

Pilot Diana entered the bridge and checked the chart where Marie had plotted the course. "Good job, Marie." She went to stand next to Pilot Kathryn.

The far talker crackled to life with static. A shouting voice came over the noise. "Station Paaku under attack. Any warships return at once." The far talker fell silent.

The Captain turned to Joan. "I know it's not something you've done before, but would you please go up to the spotters' nest?"

"On my way, Captain." She left at a run.

Minutes went by. Alexandria got up and stood by the controls for the shield, in case it was needed. "I have been missing Kira, but now I'm glad she's with Neenaa."

The Captain looked at her. "I would rather have had you stay behind, too."

The loud-box clicked on, passing through Joan's voice. "Captain, there's smoke on the horizon. I can just see the top of the mountain." Precious minutes passed and Joan's voice came on again. "Captain, it looks like two big airships circling at the station. I see flames on the ground where the ships dock."

"Good job, Chef. Be sure to look around in all directions. We don't want any surprises." He left the bridge and went to the cannon above.

The Captain looked through the far glasses and saw two gunships circling above the moored airships, firing down on them with full broadsides of cannon fire. The gunships were half the size of the Dreadnaughts but were designed for maximum firepower against other airships. He gave new orders. "Steer directly to the docking station, drop to ten feet, and be ready to start the shield. I'm going to use the cannon, so your visibility will be restricted."

The plating swung away from the cannon and covered the bridge windows. He aimed toward the two attacking ships and fired. The range was too long, and the shells fell short, but he kept a slow, steady fire. Each shot was closer. Both the attacking airships turned to face the Lady Fair and head towards them. He raised the cannon shields back up and returned to the bridge.

Alexandria looked worried. "The cannon not working, Captain?"

He smiled at her. "It works fine. I can't risk shooting at the airships. A shell could pass through and hit the Island. I just wanted to get their attention and get them to come out to us. Pilots, full stop, please. Alexandria, when we're at full stop, start the shield."

The Lady Fair lowered to just above the water and Alexandria started the shield. "Pilots, set us for a 300-foot pop-up." The Captain used the loud-box. "All hands, we'll be doing a pop-up. It will be short notice, so stay alert." He turned to Alexandria. "Please explain to Marie about a pop-up, so she can be ready for it."

They didn't have to wait long before the two gunships opened fire from 500 feet away. The shells exploded on impact with the shield. They fired shell after shell, trying to get through. As they fired, they took up positions on each side, 50 feet above and 300 feet away from the Lady Fair.

Kathryn watched the shells exploding. "Now what do we do, Captain?"

"We wait for them to either get tired of shooting or run out of shells. I just wish they were closer." He went to the loud-box. "Chef Joan, come on down and be so kind as to take cool drinks to the crew on deck. Pop back up there when that's done. Crew, act like you don't even know they're out there." He filled his coffee cup from the ever-present pot of coffee and walked down and out onto the deck.

Changing Times

The Captain made a show of strolling the deck and drinking his coffee as if he had no cares and was relaxing for the day. The cannon fire from the attacking ships increased.

Marie asked the question that was on everyone's mind. "What's he doing?"

Kathryn smiled. "Besides making them real angry, I have no idea. He's making them spend more shells, but that isn't going to make them get any closer."

"If he wants them closer, we can do that easy." Marie had a big smile and a gleam in her eye.

After chatting for a moment, Kathryn turned to Alexandria. "Everything is all set. All you have to do is push your magic button when the Captain says so. Then we'll be back. Okay, ladies, let's go see Doc." Kathryn, Diana, and Marie left the bridge.

The Captain had finished his cup and had walked to each station to tell them to look like they were polishing anything at hand. As he turned to go back to the bridge, he froze in place when he saw Doc, Kathryn, Diana, Marie, and Carter walk onto the deck with towels in hand.

"What are you ladies doing?"

"Just relaxing like you are, Captain. Lucky we bumped into Carter on the way. It's too bad Joan and Victoria are busy." They spread the towels on the deck and removed their robes to reveal that they were wearing the small two-piece swimsuits of the Island. They lay down on the towels as if sunning themselves, even though they were in the shade of the lift bag.

The cannon fire stopped. The Captain left the deck for the bridge.

Alexandria greeted him. "Welcome back, Captain. Enjoying the view?"

"I know they wouldn't abandon station without a good reason, but I wish I knew what it was. All that's happened is that they stopped wasting shells."

"Captain, you're such a simple man at times. Let me try to help you understand. If I had you stand at the bow, and you saw me strip naked here in the bridge, don't you think you'd want to get closer? Or perhaps my being naked doesn't interest you?"

The Captain blushed with the quick flash of memory of the times she had been naked under a sheet. "I get your point." He turned to stare out the window to hide his embarrassment. Both attacking ships began to drift closer. "This is not the way I was taught to fight a battle, but it is my style. Toss the rules and cheat."

Joan's voice came over the loud-box. "Captain, an airship on the horizon is approaching from behind. It looks like there are two other warships trying to intercept it. About twenty minutes away, I would guess."

"Good job, Chef."

The Captain watched the attackers on each side draw still closer. At 100 feet away and almost level, he called over the loud-box. "Pop in five!"

The women on deck waved at the approaching ships.

"Now!" The Lady Fair popped up 300 feet. "Fire when ready!"

The crew scrambled to the launchers and swung them up into place on their hinges. The Lady Fair was too high and too close for the attackers to fire, but the ballast they were dumping would get them higher soon. The Captain dumped ballast to keep above them. The crew started firing the Sunbursts into the bags of the attackers. The rockets hit the bags and the fishhooks held them in place as the rockets burned out, followed by an explosion of sparks. Spots of flame erupted on the bags wherever the sparks hit and continued to burn. In less than two minutes, both attackers were splashing down into the water. The flaming bags draped over the ships and engulfed them in fire to start the decks burning. The burning bags on the airships trapped all the men inside.

The women ran back to stations and were in place before the attacking airship's deck had caught fire.

"Pilots, turn us about and full throttle. Let's see what's happening behind us. Chief, I need the engines pushed hard. I need speed."

"We're working on it, Captain."

Shortly after, they were at full speed. With a lurch, they started to turn to starboard. "Captain, we've lost number two on the starboard side." Pilot Kathryn adjusted the rudder and the port engines to straighten out again.

The Captain waited for a report from the Chief as he knew he would report in once he knew what had happened.

The Captain looked through the far glasses to see a Dreadnaught being approached on either side by two gunships. The center one appeared to have service markings; the other two had the markings of Boschland.

The Chief's yell came over the loud-box. "Doc to sickbay; I'm bringing in Carter. She's been steam-burnt bad."

92
July 25, 1898
9:45 AM
The Bridge

"Pilot Kathryn, keep us head-on to the center airship. Keep us high." The Captain used the loud-box to alert the crew. "Stay on station; Sunbursts ready. We're going head-on to the center airship; the other two are the targets. Don't hit the center one."

Smoke from cannon fire belched from the sides of the three airships. All three were rising, trying to get above each other, but they stayed even. Cannon fire was blowing chunks out of each airship. The center airship was losing the fight, having to fight in two directions at once. All the engines of the service airship were blowing steam, and the propellers had stopped; it could no longer move to get away. The attackers were now aiming for the cannons that still fired in defense. The bow cannons on the decks of the outside airships began to swing towards the Lady Fair. Victoria picked up her rifle and took aim at the cannon crews. After four shots, the cannons dropped back into a resting position. She stood ready at the starboard bow Sunburst. Target lined up, she pressed the trigger switch, there was a short hiss, and the rockets burst forward from the mounting rack. She had fired as soon as the airship was in range and dashed to the port Sunburst. As soon as she had the second attacker lined up, she pressed the trigger. There was a short hiss, then the rockets flew, leaving a trail of smoke. As the rockets impacted the nose of the second airship, the nose of the first ship began to burn. The flames were blown back across the bag by the wind of the airship's movement through the air.

"Up and over at best speed, Pilot. Get us out of range before they wise up. Make them chase us with altitude."

The Chief's voice came over the loud-box. "Sorry for the delay, Captain. Starboard engine is ready for power."

"You heard it; full throttle, all engines Pilot."

As the Lady Fair rose and passed over the service airship, the crew manning the Sunbursts fired down on the bags of the attacking ships. Trails of smoke from the rockets showed a perfect path to each target. As the other rockets had done, the hooks caught on the fabric and held them in place. They spun and wobbled in place as if trying to bore through. When the rockets spent themselves, they exploded in sparks. The bags quickly became fully engulfed in flames. As the bags lost lift gas, the ships plummeted down over 2000 feet to the sea below.

"Pilot, bring us about and alongside. I'll be in sickbay."

The Sickbay

The Captain entered the sickbay and saw Carter lying on a bed. A wet cloth with chips of ice covered her face and right arm. "How bad, Doc?" As he spoke, the Chief came in behind him.

"She's out for now. It looks like she hit her head and knocked herself out. That was a blessing; the pain would have been extreme. I gave her something to keep her out. The right side of her face and her arm are very bad. I'll take another look after the ice cools the skin down. There isn't much I can do with burns this bad. Normally it would be soaking and removing dead skin every couple of days. I'll do my best before it comes to that."

"Any idea what happened, Chief?" The Captain rested his hand on the Chief's shoulder.

"A steam feed line blew; pipe split wide open. I think it hit her face first; then she raised her arm to protect her face. Probably fell or jerked back and knocked herself out. I found her on the deck under the steam blast. Not her fault at all. No way to know if a pipe will split like that. Doc, please give her your best."

"I'll be on the bridge. Come on, Chief, let's go see what shape the dreadnaught's in."

They headed for the bridge at a quick pace. "Don't try blaming yourself, Chief; you know it's not your fault."

"I know, but I feel bad about it."

On the bridge, they found that they were next to the dreadnaught. They were close enough to easily read the name of the ship. "It's the dreadnaught Peregrine. Looks like the engines are useless. I don't see any big holes in the bag. Fires seem to be under control. I guess it could have been worse." The Captain went out on the deck and leaned against the railing on the port side nearest the airship.

The Captain yelled across to the airship. "Ahoy, Peregrine, what assistance do you need?"

A pilot stepped out of the bridge onto the catwalk. "Ahoy, Lady Fair, we have lots of wounded; engines are down with no spare parts. No holes."

"I'll get you some help. Send over a line for a Boson's."

The Captain hurried to the sickbay. "Doc, is she okay?"

"Of course she's not." Her voice was sharp and short.

"Doc, take a deep breath. I mean, is she okay to leave alone for a while? The Peregrine has lots of casualties and could use the help."

"I don't want to leave her."

"Doc, I'll be on deck, setting up a Boson's chair. To come or not is your decision. You know what it's like with large numbers of wounded all needing help at the same time and not enough help to go around. I did tell you that someday you would be the only help for miles." A sigh escaped his lips as he made his way back on deck.

Two crew members of the Peregrine worked at the nose cannon. They put a lead ball, with a line attached, into the cannon with a light charge. They fired it across to the deck of the Lady Fair. The Chief grabbed the line and started pulling it across. Attached to the end of the line was a heavier line. As they were attaching the line to the crane to secure it, Doc appeared on deck with a large bag in hand.

"Diana and Joan are watching over Carter. I'll be back as soon as I can. Captain, thanks for the reminder." As soon as it was attached, she climbed into the Boson's chair and was pulled across to the Peregrine.

The Captain watched her as she slid across to the Peregrine. "Okay, Chief, let's rig up a tow line and get them home."

The Peregrine

Doc was pointed to the sickbay by a crew member spattered in blood. The passageway was filled with wounded men groaning in pain on the deck. She found the doctor in charge headed into the sickbay from checking the men in the passageway. "How can I help?"

"Just what I need, a nurse." He turned his back on her.

"My name is Doctor Melissa Farmer; if you don't need an extra pair of hands, I'll go back to my ship, where I have someone that will be happy for my help."

"I'll deal with the ones I can save. Go try to ease the suffering of those that are beyond help in the passageway. They have a mark of iodine on their foreheads."

She turned to go to the passageway. "Remind me to ask later if you're really a doctor."

Changing Times

Doc checked the men quickly, took a deep breath, and began to hold each one's hand, one by one, trying her best to make each one just well enough to live until proper treatment could be given. She hurried as quickly as she could. The crew watched her going from man to man, applying a tourniquet here and there and holding their hands. Each man seemed to rally, but after each one, Doc looked more tired. After the last man, she collapsed against the bulkhead. The last man kept a hold of her hand. "Thanks for caring, Doc."

The Lady Fair

The trip took over an hour to get back towing the Peregrine. The station was in shambles. Ships still burned at the moorings. Figures ran, trying to control the fires, but the ships were destroyed. The Lady Fair slowly made her way to the moorings farthest away from the devastation. They waited for an hour before a ground crew could be freed up, to grab the lines of the dreadnaught Peregrine, and pull her to a mast. The Lady Fair docked without help once she let the towline go. A steady stream of wounded were taken off the Peregrine and taken to the hospital. A Pilot made his way from the Peregrine to the Lady Fair.

"Ahoy, Lady Fair!"

The Captain leaned over the rail. "Lieutenant, what can I do for you?"

"It's your Doc; she collapsed treating the wounded. She's on the way to the hospital."

The Captain ran from the deck and all the way to the hospital, only slowing to check each stretcher as he passed. He finally found her in a hospital hallway, still on a stretcher. He knelt beside her. "Doc, Doc, wake up, Doc." He patted her hand as he talked to her. "Come on, wake up."

Doc's eyes fluttered and then opened. "Hello, Captain. What are you doing on the Peregrine?"

The Captain and the Lady Fair

The Captain heaved a sigh of relief. "You're in the base hospital. You collapsed. I think you tried to do too much. Just rest; I think, with rest, you'll be fine."

"I need to help those men."

"No, your part is done. All the men are being taken care of."

"Thanks, Captain."

"For what?"

"Making me see I was needed. I think I saved one or two."

A passing doctor stopped at her stretcher. "Doctor, you didn't save one or two. You saved all of them. I apologize for my attitude before on the Peregrine. I don't know how, but every man I gave up on is alive. You were right to question me. Compared to you, I'm not fit to hand out bandages for cut fingers. Well done."

"I should apologize to you. You had to make hard decisions based on what you could do with what you had."

He nodded then continued down the hall, looking for his crew.

"Doc, when you can walk, we'll get you back aboard. Do you want me to transfer Carter here?"

"No, they can't handle any more, and wouldn't be able to give her the proper care she needs."

It took another half-hour before Doc was able to struggle upright. The Captain helped her as they made their way back to Lady Fair. In the sickbay, he found Diana, Joan, and the Chief sitting quietly, staring at Carter. He had Doc rest in the sickbay in a chair next to Carter. She folded her arms on the bed, laid her head down, and slept.

"Chief, set up a 24-hour dual watch topside. Have them shout if they see anything bigger than a bird in the air or the sea."

93
July 25, 1898
5 PM
The Sickbay

Doc woke up to the sound of voices. Carter was awake and talking with Joan. "So, I left home and joined the service."

"Carter, you're awake. Do you hurt anywhere?" Doc slid off her makeshift bed and went to Carter's bedside.

"My face is starting to hurt some."

"The pills I gave you when you came in are wearing off. I'll fix you up right away." Doc hurried to the pill cabinet and found what she wanted.

"Doc, Joan won't tell me. How bad is it?" Carter spoke in a quiet, nervous voice.

Doc went to her side and removed the cloth on her face. Carter looked out of her good left eye; the other was swollen shut. The steam burn covered the whole right side of her face. Doc gave her the pills and a sip of water. "I won't lie to you; it's bad, but I'm going to take care of you. Don't you worry about a thing."

"Back home, I saw a man burned. He hurt for a long time and had horrible scars. Tell me the whole truth, Doc."

Doc sighed. "Carter, like I said, it's bad. Often burns like this means weeks of pain, pulling dead skin off, and, yes, scars. I'm going to try something new that should help."

"Doc, you know what hurts the most? I'll have to leave the Lady Fair."

The Captain walked in at the last comment. "Who said you have to leave? No matter where you go, you'll have to do something. You might as well stay here and work when you get better. Where else will you get a private doctor and a first class chef to cook your favorites?"

Joan perked up. "You must be getting hungry. What's your favorite?"

"Well, my mother used to make me my favorite when I was hurt or sad: beef stew, mashed potatoes, green beans, and hot rolls with lots of butter." The Captain, Doc, and Joan started laughing. "Did I say something funny?"

Joan smiled. "Now we know why the Chief likes you. That's his favorite too."

"Joan, why don't you go start some? Captain, if you leave us in peace, I'll get started with taking care of Carter."

"Yes, Doc, I'll be on the bridge. Joan, let's leave them in peace. And Doc."

"Yes, Captain?"

"Go easy, you are just recovering yourself."

Doc nodded then sat next to Carter and took her hand.

7 PM
The Sickbay

The Captain walked into the sickbay just ahead of Joan, carrying a food tray. He saw Carter sleeping and Doc with her head down on her arms. "Doc? You okay?"

She raised her head and the red eyes and tear streaks gave him the answer. "Not much of anything has changed; I failed again."

"Doc, you're still worn out. Don't push it. Relax a few days and regain your proper strength and try again."

Carter woke and stirred. "Everything okay, Doc?"

"Everything's fine. I've just had a very long day and it's made me tired and moody."

"Can you have visitors?" Admiral Archer entered the sickbay.

Carter tried to come to attention while lying on the bed. "Yes, sir."

"Relax. I heard you got hurt during the action. I trust Doc is taking good care of you. Take all the time you need to get better. I just wanted to stop in and tell you I think you've done yourself proud. Doc, I hear you saved a lot of men today. The whole crew saved lives today."

Changing Times

"Sir, I didn't do anything but get hurt." She slumped back on the bed.

"You took the risk of going into a fight and were doing your job. What else is there?" He smiled at her.

The Captain touched her hand lightly. "What were you doing in Engine Room 2?"

"I just felt something was wrong and went to check."

The loud-box carried news from Tailor in the lookout. "Captain, two ships on the horizon."

The Captain hit the loud-box. "All hands, prepare for emergency lift." He raced from the sickbay for the bridge, followed by the Admiral.

The Bridge

The Captain grabbed his far glasses and searched the skies. He found the airships low on the horizon in the setting sun. As they got closer, he could make out what the airships were. He used the loud-box. "Stand down; they're service ships. Good job, Tailor; keep sharp." The Chief joined them on the bridge. They watched the airships come in and moor up. The flags being flown showed the Admiral of the fleet was onboard.

"He's not here because of the attack." The Captain shook his head.

"No, he got here days too soon for that. I wonder what it's about."

"We both know; visiting top officers are never a good thing. Sorry, Admiral."

"I agree; it's going to be nothing good. I'll see you gentlemen later; I have to go greet the Admiral."

94
July 26, 1898
9 AM
The Admiral's Office

Admiral Yates was in his fifties, with thinning gray hair. He sat hunched over Admiral Archer's desk, speaking at full volume, with a face that grew redder the longer he talked.

"Yes, I read the messages you sent about new programs and I'm here to tell you it'll never happen. The service works just fine the way it is. As of this moment, I'm taking over this station until I can find a replacement. The programs you've started will stop now. You can also explain why all but one of the service airships out there have been destroyed."

Admiral Archer didn't say a word. He sat in the chair in front of the desk, staring out the window. He turned at the knock on the door. The secretary opened the door and stuck her head in. "Sir, Arku is here to see you."

The door pushed open and Arku walked in.

"Just what is the meaning of this? Get out of my office or I'll have you arrested."

Admiral Archer bowed to Arku and then broke his silence. "Sir, this is Arku. He represents the Island."

"I don't care; call security now and get him out of here."

Arku smiled at Admiral Yates. "You say your office. I thought this was Admiral Archer's office. I came to speak about the attack on the Island."

"*Was* is correct. He has been relieved of his duties and the Island was not attacked, just the station."

"More evil to the Island I cannot allow. You have thirty days to remove all your people from this Island." Arku turned and walked out.

Changing Times

"Ignorant native thinks he can tell us to get off the Island."

Admiral Archer cleared his throat. "Sir, in fact, he can. It's in the agreement with the Island."

10 AM
The Lady Fair

The Captain was starting to pace. He stopped at the loud-box. "Chief, please come to the bridge." He passed by the coffee, poured a cup, and paced again.

The Chief came in and saw him pacing. "More trouble?"

"Lately the feelings don't seem to stop. Chief, how many rockets do we have left?"

"About seventy or eighty."

"Load up the front racks and the aft. Spread out what's left to port and starboard. We have a weakness. When Victoria is acting as gunner on the forward racks, the bow gun is unmanned. Would you man it if we have to fight again?"

"Of course I will. We'll get on the reload now."

"Am I interrupting anything?" Admiral Archer strode in and sat down on the couch.

The Chief hurried out to get the crew and work on the racks. The Captain saw the Admiral sitting slightly slumped on the couch. He poured another cup of coffee and handed it to him.

"It's been a very long time since you've been aboard, Admiral. Welcome aboard. Something happen?"

"I felt like I wanted to be around a crazy but professional crew for a while. It seems my sending letters requesting support of the new programs was a bad idea. I've been relieved of duty. Admiral Yates has taken over command. He's killing all the programs. It doesn't matter, though; Arku has told him to get everyone off the Island in 30 days."

"I bet he's trying to deny that order. At some point, the legal people will get it through his head the clock is ticking."

"It's a big mess. There's a big mess out there to clean up too."

"Another lesson learned the hard way. The station needs two airships on guard at all times, or at least ready for immediate launch."

"Another lesson? What else?"

"Everyone we've fought thinks the Lady Fair is harmless and ignores us until it's too late. I think the women as crew makes them think we're weak. Even a nasty person like Maxmillian learned too late not all women are as weak as he thinks they are."

The Captain had just started pacing again when Marie entered. "Captain, excuse me, I thought you should know I'm back. I've been kicked out of the class. They said the contract for teaching me has been canceled."

The Captain stopped pacing. "Sorry, Marie, it has nothing to do with you as a person. I'll make sure you get training. Kathryn and Diana can teach you, anyway."

"Hello, Marie, I think it was my fault. I apologize," said the Admiral.

"Admiral, Sir, you helped on the first day; thank you. I can't see how it could be your fault."

The Admiral asked about the classes she did have, and how the instructor was. The Captain continued pacing and didn't notice her leave the bridge.

"Captain, is something bothering you? You're wearing a rut in the deck."

The Galley

Marie went to the side prep table and picked up a tart that was cooling. "Chef Joan, is it okay if I have one?"

"Sure, I'll get you some milk to go with it. Aren't you supposed to be in class?"

"Not anymore; they canceled the contract. The Admiral said it was his fault somehow."

"The Admiral? He came to your class and canceled it?"

"No, he's on the bridge with the Captain. Something must have upset the Captain because the whole time I was there he walked back and forth with a coffee in his hand he didn't drink."

"What?" Joan almost fell trying to get to the loud-box. She took a moment to compose herself, took a deep breath and, in what sounded like a calm voice, called Kathryn. "Kathryn, would you ask your sis to help me with coffee, please?"

Feet hitting the deck plates running sounded around the ship.

Marie looked, confused, at Joan. "What?"

95
July 26, 1898
11 AM
The Bridge

The Captain was still pacing when Kathryn, Diana, and Marie entered carrying some rags. They split up and started polishing brass.

"What are you three doing?"

"Polishing brass, Captain; you know we all like a clean and polished ship. Hello, Admiral." Kathryn continued to polish.

"The famous twins and Marie again. Hello."

The Captain looked out the window to the deck to see the Chief finish loading rockets in the forward rack and then run to the starboard side, loading more. Victoria strolled onto the deck with the overcoat on, headed for the forward Sunburst rack. She leaned against the railing and stared towards the sea.

The Captain turned towards Kathryn. "Is someone giving orders again?"

"Captain, I can honestly say no one gave any orders about anything. Is there something in particular?"

The Captain and the Lady Fair

"Innocent lambs. Admiral, I think I'm beginning to feel what you felt when some young Captain would go rogue."

The Admiral smiled and nodded.

"I guess you have to put up with it when you have the best there is. Yes, Marie. That includes you too." The Captain smiled.

Alexandria came onto the bridge. "Hello, Admiral. It's a surprise to see you visiting. Please, don't mind me. I'm just here to check on something." She walked over to the control box for the shield and checked it over.

The Admiral got up and refilled his cup of coffee. "Captain, is there something going on?"

The Captain snatched up the far glasses and stepped onto the walk, looking at the horizon. Seeing nothing to catch his eye, he returned inside and went to the loud-box. "Lookout, anything on the horizon?"

Tailor's voice answered. "No, Captain, all clear."

The Admiral spoke up again. "What is it, Captain?"

Kathryn and Diana put down their rags and went to the Pilot stations. Marie went to the chart table, pulled out the local chart, and spread it out. The Captain paced twice more across the bridge before turning to the loud-box.

"All hands, emergency lift."

Kathryn turned to Marie. "Get over here and take the helm."

The Chief and his crew could be seen running to loosen the lines.

The Captain opened his mouth to say something, but quickly closed it. He took a deep breath. "Pilot, my trust is in you. You, too, Marie."

Kathryn spoke to Marie. "You're on throttles." She turned to the Captain. "Engines ready, Captain." Marie wiped her hands on her pilot pants and took a hold of the throttles.

"Get us on a due north course; I'll correct as we go."

"Just like undocking the cloud, Marie." Kathryn pulled down the docking lever to unlock the dock. "Ease her back. The breeze will keep you going back and away. Good, now bring us about to a north heading." She was applying lift gas as she spoke and the Lady Fair rose to clear obstructions. Marie applied throttle to the starboard side and reverse throttle to the port causing the Lady Fair to rotate in place. The pull out was smooth and, once the heading was due north, Marie eased the power to full forward throttle on all engines.

The Captain smiled. "Great job, Marie, especially for a first lift."

The Admiral sputtered. "Her first un-dock and lift and during an emergency lift? Are you crazy? And what is an emergency lift? You need to build steam."

"Admiral, I trust my pilots. If Kathryn thought she was ready for it, then I trust her. That also means I trusted Marie to do it." The Captain turned his attention back out the window. Seeing nothing yet, he used the loud-box. "Lift all Sunburst racks to the ready and stand by."

The Admiral looked out the window to see what was going on. "What are Sunburst racks?"

"Admiral, I welcome you aboard but, first, I'll say you may see things you've never seen before. I must ask you never talk to anyone about it. Our continued survival depends on it. Because of surprise, we get an extra edge. Second, I'll ask you not ask any questions now or make comments for a while. We're busy here."

"Well, since you've taken out five airships —"

Marie cut him off. "Admiral, I think the captain was saying 'Shut up and let us do our jobs' in a polite way."

Both Pilots and Alexandria tried to hide their giggles.

"Sorry, Admiral; like I said, sometimes my crew seems to go rogue."

"I stand corrected. It's your ship."

It seemed like hours had passed, but it had been less than thirty minutes when Tailor reported. "On the horizon, five degrees to starboard, an airship."

"Five degrees to starboard, please, Pilot." The Captain raised his far glasses and could see a shape on the horizon, but it was still too far away to make anything out. "Maintain a head-on course following the lookout's directions."

The Captain and the Lady Fair

More minutes passed. "Captain, it's a service airship. Lots of steam. Probably full throttle. About 5,000 feet." There was a short pause. "Captain, a second set of steam trails. She's being chased."

The Captain grabbed the far talker. "Airship approaching Paaku Island, drop to 350 feet, maintain course and don't deviate for anything." Hearing no reply, he repeated himself, this time getting an answer.

"Who are you?"

"This is the luxury airship Lady Fair. Just do as I ask and we'll distract whoever is chasing you and give you a chance to get to the Island."

There was no response, but Tailor reported in. "Captain, she's losing altitude."

The Captain used the loud-box again. "Chief, man the nose gun. Just remember Gunner is out there at the railing, so don't jerk around too much." He used the loud-box. "Gunner, please attach a safety line." He looked at the Pilots. "I'm going topside just in case. Drop us to ten feet, stop, then shield up. Set us up for an 800-foot pop."

The Captain left the bridge. The Admiral showed frustration but refrained from asking any questions.

By the time the Lady Fair had dropped to ten feet, the approaching airship was clearly visible. Alexandria turned on the shield. The power light came on, flickered, and then went out. She grabbed the loud-box. "Captain, the shield's down. I'm not getting power."

The metal shutters dropped down across the windows. The Captain spoke on the loud-box. "All hands, the shield is not working; this is going to be a hard fight. Be ready to fire on command."

96
July 26, 1898
12 AM
The Bridge

The Captain gave orders over the loud-box. "Pilot, keep us at ten feet. Stay in the direct path of the service airship; it'll pass over us. As soon as it does, dump ballast and give lift to get above the pursuer. All hands, when you have a clear shot, take it. Chief, concentrate your fire on the bow; I want their forward guns out, or it'll be very bad for us." He paused. "My trust is in all of you."

Alexandria slammed the control box closed and tried again. It still failed. "I'm going to the engineer's room and check down there. I've left it turned on in case I get it fixed. You know which switch turns it on and off." She ran from the bridge.

The ship rapidly grew closer, but the waiting was hard on the nerves of all of the crew. The service airship was less than 100 feet away when Kathryn noticed the light was on for the shield. She released gas into the lift bags and used the loud-box. "Captain, shield is up. We'll be ready. Tailor, let me know when we're clear to lift." The Admiral went to the window with a slit in the shield, to see what was happening.

As the service airship passed directly over the Lady Fair, Alexandria's voice came over the loud-box. "Doc to the engineer's room; Carter is down." Her voice was followed by Tailor's. "Clear."

Kathryn hit the "off" switch and the Lady Fair surged upward. At the start of the rise, she heard the Captain's voice. "Fire when you have a target."

The Admiral fell to the deck with the upward surge, got up and went back to the view slit.

The cannon fire from the Captain rattled the bridge. The bow rotated from an upward position to a downward one, following the attacker as the Lady Fair rose. The Chief's guns blew steam, and the bullets raked the airship, staying on the nose.

Victoria had a revolver in each hand, firing at heads just visible in the bridge. A head dropping out of sight followed each hole in the glass.

Caught in surprise by the Chief's stream of bullets and the sudden appearance of the Lady Fair rising in front of them, the cannon crew didn't get off a single shot. The nose of the Lady Fair stopped at full down. Once above the airship, Victoria fired both sets of rockets into the bag. The port and side rockets fired as they were directly above. Once past, the aft rockets fired.

"Pilot, get us altitude." The Captain raised the metal shields protecting the bridge, then scrambled down to the bridge. "Bring us about, Pilot."

Kathryn patted Marie on the shoulder. "Bring us about 180 degrees, please."

The Captain looked at Kathryn but said nothing. She returned the smile and pointed to the shield control box. It was back on. "Did you forget? Rotating in the shield works fine. Once we see what's going on, you can decide what to do."

When they were able to see the airship, it was already down in the water. The lift bag envelope was draped on the deck in full flames. "I'm going to the engineer's room." The Captain left at a run.

The Doc had Carter sitting upright and awake. "What happened to Carter? What's she doing here?"

"Captain, I just got her awake. I was loading a bag of medical supplies and wasn't watching her. I didn't know she was gone until I heard the loud-box. Carter, please explain why you left sickbay and what you're doing here."

"I heard the shield was broken. I knew Alexandria would be on the bridge and work that end, so I came here to check this end. I ran to get here and I got weak, but I found a wire had come off. By the time I got a screwdriver off the bench, I was too tired to stand, but I got it back on. That's all I remember. Is everyone okay?"

"Everyone but you. Captain, if you would please. Carter, I'll fix you up in the sickbay."

The Captain picked up Carter and carried her to the sickbay. "You do not leave sickbay without Doc's permission, and that's an order."

"Yes, Captain."

The Captain went to the loud-box. "She'll be fine. Chef Joan, please see if you can put together a lunch for everyone. Pilot, let's do slow circles until after lunch."

1 PM
The Galley

The Captain and the Admiral were already seated as the crew filed in. The Chief came in, carrying Carter, and put her in a seat. Her head was bandaged down the right side, as well as her arm. Doc sat next to her.

"Doc?"

"It's all right, Captain. She has enough energy to join us as long as she behaves and lets the Chief carry her."

"Sorry to be trouble, Chief."

"You're no trouble; besides, I got beef stew yesterday because of you."

Kathryn came in with Marie in tow. "Captain, Diana is on the bridge; Tailor is staying on watch while we eat. They'll come down after we eat."

"Thank you. Well, Chef Joan, something smells very good. What do we have?"

"Roast pork I had cooking before all this started, a simple salad topped with fruit, cut potatoes in pork gravy, fresh corn, peas, and applesauce. Carter has a choice of warmed-over beef stew or the same as everyone else."

Carter looked at Joan with a glassy eye. "I don't know what to say. Thank you. I'll have what everyone else is having, please."

They had made a healthy start at the meal when the Admiral spoke up. "Mind if I ask questions now? What was going on with the shields around the bridge? Where do you have a cannon hidden? What is going on with the nose that moves? How the heck was Gunner hitting the people in the bridge with revolvers and what are those rocket things that stick and explode fire? How did the Lady Fair rise so fast?"

The crew laughed. "Admiral, like I said, I want those things a secret. As you saw, it kept us alive and in one piece. I have to take a moment to lecture Carter. Carter, that was the dumbest thing I've seen. Doc should confine you to sickbay." He paused and smiled at her. "Good job, Carter; I think the Chief there is about to bust buttons with his pride for you."

The Admiral stood up. "Carter, your actions have shown you don't belong in the service. The service has no place for you. You belong on the Lady Fair. I want to keep you, but if the Captain offers you a job and you want to go, I'll let you. I think you're a fine example of what a woman can do if allowed and encouraged. Well done. I wish I could guarantee things, but I can't, as I'm no longer in charge." He gave her a salute and sat back down.

Doc handed Carter her napkin. "Your eye is leaking."

The Captain continued. "Marie, I don't need the pilots to tell me you're doing a great job and learning fast. The bad news is that it won't be long before you're doing watches on your own."

The Admiral sighed. "I wish my crews had just half the skills your crew has."

"Admiral, I think this has been a learning experience for you."

"I don't know where I'll end up, but I'll fight even harder for doing things right from now on."

After a lazy lunch, and everyone had been relieved, and had eaten, the Lady Fair cruised back to the Island.

The only mooring left open was the one next to the airship they had helped. The Lady Fair docked unassisted as normal. As the ramp was put into place, armed guards took position at the sides of the ramp.

The Captain looked at the Admiral. "What did we do?"

97
July 26, 1898
4 PM
The Bridge

Three men in business suits walked across from the airship moored next to the Lady Fair as the Captain and the Admiral watched. The Captain went to the loud-box. "Chief, we seem to have guests coming. Please escort them to the bridge. Victoria, please take a look dockside." The Captain continued to watch the three make progress across the dock as he spoke to the Admiral. "Armed guards and business suits, a very strange combination. No markings or name on that airship, either. Anyone you know, Admiral?"

"I've no idea who it is or what's it about."

Just as the trio reached the ramp, a ground handler rushed up to the men. The armed guards leveled their weapons at him, and two of the men in suits pulled out handguns. The ground handler slid to a stop and was waving his arm around and pointing at the Lady Fair, while the other hand held a basket of fruit. "I see the Pilot's fruit has arrived." The Captain continued to watch out the window.

"Your Pilots have fruit delivered?"

"Admiral, you really should walk around the station and learn more about what's going on. Some things may not seem important to you, but they can be very important to others." The Captain crossed the bridge and poured a cup of coffee. As he sat in his Captain's chair, the Admiral chided him.

"Armed guards, men in suits with guns, people armed with a fruit basket almost getting shot, and you sit and drink coffee?"

"For the moment, I can't see anything I can do unless you want me to find a gun and go running down the ramp shooting everything I see. I think relaxing with coffee is a much better idea. You should try it. Grab a cup and relax, Admiral."

They could hear the footsteps make their way up the ramp; there was a pause, and then faint steps began to get louder as they drew nearer to the bridge. "Seems our guests are here."

Three men entered the bridge with the Chief close behind. The man in the lead was over six feet tall, with sandy blond hair cut very short, a medium build, and a smile on his face that agreed with his eyes. The other two men looked like twins, short of six feet, with big builds, crew-cut black hair, and blank expressions. "It seems I've been asked to deliver this to the Pilots. I would like to meet the Pilots that saved my ship today if that's possible."

A pair of boots pounding on the deck announced Victoria before she arrived. She stopped in the hatchway, feet slightly apart, balanced to move. She was in her lucky suit and had both revolvers strapped on. Two of the men in suits started to pull their weapons, and then stopped and stared at Victoria. Both relaxed and grinned. "Little girl, those guns are too big for you. Why not go bake us some cookies?"

The suit with the basket barked out. "Shut up, Jake." He turned to Victoria. "I apologize for my man being rude."

The Captain stood up and let loose a sharp whistle that got everyone's attention. "Before this gets out of hand, why not have your boys sit on the couch and pretend to be statues? Let's try introductions. I'm Captain Castellan, this is Admiral Archer, you've met my Chief at the top of the ramp, and this is Victoria, my gunner and, at present, my bodyguard. Now you try."

"Captain, this seems to have gone in a way I hadn't thought. I apologize. These two are my bodyguards and my name is Hill. I came to this Island to meet with the Admiral here. I had no idea he would be my rescuer."

The Admiral cleared his throat. "I had nothing to do with it; I just happened to be onboard when it lifted. Your rescue was strictly the

Captain and his crew. From first-hand knowledge, I suggest you take Victoria seriously."

"Thank you for the rescue, Captain. Could you please get the young lady to relax?"

The Captain sighed. "Easier said than done. She's been insulted, and that takes time to cool down. If you will allow me, I think I can make her happy."

"Please do."

"Victoria, no one is going to shoot anybody here. Trust me a few minutes and I think I can make you happy. Very slowly, remove your right hand revolver and empty it, please."

Victoria stared hard at the Captain. Slowly she did as he asked and put the revolver back in the holster.

"Thank you. Jake, come on over here and stand and face Victoria, please."

Victoria grinned and Jake looked at Hill, who nodded. Jake got up and stood in front of Victoria, who was four feet away. "Please, Jake, closer; at about two feet, I would think."

"If you think I'm going to stand here and let some tart hit me, you're out of your mind."

"Jake, I have to tell you that was a very wrong thing to say. You have insulted her again and you've insulted a member of my crew. Any mercy I felt has just walked the plank."

Hill spoke up. "Just do it so I can get on with business."

Jake stepped forward.

"Jake, close your eyes for a moment, then open them. If her gun was loaded, the next time you blink after that, you would be dead."

Victoria smiled and her eyes sparkled. Grumbling the whole time, Jake closed his eyes and opened them.

Hill commented quietly. "Strange, Captain, but you're interesting."

Jake blinked and was knocked backward onto the deck, holding his stomach. Victoria, holding her revolver at hip level, smiled at the Captain. "Do you still need me, Captain?"

"Did you have to poke him that hard?"

"Captain, I held back; otherwise there would be a hole the size of the barrel there."

"Thank you; I think things will be okay now."

Hill stood stunned. "I didn't blink and I didn't see her move."

The Admiral smiled. "I told you."

The Captain offered a hand to Jake to help him up. "Just suggestions, Jake; never underestimate or insult any of my crew. Coffee, Mr. Hill?"

"Is there someplace more relaxed?"

"Of course; the galley is the best place to relax." He went to the loud-box. "All Pilots to the galley, please."

Mr. Hill peeked in each room as they passed on the way to the galley. "You weren't kidding when you said this was a luxury ship. How in the world did you take out that dreadnaught chasing us? It had already taken out our escort."

"Just luck, Mr. Hill; just luck."

They entered the galley and were greeted by the smells of baking pies and cakes. "This is Chef Joan, the heart of the Lady Fair. Please pull up a seat. You said you came to meet the Admiral?"

"Yes, I did. Admiral, I wanted to talk to you about a letter I received."

The Pilots came through the hatchway. "Yes, Captain?"

"These are the Pilots?" He smacked his forehead. "I knew I had heard of the Lady Fair. You must be Kathryn and Diana. I am very pleased to meet you in person. Now I know why your Captain did his extortion on the Admiral. A gentleman on the dock asked me to bring this for you." He extended his hand with the basket.

Kathryn looked puzzled. "Should we know you?"

"My apologies; I haven't been fully forthcoming. I am President Hill. I signed your tickets."

Changing Times

"My pilot will be upset. He talked very highly of the nerve of the pilots to hold that low over the water while another airship passed over them, then the nerve to take on a gunship to rescue us with no weapons in sight. He was in awe as you moored with no ground crew. I think his words were 'As gentle as a mother's kiss.' I'm sure I'll get a laugh at seeing his face when he learns it was you two. Wait; there are three of you."

Kathryn smiled at Marie. "Sir, this is Pilot Trainee Marie. She handled the engines during the rescue and mooring."

"Very impressive; my Pilot will collapse. How many months have you been training?"

"Two weeks, sir."

President Hill sat silently for a moment and then smiled at the Captain. "Captain, when you decide she's ready for a ticket, write me and I'll send it to you myself. Just give me at least a few days to get back before you request it."

"Admiral, you sent some letters to your commanders. It seems some secretaries were in the path of the letters and decided I should have a copy. I received several copies. I decided it might be a good idea to talk with you about it. I thought I'd take a short vacation and visit here. What programs are you doing now?"

"None, sir. All the programs were canceled, including Marie's navigation school. Admiral Yates has relieved me of my command. I should also mention we have thirty days to get everyone off the Island."

"Chef Joan, is it? May I have a piece of that pie I smell when it's done? I can see we are going to be here a good while. I want to hear about the programs and any information you gathered, and I want to hear about what the heck happened to this station."

"It'll be a long night. Chief, could you go ask Neenaa to round up the committee that was set up and ask them to bring everything they've gathered?" The Admiral stood and refilled his cup.

The sun was setting when Chef Joan called for an interruption. "Gentlemen, dinner is ready and, if you've not overstuffed yourselves on my pies, I'll serve up soon."

Alexandria cradled Kira. Neenaa had brought her when she brought the women on the committee. "Joan, let me help with something."

The President stood and stretched. "Dinner will be fine by me, thank you. You're sure General Tarki is dead and no more a threat?"

"Yes, I saw his flag as we passed over. He was onboard. That had to be his last ship, or he wouldn't have braved doing it himself. We were also lucky he was an idiot and knew nothing about airship battles and seemed to have given his pilots and commanders specific orders on how to engage." The Captain stood and stretched as well.

"I need to talk to Arku." The President sat back down and moved papers off the table to the floor under his chair.

"What would you wish to speak to me about?"

Arku entered, followed by Martin, and looked at Chef Joan. "Can you spare some pie for an old man?"

Chef Joan bowed. "Anything for you." She went to the loud-box and announced dinner would be served in thirty minutes.

The president stood and bowed to Arku. "You look well."

"The Island is kind to me."

Martin sat in the first empty seat he came to. Rubbing his hands, he smiled at Chef Joan. "I have perfect timing."

"So does Arku, it seems." The Captain stood and bowed. "Welcome to our table."

Arku walked over to the President. "You are still strong and have done many good things for many people. You should visit more often, Little Bird."

Changing Times

"Little Bird?" Joan looked at the President.

The President laughed. "That is what Arku called me when I was a young boy because I flitted here and there like a bird just finding its wings. My father was stationed here in the Navy for several years. After we left I came back as a young man but, as I got deeper into politics, I came back less often, and then my visits stopped."

"There are many bad men that are here and the new Admiral is worse than any." Arku frowned.

"In the morning Admiral Archer will be back in charge. Admiral Hatcher will have a new job in a place as cold and without mercy as he is. Admiral, as far as I can see, by the general flying the flag of Boschland and attacking this station and service vessels, we are at war. This means you have many powers until it is straightened out."

"Good, I have moles to round up and one other thing: Petty Officer Carter will be made Lt. Junior Grade instead of an Ensign."

The crew began to file in for dinner. The Chief waited until the last minute and rose from his chair. "I'll go bring Carter for dinner."

As he left, Tala, followed by Doc, came through the hatchway. "Good evening, everyone."

Martin rose and escorted Tala to a chair next to his.

"Martin, would you please introduce your guest?" The Captain smiled at Tala.

"I'm sorry, Captain; I thought you all would know her. She lives on the Island. This is Tala, my friend and guide."

The president tapped his lips with his finger. "Tala. Tala." He smiled as a memory came to him. "Arku, I remember the last time I was here, a girl was born. Could this be the same Tala, grown to become a beautiful woman?"

"Yes, the same." Arku sat up straighter and smiled at Tala.

The President got to his feet and bowed to Tala. "Please forgive my rudeness, Princess Tala, Granddaughter of Arku."

Martin sat in shock, mouthing the words "princess" and "granddaughter."

The table started an excited chatter and then fell silent as Carter entered. She wasn't wearing any bandages and had no burns, only pink, new skin where the burns had been.

99
July 26, 1898
8 PM
The Galley

The Captain spoke for everyone. "Doc, I see you …" He paused and looked at the Admiral and the President. "got your new treatment to work."

"I had help from Tala; it seemed to work much better with her helping."

"Carter, you look great." The Chief's eyes were watering.

The Admiral muttered to himself. "The whole crew does impossible things as if it's nothing."

Arku's voice took on a serious tone. "Young Martin."

"Yes, sir?"

"You have been seeing my granddaughter a great deal."

"Yes, sir." Martin blushed.

"You have been seeing her all day, and well after the sun has set, and the moon has risen."

"Yes, sir, I have, but we were just talking and lost track of time."

"There is a saying where you come from. Are you going to do the honorable thing?"

The crew around the table waited for the answer.

"Yes, sir, of course I will and I will admit I love her." He took Tala's hand under the table.

"I am getting old; don't make me wait too long for the event. A man that stops to feed helpless birds has a good heart,"

"Yes, sir." He looked at Tala and whispered. "How does he know? I was alone."

Tala smiled at Martin. "No, you weren't." She put her finger to her lips.

Joan served dinner. The President rose and went to the hatchway. He returned with his two bodyguards from outside the hatchway. "Gentlemen, please take a seat."

When Joan was serving the bodyguards, she noticed one was rubbing his stomach. "Do you have a stomach problem? Maybe Doc can help."

The second bodyguard laughed and slapped him on the back. "He had a slight run-in with a devil in red." He immediately held up his hands at Victoria. "Sorry, sorry. I didn't mean it in a bad way."

Joan patted the man on the head. "Odd that you're still alive." She smiled at his stricken look. "Devil in Red … Red Devil … that would make a good nickname, I think."

Victoria was fast to comment. "Don't even think it, Shorty."

The President joined in the laughter around the table. "Captain, there is a great deal I don't understand about you, your crew, or your airship. There is a lot you're not telling me, but I'll have to accept that. Someday, before I die, please tell me the whole story."

"No promise on that, Mr. President."

He continued. "Admiral, tomorrow, meet me at nine AM in your office. I will have had a chat with Admiral Yates by then. We'll meet with that committee again and set up whatever programs you want or need. I'll sign paperwork, making it a Presidential order so you won't go through this again. I will say, for now, I will not make any other stations follow suit. This will be a test station to see how things go. Captain, I agree two ships should be overhead at all times, and I'll make that an order here and at all other stations."

The Admiral was smiling. "Captain, how is it you can always launch so fast?"

"That one is simple, Admiral. We stay hooked up to land water, and keep the water supply topped up. We keep the boilers on all the time.

The Captain and the Lady Fair

Every two days, we top up on fuel. That keeps us at over a two-week supply. We do that to be ready. Besides, I like hot showers."

Chef Joan and Victoria whispered to each other for a few minutes. Joan spoke up. "Tala, when dinner is over, come to our cabin and we'll make wedding plans." Martin started coughing. Arku smiled and nodded.

A voice at the hatchway made them all turn. A young man stood there holding a large black bag. "I'm sorry to interrupt, but our Doc asked me to return this to your Doc. He says he restocked it as best he could." He lifted up Doc's bag.

Kathryn got up and took it from him. "Lieutenant Meyers, what a surprise. Join us for a bite to eat. Look, sis, it's the nice Lieutenant we met at Bernard's."

"I said it before and I'll say it again, the two best pilots in the world; now I have to add the best crew to that. Thanks for the rescue. The Peregrine would never have made it. We were losing that fight. My Captain is still busy with the damage to the Peregrine, or he would have come himself. We're trying to get her back to status as fast as we can, as she's the only ship that can be salvaged. We're stripping engines and everything else we need from the other ships."

Kathryn pointed to Marie. "Meet Pilot trainee Marie. You can add her to your best list."

The President nodded to the Admiral. "It seems you have allies in your camp."

The Captain looked at the Chief. "Chief, would you like to lend a hand with the repairs?"

"Of course, Captain; can I have a trainee along? That is if she still wants to train with me."

Carter was quick with an answer. "You bet, Chief. I've been doing nothing, and I'm ready for some grease on my hands."

The Chief beamed. "Lieutenant, you have myself and Lt. Junior Grade Carter to help your ship, starting tomorrow."

Carter looked at the Chief in surprise. "What? Lt. Junior Grade?"

The Admiral laughed. "Sorry, I forgot to tell you. You've been promoted, effective about ten minutes ago." Everyone in the room applauded and offered congratulations.

The President smiled at the Captain. "Please invite the Lieutenant to stay for dinner. I think I want to hear his version of the rescue."

The dinner was Chef Joan's usual tasty delight. Light conversation continued well into the night.

100
July 27, 1898
11 AM
Control Tower Roof

Victoria stood at the front edge of the Control Tower Roof, overlooking the docks. She was in her lucky suit and wore both of her revolvers. Directly in front of her were the burnt-out hulks of the destroyed airships. She used far glasses to scan the docks and watched aircrews, dockworkers, and ground crews working to clear the wreckage. Burnt-out timber was being placed in one pile at the edge of the field; salvageable parts were placed in another pile on the ground next to it. They were working hard to clear three mooring masts to be available for any incoming airships. She could see the Captain, Admiral Archer, and President Hill, with his two bodyguards, standing at the center of the disaster.

The Docks

Admiral Archer shook his head. "It'll take days to clear this. I need to have big pumps installed to the sea so there's a bigger supply of water for a fire. Perhaps even a nozzle at the top of each mooring tower. Water could be directed at an airship and the neighbor mooring."

The Captain and the Lady Fair

The President agreed. "Yes, and perhaps even some ground guns for defense. Speaking of defense, my bodyguards are enough. Stop worrying, Captain. Please don't ask me to get off the docks, for my safety, again."

"The service plays by the rules; attackers don't. I asked Victoria to keep an eye out for you while you're on the docks. We need to rethink everything. Defense tactics, attack tactics, ground defense, and even ground safety. We've been complacent and blind. I should go change and lend a hand."

"I may be an Admiral, but there are times when rolling up the sleeves is a good thing. I'll change and join you. Where's Victoria? I don't see her." The Admiral was looking around the docks.

"I have no idea."

The Control Tower Roof

Victoria's attention was drawn to a man who was doing no work. He walked from one spot to another, never picking anything up, unlike all the other workers. He was slowly working his way to the Captain's group, taking a very indirect course, zigzagging across the area. Each pass brought him closer.

The Docks

The Admiral cleared his throat. "I know it is bad etiquette for me to ask, but where's Admiral Yates?"

"He's been assigned to lookout duty to allow him time to reflect on the wisdom of arguing with me. He's up on a hill somewhere. This trip has been a great revelation on the state of the service. It has suffered from lack of progress and bad attitudes. Little kingdoms over people wanting to do a good job, but who can't because of others' family connections, or just the bad attitudes of those in charge."

"Guilty as charged for leaving things as they are and not getting out and seeing things for myself."

Changing Times

The Captain clamped his hand on the Admiral's shoulder. "Don't worry; we'll salvage you yet."

The Control Tower Roof

Victoria watched the man get behind the group. Everyone in the group was facing the direction of a dock being cleared. The figure started a rush from behind and drew out a revolver.

The Docks

The Captain heard fast-approaching footsteps and started to turn. So did the bodyguards. They saw a man rushing forward, aiming a gun at the President. Before they could draw their weapons, the man's head exploded, followed by the sound of a loud gunshot. He fell to the ground. The bodyguards pushed the President to the ground and looked around. They could see a figure standing on the roof of the control tower, putting a gun back in a holster. Jake had started to raise his gun when the other bodyguard stopped him. "I would suggest you don't aim a gun at the Red Devil. It wouldn't be healthy. Besides, you'd never hit her from here."

Jake watched the figure on the roof pick up far glasses and look around the docks. "Anyone have any ideas what to get her as a gift so she won't be angry at me? From up there to down here, to hit a moving target, with a handgun, is very … I don't know. Maybe she is a devil."

The President got up, brushing himself off. "You and your crew, at the right place, at the right time again, and with skills I can't even describe. Can your crew teach any of that to any of my service people?"

The Captain and the Lady Fair

The Peregrine

Carter, in overalls, finished tightening the last steam line to the engine she and the Chief were working on. "That's two, Chief. Start the third, or start after lunch?"

"Just like a woman; has to go do her nails. You might want to check those connections; they're probably hooked up all wrong." The voice came from behind them.

The Chief turned and looked at the petty officer. "What's your name?"

"You don't need to know. I don't answer to civilians."

The Chief's neck veins throbbed and his fists clenched. "Boy, one thing you forgot when dealing with civilians. We don't follow rules." The Chief's fist hit the petty officer square and knocked him back several feet flat on his back. The Chief walked over and looked down at him, waiting for him to regain his senses. "Please, do get up and spew out another insult."

"I'll have you arrested and they'll throw away the key."

"Good morning, Chief."

The Chief turned to see Captain Morgan from the Peregrine climbing down a ladder.

"Good morning, sir."

"What do we have here?"

Neither the Chief nor Carter said a word, but the petty officer on the ground started talking fast. "He hit me for no reason. I want him arrested and charged with assault."

"I see you hit your head pretty hard. It scrambled your brains. I heard you throw insults at the young lady, even an insult to the Chief. I saw you fall backward, tripping over your own feet and hit your head. Is that what you saw, Chief?"

Carter snapped to attention and saluted.

Changing Times

"I think that just might be it, Sir. Allow me to properly introduce you to my engineer trainee, Lt. Junior Grade Carter, currently assigned for training aboard the Lady Fair."

Captain Morgan returned Carter's salute. He looked down at the petty officer on the ground. "When you can get up, report to my office. You and I are going to have a long talk about disrespect to a superior officer, your conduct towards civilians that volunteered to help get the Peregrine back in the air, and what your future work assignment will be."

They heard a gunshot and turned to see a man down on the dock, the men nearby looking at the tower. "Chief, isn't that Victoria up there?" Carter was squinting to see the figure on the tower roof.

"Yes, my guess is that she took out an attacker."

Captain Morgan returned to the business at hand. "If you're training under the Chief, I feel confident these engines will work perfectly for a long time. Thank you both for helping. One of my pilots has driven me to distraction about the crew of the Lady Fair, especially the women onboard. I've seen her pilots dock many times unassisted, and now I see you. I'll guess that this Victoria is a member of your crew, too."

"Yes sir, she is. She's our gunner."

Captain Morgan gave a small grunt. "That figures, I guess. I've got to start thinking about getting women on my crew."

The Docks

Jake managed to pull out some papers from the attackers' pockets. He handed them to the Admiral.

"I know this name; it was on the mole list. I guess he hadn't heard his general is dead. If you'll excuse me, I have to go stoke the fire under security and get the moles rounded up. I'm sorry, Mr. President; I should have had them all picked up by now."

"Don't be sorry. I'm fine and I got to see that young lady do an impossible shot. Captain, I'll take the advice you gave me, to get off the docks, albeit a little late."

The Captain shook the President's hand. "That'll be best. Thanks for helping the Admiral. Excuse me; I'll go change and get to work. It seems I'm the only one of my crew not working."

101
July 29, 1898
11 AM
The Galley

The crew had just sat down for lunch together when Martin came in with Tala. "Hello, everyone; may we invite ourselves for lunch?"

"Welcome, Martin; welcome, Princess Tala." The Captain stood and bowed to Tala.

"Please, as a favor to me, stop the bowing and just call me 'Tala.' I would much prefer that." Tala and Martin took seats.

Chef Joan started serving. Alexandria got up, with Kira in her sling. She went behind Tala and whispered in her ear.

Tala looked at Alexandria with a sad face. "No, I'm sorry. It is well beyond my power. Doc already asked about it. I truly am sorry."

Alexandria put on a smile. "I had to ask, and I'm sorry if I've caused you any discomfort." She put her hand on Tala's shoulder for a moment and went back to her seat.

"Is this a private party or can anyone join?" Admiral Archer came in and headed straight for a seat. "I have lots of news."

"You're always welcome, Admiral. I know you only came for Chef Joan's cooking."

"Of course that's an added bonus, but I do have news. The first moorings have been cleared just in time. A supply ship will be here later today. Joan, I checked and the item you ordered is on the ship. Chief, there's lots of parts for the Peregrine that should let you finish her."

Changing Times

Joan went to stand behind Tala and put her hands on her shoulders. "Tala, I've been bad. I forgot to pass on to the crew the invite to the wedding at noon tomorrow."

"It's okay, the invite is delivered now. Just don't forget to make the wedding cake you promised."

"I'll start it right after lunch."

"I have news for you too, Martin. The President asked me to tell you; he wants you to take on the job of being his direct representative here on the Island. I'm sure that'll make things easier for you." The Admiral looked expectantly at Martin, waiting for an answer.

"That's great news, Admiral; thank you."

"One last piece of news. An offer of a contract. This one requires the approval of not only you but Kathryn and Diana as well."

"What would that be, Admiral? I'm sure, if it's a contract involving them, I'll leave it up to them."

"Good enough, then. When available, to evaluate the Island's service pilots and train them, as needed, for improvement. The pilots will be informed that the evaluations and training are voluntary. If they refuse and are not passed within a year, they'll be assigned off dreadnaughts and reassigned to supply ships or smaller."

Both Pilots looked stunned. "You're going to have some upset pilots, sir, but we'll do it."

"There is a touch more. The school that wouldn't ticket you is being informed to advise students in advance that any pilots coming for duty on this station will not be allowed to pilot until passed by you both."

The crew broke into laughter. The Captain was still chuckling. "That's going to really stick in their craw."

"I've already had a request for training from a Lieutenant Meyers from the Peregrine. He said he wanted to be the first."

Kathryn could hardly speak. "Thanks, Admiral, for all you've done. Lieutenant Meyers will be easy. He already has a good attitude and an open mind."

"This station will be assigned new airships and lots of supplies. Extras will be here quick. As the President is going to drag his feet about resolving the war issue with Boschland, that will give me extra powers for a while. Because of that, most of the women assigned here will be promoted one rank, and the rest two, based on the information the committee had gathered about reviews versus promotions. As a point of pride for me, there are already women asking the committee about how to apply for new careers."

"That's good news, Admiral. Progress is starting." The Captain patted the Admiral on the back.

"The better news is I'm starting to get requests from some of the men to be reassigned off the Island. They've heard of the programs and attitude change from the top and don't like it and want to get out of its path."

The Chief laughed. "Good luck to them. I'm sure it will follow to other stations before too long."

102
July 30, 1898
Noon
The Wedding

As at Joan and Victoria's wedding, the shrine was decorated in white cloth. This time, the food table was much larger and had not only fruits and breads but meats and pastries as well. In the center of the table was a huge wedding cake. Many native families were in attendance. The crew was dressed in their best white uniforms. Martin was wandering around the clearing and being congratulated on his new job.

Joan came up to the Captain and Alexandria. "This is so beautiful; don't you think?"

Alexandria agreed. "It's a dream wedding."

Changing Times

"Would you do me a favor? I want to stay out here and keep the children away from the food. Can you go to the tent and see to Tala? I'll take care of Kira. We haven't had a chat in a while and I wouldn't want her to forget my voice."

"Sure, I'll be happy to help. I haven't done a thing for the wedding; I was beginning to feel left out." Alexandria made her way to the tent.

Tala gave a big smile and spun in place when Alexandria entered through the tent flap. "Have you ever been in love?"

Alexandria gave a wistful smile. "Yes."

"That's a funny expression on your face. By any chance, are you in love with the Captain?"

"Well, I … I mean he …."

"That means 'yes.' Isn't love a wonderful thing?" She did another spin.

Martin

Martin tapped the Captain on the shoulder. "Sorry to trouble you, but will you be my best man, Captain? You're the closest thing I have to a friend here."

"I would be honored. I guess the time is near; Arku is in place at the altar."

Martin took a deep breath. "Yes, now is the time." As they walked towards the altar to take their positions, Martin asked, "Have you ever been married, Captain?"

"No, I never slowed down long enough."

Martin laughed. "Thanks, Captain; I needed a laugh about now. I can't tell you how nervous I am about this. If I mess up, I'll be dead by morning. I've noticed you didn't slow down for Alexandria; you came to a complete stop for her and Kira. Ever think about asking her to marry you?"

"No need to be nervous; you'll be fine. Alexandria is a very good woman. She deserves better than me."

Martin chuckled. "I'll take that as a 'yes.' " They arrived at the altar and took their places.

Tala

"Thank you, Alexandria; I think we can be good friends. You've told me all I need to know." Tala peeked out of the tent. "I see Martin is in place." She raised her voice. "Sir, please come in and escort the bride."

A man entered through the entrance. A short man with a barrel chest and large biceps, which strained the jacket he wore, spoke in a deep, raspy voice. "I never thought I would see the day."

Alexandria spun around. "Uncle! I'm so happy to see you, but how did you get here and why are you here?"

"To escort my little girl and give her away." He took her arm in his and headed out of the tent.

Alexandria talked quietly out of the side of her mouth to avoid attracting attention. "But I'm not getting married; Tala is."

"Just humor your uncle and come along; everything is arranged and your Auntie will be upset if you mess up the wedding she always hoped she'd see. She really wants to meet your young man. We've already heard lots of stories about him. Everyone likes him and it seems you forgot to tell us he saved your life more than the once." Nervous steps carried her to the altar.

Martin stepped back into the crowd of guests and the Chief stepped up to the Captain's left. "Don't mess this up or Victoria will fill me with holes, and Joan will bake me in a special pie."

"What?" He turned from the Chief and looked toward the bride's tent. He saw Alexandria on the arm of a man he'd never seen before coming to the altar.

Once the Captain and Alexandria were side by side, Arku began.

Arku raised his arms and his voice as the crowd moved closer. "Friends of Captain Castellan and Alexandria Castle, this day starts a new beginning." He took the Captain's right hand and Alexandria's left and joined them.

Both the Captain and Alexandria were too stunned to say anything. The Captain smiled and squeezed her hand. A tear came to Alexandria's eye as she returned the squeeze.

Arku smiled as he smelled Jasmine and Gardenia in the air. He spoke to the Captain first. "Captain Castellan, have you given your heart and spirit to Alexandria?"

"Yes, I have."

"Alexandria, do you accept what is given to you?"

Alexandria whispered past a tight throat. "I do and have."

"Alexandria, have you given your heart and spirit to Captain Castellan?"

"I do, and I have."

"Captain Castellan, do you accept what is given to you?"

"I do and have. This is one time I know exactly where I'm supposed to be."

"You are witnesses to the merging of two spirits to become one in life." He drew a circle on the Captain's forehead. "The circle of life." He drew another circle so the circles were linked. "Two lives joined." He did the same to Alexandria. "Your friends bless your join, I bless your join, and the spirit of Paaku blesses you. Your spirits joined, shall be stronger than alone."

"Our ways are simple, the spirits are now one, but your world is different and we honor that here. Who gives this woman, Alexandria, to be joined this day?"

"I, her uncle, do." Uncle John stepped back and joined a weeping Aunt Helen. Victoria let Uncle John take over, supporting her.

"Who says this man is to be given on this day?"

"I, his friend, do." The Chief didn't hide his huge grin.

"You both have been given. Do you, Alexandria, accept what is given to you?"

Alexandria choked out "I do."

The Captain and the Lady Fair

"Captain Castellan, do you accept what is given to you?"

The Captain cleared his throat. "I do."

"Spirit has been given and received. Now a symbol of the joining."

The Chief pulled a ring from his left pocket and handed it to the Captain. The Captain looked at the silver band and the inscription inside, which read "Two spirits as one." He slid it onto Alexandria's finger.

Victoria stepped forward and handed Alexandria a ring. She placed it on the Captain's finger.

Arku turned and picked up a silver cylinder. "Today, two spirits have joined as one. In this cylinder is proof of that. On this great occasion, there is more." Arku opened the end of the cylinder and pulled out two documents. He laid one on the table and handed the other to Alexandria. She read the document and collapsed to her knees, crying. "The document I gave Alexandria Castellan states that the child known as Kira is now Kira Alexandria Regina Castellan, the daughter of Thomas Hewitt Edward Castellan and Alexandria Castellan. It further says that Kira Alexandria Regina Castellan is a child of this Island. It is signed and sealed by my hand and by the President from the land that Captain Castellan comes from."

"Crew of the Lady Fair, honored guests, welcome the joined spirits of Captain Castellan and Alexandria."

The guests applauded and congratulated the newlyweds. Alexandria hugged Aunt Helen tightly. "How did you get here?"

"We came in on the supply ship yesterday. We were hidden away, so it would be a surprise. We weren't told you were getting married until this morning. Why didn't you write and tell us?"

"You had more notice than I did. I didn't know until Uncle John told me. There are some people around here that have a lot of explaining to do."

Aunt Helen held her at arm's length and looked her up and down. "A bare belly and a naked leg showing up to you know where." She paused and then whispered, "Everyone can see you're not wearing underwear."

Changing Times

She pulled her close again into another hug. "You're the most beautiful I've ever seen you."

Alexandria introduced the Captain to her aunt and uncle. Aunt Helen took the Captain's hand. "Alexandria has written us with wonderful things about you and your ship and crew. I hope to see the ship before we go back."

"You'll see it. We'll fly you back home when it comes time to do that. We'll have a cabin onboard for you during your stay here."

"Good, then we can hear all the stories we've not been told." Aunt Helen stared at Alexandria.

Joan, with Kira in her sling, tapped Alexandria on the shoulder from behind. "I have a young lady here that would like to be with Mummy." Joan raised the sling off her neck and placed it around Alexandria's.

"Aunt Helen, Uncle John, meet my daughter, Kira." Helen made a big fuss over Kira and the sling that kept Kira close.

They all went to the food table where everyone was taking seats.

There were two seats at the head of the table for the bride and groom.

"Thank you all for coming to our wedding that we didn't know about. With all the aunts and uncles Kira has, I fear she may grow up to be a very smart, gun-toting renegade that can cook food fit for the Gods. I expect to hear the details of how it came together." As the Captain looked down the table, he saw Joan and Victoria with heads down, not looking at the Captain. "Joan, please entertain us with the story while we all enjoy this wonderful food."

Joan slowly stood up. "Captain, it was your idea."

"Mine?"

"You did it first. Everyone knew Alexandria was in love with you except you. Everyone knew you loved Alexandria, except you and Alexandria. So, we just helped. You're worse than a schoolboy. I got Kathryn to ask the Admiral to get Alexandria's aunt and uncle here, so he arranged that without telling them why. He also arranged the rings for us, and the cylinder like the one you gave us. Tala and Martin's situation allowed us to talk more openly about wedding plans. We just never said whom the plans were for; we just let you and Alexandria think it was for Tala and Martin. Arku arranged the adoption. We all pitched in on the plans, decorations, and food. We were worried, with all the trouble and the station being a mess, that her aunt and uncle wouldn't make it."

"That was the package that the Admiral said you special-ordered."

"Yes."

"Joan, you and Victoria have gotten too sneaky for me."

Neenaa stood up. "Everyone here is our friend, too. I need your help in controlling my sweet, lovable husband. I know this is the bride's day, but I can't think of a better time."

Aunt Helen leaned over to Alexandria. "That tiny girl and that huge man? I thought she was his daughter, and she's so young."

"Yes, Auntie, there's another marriage surprise in store for you, but that can wait."

"I know him well and he'll overreact and I need help to keep him reasonable." She looked at the Chief with his worried face. "You all know he has become attached to Carter like a daughter. He is as proud of her as any father should be. Carter, would you like a little brother or sister?"

"What?" Carter's face showed she had no idea what Neenaa was talking about.

"Sweet husband, you're going to be a daddy in about seven months."

The Chief stared wide-eyed; he leaped to his feet, taking Neenaa by the shoulders. His voice was panicky. "Sit down; don't stand on your feet like that. Fresh fruit, you need fresh fruit." The whole table of guests laughed at the Chief's panic while Neenaa made a laughing show of yelling for help.

"Auntie, before I forget. About that red suit you made for me …."

Changing Times

Sunset

Arku and Tala escorted the Captain and Alexandria up a long path. "Where are we going?" The Captain was looking around to see what was on the path.

"You'll see; it's just around that bend." Arku pointed.

They turned the bend and a clearing ahead revealed a white-walled cottage similar to Neenaa's.

Arku waved his hand. "Your new home."

Arku and Tala turned and went back down the path.

"They gave us a house?" Alexandria was looking over the cute cottage. They went in and found it to be a two-bedroom cottage with everything already in place. There was even food in the pantry and a food chiller. "Captain, it's beautiful. What's this?" Alexandria looked down at the table in the center of the room. On it were two books, with ink bottles and pens next to them. "Diaries. This is so thoughtful."

"You know you can stop calling me Captain and just call me Thomas."

"I've called you Captain for so long, it just feels right. Do you mind?"

"No, I don't mind at all."

They talked and explored the cottage and found the second bedroom had a cradle for Kira. Alexandria put the sleeping Kira in the cradle and tiptoed out.

They sat on the couch talking quietly, to not wake Kira. "Captain, someday tell me about your past. It bothers you or you wouldn't keep it secret. I want to help you get over it, whatever it is. Maybe you could tell me how you can afford the Lady Fair."

"All that is a long story best left for another time."

As the sun began to set, they sat in front of the cottage eating a light salad. The Captain looked at his food. "I do want you to do something for me. I want you to teach me to cook."

Alexandria laughed hard. "From what I hear about your cooking, it will take me the rest of my life, to teach you to slice a melon."

"This was all so planned out, I wondered if those two thought of clothes." She went inside to look. It was several minutes before she returned.

The Captain looked up to see her standing in front of him in a very tight, blue, silk gown she had bought in Feast Town.

"Come on." She took his hand and led him inside to the couch near the window. They fell asleep on the couch holding each other, learning to be comfortable with touching each other.

A full moon had risen. Kira's room filled with the scent of Jasmine and Gardenias. Next to Kira's crib, an orange glow began to appear. It grew taller and changed to a soft white light in the shape of a woman. The ghostly figure leaned over the cradle and touched Kira's cheek. Kira woke and giggled. She tried grabbing the hand that touched her, but her tiny hand passed through. Kira giggled more. Her tiny mouth formed an O, and then she cooed. The figure slowly moved away. Kira's eyes followed the glow as it crossed the room. The moonbeam through the window made her giggle more.

Not The End   A Beginning

End Notes

In writing this steampunk novel, I tried to stay within the bounds of 'could have happened' as much as possible. Some of my beta readers hit me on a few things and I had to explain that yes, many things did happen long before they thought they were used or invented. These notes cover some of them. I wanted to stay with reality as much as possible so when I wrote of things far beyond reality, it would be more acceptable than if everything was unreal. Two big ones, Talent and Air Sharks.

1 Women as doctors :

The Women's Medical College of Pennsylvania opened in 1850. By the end of the 19th century, 19 women's medical colleges and 9 women's hospitals had been established. The struggle for coeducation, however, was initially successful only in a minority of institutions, hampered in large part by the theories of Harvard professor Edward H. Clarke (1874) who proclaimed that women seeking advanced education would develop "monstrous brains and puny bodies [and] abnormally weak digestion." As Mary Putnam Jacobi wrote (1891), "It is perfectly evident from the records, that the opposition to women physicians has rarely been based upon any sincere conviction that women could not be instructed in medicine, but upon an intense dislike to the idea that they should be so capable." In short, the 'Good old boy' attitude prevailed.

2 Dissolving sutures

Physicians have used sutures for at least 4,000 years. Archaeological records from ancient Egypt show that Egyptians used linen and animal sinew to close wounds. In ancient India, physicians used the heads of beetles or ants to effectively staple wounds shut. The live creatures were affixed to the edges of the wound, which they clamped shut with their pincers. Then the physician cut the insects' bodies off, leaving the jaws in place. Other natural materials doctors used in ancient times were flax, hair, grass, cotton, silk, pig bristles, and animal gut.

Though the use of sutures was widespread, sutured wounds or incisions often became infected. Nineteenth-century surgeons preferred to cauterize wounds, an often ghastly process, rather than risk the patient's death from infected sutures. The great English physician Joseph Lister discovered disinfecting techniques in the 1860s, making surgery much safer. Lister soaked catgut suture material in phenol making it sterile, at least on the outside. Lister spent over 10 years experimenting with catgut, to find a material that was supple, strong, sterilizable, and absorbable in the body at an adequate rate. A German surgeon made advances in the processing of catgut early in the twentieth century, leading to a truly sterile material.

3 Use of Oxygen

Oxygen has been in use for over 200 years. Airships going to high would find the air 'bad' and Doc would have latched onto the idea of using oxygen as a supplement. It was first used as a therapy by Thomas Beddoes in 1774.

This is an article printed in the medical Journal Lancet in 1857

ON THE THERAPEUTIC USE OF OXYGEN
by S.B. Birch, M.D. The LancetAugust 1, 1857

In venturing to call professional attention to the subject of this paper, I may safely premise with the remark, that it is one respecting which there exist great diversity of opinion and very little practical knowledge. The therapeutic use of oxygen gas, either alone or as an adjunct, in various intractable diseases, is a subject of vast importance to my professional brethren, enhanced in value as it is by an impartial reflection upon the still very uncertain and unsatisfactory state of our knowledge of medicinal *modus operandi*. Thus far, excepting to a few individuals and to a very limited extent, this gas, although so well known in its physiological relations, has been practically litttle better than a "secret" in it therapeutic bearings. Notwithstanding that from the time of Dr. Beddoes and Sir Humphry Davy several practitioners have made successful trial in private practice -- notwithstanding that the researches of modern chemistry have made us more scientifically cognizant than formerly of the relations of oxygen to the other elements of the vital organism -- notwithstanding that the daily observations of every man who has disease to treat shows him that the patient needs plenty of pure air, more air (in other words more oxygen) than he can possibly obtain under many circumstances and in many diseased states from the atmosphere around him -- the idea seems merely to float through the professional mind, without any resulting general endeavor to make a practical application of it.

It would not be difficult to show cause why the use of this remedy has been neglected. It involves some trouble and loss of time to the practitioner, and consequently, the very want of practical knowledge still existing may be justly attributed to the neglect to carry out fair trials on a sufficient scale in practice. Thus the profession has been led to overlook or ignore oxygen as a medicine, even though chemical science tells us decidedly that it ought to be a most valuable remedial agent. A single trial, or several trials on several patients, are no evidence, if they fail, against its value; they are only proof either that it was not suited to the case, or that it was not properly exhibited. Drs. Beddoes, Thornton, Hill, and others, who have tested this gas in a sufficiently large number of cases, afford conclusive evidence that it is a powerful, therapeutic; while occasional experiments, in which it has been unsuccessfully tried, can only be accepted as proof that, were we to seek an "universal pancacea," oxygen is not thar remedy. True, medical science will learn to value it at its intrinsic worth only when it is allowed to have a fair and sufficiently extensive trial.

4 Radio

This is hard to nail down as there is a difference between who gets the credit and who actually was the first. I find reference to tests and demonstrations as far back as 1878 that could allow a person to modify and have a radio by the mid 1890's.and as an additional note on the subject. In 1871 Mahlon Loomis submitted his patent for wireless communication. By the late 1870s there were rumors he was working on a wireless telephone.

5 Transfusions

1818 British obstetrician James Blundell performs the first successful transfusion of human blood to a patient for the treatment of postpartum hemorrhage.

6 Air Shark

This one was a big stretch, Years ago I read an article about the first steam powered aircraft. I could not resist the urge to use it. The first practical steam powered aircraft was demonstrated by the Besler Brothers on April 12, 1933 over Oakland California. It was powered by a steam boiler that was so quiet that spectators on the ground could hear the pilot calling to them. 10 gallons of water were sufficient for a flight of 400 miles.

Be sure to read the sequel

The Captain And The Lady Fair

Pathfinder